Wakefield Press

101 NIGHTS

101 Squadron motto:

Mens agitat molem
Mind over Matter

101
NIGHTS

RAY OLLIS

Edited by
Robert Brokenmouth

Wakefield
Press

Wakefield Press
16 Rose Street
Mile End
South Australia 5031
www.wakefieldpress.com.au

101 Nights first published 1957; this edition published 2016
Reprinted 2020

Cover designed by Liz Nicholson, designBITE
Typeset by Wakefield Press

National Library of Australia Cataloguing-in-Publication entry

Creator: Ollis, Ray, author.
Title: 101 nights / Ray Ollis; edited by Robert Brokenmouth.
ISBN: 978 1 74305 405 5 (paperback).
Notes: Includes bibliographical references.
Subjects: World War, 1939–1945 – Aerial operations,
                    British – Fiction.
Other Creators/Contributors: Brokenmouth, Robert, editor.
Dewey Number: A823.3

CORIOLE
McLAREN VALE

Wakefield Press thanks
Coriole Vineyards for their
continued support.

Contents

For

Dr Biaggini

of Adelaide University

and for

two Rays, both fathers, both taken from us far too early.

Acknowledgements

Sam Brookes, David Champion, Craig A. Chidley, Stephen Clarke, Matt and Justine Harrop, Nick Hector, Graeme Inkster, Clive Jackson, Richard Morris, Stephen Oakley, Margaret Rose Ollis, Marjory Ollis, Jonathon Ollis, Timothy Ollis, Michael and Susan Treloar, Mandy Tzaras, David Vincent, Paul Wilkins, Andy Wright.

Stay with me, God. The night is dark,
The night is cold; my little spark
Of courage dies. The night is long;
Be with me God, and make me strong.

From *A Soldier – His Prayer*, by Gerald Kersh.

'Man – the animal Man – is not a very romantic creature. He tries to laud his spirit and forgets that, in his body, he is not superior but actually inferior to most other animals. For all his dreams of mind, of homo sapiens, the articulate, rational being, Man's body rules him.'

Ray Ollis, *101 Nights*

Introduction

'We must be rather careful in what we cast aside as unimportant and of no value. Every experience in life, whatever it may be, is of value if – and such a big "if" – rightly applied.'

Her Highness Princess Marie Louise,
My Memories of Six Reigns, Evans Brothers, 1956

'What really struck me about *101 Nights* is the references to things which did happen.'

Margaret Ollis

Upon noting that *101 Nights* was written by 'a veteran', the first question most history buffs ask is – how much truth is there?

As Ray puts it in his 'Briefing', 'some events, times and one significant code-name have been changed either for security or art.'

Ray's log-book places him squarely in the latter part of the war, flying as a navigator with 101 Squadron. Fascinated with his new squadron, Ray places his character, a dead ringer for himself – in 101 almost from the beginning of their special operations, meticulously covering their failures and successes. *101 Nights* is vivid in the way most military memoirs are not because the fiction has allowed Ray's thinly-disguised facts to be published at a time when most first-hand accounts kept determinedly away from the real horror of war. Most first-hand memoirs focused on light-hearted antics and a somewhat jingoistic black-and-white reality, a 'preferred truth'. Even the German accounts which appeared in England at this time were often self-serving and bombastic, also playing into the preferred memory of the war.

When Ray writes, 'All the characters are imaginary and have no connection whatsoever with their true-life counterparts. I know of no true instance where a flyer was charged with sabotage, where a flight commander was posted from the squadron during a tour, or where a German "Special" baled out over his homeland'; fiction allows Ray to point the finger but not too precisely, thus avoiding potential legal action. Indeed, it might be more embarrassing to bring suit against the publisher ...

We are forced to conclude that *101 Nights* is as vivid a portrayal of one man's experiences in Bomber Command as can be imagined. Ray has used a little creative license in order to make points; equally clearly, the 'made-up' events represent Ray's experiences and impressions of the men around him.

Everyone has a different reason for writing a book, whether that book be factual or fictitious. After all, history visits and vanishes in the blink of an eye, the everyday writ large.

The genesis of Alexander McKee's *Dresden* came 'when I was with the British 2nd Army in the Rhineland and Ruhr, I heard the first whispers. Something very terrible had happened over there in the East near the war's end, I was told, but no one could explain why it had been so much more cruel than the fate which had engulfed most of Europe, burnt with fire from heaven or tornadoed into rubble by the passage of the armies.'

When he came to write *101 Nights*, Ray Ollis had lived an exciting life and, as his logbook shows, he was proud of it. Usually blunt, straightforward affairs, logbooks are often cryptic, perhaps with a few blackly humorous comments, and sometimes remarkably revealing. Many fliers treat their logbooks like a kind of 'score-sheet', as if flying were some grand game of cricket. To some extent it is a record of their prowess, also an expression of their self-identity.

Guy Gibson's logbook is 'a fascinating document ... [with] many of its entries ... made at a single sitting, discernible from changes of pen, ink or variable handwriting' (Morris). This is true of most logbooks. However, Morris also concludes that 'Gibson treated his logbook as a kind of score sheet, as much a record of accumulated experience as of his flying.'

More flamboyantly, Ray Ollis's logbook is littered with newspaper clippings of the raids he has flown, a chunk scissored from one leaf has the result of both pages being rewritten on a following page, and there are later emendations. Ray's 1956 London-to-Sydney flight in a Percival Proctor 3 is accompanied by newspaper cuttings and an article published in *Flight* magazine in 1957.

Predating the mid-1960s wave of British action-thriller and military nostalgia, *101 Nights* was reprinted only once by Cassell, the same year it was published, 1957; WDL also put out a paperback edition in 1957, and there was an Italian translation; *Cento e una Notte*.

Ray Ollis tells of the many dramatic shifts in the long night war between Bomber Command's offensive and the German defences. In a novel, trifling matters such as re-arranging actual events to suit the story do not detract. Indeed, because *101 Nights* is a remarkably accurate depiction of a Bomber Command station at war, with the special nature of 101 Squadron thrown in, the novel is that much more compelling.

101 Nights compares favourably well with the attitudes and literary concerns predominant in novelists writing in WW2; Ray Ollis bears a curious – even eerie – kinship to the war novels (and life) of Nevil Shute. Also, at least two modern novels were clearly influenced by *101 Nights*.

However, with the exception of aviation and military buffs who appreciate *101 Nights'* strong factual, eyewitness quality, the book has been forgotten for almost sixty years. A difficult book to find today, I discovered *101 Nights* in 1992 at a Red Cross sale.

I later discovered *101 Nights* in the collection of several Bomber Command veterans. Here was a novel written by a veteran unable, at the time, to describe his actual experiences. Fiction allowed Ray Ollis to tell his story in a way that non-fiction would not, could not allow. While novels based on a man's wartime experiences cannot be taken as an accurate depiction of characters or events, their impressionistic immediacy has great appeal. However, because there are so many things in *101 Nights* which are described, as near as my research can tell, very accurately indeed, one is drawn to the conclusion that *101 Nights* is less fiction than a sort of 'fictionalized memoir'.

With my task with John Bede Cusack's *They Hosed Them Out* (Wakefield Press, 2012) completed, I came to realise that *101 Nights* could be re-examined and brought to a new audience, an audience curious about the way things were during World War 2, sophisticated enough not to be captivated by the war-as-boys-own-adventure, but to look more closely at the turmoil in the human condition such conflicts reveal.

Some detective work coupled with some research from scientist and genealogist Stephen Clarke, allowed me to track down Ray Ollis's widow, Margaret.

Editing *101 Nights* was mostly confined to spelling, harmonisation of tenses, punctuation, editing for sense and a few slight rearrangements within the text. The original edition's transposition of several pages has also been attended to.

One of the most awkward things for someone unfamiliar with the setting of a novel is the acronyms and closed-shop terminology essential to the setting. Because *101 Nights* was one of the first Bomber Command novels, on the evidence of the original edition, a few small textual inconsistencies flourished. On the ground a bomber crew had names and nicknames; in the air the crew would be referred to by their job titles to avoid confusion over the intercom; in the original edition either the author or the original editor has occasionally confused matters. For example, Hyde's function of skipper sometimes rates a capital letter when he is addressed directly, but not when he is described by his job.

Also, Ollis mostly avoids capitalising code words such as GEE, presumably in order to express the story as simply as possible; I decided to follow his lead. A reader more familiar with Bomber Command literature will recognise terms as they now normally appear; for example, 'window' is more usually 'Window' instead of its official code name WINDOW.

The only exception involves a character who appears at the beginning of Part Two, who seems to require Very Formal Capital Letters; the author's decision to use 'VFCL' is amusing and descriptive in its own right. My editing revealed far more understated humour than I recalled from my initial reading.

In compiling the biographical section, I have relied on extant sources as well as Ray's extraordinary logbook, fragmentary memories (most of which are understandably reluctant to surface), books and references of the day as well as recent histories. Because this is a novel, I have also utilised references from popular literature of the day, and today.

Much of what Ollis obsessively wrote of himself was, at the time, unavailable to the editor; at least one of his voluminous diaries was destroyed, the rest proved inaccessible. Similarly, much information remains hidden; perhaps a later edition will enable me to provide a fuller portrait of the man; if the diaries ever surface, they would make a revealing, informative and entertaining book in their own right.

I must emphasise how significant it is that most of the information Ray provides is substantially correct; my notes are intended to amplify our understanding and to encourage the reader to dip into the many topics introduced, or even to pursue them in detail. Writing between 1954 and 1956, Ray Ollis had no vast resource of information at his fingertips; the first official history of the Strategic Bombing Offensive appeared five years after *101 Nights* was published; if Ray's memory is at fault, we forgive his humanity.

There is also a brief bibliography for intrepid newcomers to this bewildering and busy historical subject.

History is often misrepresented; when computer games are based on historical battles they inevitably alter the history they represent. Photoshopped photographs polish and edit history, and truth is concealed, not revealed. History is not tidy, bright and sharp, but blurry and indistinct, messy. History is what happened yesterday. How often have we discovered that, in discussing a minor car accident or a fight at a bar, we all see and remember things differently.

On seeing Steven Spielberg's film *Saving Private Ryan*, a friend observed that the damage done by bombing to the villages depicted in the film was 'somehow ... too much'. As a general rule, the Allies did not deliberately bomb or shell small villages. There were exceptions, and there were many, many accidental bombings by both sides during WW2. But the damage depicted was real enough, as anyone who has seen photographs of Europe immediately after the war knows.

Conversely, when a combat veteran writes a novel which draws from his experience, it is important to place the book on the shelf adjacent to the military memoirs. Sixty years ago Ray Ollis wrote a fine novel which stands on its own, based on a time in his life which defined his generation.

Long may we remember them.

Robert Brokenmouth

101 Nights

Briefing

This is the story not of the few but of the many; the true story of Bomber Command. A special security release has enabled me to base the story on the hitherto secret activities of 101 Squadron. This is not a squadron history. Some events, times and one significant code-name have been changed either for security or art.

All the characters are imaginary and have no connection whatsoever with their true-life counterparts. I know of no true instance where a flyer was charged with sabotage, where a flight commander was posted from the squadron during a tour, or where a German 'Special' baled out over his homeland.

Fort Smith, Kenya, Ray Ollis

Part One

Hyde

It will be strange flying with another crew. I had grown used to our shower. My new squadron is 101, based at Ludford Magna, right on top of the Wolds. They've got Lancasters already. I'm to navigate for a Squadron Leader Parke: he's B Flight commander. I've heard that 101 are on some new special duties lark. I hope not. Special duties usually mean you stick your neck out even further.

At times I almost wish I were in that comfortable hospital with you. It gets a chap a jinx reputation being an only flying survivor ...[1]

Nothing in Vincent Farlow's letter to his ex-skipper showed how bewildered he felt arriving at his new squadron. Previously he had moved with his crew and they had bolstered each other. Here, he was alone.

Pausing, he looked around at the tiny village of Ludford Magna.

'If this is *great* Ludford,' he reflected, 'then *little* Ludford must be non-existent.'

A forty-minute walk past the village, down a path that forded the creek, over three fields of waving grain and half a mile around the aerodrome perimeter brought him to flying control: a fortress of stone made brittle with walls of glass.

Above its observation roof was the revolving searchlight, stilled now by the embarrassing brilliance of day. Beside it, three spinning cups measured wind-speed. Their message was repeated on two dials inside control; one upstairs in the control-room itself, another in the ground floor Meteorological section.

Vincent Farlow came to the door marked 'Met' and frowned, undecided. His indecision did not seem to arise from nervousness. He was tall and blond and his blue eyes had a twinkle as frank as a puppy's tail-wag; there was no trace of nervousness in him. His pause was more a serious, deliberate reckoning to decide the right move. He gave three firm raps on the word 'Met' and entered confidently.

His glance took in the Waafs sitting at two plotting tables, the met officer leaning against the teleprinter, and came to rest on a squadron leader with pilot's wings who sat on the desk, dangling his legs and grinning at a joke he was recounting.

Vincent saluted and, because he was the only one not laughing, waited awkwardly until the squadron leader finished speaking. Then, still smiling, the met officer asked: 'Can I help you, Flight?'

'Yessir. I was told if I asked in flying control you could direct me to B Flight.'

The squadron leader hopped down off the table. 'I'm going to B Flight now,' he said. 'Whom do you want?'

'The Flight Commander, sir. I'm his new navigator.'

'Well, you clot, why didn't you say so?' The pilot seized Vincent's hand heartily. 'That makes me your skipper. Parke's the name. Really delighted to see you.'

By the time the two men reached B Flight Vincent had warmed to the idea of having Parke as his pilot. Patrick Parke looked a reassuring genealogical paradox with almost prehistoric features: broad, jutting forehead, full lips, heavy jaw and strong, prominent teeth, but with a strength of purpose and sense of humour in his manner that made him as modern as tomorrow. Here would be a jolly, roistering companion, loud and lovable; or an enemy dark-lowering and fierce as the jungles from which he seemed to have sprung.

As they entered Parke's office seven men who had been waiting hurried to attention. Parke's eye sought the wearer of pilot's wings. 'Hello, who are you chaps?'

'A new crew, sir. My name's Buckley.'[2]

'Ah, Buckley. I expected you earlier.' Parke moved across and sat on the corner of his desk.

Vincent watched approvingly. Here was an easy-mannered leader. Yet nothing in Parke's manner suggested that he would brook a breath of disrespect. Here was perfect informality. Even his brusque 'I expected you earlier' combined unquestionable authority with a nice friendliness.

'Look out the windows at those Lancs,' Parke said, waving towards the aerodrome. 'See anything strange about 'em?'

Vincent had been curious about the additional antennae which made the 101 Squadron Lancasters differ from any Lanc he had previously seen.[3]

Parke looked quickly at Buckley's silent crew and continued: 'They've got extra radio. Lots of it. This squadron is the RAF counter to German night-fighter radar. The Germans are too short of radar to mount sets in individual night-fighters as we do.[4] Instead they have giant radar sets called Wurtzburgs on the ground. They work in pairs, one Wurtzburg tracking a German fighter while the other searches for our bods. When they find us they plot our position and radio a course to the fighter so that he can intercept us. Now do you see why we carry extra radio? So that we can intercept those messages and counter them. We carry an extra wireless-operator, too, who speaks German as well as the Germans themselves. In fact, many of our chaps *are* Germans. These Specials, as we call them, have a receiver and a transmitter. As soon as they pick up a radio-message they tune their transmitters to the German frequency and, before the German on the ground can tell the fighter what course to fly, they transmit from a microphone in one of our engines all the clatter of a Rolls-Royce Merlin on the wavelength that the poor bloody German is trying to listen to.[5]

Vincent laughed and Parke gave a grim grin in reply.

'That's not all. Our Special then eases off his jamming and, using the call-sign he's just overheard, gives the fighter false directions. Often there's a ginormous flap between the German on the ground and the German fighter in the air, with the German-speaking Special in our plane stirring it all he can. By this time the bomber and the fighter are so far apart that the Wurtzburg boys downstairs have to start all over again and we have frustrated another interception.'

Parke looked around. 'Of course,' he continued, 'we also do the work of a normal bomber: full bomb-loads, usual targets, the lot. You chaps hardly know you've got a Special with you.'

Parke paused again and Vincent said quickly, 'But we must constantly break radio silence. They could pick up 101 Squadron aircraft using ordinary radio-direction sets.'

'Yes,' said Parke calmly. 'That's why this squadron wants very good gunners. In protecting the bomber force as a whole, we attract fighters on to ourselves. Any questions?'

Nobody spoke. Each man was repeating mentally: *We attract fighters on to ourselves.*[6]

'Well, that's the story, chaps,' Parke finished breezily. 'Do your job, stay alive, and we'll all be very happy. Welcome to 101 Squadron and the best of luck.'

The interview was over. Parked moved into his chair. 'Take your crew to dispersals, Buckley. Introduce yourselves to Chiefy Mitchell the mechanic and ask to look over a Lanc. Touch nothing but learn all you can. Be here again at 1400. Farlow, wait here.'

Buckley saluted and left smartly with his crew.

'Well, Farlow,' said Parke, lolling back and resting his size-ten shoes on the desk, 'sit down and tell me about yourself. First of all, what's your Christian name?'

Flight Sergeant Joe Trinket, a lanky, wiry, grey-eyed gunner, nimble of body and wit, murmured 'Grog's the shot!' and drank half a pint at a gulp. There was silence between the three men for a moment until Joe said, 'Well, will we talk about it now or just wait till it crops up?[7]

'No, we won't talk about it,' said the oldest of the three, a tubby, clumsy little man whose balding head contrasted with the youthful faces around him. Sergeant Bill Graham was a Yorkshireman, blunt and direct. 'We'll talk about this new nav. How'll we recognize him?'

'Skipper says he's tall and fair with an 'O' wing, and he's got a BEM.'[8]

'How'd he get that?'

'Dunno, mate,' said Joe Trinket, his accent leaving no doubt that he was Australian. 'He wouldn't talk about it and the documents just say he got it in Crete – no details.'[9]

Joe gulped his drink then turned to the trio's third member and said, 'Your shout, Yarpi.'

'Hell, man,' protested Yarpi, raising his pale eyebrows so high that his long, thin face looked even thinner. 'Why my shout? It's only our second drink, man.' His voice was shrill and indignant.

'Because if it's Bill's turn to buy the last drink then we know we'll get a last drink.'

Yarpi flushed, ordered the drinks, and got back onto a safer subject. 'This chap's got the luck of a Parke navigator anyway. I hear he wandered into the mess, asked a chap to play him table-tennis, and who did he pick but the squadron champion.'

'And got trounced, eh?'

'Well no, man. I heard he won.'

Joe pointed to the door. 'Then ask him. This looks like him coming in now.'

Joe presented himself to Vincent and introduced Yarpi and Bill. Then he asked: 'Ready for a night out?'

Vincent wasn't sure. 'Really, I should do some work.'

'Work! Work is the downfall of the drinking classes. Besides you've gotta meet the crew here. Skipper's orders. The only other NCO member is Roger North the engineer. Attractive chap, Roger.'

'Attractive?' echoed Vincent. 'Then doubtless you call him 'Magnetic' North.'

The group groaned and Joe continued: 'Call him a nice chap then. He's now with the bloke who usually flies Special with us: young Johnnie Muller. They're in Grimtown.'

'Grimtown?'

'Grimsby; our leave town. Roger's trying to put Johnnie on to a popsie.'

'Why can't Johnnie find his own popsie?'

Joe smiled and said: 'Johnnie loves popsies but popsies don't love Johnnie. I've put him on to some of the surest things in Lincolnshire and still he's missed out. I've even lingered until I felt it was indiscreet to stay another instant. But Johnnie seems doomed to be a sexual sprog forever. But still we keep trying and Roger's trying tonight.'

Joe drained his drink. 'The other guy,' he finished, 'is Krink. Krink Krynkiwski, our wireless operator.[10] A Flying Officer and, as you may recognize from the old Ukrainian name, an American. He and the skipper are due here any minute.'

The pub was crowded by the time it fell Vincent's turn to buy drinks. While he waited for bar-service he eyed his crew. Krink proved to be stockily built with a round, baby face and curly hair. Krink said little but sat quietly in a corner entangled with a lithe blonde night-fighter.

Roger, who had arrived with the news that Johnnie was fixed up with a reliable popsie old enough to be his mother, had slight, aquiline features. About thirty, he did not seem old in the way Bill did. To these youngsters any flyer nearing thirty was old.

Vincent eyed Joe calculatingly; 'Noisy, yes; but not shallow. Yarpi van Rijn the South African: hmmm. Doubtful. Seems sly. Sloppy mouth and shifty eyes. I'll watch him. But Parke was the salt of the earth. Probably just a good-natured nobody back in Ireland but a man who thrived during war. Permanent RAF; a born leader and, he'd vouch, a sound pilot. All the regulars were. Bill Graham was a contradiction. Rock-like in some ways, yet he seemed nervous. Flak-happy?[11] Perhaps. This crew had just had a dicey do; the navigator he was replacing had been killed.'

Vincent picked up the tankards and headed back. In front of their table a giggling girl blocked his way. 'Excuse me,' he said, but she did not move, whereupon Parke seized her around the waist, and lifted her bodily aside.

'Hey!' she protested. 'You've got a hide!'

'But of course,' said Vincent, distributing drinks. 'Squadron Leader Parke has all the hide of the entire Parke family. That's why they call him 'Hyde Parke'.[12]

The pun was appreciated. There was immediate approval and it was suggested that Parke should be known as 'Hyde' hereafter. He seemed delighted, and proposed that Roger might also accept renaming at Vincent's hand, and be called 'Magnetic'.

'Grab 'em, you blokes!' shouted Joe. 'Here's a rag! We're gonna christen Roger and the skip!'

The table rocked as the men struggled to restrain their two crew-mates. Parke and Roger were soon secured in their seats, laughing with some misgivings at their imminent christening. Their caps were found, part-filled with beer, and plunked squarely on their heads to cries of 'I dub thee 'Magnetic' and 'Arise, Sir Hyde, sir,' while the foamy beer ran down their faces and trickled stickily under their collars.

There was a great deal of noise and it was not until the rumpus was subsiding that Vincent noticed a short, swarthy sergeant standing watching them, not only unamused but positively miserable. Johnnie Muller said a sad and serious 'hello'.

'Johnnie,' Magnetic said. 'You haven't missed out again? Not with Bag Bertha!'

Johnnie nodded and glanced floorwards. His big eyes, sad and shy as a newborn heifer's, were actually misty. 'She slapped my face,' he whispered.

'Bag Bertha! Slapped your face? Are you sure you didn't faint and she was trying to revive you?'

Magnetic looked sidelong at Johnnie. 'There's something mysterious about you, chum. Why, Bag Bertha wouldn't take offence at Jack the Ripper.'

— 2 —

There were a few shuffles, a few coughs, then expectant silence. The entire end wall was covered by curtains. The Wingco[1] pulled a cord, the curtains parted from the centre to reveal a map, and the tightly-stretched red cord which snaked deep into Germany.

'Leipzig', said the Wingco.[2]

One hundred and ninety-six lips made one hundred and ninety-six low moans. No target is ever received with silence. One voice was heard to suggest an improbable feat that the Wingco might perform with Leipzig, and there was a general nervous titter.

The Wing Commander generalised on the attack. A red-haired Waaf officer Vincent had seen in Met told the weather story. Gunnery leader, wireless leader, bombing leader, engines leader, Specials leader the Hon. Holbrook-Hardwicke; all gave directions to their own particular charges.[3] Orders, tips, advice, a word of encouragement and a wish of good luck. The navigation leader, his own section busy elsewhere plotting winds and tracks, came to advise on navigational hopes and hazards and to synchronise watches.[4]

Then the Wingco summed up. 'It's a 4 Group bash tonight.[5] But they want Wurtzburg cover, so we fly too. One more point: this squadron, or rather our anti-Wurtzburg function, is to have a name. We are to be known as the XYZ squadron. Command say it stands for X-ray Your Zebra. Doesn't make sense to me but there you are, security measure I suppose. But I want you to take it as your title. I'm coming with you again tonight. Make me proud of XYZ.'

Dusk and the perpetual mist quickly hid Ludford Magna behind and England, fading below, became more misty than a dream. Her fields were drifting haze, her rivers imagery, her towns merest mirage. All that was behind seemed misleading memory; only this hurtling, roaring life in the air was real. The dream that was behind could not be true. There was no fireside calm, no bar-room warmth, no friends, no sympathy. The earth below was nothing but a platform for guns and a launching-ground for fighters. The flyers looked down with loathing at the wrinkled sea and hostile coast that crept towards them.

They were to cross between Boulogne and Calais: both defended.

'Flak port bow high,' said Yarpi in mid-upper.[6]

'Calais,' said Vincent.

'Flak starb'd bow level', said Bill in the nose.

'Boulogne,' said Vincent. 'Good. We're between them.'

'Here's a perfect pinpoint, nav,' said Joe. 'When I give the word we're crossing the coast slap over Cap Gris-Nez. Dead over it – now!'

'Then we're bang on time,' said Vincent. 'Thanks, rear gunner.'

Looking down over the port nose Hyde smiled to himself. They seemed to have settled down to work smoothly together. Farlow was starting well, anyway. Cap Gris-Nez was dead on track.

'Nav to skipper. At 2002 alter course four degrees port to 092 compass, and reduce airspeed five knots to 210 indicated. That'll make groundspeed 257 and ETA point F: 2018.'[7]

'Is that early or late, nav?'

'Bang on time, skip. If it's right.'

'Won't a port alteration bring us into the Ruhr?'[8]

'No, skip. We were slightly south, away from the Ruhr. We are now converging on point F.'

Five miles away on the port bow, flak confirmed the position of the Ruhr. Suddenly, amid the dancing flashes, a larger fireball flared, glowed, for an instant lighting the countryside for miles around; then darkened.

Somebody's bombload hit by flak.

Unsatiated, the flak flickered on; delicate flashes as fast as sight, every twinkle a white-hot thunderbolt scattering death like a grindstone scatters sparks. They burst in threes, triangles of tragedy, each group representing a battery on the ground, each battery directed by a Wurtzburg.[9]

Listening amidships, Johnnie Muller could not outwit these saboteurs of sheltering night. The wind-fleet shells sped unalterably upwards.

It would be the same with the fighters, too – open season for hunters and every fox painted white – were it not for 101's twenty-eight Specials rallying at the German 'Tally-ho', turning the tantalizing scent into an infuriating stink. Twenty-eight nightingales, not killing enemies but saving airmen's lives.

The flak was dead abeam now. Coming up from Bonn, Vincent took a bearing, plotted a reciprocal position line from the city on his chart and checked his ground speed. Treacherous even to its maker, flak betrayed the homes it defended, providing navigation facts that sped the bombers on to Leipzig.

The flyers watched the flak drifting behind under their port wing, almost mesmerized by its fatal beauty. A blossoming ribbon of flame unfurled across the sky, lighting the Halifax that fed it.[10] Another flourished suddenly nearby; another plane, another crew, another fiery finger pointing home. Then, as if they had rehearsed twin suicide, both planes fell away gracefully in arcs of fire.

The crew of Q-Queenie did not speak.[11] To them it was a log entry: '2006, two Halifaxes and one unidentified aircraft destroyed over Bonn 3 miles port', wrote Vincent. Three miles. Less than a minute's flying, and those three crews had strayed just fifty seconds too near to death.

Turning northwards now, around the Ruhr for a spoof attack, the force would head straight for a German city. German defences, it was hoped, would muster their fighters to protect the spoof target, only to see the attackers veer around and fly by just out of range. This forced fighters into the air too soon, wasted their petrol and, RAF planners hoped, caused them to land and refuel just when the real attack opened.

Johnnie Muller confirmed it. 'Special to crew. Increased fighter activity.'

'Muck 'em about, Johnnie!'

It always delighted the 101 Squadron aviators to picture the consternation they caused. Fighters anxiously airborne, waiting for orders that never got through. Guns, chock loaded and hot for the fray, but always pointing into empty air.

Over Eastern France and around the Ruhr the weather had been fairer than forecast. But now, as they flew deeper into Germany, it was growing worse. They had seen nothing but cloud below them for a hundred miles. No pinpoints here. Nothing but stars to point the way.[12]

Suddenly: 'Rear-gunner to crew. Bandit! Port quarter up.'

'What is it?'

'Me 110, skip. Six hundred yards on parallel course. I don't think he's seen us but prepare to corkscrew port.'[13]

Seconds dragged by. No sound save the drum of five-thousand horsepower and the rushing, two-hundred-mile-an-hour wind.

'Where is he, gunner?'

'Still there, skip. Five hundred yards.'

'Mid-upper. Search starb'd.'

It was not unknown for one German fighter to fly where it could be seen, even with all its lights on, while a second fighter attacked from the other side hoping that preoccupation with the first fighter would leave the prey a sitting shot.[14]

'Still there. Four hundred yards.'

It was not RAF policy to open fire. A single burst of tracer lighting up the sky would bring every bloodhound from fifty miles around, barking at their presence and calling the pack to destroy them.

'Nav to skipper. We have time to spare to fly a dog-leg.'

This was a manoeuvre designed for wasting time if flying ahead of schedule. The aircraft would alter course 60 degrees starboard then, after a minute, 120 degrees back again, flying two sides of an equilateral triangle. In this way it took two minutes to fly to a point which would otherwise be reached in one minute. To do it successfully now would place the fighter three miles in front; more comfortable than having him 400 yards behind.

Danger accompanied the move, however; should the fighter see them and attack while they were turning they would be left at a tactical disadvantage. Hyde weighed the wisdom of evasion against the mortal risks of either altering course away or remaining close to combat.

'Okay, nav. We'll try it. Rear-gunner! Shout if he starts a curve of pursuit and I'll dive hard port.'[15]

The big bomber slid around quietly onto the new course. The fighter quickly dwindled into the darkness. All eyes strained to see through the night that hid them.

Nothing.

They altered course back towards track and, a minute later, swung again towards the target.

'Nav to skipper. Better speed up a bit and regain some of that lost minute. New airspeed 215 indicated.'

'Engineer to skipper. We'll eat petrol at that speed. Should we alter boost?'

The engines settled on to a new, higher note. The crew returned to routine work. The German fighter, still concentrating perhaps on nothing but his prankish radio which Johnnie could beguile, flew on unheeding three dark miles away.

Below them, now, the cloud was thicker and darker than before. Above, the stars rocked gently with the movement of the aircraft, quietly defying the sextants down below to shoot them with that arrow through the heart which gives the perfect fix. Vincent's aerial sextant, marking horizontal with only a dancing, spirit-level bubble, took sixty separate sights and reduced them to a single average. Yet still the reading could not be trusted nearer than a few wide miles: the difference in bombing between a direct hit and a wild miss.

Bright stars above. Thick cloud below. And all around more than two hundred aircraft. But nothing to be seen, not a damned thing. Were they on track? Q-Queenie still hit occasional slipstreams indicating they were in some sort of concentration.[16] But the night that hid them from attack concealed their target too.

The met forecast had misplaced the area of good visibility. They should have bombed south-east of the Ruhr. Visibility over Coblenz was perfect. They could have bombed successfully there and been half-way home by now.

'Five minutes to TOT,' said Vincent. Time-on-target in five minutes and not a sign of action. Not a flare, not a few early bomb-flashes, not even any flak. Too often it was like this. War by guesswork.

'H-Hour!' announced Vincent at last. 'The attack should open now.'

Ahead of Q-Queenie the leading bombers released their loads, bombing blind on ETA.[17] A dull glow showed under a wide expanse of cloud, and instantly the night went wild with flak. Preferring not to shoot at first rather than betray their position, the Huns had nothing to lose now and opened fire. Q-Queenie lurched from the blast wave of a nearby flak burst.

Hyde dropped the nose a few degrees. A shallow dive through the target got clear of danger faster. The ASI showed 240 knots; with the following wind they would be tracking over the target with a groundspeed well over 300 mph.

'Five, four, three, two, one, *now!*' counted Vincent. Bill Graham pressed the tit. 'Bombs away!'

Another thirty seconds Hyde held her, dead ahead, hurtling in that shallow dive. The sky around and behind them bubbling with molten shrapnel and dotted with burning aircraft.

Clear of the target Hyde turned north-west for home.

A loud, rapid order shouted in their earphones. '*Corkscrew port, go!*'

Hyde slammed the stick forward, jammed on left rudder and dropped the port wing. The Lancaster lurched downwards and Vincent's instruments floated up off his desk as he scrambled to catch them.

'Up!' shouted the voice.

The men were anchored to their seats and the floating navigation instruments crashed to the floor as the heavy aircraft, mercifully free of her bomb load, strained out of her dive.

Tracer shells zipped under the starboard wing and a new vibration shook her as two machine-gun turrets returned fire at a rate of over a hundred bullets a second.

Cordite fumes filled the fuselage, penetrating into their oxygen masks.

'Up starb'd!' ordered the gunner.

Grinding around in tight turns trying to bring his own guns to bear, the fighter followed.

Q-Queenie's antics made shooting difficult for fighter and bomber alike, but for just an instant the Hun was steady in Joe's sights. Joe squeezed his buttons and the exchange was switched on again.

'Dive starb'd!'

A sickening, empty lurch and again the Lancaster plunged down, chasing its wingtip. The firing stopped.

'I think we've lost him, skip.'

The bomber eased back on course. Hyde checked on phones that everyone was unhurt. Men tested equipment for damage. Better find faults now rather than wait until they gave way.

Vincent crawled around rescuing equipment from the floor. To every navigation instrument – protractors, slides, computors[18] – was tied a piece of string. Vincent found his strings, lifted them all together and deposited his missing equipment on the plotting desk. That trick for finding things might save a minute.

A minute might save their lives.

Even now the aircraft was rocking again as more flak found them.

While they were over the target there had been a private little incident going on amidships. Johnnie Muller's task over the target was by the photo-flash chute. A few thousand feet behind the bombs, the photo-flash is released. This is a flash bomb timed to burst in the sky an instant before the bomb load explodes. Its flash lasts only one-fiftieth of a second; its three million candle-power acts as the exposure for the open-shuttered camera waiting in the bomber above. Johnnie stood duty to see that this HE flash did not jam in the chute.

As he waited for the flash to fall Johnnie drew from inside his battle-dress blouse something about the shape and size of a good trout. He poised it behind the flash, nose downwards. The mechanism clicked, the flash fell away, and directly on its tail the German boy released his own private missile to fall on his native land.

It was a tiny bomb. An 11½ pound practice bomb, used by bomb aimers in training. A puny puff of smoke in the wake of more than four tons of high explosive already released by the bomb-aimer.

Johnnie returned to his radio pleased to have added his mite. This radio, he knew, was valuable. Valuable, yes; but passive. But he *hated* Nazis and he, personally, wished to wound them.

The Hun had the situation worked out by now. He knew where they had been and where they were going. Fighters mingled with the returning stream, slashing like hawks in a flock of pigeons. Once more Joe shouted evasive action and Queenie corkscrewed out of danger.

Later, Joe and Yarpi yelled simultaneously to 'Corkscrew starb'd, go!' as their four eyes and six guns turned together on a single foe. But not a shot was fired, neither in attack nor defence. In each clash the fighter was lost during the first evasive dive.

Some aircrew believed that few German fighters followed a bomber which took evasive action. Perhaps it was true. Why risk their German necks in what would probably be a futile chase after a gunner who has already shown he is wide awake and knows what he is doing?

The mediocre gunner with good eyes who kept alert was therefore a better defence than the crack shot who dozed. Joe always said he was 'too bloody scared to fall asleep', and his crew loved him for it.

Johnnie eased the tension. 'Special to crew. Fighter activity has stopped.' It was usually like that. Ordered into the air at the same time, the fighters were all forced to land at the same time for lack of fuel.

'Skipper to gunners. Keep watching in case there's a stray.'

Flak still sprayed occasional brilliance into the sky. For a few minutes it seemed more intense, forming a line of bursting stars running across their bows from left to right. Vincent spoke; 'Crossing the coast out now.'

Now came the dull sea-leg home. Men were getting tired, and the relaxation made them realize it. Johnnie's radio still scanned the crackling ether but Fritz was silent. The gun-turrets still swung left and right, sweeping the empty sky with gestures of extreme distrust at its quietness. The engines drummed softly, throttled back now as the aircraft, hurrying still, gained speed in a gentle dive. In watchful monotony, Q-Queenie was returning home.

Hyde broke the long silence. 'Ten thousand feet. You can take off oxygen masks.' What a joy to tear the restricting rubber from one's face!

'Skipper to engineer. How are fuel levels? I smell petrol.'

'I smell it too. But the levels are okay. I've checked.'

No sooner had he spoken than the sky ahead was lit with a sickening orange flash. Its tailpiece blown off in a flurry of oval fins, an aircraft crashed, burning, into the sea.

'Skipper to crew. Anyone see that? It looked like a Lanc.'

'I thought so too. Have 4 Group got Lancasters?'

'I think they're all Halifaxes.'

'Must be a one-o-one bod,' said Hyde. 'Either they were on fire or else at 'oxygen-masks off' some clot lit a cigarette.' It was not idle chatter; the crew sniffed the petrol-laden air and reconfirmed their decision never to risk blowing up for a premature smoke.

'English coast ahead.'

'Looks damned misty.'

'Met said there might be fog.'

'Oh hell!'

'Any word of a diversion, Krink?'

'Something coming in now. Wait a sec.'

If Base were under fog they may be diverted to land elsewhere. It often meant acute discomfort; landing on some dreadful training field that lacked facilities, sleeping in make-shift accommodation, then hanging around maybe for days of bad weather without a shave or a change of clothes.

'Here it is,' said Krink. 'Diversion. But not for us: 4 Group. Some of them have to land at Ludford.' Ludford Magna, perched on top of the Wolds, was the highest aerodrome in Group and was frequently the last 'drome to be closed for fog.

They found Base, called up for permission to land and were told to wait; Ludford was handling four times its usual number of aircraft. Q-Queenie circled for almost another hour before landing. They taxied to their pen and cut engines.[19] The still silence seemed strange after ten hours and forty-two minutes of roaring vibration.

The waiting ground-crew jammed a ladder under the exit and, slowly and stiffly, one by one the crew climbed out. Hyde called to Chiefy Mitchell; 'Give her a good check, Chiefy. I didn't think we'd been hit but there's a helluva stink of petrol.'

Somehow, suddenly, the men did not feel tired. At debriefing nobody is. There is the excitement of another trip finished safely. The reaction after hours of comparative silence. There is so much to remember and discuss.

'Who blew up over the North Sea?'

'Looked like a Lanc.'

'We had six combats. Six!'

'Anyone missing?'

'The natives, my dear chap, were positively hostile.'

'... a ginormous explosion.'

'I believe Willard bought it.'

'Six combats!'

'Who got that Ju 88?'

'… fantabulous …'

'… coned over Bonn.'

'Target was a shambles.'

'Shhh!'

'Who blew up over the North firkin Sea?'[20]

The men queued for coffee and biscuits and their tot of rum. They were excited and talkative; most of them were really only boys. The rum would make them talk even more. That was just what the intelligence officers wanted.

As each crew repeated their story the raid took shape in the intelligence reports. There was cloud. Opposition average. Crews bombed on ETA. Bombed area reasonably concentrated. Possibly successful. Photographic reconnaissance would decide.

Outside de-briefing they bumped into Chiefy Mitchell. 'You didn't think you'd been hit? Queenie's got a hole in her so big that if she was round you'd think she was a doughnut.'

He turned wide eyes on Vincent. ''Ere! You the new nav? There's a piece of flak the size of twenty Players hit back of you and shot out the top behind the skipper. If you was sittin' in your chair it would've passed clean through your skull. You had a mite of fine fortune to miss that one.'

Vincent laughed hollowly and noticed he was the only one who did.

The crew-bus came and they climbed in. 'Vincent,' said Hyde. 'I haven't told you this before. You are my fourth navigator. The other three were all killed. You are the first one who ever had a shred of good luck.'[21]

Vincent felt a shiver run up his spine. 'I though we ran close to some flak when I was groping around finding instruments after our first combat. It must've been then.' He added brightly: 'I had a reputation for very *good* luck on my last squadron.'

'Fine,' said Hyde. 'Keep it up with one-o-one.'

— 3 —

Aircraftswoman Pearl Yewster (known naturally enough as Pearly Oyster) flitted about guarding the Nissen hut[1] of B Flight officers' quarters which contained her four sleeping charges. One of these charges was Flying Officer Kyrynkiwski, 'that ever-so-friendly American gentleman'.

Krink liked Oyster. She was a batwoman worth her weight in strategically placed armour plate. But he was not altogether kind to Oyster. 'Maybe Pearl Yewster,' Krink had said the first time he saw her, 'but I'll bet Pearl doesn't any more.'

Ac/w Yewster was old enough to be mother of them all. No real mother could have guarded and cared for her sons better than did Oyster. When the returning aircraft wakened her she had slipped from her bed into the pre-dawn cold to light the fire in their hut. She waited up to greet them and make sure they were safe. 'Never any of *my* boys missing', she would boast, as though her broody, earth-bound clucking and fussing had preserved her high-flying chicks from the Hun.

Soon she would wake them for lunch. Their morning tea and shaving water was heating over the fire in the centre of the darkened hut. It was dark because Oyster had left up the blackout screens to foil the sleep-distracting sunshine. The top of the stove glowed a heart-warming, fire-brick red.

Startled by a noise outside, Oyster rushed to investigate. She waved admonishingly and tried to shout a silent 'Shush' at three airmen walking noisily along the nearby road. 'These poor exhausted boys are trying to sleep,' she said. The airmen suggested another, and not altogether unpleasant, occupation for the 'poor exhausted bastards'.

Bill Graham propped himself up on one elbow and scowled over the blankets at Sergeant Gotleib Heindrickson and Johnnie Muller who lay in the next two beds. 'If thee don't stop yabbering bludy German right soon,' Bill threatened, 'I'll take fist and stop thee m'self.' Bill often reverted to dialect when he was either excited or half-asleep.

'Bravo, Bill,' said Magnetic.

'Oh, pipe down, the lot of you,' complained Joe.

Vincent sat up and yawned. 'What time is it?'

'What a navigator!' said Joe. 'Gets a Longines Astro on issue and has to ask the time.'[2] Joe disappeared completely under his blankets.

'Half-past twelve,' said Magnetic.

In the end bed, Vincent reached out and opened a window. 'This place stinks. Eight men asleep and a fire burning, and not a window open.'

Magnetic touched a tentative toe from under the blankets and touched the stove. 'Except that the fire is not only out but is as cold as a frog in a frozen pool; as cold as the tip of a polar bear's tail.'

The blankets of Joe's bed erupted into a heap on the floor. 'Might as well go and eat,' he said. 'Can't sleep in this freezing Babel.' He ran a finger down the curved iron wall of the Nissen hut and watched the rivulet of water he caused dribble to the cement floor. 'I'm so bloody cold,' Joe told nobody in particular, 'that if I was a passionate Eskimo and you a receptive Eskimiss I'd freeze your assets.'

He opened a window and stuck his head out. 'Hey, cock-head!' he called to a passing NCO. 'Is the water hot?'

'Not bloody likely!'

'Oh, blast!' said Joe. 'I'll shave after lunch.'

Magnetic and Vincent, in greatcoats and slippers and carrying towels and toilet-kits, walked out to the wash-shed. Cursing, Joe followed them.

By the time they returned only Yarpi was not out of bed. 'That loafer will sleep through Domesday. Let's toss him out.' Four men took hold of Yarpi's bed and hauled lustily. Yarpi fell heavily, dragging the bedclothes with him as he bumped on to the moist cement. The fall just managed to stir him. He blinked.

'Oh hell! What a stink!' cried Joe.

'Unless tha change thy sheets for clean ones soon, lad, we'll find thy stuck to 'em. Tha's only got to take 'em 'cross t't bedding store.'

'Here's your tea, sir,' said Corporal Tommy Tucker, NCO i/c B Flight quarters. Apart from the boiler attendant ('laziest sod unhung'), Tucker was the only male on domestic staff. He shook Squadron Leader Parke's shoulder gently. 'Tea, sir.'

'Mm? Oh, thanks. Put it on the table.'

Tucker set down the heavy china cup and saucer. 'And, sir,' he arrested Hyde's inclination to have another forty winks, 'Wingco phoned, sir, and said conference thirteen-thirty.'

That woke Hyde properly. 'Dicing again tonight?'

The batman expressed no surprise at the Flight Commander asking him if the squadron was operating. 'Looks like it, sir. Petrol load's announced.'

Hyde shuddered. 'Tell me softly,' he said.

'Twenty-one fifty-four, sir.' Hyde shuddered again.

The only indication of the target given to general ground staff was the petrol load. This information seemed to be instantly transmitted by the tanker drivers to the entire station: upwards of a thousand people. Hyde had once been told the petrol load by 'Old Meg', Ludford's village post-mistress.

Hyde reached for his tea and mumbled, 'Twenty-one fifty-bloody-four.' Maximum load meant another long trip.

'I've ironed your battle-dress, sir,' said Tucker. 'And here's your clean shirt and socks.'

'Oh, thanks.' Hyde swung his feet out of bed.

'Bring my shaving-water, then nip out smartly and start the car; key's on the dressing-table. I want to dash up to flight office as soon as I've shaved and that engine takes the devil's own time to warm up.'

The crews stood disconsolately outside the briefing room watching the cloud thicken.

'Cloud base two hundred at most.'

'And tops forty firkin farsand.'

Rain started to fall and a disgruntled murmur signalled general discontent. The black cloud base swept still lower and gusts of cutting wind made the coatless men stamp their feet and bury their hands deeper in their pockets. The briefing room door opened and the clustering flyers spilled inside. By the time the last men were in, the raindrops outside were large and cold and growing heavier.

'If they told the dock workers to work in this they'd go on strike.'

'If they told those loafers to work at all they'd strike.'[3]

'And we've gotta fly through it.'

Momentarily, morale was low.

The roll was called. The map slid back. The measured, red cord miles spread east and east and east. Beyond Berlin and north to ... 'Stettin!'

Red-headed Section Officer Wendy Marlborough-Jones was briefing again. She looked almost fierce as she spread her map. As though she had been forced to do something that she knew full well was suicide.

Nobody whistled; nobody wanted to. Every man sat and gazed sullenly at that vicious, arctic trip of over two-thousand miles return. That's if anybody *did* return. Wendy for all her beauty could almost have walked in front of those two hundred young men naked and nobody could have raised a whistle ... so preoccupied was every man with the thought of this dreadful trip on this dreadful night.

'The weather,' Wendy began, the copper gleam of her eyes flashing around the room, 'the weather, we are assured, is fair for this difficult target. We are told,' and she accented 'told' as if to imply she had been ordered to agree, 'that a cold front lies down the Irish Sea. You will take off before it reaches Base.'

'But the bloody thing's here now,' somebody grumbled, and the Wing Commander had to call for silence.

'This frontal system of severe weather will take eleven hours to pass over England. You could not possibly land during that time; that is why a distant target is considered ideal, so that you will remain airborne the whole duration of bad weather over Base. Behind a cold front, as you know, is much cloud but good visibility. In these patches of good visibility you will land.'

'I know the only patch we'll land in. A six-foot one.'

There was another angry murmur from the men and Flight

Lieutenant Marshall, the Signals-leader, remarked to the Hon. H-H that he had never seen a squadron so disinclined to fly during his eleven years in the RAF.

The Wingco was again obliged to call for silence. He was to fly this trip himself and it was to his credit that he restrained the men, whose misgivings he must have shared completely, with such military severity.

An intelligence officer entered from the map end of the hut and whispered to the Wing Commander. Every eye watched him.

The Wingco stood, motioned Wendy to stop briefing, and announced: 'The operation has been cancelled.'

'Scrubbo!'

'Trip scrubbed!'

'Thank Christ!'

'Scrubbo!'

Every man had heard, yet every man was happily telling his neighbour.

Wendy looked as pleased as the men. Her eyes sought Hyde's and she wrinkled her nose in a grin. Hyde said to Johnnie: 'I'm being mothered from a range of thirty feet now.' It was clear he did not like it.

The flyers were tumbling out of the briefing-room into the squall-driven rain, but now they did not complain. This weather could only wet them now, they did not mind; it was when it could kill them that they hated it.

Whenever a short or easy trip is cancelled, aircrew are often heard to say; 'I really wanted to fly tonight. Not just because it was an easy target; I really felt like flying.'

When a tough target is scrubbed there is an equally frequent reaction; 'Let's get stinko!' Escape demands celebration and the bar is rushed. Spirits, so low ten minutes before, soared as the men rocked in the crew bus bound for the warm mess with its cheerful fires and cheering bar. More than momentarily, it seemed, morale was high.

Somebody struck up a popular hymn, but these were not words of heavenly praise that the bus-load of young men started singing:

An airman told me before he died,
I have no cause to think he lied,
No matter how he tried and tried
His wife could never be satisfied.

So he built her a ...[4]

There is a sameness about most of the hymns in Ancient and Modern. It might be said that they had 'one theme'. So was there a sameness about the words these young servicemen sang to many of the hymns, perhaps because they had 'one theme' too? As the crew bus rumbled through the village, Ludford Magna's rustic citizens could be excused for any nostalgic longings they may have nurtured for their pre-war sleepy town.

'No we come to the tragic bit:
There was no way of stopping it ...'

The airman bus driver jammed on the brakes outside the sergeant's mess and the song was lost in tumbles and grumbles as the standing sergeants fell forward in a blaspheming jumble.

Although Yarpi bought the first round he was still in the chair when Vincent arrived from distant nav section so, despite his wile, Yarpi bought drinks for all.

'Whacko the scrub, eh?' Joe greeted Vincent. Having mixed with Australians in Crete Vincent understood, and replied: 'It's okay for you blokes. I had almost finished a two thousand mile flight plan.'

'Eeeh! Well let's bludy-well fly then, lad.'

'Can't waste your flight plan, man.'

'Let's not bloody-well fly, eh?' Vincent smiled.

Joe glanced at Vincent more approvingly. It was the first time Joe remembered having heard Vincent swear, and he drew reassurance from it.

When it fell his turn to buy, Johnnie Muller turned towards Joe and asked: 'Can you led me a pound, Joe?'

An RAAF flight sergeant, Joe earned twice as much as Johnnie. Johnnie's pay was a constant problem; he had even asked the Adjutant to investigate if pay section really was entitled to deduct income tax from Germans. He knew Joe paid no income tax. But maybe King's Regulations had foreseen Australians as Allies and made allowances.

Joe said: 'Gee, I'm sorry, Johnny; I'm so broke that if Christmas turkeys was fourpence-a-dozen I couldn't afford a tom-tit's ear-hole!'

Bill Graham was standing next to them. He slipped a pound into Johnnie's hand with no more than a finger placed to his lips.

Presently, Dickie Bird strolled over to Vincent and asked to play him table-tennis. Joe leapt at the chance of a contest. 'For the squadron championship!' he demanded.

'I was just thinking of a friendly game.'

'No sleeping champions here, lad. Defend your title or give it up.'

'Hey! Just a tick,' said Vincent. 'I'm half-stinko.'

'Half?' echoed Dickie. 'I'm three-quarters.'

That was taken as acceptance. Joe announced to the mess (which took little notice but continued on its own noisy way) that this was to be a rubber for the championship, and the game was on.

Despite their protests about drinking, both men seemed very swift of action and keen of eye. Because Vincent was a newcomer most of the spectators favoured Dickie. The Parke crew, however, gave lusty support to Vincent. It was the Parke supporters who cheered most frequently as their entrant steadily drew ahead.

During normal play Vincent and Dickie were closely matched, but each time he took the service Vincent would gain a point. Vincent won the first game and when it fell his service and when he was up 19–16 in the second, the result looked a foregone conclusion.

At 21–17 Joe shouted: 'The champ! A beer for the new champ!' and led Vincent triumphantly to the bar.

The cold front of severe weather that was to have taken eleven hours to pass over England in fact moved diagonally down the Channel, finally blowing itself out on the morning of the third day.

The rest had left the aircrew refreshed, so when the Tannoy blared out the special mealtimes for navigators that signalled another operation, there were few complaints. Instead, the expert eyes appraised the clearing skies and most men agreed when Joe said: 'It should be bang on for dicing tonight.'

The target was Karlsruhe, near the Ruhr. But at least they would be there and back in six hours. By the look of things there would be a good chance of finding the target visually and bombing accurately. That was always gratifying.

'I don't so much mind sticking my neck out,' Bill would say, 'when I get something good in my bomb-sight and know I've pranged it well.'

After the briefing, Flight Lieutenant the Hon. Holbrooke-Hardwicke was surrounded by his brood of Specials in a more excited mood than usual. Clear skies meant a busy night for fighters.

'Sir,' one of the Specials called, 'I can never think of anything to say except 'fly such-and-such a course.' It sometimes sounds unconvincing. What else could I say?'

'Say any jolly thing you like,' said H-H.

'But what, sir?'

'Well, any dashed thing. If you don't want to give an actual course just say, er, 'Fly north and await instructions.''

'And what will I say?'

'The same, if you like.'

'And me, sir?'

'And I, sir?'

Again H-H cursed the day he had volunteered the information that he had spent his youth in Germany and spoke German perfectly. No Continental, he was sure, would think for himself if he could find an officer to think for him. 'Oh, for goodness' sake, *all* say it,' he said curtly. 'Everybody. Just keep repeating 'Fly north and await instructions.''

Johnnie tried the phrase in English, then in German. He liked the ring of it.

With the exception of Vincent who was finishing his flight plan, the crew arrived early at the aircraft. It was not yet dark and they lolled around happily, enjoying the evening quiet. Hyde passed around the cigarettes, carefully including the ground-crew whose work was so vital and whose approval he always strove to win.

Hyde was surprised, though, that Joe refused. He noticed, too, as Joe wandered away from the group towards the mechanic's hut, that his usual exuberance was gone. After lighting the cigarettes all round, Hyde walked over behind the hut where Joe had disappeared.

Joe was leaning on his arm against the hut, vomiting violently. Hyde placed a friendly hand on his shoulder. 'What's up, Joe?'

'Nothing,' said Joe, averting his ashen face and watering eyes. 'Just a bit crook in the guts.'

'Sure it's only biliousness?' Hyde translated the lurid Australianism.

'Quite sure,' said Joe, 'I'll be okay in a minute. It always goes as soon as I get in the air.'

'You've had it before, then?'

Joe had not expected that. But he forced a wide smile. He really did seem to be recovering. 'Yeah. I've had it for years.'

Hyde did not believe that, but he could hardly say so. 'Certain you're fit to fly?' he asked.

'Quite certain. I tell you it's all right as soon as I'm airborne.'

By the time the two men had walked back to the group Joe seemed almost recovered. 'I'll have that smoke now if I may, mate,' he said. Either he really was better or he was making a terrific effort to appear so.[5]

Vincent arrived, weighted down as usual with equipment. As he tossed his nav-bag on the ground, Hyde noticed the contents included gauntlets.

'Hey, Bill, Joe!' called Vincent. 'Spare a minute?' Vincent brought out his chart and maps and pointed. 'There are four pinpoints I'd like to get. If either of you see them let me know. On the coast-in here … on the bend of this river; should be easy, that bridge will be up-moon … this railway junction at the bridge here … and this town; you can't miss those canals. I've written down on these two pieces of paper our approximate times over each point. If you could find those for me we'll be bang on.'

'Okay, Vin,' said Joe. 'And if I've got a minute I'll scout around for a few fighters, too.'

Part One

It was a fair retort. Every member of aircrew feels that the whole aircraft is there to further his own particular job. In a way, that is. That is how eight men become one crew.

Further around the airfield an engine started. 'Let's go,' said Hyde.

Daylight still lingered. Aircraft taxied quickly into position and took off close to each other's heels.

'Pity it isn't a little lighter,' Hyde thought. 'I could've taken off to the mess.' It was squadron practice, a sort of game, to do a flashy take-off or landing to the audience in the mess whenever daylight allowed the audience to see. However, with anything up to eight tons of bombs on board and the same weight of petrol, the flashiness was seldom flamboyant.

Hyde recalled the cat-calls and cracks after his last daylight take-off. Tied to the tall XYZ aerial of Q-Queenie had fluttered a pair of scarlet-dyed Waaf-issue bloomers known to Waafs (and, it must be admitted, to airmen) as 'romance wreckers'.

'I wonder what happened to those romance wreckers?' thought Hyde. 'Probably blew down into Germany where some fat old Frau is wearing them now. Well, if she lives in Karlsruhe, she'll have to wash 'em tomorrow by the look of this weather.'

As they lumbered, heavy-laden, into the air Hyde's eyes approved the clear horizons and bright skies. This trip should be fun.

As usual with a dusk take-off they were to cross the coast-in at low level. Sunset occurs later at altitude than on the ground directly below. Twenty thousand feet up, the flyer can peep over the rim of the earth and see the sun almost half-an-hour after the rays have deserted the groundlings beneath him. Even flying low, in the shadow, it seemed to Hyde that the enemy coast would catch them still visible in the dusk.

But men who plan RAF attacks do not make such mistakes. They flew into the night a meagre minute before the shores of France rushed under their bomb-crammed belly. Once into France their climb to height began: a dragging, clawing climb four miles into the sky. Hyde knew Q-Queenie well. He had flown her often and she had never let him down. Now he eased her up and up, aimed at a star, and she rode it like a lifeboat rides rough seas; fighting, straining, shuddering, but never for a moment anything but absolute master of her element.

As they rose from the cover of coastal hills, German radar started to pick them out. Johnnie made his first contact and promptly ordered; 'Fly north and await instructions.'

The flak started. Light stuff. Until an aircraft is at height the big anti-aircraft guns cannot train on it accurately. The more manoeuvrable light guns, however, are effective up to eleven thousand feet. The bombers were still well below that, and the light guns sprayed the skies with a dazzling pattern of criss-crossing tracer.[6] But the risk of light flak seemed worth the entertainment. Shells fired upwards spiral forward as if following a fine-spun corkscrew. This dainty pattern of light is seen nowhere to better advantage than from an aircraft towards which the shells are travelling. The flyers, light-hearted in the face of this paltry opposition, watched the vivid counterplay of streaking lights with delight.

Then, suddenly, the ground below seemed to erupt in a chain of great explosions. Nine distinct blasts in a straight line: eight big and one very big. Q-Queenie rocked as the shock-wave hit her. 'That was a bomb-load,' announced Bill. 'Eight thousand-pounders and one four-thousand-pound cookie. Jettisoned!'

'Hell!' said Joe. 'Is that what we drop? I'm glad we're flying. It must be dangerous down there.'

Turning away from the bomber stream with both port engines ablaze, the Lancaster that had jettisoned its bombload was struggling to maintain height. Westward they flew, visible as twin flying fires, back into the tracer that had wounded them.

'With luck they'll make it,' said Hyde, 'provided a fighter doesn't jump them. How is fighter activity, Special?'

'Fairly brisk, Skip,' said Johnnie, 'but I'm telling them all to fly north.'

It had grown quiet. The light flak faded behind. At operational height the bombers were quickly covering the miles to the target. 'Skipper to gunners. Seen any combats?'

'Nothing, skip.'

Nobody liked to tempt Fate by speaking his thoughts on the subject, but everyone was thinking the same thing: there should be more fighters on a bright night like this.

The bomber stream seemed well concentrated. Joe and Bill found Vincent's pinpoints. The usual flak, wide to left and right, punishing planes which strayed off track, did not appear. The miles sped back below them; Karlsruhe was at hand. Still the lack of those tell-tale bursts of horizontal tracer revealed the absence of fighters.

'Five minutes to TOT,' said Vincent.

The flak started coming up dead ahead.

'I've got it!', Bill announced excitedly. 'I can see it perfectly. Oh, wizard! Left, left, Skipper. Steadee ...'

The attack opened dead on time. The sky was filling with flak but the flyers, intent only on this vulnerable target, were not diverted.

'Right a bit. Steady, steady. Right-right steady.'

Bill was excited but calm; his voice told of a Karlsruhe square in his sights. 'Steady, steady, steadee ...'

'It's as slow as this at two hundred and fifty mph. My heart's knocking chips off my ribs', thought Joe.

'*Bombs away!*'

Q-Queenie shuddered rhythmically as the nine heavy weights dropped away one after the other, then lurched upwards as her sudden lightness gave her extra lift. Hyde re-adjusted trim and Queenie was in level flight again.

The attack was absolutely copybook. Every bomb-aimer was locating the target and every bombload was hitting its mark. String after string of close-knit explosions sprinkled across the wretched city. The flak was getting erratic: 'Bombed off a good length,' as Joe put it. Fires had started and were spreading as hurtling explosions flung burning masonry high and wide.

And still the fighters did not appear.

'Absolutely bang on,' said Hyde.

'Wizard prang!'

'Poor bastards!' Even as they bombed some airmen could feel pity.

'She'll *never* get 'em clean,' laughed Hyde.

'What's that, skip?'

'Oh, nothing. I was just thinking.'

They left the target searchlights and burrowed into the night, diving away from danger for home. It was all Joe could do not to spoil his night-vision by staring at the flaming mass that was central Karlsruhe.

'We won't have to bomb Karlsruhe again.'

'I'll bet they'll be glad to hear that.'

'Last time I operated here,' announced Hyde, strangely talkative, 'we dropped leaflets. Each one had written on it in German, 'This might have been a bomb.''

'You dropped *only* leaflets?'

'Well, in theory, yes. But in fact I brought along a ginormous housebrick, wrote on it in German, 'This might have been a leaflet', and tossed *that* out.'

Before they could laugh they were snapped back to the present. 'Mid-upper to rear-gunner. Can you see anything dead behind, up fifteen?'

'It's a Stirling.'[7] Joe's prompt identification showed he had seen it before; a friendly bomber.

'Didn't know Stirlings could get this high.'

'Okay,' snapped Hyde. 'Less natter. Settle down.'

The 'wizard prang' plus the light opposition was making them relax. To relax once over Germany might prove once too often.

'There's a combat!', Yarpi shouted through the unwelcome news that armed their fears.

It was the first they had seen tonight.

'Keep on your toes, then.'

A few more squirts of tracer gashed the sky. But opposition remained tentative and half-hearted. The arrogant bombers flew home almost unmolested.

The weather held. At noon the Tannoy spoke again. Another battle order. Already the aircrews had been up for hours to call at Photographic Section and see the bombing photographs each plane had taken of the Karlsruhe raid. These five-inch-square contact prints showed seas of fire and hot chaos. From the time-on-target written on each frame it was possible to follow the whole course of the raid. In safety they relived the excitement of the night before.

Bombing photographs were still the main topic of conversation while the aircrews waited in the big briefing room for the night's orders. Spirits were high. Last night the squadron had flown without loss. And tonight's petrol-load was eighteen-hundred so it was not to be a long trip. They waited eagerly to be airborne again; weather and morale were good.

The Wing Commander, when he rose to speak, did not straight-away draw back the curtain and name the target.

'Well, chaps,' he started, 'you'll all like to hear Command's comments on yesterday's raid, I think. This morning's photographs show that central Karlsruhe is more than half destroyed. And it's still on fire. This is one of our most successful large-scale attacks. Shows what we can do when weather's kind and we try. The oil stores we particularly wanted to get are completely destroyed – rather they will be by the time the fire has burnt itself out. Several other delectable targets have had it, too, including a rolling-stock works that had been marked down for future attack. All of which is splendid news.

'But that's not all. Most of you observed the lack of fighters last night. As a result of this our losses were kept down to five aircraft: less than two per cent of the force engaged. And what delights me is Command's news that the credit for this is due entirely to us; to one-o-one, the XYZ squadron. It seems that Flight Lieutenant Holbrook-Hardwicke conceived the idea of telling his Specials to repeat over and over again the order 'Fly north and await instructions', and with twenty-odd voices all repeating the same order the Huns followed it almost to the letter. While we were down in Karlsruhe most of the Luftwaffe were well on their way to Denmark.'

The Wingco pulled a tuft of hair down over his forehead. 'Hitler's positively *livid*!' he mocked. The men were delighted. 'And even that is not all,' continued the Wingco. 'These Hun fighters, when told to await instructions, really seemed prepared to wait. Figures received so far from MI5 show that at least sixty-seven of them were still awaiting instructions when they ran out of petrol anywhere between the Frisian Islands and Sweden. There they were obliged to forced-land and many of them got severely bent.'[8]

The Wingco was extracting the most out of this victory. 'Those poor German pilots. It's inconvenient having a U-shaped Ju 88 in a field ten miles outside Wilhelmshaven when your aerodrome and your toothbrush are six hundred miles south in Stuttgart.'

'Hitler's night-fighter chief – a fellow called Hans Jeschonnek,[9] whom I look upon as our opposite number – must be as miserable tonight as we are delighted. We must keep it that way. Keep jamming him on XYZ.'

The men had become excited and noisy; the Wing Commander cut it short suddenly. 'Settle down now, chaps, and listen. Tonight we're going to do it again.'

He drew aside the curtain. There was the target: eastern Ruhr. A sobering thought.

'Here is your target. A factory block north of Remsheid which makes the very special carburettors for the He 113. This carburettor is trickier than most so if we succeed the He 113 will not fly in numbers for a year.[10] Now, here are your tactics. We go in north and fly down past the Ruhr as though we were striking at Frankfurt. Then, dead east of Remsheid we cut back into the Ruhr, bomb, and fly straight through between Düsseldorf and Cologne. It's a small target and a small force; just ourselves and our neighbours 460 and 100 Squadrons. That means seventy-odd aircraft on overlapping circuits so be careful on return.'[11]

Once again it was a daylight take-off. With a long sea-leg to fly before they reached the Continent they would set course before dusk. Hyde hurried out to Q-Queenie to tell the ground staff the good news about last night. Too many flyers left the ground personnel to look after themselves and get on with their jobs, isolated from the work the squadron was doing. Hyde knew that good ground crews doing their work conscientiously often made the difference between getting home after a dicey do or failing to

reach home at all. They were vital and they deserved every attention. Chiefy Mitchell and his boys fully shared the flyer's delight
at the German fighter fiasco. Hyde told the story well, and Johnnie
added zest by breaking in at appropriate moments with fierce
outbursts of German. Johnnie's phrases were meaningless to the
Englishmen, but he was so amused himself that at one point he
actually doubled up.

As he did so a heavy object fell from his battle-dress blouse.

A practice bomb!

The men stopped laughing and stared. 'What's this, Johnnie?'
asked Hyde.

Johnnie coloured pathetically. His sensitive lips twisted, his
eyes, which always seemed near to tears, grew moist and he looked
pleadingly at his skipper.

Hyde said, helpfully, 'I know it's a practice bomb, but why are
you carrying it around? Especially on operations?'

'I, I drop it out,' Johnnie managed to say. 'Over – the target.'

'But how? And why?'

'Down – the – flare-chute. I – want to feel – that I, personally,
am – bombing – Germany.'

He seemed suddenly to be quite overcome with emotion, for
he half-shouted, half-sobbed: 'I want to *kill Nazis*!', then instantly
turned away to hide his face.

'Now come on, old chap,' Hyde said, walking Johnnie away. 'We
can straighten this out without getting all upset. Anyone'd think we
don't like people who drop bombs on Germany.'[12]

When Hyde came back to the group he announced: 'Johnnie's
okay. I've said he can drop his bombs but that I mustn't know about
it. So nobody say a word and it'll be all right.'

Hyde looked around. 'Where's Joe?'

'He walked away over there.'

'Oh, hell! Not another one!' Hyde strode off to where Joe could
be seen on the other side of Q-Queenie.

'Have you been sick again, Joe?' Hyde asked sternly. He was
exasperated with all this emotion and his voice sounded terse.

'Just a little, Skip,' said Joe. 'It's gone now.'

'Well, you'll have to cut it out,' snapped Hyde, and immediately realized how unreasonable his order was. 'If it happens any more you must report sick,' Hyde explained more kindly. 'I don't know whether I'm running B Flight or a female dramatic art school,' he complained. 'Great bloody show if Johnnie burst into tears and you were sick smack over the target.'

From the mess windows as they chatted over cakes and afternoon tea, watching squadron officers saw only a dull, copy-book take-off by Q-Queenie; too many 460 and 100 Squadron aircraft nearby for any trick flying. Bound for the Ruhr and a hundred hazards, Hyde raised his hat to caution.

From Ludford Magna north-east to the sea is only twenty miles. Including take-off and circuit on to track it is less than ten minutes flying time. Something happened, however, in those few minutes that Q-Queenie's crew long remembered, some of them until the day they died.

Magnetic saw it first: a field of ripening wheat, and growing amongst it a blaze of scarlet poppies.

He pointed it out to Hyde and then to Vincent. They were still low enough to see the rows of wheat drawn like threads of straw across the field. The setting sun caught each poppy with a touch of blood-red fire, then a ripple of wind set the wheat-heads dancing, and the whole field became a sea of flashing scarlet sequins.

'It's like coarse-weave linen dyed in Ireland's blood,' said Hyde.

'What is?' asked Yarpi, who was staring straight at it.

'It's bloody bad farming an' all,' said Bill. Then, snapping them all back to reality; 'I'll give you the exact time we cross the coast-out, Nav.' In an instant all were back at work. Beneath was restless sea and ahead lay the night.

By the time they reached the Dutch coast they were at twenty thousand feet, and the temperature outside Q-Queenie was minus twenty-six degrees centigrade.

'That coast must be five miles high', thought Hyde, for up there in front of them were twinkling the million lights of Holland's Blackpool.[13] Hardly designed to attract visitors, these; unless the guns below hoped to win for ever the passing travellers.

There! There was one crew for whom the lights of the fair proved too much temptation. Down they hurried unwillingly, down to the evening boulevards and the black night sea.

'Special to crew. Not much fighter activity.'

'They can't still be flying north!'

'After sixty-odd losses they'll still be disorganised.'

'Muck 'em about, Johnnie.'

They were well into Germany when the rear gunner reported: 'Predicted flak closing in behind. Prepare to dive starb'd.'

He watched the regular bursts ranging closer then yelled, 'Go!'

Q-Queenie nosed sharply down, dropped her right wing and started to turn after it.

Immediately she shuddered as the blast of three shells, heavy 5.6 flak, burst just above her.

She was unharmed. Flak bursts upwards. The gunners below would have to find her again now.

Hyde held his dive for a thousand feet. 'Make 'em think they've got us and they'll stop,' he reasoned.

Then Q-Queenie was back on course again. Vincent was busy collecting strings. Joe thought, 'Thank God we're not Yanks who have to fly formation and can't take evasive action. That burst would've got us.'

The sky over Munster was boiling. They took a bearing on it and checked their ground-speed. Bang on time – good. Some aircraft must be off track, though; else the Munster gunners would have nothing to shoot at. But for the most part the concentration looked tight. Bombers were actually visible all around them and Queenie bounced over many a slip-stream.

The force flew on past the Ruhr. In Frankfurt the sirens sounded the alarm. In Remsheid they unwittingly signalled all-clear.

Then the stream wheeled westward. Throttles rammed forward, noses dropped, airspeed indicators pointed towards 250. Surprise demanded speed and every aircraft was straining forward. The Remsheid sirens, recently so smug, changed their minds and tunes to quick alarm. Fighters circling over Frankfurt received frenzied orders to hurry to Remsheid.

But the bombers had a fifty-mile start. Tactics had succeeded.

'Nav to crew. Five minutes to TOT.'

'I see it,' said Bill. 'Ten port, skip. Left a bit more. Left-left steady. Steadeee.'

Bill set the wind on his bombsight and prayed that it was right. A perfect run could miss badly if the navigator's target wind was incorrect. Bill prayed and stared ahead. 'Oh, good shot!'

The instant Bill had identified the factory the first bombs had landed. They were dead centre. Q-Queenie's dive from the turn-in point, eighteen minutes behind, had brought them down to twelve thousand feet. From this height the target lay clear and vulnerable. Bombs were hitting. Bill was hard-pressed to keep his eye on the factory itself and not be distracted by the explosions. 'Left-left. Left-left, too much; right a fraction. Steady, steady, steadee ...'

It always took an age over the target. If only time could keep pace with their racing hearts.

'Steady, steady, steadee ... *bombs away.*' Q-Queenie jumped for joy as the heavy bombs flicked off.

So intent had the men been on their bombing-run that they had not given more than a glance to the sky about them. This was the Ruhr. Naturally all hell would break loose.

But now they turned to watch and what they saw made them think that they had blundered into a war of the stars. They sailed upon a sky of liquid lightning. Flashes and crashes surrounded them. They could smell flak in the smoke they flew through. Q-Queenie rocked and shuddered in the grips of blast and counter-blast from shells all around her.

Pointless to try evasive action in this. Flak was everywhere. Straight and fast was the quickest way out. The war of the stars went on, intensified, filled all space. They seemed to be flying in the tail of a comet.

This was the Ruhr. Naturally all hell would break loose.

This was one of the reasons they had attacked from the east, the Remsheid side of the Ruhr. To fly through such frantic opposition *to* a target scatters the force and puts all but the bravest men off their aim. This way they bombed first. Now they flew without bombs, too. They were lighter, faster, less vulnerable. And besides, those bombers they could see crashing now, they had already bombed, they had finished the job

It was reported that 'Bomber' Harris, Chief of Bomber Command, had said that 'an aircrew had justified their training and the cost of their aircraft if they flew two successful missions and were lost on their third *after they had bombed.*'[14]

Perhaps this attack from the long way round had turned one or two of these crews from a loss into a profit. A reassuring tick on the credit side, and all for the price of only seven telegrams. How reassuring for the wives and mothers who read them.

At least they did not have to worry about fighters as long as this kept up. The fighters would wait above, wait to subdue with guns those bombers who survived this trial by fire.

Q-Queenie, pushing home with growing confidence one instant, found herself hurtling down towards hated Germany the next. Three flak bursts, under her starboard tail, had flung her fins into the air.

Hyde struggled with the controls that had been wrenched from his hands, straightening Queenie in her dive, then eased her out and back to level flight.

'Anyone hurt?' Hyde asked on intercom. 'How are you, nav?'

It was the answer to this question he had come to fear the most. 'How are you, nav?' he repeated.

Silence.

'Skipper to navigator. Are you okay?'

Silence!

'Engineer. See if the nav's okay.'

Magnetic, standing beside Hyde rubbing a bruised elbow, did not hear. Intercom was smashed. Hyde tore off his mask and shouted to Magnetic to check that the crew were unhurt.

Magnetic shouted back; 'Watch the starb'd outer. I think it's been hit,' unplugged his intercom and oxygen leads and walked aft.

By the time Magnetic returned with the heartening news that nobody was hurt and nothing important seemed broken, it was quite obvious he was right about the starboard outer.

'She's very rough,' he shouted, as Q-Queenie rattled at the uneven revolutions. 'Should we feather?'

To feather a propeller is to stop the motor driving it and turn the propeller-blades edge-on so they cause minimum wind-resistance. Engineers liked to do it because it saved the engine. Other aircrew did not like to do it because it lost them power and speed. No use saving an engine for the RAF if it never got back to England.[15] Hyde was pondering the wisest move when Q-Queenie was hit again.

Again the burst was to starboard and again they were flung into a headlong dive. This hit was less serious. Hyde quickly had Queenie under control, but by the time they were on an even keel the starboard outer had seized. That not only meant no power, it meant a devilish drag as well – seized blades could not be turned into wind. But at least another check revealed the crew unhurt.

The murderous flak continued. It was mostly above them now. That was where they should be, too. Up there with the main force. Radar could isolate them alone below. Their dives had lost them five thousand feet and now, flying on three engines and with one dragging, they would be struggling to regain altitude.

Then suddenly the flak stopped.

Far below, a German voice had switched it off.

That meant the fighters were ready.

Q-Queenie's plight was instantly serious. If they were attacked they would just fly on; a sitting shot. Hyde would not hear Joe's evasive orders on a dead intercom.

Every one of them knew this. Every man knew that any danger they may meet would find them dumb.

Bill edged back in his bombing compartment; from here he could see the skipper.

Hyde loosened his harness; might as well prepare for the quickest getaway possible.

Magnetic pointed to a gauge that told that the starboard inner was overheating. That would leave them with only two.

Vincent computed their next course and wrote it on a slip of paper to hand to the skipper.

Krink was tinkering with the intercom and cursing the dark; maybe his compatriots were wise after all to fly in daylight; at least they could see to fix things.

Johnnie was terrified, but grimly intent upon his sets; the Hun he was diverting now might be meant for Q-Queenie.

Yarpi, too, was terrified. The only chance, he was thinking, was to bale out before they were shot from the sky.

Joe was straining his excellent eyesight to its limit; if a fighter attacked now Q-Queenie would simply have to shoot it down before it shot Q-Queenie down. That was their only chance. That chance might have to be taken; the sky was full of combats.

It would be another hour before they were out. A wordless hour. An infinitely worrying hour. A dreadfully dangerous hour. Every man knew that.

Eight subconscious imps knew that too. Now was the time to work on these men. Now they are afraid! Bombard their minds with terror now and perhaps they will crack. Make their fear unbearable and perhaps they will never fly to worry us again. Nag their minds. Nag, nag, nag. Drive them mad. Destroy their courage. Worry, worry, worry … Snap their nerves. You were fools to think you could survive! It couldn't happen to you? Give up! Crack!

He's out there now: it's a Ju 88. Joe can see him but Joe can't tell the skipper. Here he comes! He's telling himself you're a dead duck. His finger's on the trigger … Wait for it … Joe won't get him: Joe with four machine-guns. The Hun has four cannon and ten machine-guns. They were learned imps; masters in the art of the nervous breakdown. They would keep nagging a long hour or more.

'W/op to skipper. Testing.'

'Skipper here. Okay! I can hear you. What have you done?'

'I guess I've fixed it, skip.'

'Oh, good show!'

'Whacko!'

'Thank Christ!'

'Good effort, Krink.'

'Bless thee, lad!'

Every voice spoke eagerly, delighted at its own sound. Only Yarpi did not speak. His imp had proved too strong. Yarpi was unconscious; slumped over his sights, his face twitching, fingers misshapen hideously like twisted claws.

Now, the others felt, they could make it. Queenie wouldn't let them down. Even if they did have to feather the starboard inner, Queenie could make it on two. Simply because they could speak and hear they felt that they had conquered war. Not long now. They would soon be home.

The starboard inner held until the French coast. Maybe it could last the whole way but Queenie could fly on two; better to save the engine.

It was while Hyde and Magnetic were discussing the feathering that Yarpi came to. He heard the voices.

He looked down and saw sea.

He must've collapsed. Must pull himself together.[16]

'Special to skipper. Want to hear something funny?'

'What is it, Johnnie?'

'Listen!' Johnnie plugged his receiver into the intercom circuit. The fighters, game to the last, were still trying to cut off the stragglers. A frantic, three-way squabble was going on in German. A German pilot, a German Wurtzburg operator and a German-speaking Special in a 101 Squadron aircraft were arguing like Italian lovers in an opera. Yelling, swearing, cursing. Perhaps the words were unintelligible, but their meaning was transparent. Perhaps it wasn't much fun being a German fighter pilot, either.

Q-Queene did not have to wait when she returned to Ludford Magna. Their 'Request emergency landing on two' was answered instantly with a green and they came straight in. As it was they were late. Even the valiant Queenie could not maintain timing, minus half her engines.

'Gee, you look crook, Yarpi,' Joe said, as soon as the crew were indoors in the light. 'Anything wrong?'

'No, I'm okay,' Yarpi answered, and instantly his imp resumed its tormenting. 'You fool! That was your chance. You only had to tell them. You've had a sort of fit. You're too sick to fly. Tell them!'

But Yarpi was afraid to tell anyone. His imp resolved never to cease torturing Yarpi about that lost opportunity.

Hyde and the Wingco drank late into the night. They were waiting for the reports. 'I've phoned Four-sixty and One-hundred Squadrons,' the Wingco said. 'They say the same as we do: "very successful but expensive". One-hundred Squadron lost three, Four-sixty lost two and we lost three. Eight out of seventy-eight. Over ten per cent losses on one trip.'[17]

'And thirty to a tour', mused Hyde.

'And Buckley's plane's a write-off. Flak holed their port landing-wheel and they ground-looped on touchdown.'

'Anyone killed?'

'No. But three injured. Their first trip.'

'The force was too small,' Hyde complained. 'The more kites the fewer losses. We proved that in May in the first thousand-bomber raid on Cologne when One-o-one flew without loss. At least the weather was kind tonight and we got the target. But another five hundred bombers raiding nearby towns could've done good work and halved our losses. We were promised progress if Cologne succeeded. Well, it did. But what's happened? Nothing!'[18]

'Expensive if a thousand bombers miss the target.'

'Then give 'em this radar we're told is coming.'

'Not enough of it.'

'Then give it to the lead bombers and let them mark the target with flares or something.'[19] Hyde jumped up. 'I say, let's pop into photo-section and see if the target shots are ready.'

When they had studied the target photographs the two officers felt better. H-H was there and the Wingco chided him: 'No fighters for you chaps to jam if we keep this up. Germany now has over four hundred He 113s and no carburettors.' He pointed to a photograph taken late in the attack. 'Absolutely wrecked! I'm to phone Group and tell 'em. I'll use this phone here.'

He spoke to a wing-commander friend and insisted there was no need for photographic reconnaissance. 'Send 'em as a formality; but I tell you the place is wrecked.'

Then he listened for a moment. 'Who? Holbrook-Hardwicke and Parke? They're with me. Certainly, old boy. Gladly. I'll tell them now.' He hung up.

'Tell us what?'

'You've both been awarded DFCs. Congratulations. Yours was recommended after that last dicey-do, Parke, and is now confirmed. A press-on gong. Yours, H-H, was recommended last night. But it's so certain it's come straight through.'

'But what's it for, sir?' H-H looked amazed.

'Getting sixty-seven fighters, that's what for.'

'But that was a mistake, sir. I just *said* that. I just couldn't think of anything else.'

'You didn't need to!'

'But it was unintentional. Quite an accident. Honestly!'

'Look,' said the Wingco, sternly, 'did you tell your chaps to say "Fly north and await instructions" or not?'

'Yessir. I did, sir.'

'Right! Then you destroyed sixty-seven German fighters and I've given you a DFC and that's that. Now come and have a drink before Parke tells me he wants to give his back, too.'[20]

Section Officer Wendy Marlborough-Jones lay in the darkness of her room watching the rain running down the window.

What was it Krink had said? 'I've got a couple of night-fighters lined up at the Wheatsheaf. Coming?'

And Hyde had jumped up and said, 'Sure. Let's go shoot 'em down in flames.' Then Hyde had patted Wendy's knee and left the mess.

Just how much did his metaphors imply? Did Hyde actually make love to these women? Oh, why was she so terrified of such things? Hyde had kissed her once and she had jumped back a foot. Literally jumped back a foot out of his arms.

He had laughed. He apologized immediately and said it was because she looked so funny, but that hadn't helped. If only she could have flung her arms around him and kissed him back. But what if he had gone any further? She could not bear that.

The thought left her frightened and confused.

'Are you really a squadron leader?' she asked, fingering the three rings of braid. As a night-fighter she looked above average; straight, black hair like a ballerina, large, lash-swept eyes, flashing teeth and vivid mouth.

Krink's girl was a blonde edition of the same book. There were differences, yet the two girls seemed cut with the same pattern, painted by the same commercial artist. Their names even came from the same comic-strips: Blondie and Daisy Mae.[21]

'Are you really a squadron leader?'

Hyde's body stayed very close to the night-fighter – legs together from toe to thigh and her shoulder snuggling under his encircling arm – but his mind stayed aloof.

'Why', it was asking, 'why do these stupid girls talk to us as though we were babies?' He knew she'd tried that 'Are you really a Squadron Leader?' gag a dozen times. Or perhaps none of them wanted anything but periphrases. To delve might be to find too much, like an anthropologist who discovers the missing link, only to prove that Man is still a monkey and cannot really think at all.

When the two couples emerged from the bar, icy rain was falling. They ran, the girls squealing, and scurried into Krink's car. It had only been a twenty-yard dash but the girls' flimsy clothes were wet through. Krink saw Blondie shivering and offered her his jacket. Hyde, lacking the American's consideration and wondering why all the British Raleighs had emigrated, was obliged to offer the same to his own partner in the back.

'I'm sure your jacket's nice and warm,' Blondie said to Krink. 'But I'd still freeze. My blouse is wet.'

'Take it off,' said Krink.

'But my bra's soaked as well.'

'Take 'em both off.'

Blondie looked sideways under suspicious lids, then said: 'Okay!'

Hyde swallowed, and thought: 'Well, well! The history books

didn't tell you Sir Walter's ulterior motives. Krink's certainly a smooth operator.'

The car's four occupants, hidden in the darkness of the blackout, started disrobing. The girls were soon stripped to the waist; the flyers' eyes, trained to see in darkness, could just discern exciting outlines. The men slipped their warm jackets over the naked shoulders.

This, Hyde felt, was the embarrassing stage in the alchemical period when stranger turned to lover. Now was the vortex in between. They had lost the strangers' decorum; now coyness – a brazen coyness perhaps, but a definite conventional shyness demanding a decent interval before beginning to surrender – now coyness left a vacuum.

Hyde paused, content to kiss discreetly as though he did not know soft breasts were near, defenceless against premature caresses.

'I had thought we'd go along to the Cafe Dansant for some coffee and a dance,' he said. 'But we can hardly do that in this garb.'

He rattled his gold RAF cuff-links against the button on Daisy Mae's tunic. 'So where to now, Krink?'

Smothered in the depths of voluptuous kissing, Krink's answer was indiscernible. Hyde thought: 'So Krink's already airborne, eh? Quite a hot-house chrysalis!'

'Let's go to my place,' said Blondie. 'I want to get out of this flying officer's tunic before Daisy Mae pulls her rank on me. So let's go, Krink.'

There was a pause, then she said petulantly: 'Well you can't drive and nuzzle at the same time. Put it on ice till we get home.'

'Blondie's place' was neat but mean, the top two stories of a single-front terrace-house. As she turned her key in the latch she said, 'Don't turn on the lights yet. I want to check the black-outs.'

While they stood in the dark room Hyde could see Daisy Mae doing up the buttons of his tunic. She need not have bothered. In clothes cut for Hyde's massive measurements her dainty figure was but scantily hidden.

'Can't see why you wear uplifts, Daisy Mae,' said Krink, and Blondie looked daggers at him.

'I'll go put on some coffee,' said Blondie, heading for the kitchen.

'Can I come?' asked Krink.

'Why?'

'I want to go with you everywhere, like a devoted lap-dog following his, er ...'[22]

Hyde and Daisy Mae were left together. He could usually take this situation easily but tonight it unsettled him. His gaze travelled the tiny room, then fell on a divan. He instantly averted his eyes, as though the divan was a vulgar villain hissing lush, off-stage suggestions in a whisper all the audience could hear.

He stared around for a diversion. 'Shall we light the gas-fire?' he asked.

She smiled radiantly and said, 'Oh, yes; wonderful!' most reassuringly.

Blondie and Krink returned, giggling childishly. 'I'm going up to change,' she said. As she headed up the stairs Krink followed. 'Where are you going, big boy?'

Krink's baby-face wrinkled into an innocent grin. 'I'm just that devoted little lap-dog, remember?'

Blondie answered with a smile that said nothing. But as Krink followed her upstairs she did not stop him.

Daisy Mae had sensed Hyde's restraint. 'Funny,' she thought. 'He didn't look the kind of a chap a girl has to lead.'

He was shuffling around now, actually embarrassed.

'Give me a hand with the divan,' she said. 'Over by the fire.'

They slid the divan across the linoleum. As she lay down and turned back towards Hyde she blinked up at the light. 'Just fire-light, huh?'

Hyde obediently flicked the switch, then stood looking down at Daisy Mae in the fire-light as she nestled back, pillowed in cushions, smiling encouragingly.

It was an open, pleasant smile. For all he knew this girl might slap his face if he got too fresh. So why did he feel this revulsion?

Daisy Mae thought, 'Next thing I know he'll be talking philosophy.'

So she took his hand and drew him gently down. 'Now tell me,' she said. 'What is it you like most in a woman?'

Hyde kissed her. A fatherly kiss. On the forehead. 'You know,' he said, 'it's funny, this sort of thing. Isn't it?'

Daisy Mae thought, 'Ho-hum!', rolled on her side and cupped her chin in her hand. 'Here it comes. Philosophy! Who will it be tonight? Schopenhauer? or Spinoza? I'll give him ten minutes. Then, if I feel I've still got the strength, so-help-me-god I'll rape him!'

— 4 —

My dear husband,

There's nobody like you at writing love-letters, Passion-pants. And Cuddles-pie honey, I'll stay true to you, too. How can I even look at any of these aviators here at the Fort when I've got my own Yank in the RAF?

Sugar, these guys do have nicer uniforms, though. Nicer than that photograph you sent, anyway. And where are your medals? These guys all got medals. Ruffles (he's my room-mate's boyfriend; she's single) says if you been to England you must have a medal too.

Do you have to fly clapped-out old fan-beaters like he says they have in the RAF? He says our Flying Fortress flies higher, faster and further than any ship in the air. Fortresses are bombing Berlin night after night.

Say honey, I'm going to finish now. My room-mate is pitching woo with her boyfriend (a dumb mechanic called Willis) and their breathing's getting so I can't concentrate. Makes me think of you, Passion-pants …[1]

Magnetic and Vincent were waiting for the bus to Grimsby when brakes screeched beside them and a car horn honked. Krink's head appeared out of the driver's window. 'Going to Grimtown?'

'Yeah!'

'Hop in.'

Everybody in the queue rushed forward. 'Hold it, youse guys,' yelled Krink. 'Slow down to a gallop, eh? I can take five. My two buddies here and the three prettiest Waafs. You, you and, er, you.' Krink chose them carefully.

Vincent recognized a pretty Waaf from the met office. At this range he recognized, too, why she was nicknamed Paps. He murmured a shy hello and was surprised that she remembered him. 'Patrick is always talking of his crew,' she said. 'The met staff know you all. It's your crew's gong party tonight, isn't it?' Before anyone could answer, she added: 'Wendy's going. Patr ... I mean Hyde asked me, too.'

'Great!' said Krink. 'We'll see you there.'

'I really don't know whether to come.'

'Gee, honey. Why not?'

'Well, with squadron leaders and such. And Wendy. She frowned a bit when Hyde asked me. I really don't know ...'

'The Limies and their officers; phooey to officers!' said Flying Officer Krynkiwski. 'You come along.'

'I will, then,' decided Paps. She was obviously eager to be talked into it.

'I hear Mr Holbrook-Hardwicke's fiance is coming up, and I'm crazy to meet her. I saw her in *Tatler*. She's gorgeous and her father's a millionaire.'

'*Tatler* was under-estimating as usual,' said Krink, as he unleashed his gaze to feast upon the lovely Miss Barbara Cunard.[2] 'Even Hollywood couldn't do her justice. Imagine! All that and a million dollars, too.'

'A million pounds,' said Joe.

'Eh? Oh, pounds, yeah. Say, that's four million dollars, ain't it? That doll looks lovelier every minute.'

No less doll-like beauty than Barbara Cunard's could be imagined. True, her hair was perfect blonde and her eyes were large and blue. But there the likeness ended. Her features were smooth and adult: one sweeping curve from the top of her forehead to the tip of her nose. Yet it was her voice and grace which turned her loveliness into charm. To watch her move, whether to dance or to light a cigarette, could have taught something of grace to a ballerina.

She captivated everyone. Her influence made even Yarpi attempt refinement.

H-H quite obviously adored her, but his adoration was typically English; restrained and tasteful. One sensed his affection, not because he gazed lovingly or whispered romantically, but because this creature he obviously treasured. He had chosen her; naturally she was a goddess and he worshipped her.

After dinner, the party moved from the Wheatsheaf to the Cafe Dansant. The move displeased Krink. 'Blondie'll turn up,' he told Hyde. 'Blondie is terrible sick. Bells ring in her ears; wedding bells.'

'Nonsense!' Hyde said. 'Anyway, she's married. So is Daisy Mae.'

'Blondie *was* married. But Poppa got the chop. Merchant Navy. Now she's got her merry widow eyes on me.'

'You're imagining it.'

'No such luck. 'Isn't it wonderful,' she says. 'Dear Herb is dead. Now we can get married.' Those were her exact words.'

Krinks' tone implied that Blondie had donned the black cap as she spoke.

'Isn't this music romantic?' asked Paps.

'Yes,' said Vincent.

'A waltz. I love to waltz.'

'Yes.'

There was a pause while Paps looked at Vincent and Vincent stared at his drink.

'Ah, the waltz,' breathed Paps again.

'Er, would you like to dance?' Vincent asked.

'Oh!' Paps turned to him quickly. 'Why, yes,' she said, and they joined the kaleidoscope of dancers.

'Crowded.'

'Yes,' said Vincent.

'Nice, though.'

'Yes.'

'We'd take less room if we danced closer.'

Vincent started at a tap on his shoulder. 'Excuse me, mate,' said Joe. 'I'm cutting in. You're wasting this shapely armful dancing at that range.'

Joe took Paps around the waist. 'Clear the decks for a navel battle,' he joked, and they waltzed away, dancing very close.

Vincent headed for their table, but Hyde and Wendy were there, alone, so he walked over to the bar and watched them.

She was smiling now. Shyly. Smiling at something Hyde had said. 'Her coyness has a charm all its own', Vincent thought. With Wendy he would be able to relax.

'So having asked her to marry him,' Hyde was saying, 'Krink is now flabbergasted to find she's in a position to accept.'

'But does he want to marry her?'

'Hell, no!'

'Then why did he ask her?'

'Well,' he said, and he shot a glance at Wendy. He thought, 'she honestly doesn't understand.'

'Well, just to make her feel better about things.'

'But how could it?'

'Because she'd think the *affaire* less casual if she thought he would marry her if he could.'

'*L'affaire de coeur*?' Wendy could not hide her surprise.

'Of course.'

'Then he *should* marry her.'

'Not if Krink can help it.' Hyde thought this was getting out of control. But he wanted to gauge Wendy's feelings. 'So he's devised this elaborate scheme. If they should turn up here tonight ...'

'They?'

'Yes. Blondie's got a chum. Another night-fighter. They always fly formation.'

'A night-fighter?' Wendy's voice faltered.

'Yes. If they turn up tonight, Krink's going to ...'

'A couple of night-fighters,' Wendy was thinking. So her fears *were* well-founded. Hyde had not admitted the other was his own mistress, but asked about Krink he had said 'of course' as though doubts were foolish. Oh, it was monstrous! To ask her out then tell her this! But, had he asked her out? He had also asked Paps. It was a party. If these horrid night-fighters arrived he would probably ask them to join the party, too.

'It's the funniest situation in years,' Hyde was saying.

But Wendy did not hear. Emotions were thundering against her ears and she was lost to every other sound.

'But a situation I carefully avoid,' Hyde continued. 'I've been looking for something more honest and sincere.'

Wendy sat deaf to everything but the fear that she had made a fool of herself. This man had exchanged a few pleasant remarks with her, he had been friendly and amusing, and she imagined he was courting. She had flung herself at him as brazenly as she knew how. And all the time he had been laughing at her and making love to other women.

'Wendy,' Hyde said solemnly, and took her hand. 'Wendy, my dear ...'

His action returned Wendy's mind to the present. This ... this monster was caressing her! She jumped to her feet.

'Excuse me,' she said coldly, and walked quickly across the room, where she found herself standing next to Vincent. She did her best to smile at him and said, 'Buy me a drink, please.' She raised the glass with trembling hand and drank greedily. Then she murmured 'Excuse me,' and started to leave.

As she was collecting her cap and great-coat, Vincent appeared. 'May I see you home, m'am?' he asked softly. 'Yes,' she said. She did not have to try to smile this time. 'Yes, I would like that. Please do.'

As they walked to the door, two girls came in: two very pretty girls. One was tall and blonde, the other had straight black hair like a ballerina, lash-swept eyes and vivid mouth. They were fresh, sweet-looking girls. Especially the one with dark hair. 'She won't be safe in the same room with that monster,' thought Wendy.

Hyde glanced approvingly at Daisy Mae. A real woman with some understanding of the world, who knew what it was for, and had a sense of humour.

He could relax now. With Wendy he was always acting.

'It's unreal,' said H-H. 'Having you here, Petal, is utterly unreal. In this vulgar world around the squadron I did not think you could exist.'

'You exist here. That's all I need.'

'But surely you are loftier, Petal. Isn't this too earthy?'

'I'm feeling earthy. We're in love and that happens at all altitudes.'

'Even in different worlds?'

'Any world with you is heaven.

Their bright eyes kissed across the table.

There was a crash and a nearby ATS girl leapt to her feet with gin-and-it spilling down her tight khaki skirt.

'Oh, you clumsy sod, Kiwi,' she complained to the young airman trying to wipe her dry with a handkerchief. 'Here, give me that,' she said, taking it from him. 'It's bad enough getting a wet skirt without you pawing at it.'

The rough diversion snapped H-H back to earth. The vulgar dialogue and the smell of gin eclipsed the stars in his eyes. 'No, Petal,' he said. 'This wouldn't work. We agreed to wait. Let's stick to that. It isn't as if we must deny ourselves everything.'

Barbara lowered her eyes and H-H said quickly; 'Waiting a month, or a year we'll forget before our honeymoon is ...'

He was interrupted by a dark, saturnine young air-gunner.

'Yes?' asked H-H, trying to keep the irritation out of his voice.

'I should like to buy you and your lady friend a drink, sir,' said the youth. 'If you would permit me I should be honoured.'

'Really? Oh, that's jolly decent of you.' H-H was almost embarrassed. 'Darling,' he said to Barbara, 'may I introduce Sergeant Schydt, one of my Specials.'

'To your fiance,' said Schydt to Barbara, when the drinks arrived. 'A born leader and a brilliant tactician.'

'To One-o-one Squadron,' H-H responded, embarrassed. 'They're the ones who got the original brain-wave.'

H-H instantly cursed himself for saying the wrong thing; in trying to pass the credit to XYZ itself he implied that credit did exist.

'It *was* tactics then, sir?' asked Schydt. 'I knew it! You made it seem so casual; almost unintentional. But you knew if we understood the role we were playing we might sound forced and unnatural. Brilliant indeed!'

Again H-H cursed the un-English minds of his Specials; minds that showed too much emotion, too much excitement. They injected drama into every tiny aspect of life. He decided to change the subject. 'Have another drink,' he offered. He did not wish to keep this fellow in the party, but another drink was the first other subject he could think of. Schydt had no urge to leave; he accepted readily.

'Here's fun,' H-H said quickly.

There followed a moment's silence. Evidently it was what Schydt had been waiting for, because he drew his chair nearer and said, seriously: 'There is a little thing you could tell me, sir; what prospects have we Specials of being commissioned?'

So this little crawler wants promotion! What a slimy, un-British way of going about it! A sip of whisky and a mouthful of flattery.

'I'd bust him to a corporal if I could,' thought H-H. He would deal with Sergeant Schydt. But not now and not in front of Barbara. 'That is your flight commander's decision,' said H-H. 'See him about it.'

'Squadron Leader Parke, sir? He's over at the bar. Could we see him now?'

What an insufferable little dandy! A cheap attempt to win favour and now this blitzkrieg to enforce an imagined advantage. 'This is hardly opportune,' said H-H coldly. 'I do not suggest you approach him here.'

'We don't have to, sir,' said Schydt, happily. 'He is joining us.'

No sooner had Hyde's group joined the party than Schydt returned to the attack. 'This is indeed fortunate, sir,' he said to Hyde. 'I have been ordered to approach you on the matter of my commission. Flight Lieutenant Holbrook-Hardwicke seems to comply for he has referred me up to you.'

'Then I would refer you to the time: close on midnight. And the place: a party at Cleethorpes. And the company: mixed and informal. If you consider yourself worthy of commissioning – despite this untimely intrusion – apply in writing through the proper channels.'

If Sergeant Schydt was quick to sense and press and advantage he was equally quick to recognize a rebuff. Without a word he clicked his heels, gave a stiff little bow, and left.

It was not long before H-H said that he and Barbara must be going.

'Where are you staying?' Daisy Mae asked Barbara politely.

'The Dolphin.'

'I thought I might stay in town tonight,' offered Krink. 'I asked at the Dolphin but they only had double rooms left.'

Barbara coloured to her eyes but H-H responded quickly: 'Then Miss Cunard must have booked before you.'

Daisy Mae and Blondie started talking about Barbara the second that she and H-H were out of earshot, and every word was praise. They liked her looks, her clothes, and most of all her charm.

'Not at all stuck up.'

'She's less of a snob than my manageress.'

'H-H is a lucky boy.'

'She's lucky too. He's cute.'

The foursome was all that remained of the party and, having exhausted the Barbara and H-H topic, they remained silent.

'Another drink?' asked Krink.

'I've got some Scotch at home,' volunteered Blondie.

'Good!' said Daisy Mae, and she squeezed Hyde's hand. 'Let's all go to Blondie's place.'

The Air Vice-Marshal had arrived at briefing and 101 Squadron were suitably impressed. Ludford Magna housed Base HQ as well as Squadron HQ, but AVM's only attended briefings on very special occasions.[3]

The AVM confirmed it. 'Tonight we use new tactics. Your target will be illuminated by specially equipped aircraft called Pathfinders. They will find the target using radar navigation, and mark it three minutes before the first main-force attack with bombs which will burst on the target and continue to burn in several vivid colours. These tactics will necessitate closer bomber concentration. The XYZ function of 101 Squadron will therefore be all the more vital.'

Q-Queenie had just crossed over enemy territory when Johnnie Muller's voice, seldom heard on intercom, interrupted excitedly.

'Special to crew. Here's a problem. The German fighter instructions are being given by *women*. What shall we do?'[4]

The seriousness of this change quickly sank in. With female voices directing them from the ground, the German fighter pilots could not possibly be tricked by false orders from the 101 Squadron Specials. The German counter was one of those delightfully simple but devastatingly effective inspirations. The loss of almost a hundred night-fighters had seemingly provoked the Hun to combat 101's counter-fighter tactics. 'Fly north and await instructions' was being avenged with this counter counter-fighter device. And twenty-six airborne Specials were puzzling vainly to evolve a counter-counter counter-fighter scheme. Where would it all end?

But Special number twenty-seven, Flight Lieutenant Holbrooke-Hardwicke, who was flying with A Flight commander, had already worked it out. Defying the radio-silence orders in consideration of the urgency of his message, he broadcast tersely: 'All Special to jam only, no speech. Repeat: jam only, no speech. Do not acknowledge. 'Brylcreem' captains advise crew. Out!' ('Brylcreem' was the 101 code call-sign, in deference to advertising and the title 'The Brylcreem Boys'.)

Tonight, of all nights, it seemed that there was greater radio activity than ever. The sky was full of fighter messages. Johnnie's hand was seldom off his key. Once he jammed a message and, having finished with apparent success, searched for new transmissions to obstruct. He quickly found one and began jamming it, but not before he had been able to recognize it as the same message he had just finished jamming. There were, obviously, new tactics to be surmounted tonight.

Alert to the many new complications, H-H had sent a coded message back to England by morse advising that many listening-out radios be set to find out what the Germans were up to. He hoped that, by studying and carefully timing every transmission that went out, he could later analyse them and discover any system of duplication that the Huns might be using.

'Huns', he told himself, 'were suckers for systems. And systems were easier to crack than random operations. So first find the system and soon would come the answer.'

Meanwhile it was obvious that the Hun tactics were succeeding.

XYZ jamming was impeding them but not decisively. Combats filled the sky.

H-H was cursing the luck that had fated this new German counter to coincide with the RAF's first Pathfinder attack. Perhaps, if tonight's losses were unreasonably heavy, the brass-hats would blame Pathfinder concentrations and abandon their welcome protege with all its brilliant prospects. Not only XYZ, but perhaps the future of the whole Pathfinder force was threatened tonight.[5]

Nor was that all. Most men, flying this fighter-lined gauntlet, would arrive at the target shaken and jumpy. The attack would not find them at their calmest and best, so the likely success of the new tactics would be further threatened.

These were the fears that spurred the Specials' efforts. Their fears were well-founded and their efforts extreme and well-directed. But the German transmitters were too many; the fighters hammered at the bomber stream repeatedly, and it was indeed a jumpy, shaken force that beheld the first ever attack marked with vivid-burning candle bombs.

Pathfinder markers were dropped, it is true, and remained clearly visible from the air. Some of those markers were spot on the target. But others were too wide to be anything but confusing. Clusters of candle bombs were burning over an area many miles across.

The main force saw them all right. Bill saw the first batch go down and shouted, 'Spot fires fifteen starb'd!'

'Turning on,' said Hyde. They tracked towards the burning bombs with careful confidence.

'This is a piece of cake,' said Bill.

Then the next cluster dropped, but at least a mile beyond and ten degrees port. Then another cluster somewhere between and two more far out on either side. 'Eeeh, hold on, lad!' Bill exclaimed. 'I can't bomb six places at once.'

'Can you see any substantiating ground detail?' Hyde asked, quickly grasping the situation.

'Can't see a thing through that glare,' said Bill, and added, 'Left, left.'

'Don't bomb yet,' said Hyde. 'That first cluster seems wide. I'll fly over the centre. See if you can recognize anything.'

Bill cursed under his breath, stopped looking through his bomb-sight and squinted over it, trying to recognise the target. The spot markers helped by lighting some of the countryside around them but they also hindered by dazzling the bomb-aimer's vision.

'I can see a factory chimney-stack between those two reds on the port bow,' said Bill. 'It's obviously something worth hitting.'

'Right! Going round again.'

Q-Queenie completed her sweeping, five-mile circuit and turned her nose once more the target. Bill had just given a rough alteration on to the markers when, one by one, they started going out. Suddenly he remembered the warning at briefing; 'Each cluster will burn about three minutes.'

Hyde had seen it, too. 'Line up on the spot as quickly as you can. Keep it in sight even if the fires go out completely.'

'Left-left. Left-left, steady.' Bill spoke quickly, his voice high-pitched and strained. 'Steady, steady, eh, drat it! They've all gone out. Hold her steady, lad, I can still see target.'

It was now seven minutes since Queenie had started her first bombing run and nerves were fraying fast. As Bill's voice droned on – 'steady, steadee' – seven other voices were aching to scream 'Bombs away for Chrissake!' But when it came, the voice that spoke was Joe's;

'Rear-gunner to bomb-aimer. Hold it, there's a Manchester straight below us.'[6]

'Would our bombs hit him?'

'Sure to. He's dead below.'

'This be proper muck-up an' all.'

Bill dared not take his eyes off the target. He could only just keep it pinpointed as it was.

And then the flak got them. Three shells burst below. Far enough below, fortunately, for Queenie to miss most of the shrapnel, but close enough to be flung in the air by the blast.

Magnetic spoke on the intercom, his clear voice perfectly calm and modulated; 'Have you ever had one of those days when every-thing, but absolutely *everything*, goes wrong?'

'Get off the bloody air!', Hyde snapped viciously. 'Bomb-aimer!

Can you still see a target?'

'Yes, skipper. Left a bit.'

'Gunners! Is that Manchester still below?'

'Yes,' said Joe.

'No he's not!' screamed Yarpi. 'He's clear port. The flak blew us off him. He's clear, man! For Chrisake bomb!'

'Okay,' said Bill. 'Steadee ...'

The next instant three voices spoke simultaneously. Joe said, 'He's dead below!'

Hyde said, 'Hold it!'

And Bill said, '*Bombs away!*'

It takes seven seconds for bombs to fall the first thousand feet. Aboard Q-Queenie the count was made in utter silence. With every eternal tick the referee's finger of Fate pointed over the Manchester and its crew below. *One. Two. Three. Four.*

The Manchester lay on the canvas, not hearing the mortal count above.

Five. Six. If only it could stay there, take a count of nine, then they would know it was on its feet again and still in the fight. *Seven!*

Queenie shuddered and groaned with her crew under the impact of two bomb-loads and an aircraft blowing up just a few hundred yards below her. Nobody spoke. Queenie turned for home. She had a lump in her throat.[7]

Back at Base the radio message from H-H had set every available wireless-operator in Bomber Command system. Already they had discovered the new German tactics. 'They transmit every message on three channels,' the Station Commander explained H-H. 'We assume the German pilots have receivers with three-switch positions. If they encounter XYZ jamming on one, they switch straight over to another and we've only caused them a moment's interruption. We'll simply have to copy them; jam all three channels simultaneously.'

'How do we know they won't change their channels, sir?'

'We don't know. But we can check at the start of each raid and adjust transmitters accordingly.'

'Adjust them in the air, sir?'

'Yes. In the air.'

H-H reflected on this complication. 'And what about the female operators? Couldn't we carry women, too, sir?'

'Women? In our bombers?'

'Why not, sir? I'm sure we'd find volunteers.'

'We'd find aircrew volunteers to rescue these female Specials at any sign of trouble.'

H-H smiled. 'But what alternative is there, sir?'

'I don't know yet. But if there is no alternative I don't doubt we'll issue Waafs with chastity belts and send them flying with you.'

— 5 —

The CO had called a Flight and Section Commander's conference for 0930 hours the following morning. As Hyde walked into the cosy, usually informal little office, he was surprised to see it crowded with every senior technical officer off the squadron. Both the Station Commander and the Base Air Vice-Marshal were present.

As soon as they were all present, the CO handed over to the AVM who went straight to the point. 'One-o-one must beat these German tactics,' he said, 'and here's how we're going to do it. To jam all three simultaneous channels used by the Hun we shall transmit our jamming signal on the same three wave-lengths. That will mean more equipment in every aircraft. And we're not going to put in just enough – three channels – we're going to put in four, in case Jerry has an extra one up his sleeve too. Now, I can see Mr Marshall bursting to tell me the Lancaster's wiring won't stand the load. I know that. What we've got to do is put in more wiring. I know, too, it's a big job and a fiddling one. And what's going to make it even more fiddling is that Harris won't let us take the squadron off operations to make the conversion. The war must go on. You'll do the job when the aircraft are here to work on and they must not at any time be non-operational.'

Several officers exchanged glances and their eyes groaned.

'But it's an ill wind that blows no good,' he continued, 'and we do get something out of this. It'll mean even more work for the ground staff but I know it's going to delight the aircrew. While we're boosting our Lancs' wiring we will also fit them to take Gee[1] for radar navigation. This means work. I know it. But I also know you'll do it and do it quickly. Let this thought spur you on: until XYZ is functioning efficiently again men are being killed every time we fly, men who would otherwise have survived. Keep that in mind and I know you'll break records. Now I'll leave you to your CO who'll set you each to work in your own way. Work with a will. And if there's anything you want, tell me about it straight away and if it's humanly possible I'll get it.'

Then he left the meeting. Quickly. The brisk way he slammed the door behind him added even greater urgency to what he had said. Inspired, the technical staff were already settling down to the business they liked: getting their teeth into the job.

'If we're likely to have *women* in our crews ...' H-H left the sentence unfinished.

'What's suddenly so repulsive about women?' asked Krink.

'How could you ever feel love and tenderness for a woman after you'd been to war with one?'

'Easy!' said Krink. 'It'd be a new approach. 'Weren't we over Berlin together?' The romance of that'd lay 'em cold.'

'Exactly,' said H-H. 'Cold! I want women tender and soft, not athletic and valiant.'

Krink turned to his neighbour – a pilot in the khaki uniform and rank of the South African Air Force – and pleaded for support. 'What do you say, Bob? Would you kick a girl out of bed just because you discovered she'd had a distinguished career as an aviator?'

Bob – Lieutenant Robert Cahill – ran a freckled hand through his unkempt hair and smiled boyishly. 'I doubt that in those circumstances I'd have broached the flying topic,' he said.

'Could a woman walk into debriefing after a raid,' asked H-H 'and then leap screaming onto a chair at sight of a mouse? She'd lack the courage to appear so uncourageous.'

They were interrupted by the Air Vice-Marshal coming in to briefing.

'Is that guy always around?' asked Cahill.

'He's usually around if anything important is happening. You just happen to have joined the squadron at a crucial time.'

That this was indeed a 'crucial time' could be felt in the air. Despite the AVM's warning that all aircraft must remain operational during conversion, One-o-one had not been called upon to fly for several days, and during that time the modifications had been completed. Navigators and bomb-aimers had been training to use the new Gee; really working hard. The Specials were eager to air their new equipment.

'Tonight,' the AVM began without preamble, 'Bomber Command will use, for the first time, a weapon that has been the topic of heated argument throughout top-level talks of all three services for a year. It is to be called 'window' and for once it is no secret. You can tell your Mum all about this one, because Jerry's going to know before you even reach tonight's target. In every aircraft are bundles of tin-foil, usually called 'silver paper'. When you come into range of enemy radar you will start throwing these paper strips out so they will float in the sky behind you. Every metal strip will echo back a radar signal and be picked up on German radar screens. The boffins assure me that ten aircraft dropping window appear on a radar screen rather like a formation of a thousand. How the six hundred of you flying tonight will look I almost hate to think. Cologne got a shock when a thousand bombers appeared on their screens; tonight, Nürnberg will have a fit because they're going to see what'll look more like sixty thousand.'[2]

The flyers goggled with delight at this picture of German perplexity.

'This is not a new thing; we've had it a year or more. But British military policy forbids the use of any weapon for which we have no counter-measure. For window there is no counter. So we have not used it. But bomber losses have been so heavy that Command want to use it even so, and have constantly pleaded for permission to do so. At last, contrary to policy and still against much opposition, we have that permission.'[3]

'Tonight you have added radio coverage too, so be sure you let

no messages through; always assuming the German radar operators can untangle the mess on their screens sufficiently to find a
message worth sending.'

Then he grew suddenly more serious. 'There is one man they
will be able to discover, though, and he's the man who gets off
track and outside the bomber-stream. He will appear as one, solid
radar dot, unhidden by the responses behind him caused by his
own window. Hereafter, more than ever, these stragglers will be
attacked. So you'll have plenty of vital XYZ work to do. And make
sure that *you* are not amongst the stragglers. You're lucky to have
Gee. But it means more work, not less. More work for greater
accuracy. As your aids improve your work doesn't get easier; it gets
harder. Remember that, and put those aids to work.'

Out at the aircraft the excitement of briefing gave way to the
wilder, more intense excitement of the approaching raid, and the
flyers were inside Queenie long before necessary. They wanted to
see their new aids.

Johnnie was giving himself a final check on his band transmitters; closing his eyes and putting his hands on each unit in turn;
checking that he literally could do it in the dark.

Vincent was admiring his Gee-set. The grey metal box, like
a four-gallon kerosene tin on its side, with a round, green glass
screen and many coloured knobs facing his desk, looked more like
a toy than a weapon of war. It could not be switched on until the
engines were running, so they just gazed lovingly at it.

Then they all studied the 'window'. It, too, had little entertainment value in its present form. But still the flyers, hardly more than
boys and all just boys at hears, fingered and admired their latest
toys with gay anticipation. Like the children they had been only a
few years before, on Guy Fawkes' afternoon, playing with fireworks
which, until the night when they would be lit, were just so much
trash.

Students of natural history have studied flocks of birds altering
course in flight. Every wing dips and turns on an instant, as though
to a word of command. Some theorise that the command is given
telepathically. Any aviator who has flown in a bomber stream, even

isolated by radio-silence, can believe this theory. Waves of feeling – excitement, fear, exhilaration, even panic – can sweep through a flight of aircraft influencing every sensitive man and making him respond to its message. Such a wave swept the stream now. The first bombers to come abreast of the French coast started windowing. Perhaps it was their joy that permeated through to their comrades as the leading crews released the first ever life-saving window used in action. Perhaps it was an amused awareness of the German panic as they saw thousands upon thousands of solid blips dancing on the searching radar screens. Perhaps it was just a primitive, intrinsic awareness; a mob instinct. Whatever the explanation, the crew of Q-Queenie caught the sudden impulse of joy.

'One minute to French coast-in,' Vincent said. 'Start windowing now.'

And, as the bomb-aimer started dropping the tinsel strips, a few at a time, each man had become a part of that wild, unspoken paroxysm of soul-felt joy.

'I'll give you the exact time we cross the coast, nav,' said Joe.

'No!' said Vincent. 'Let me tell you. I've got it spot-on with Gee. We're dead over the coast at latitude fifty degrees eighteen minutes ... *now!*'

'Half a second late,' laughed Joe. 'Haven't you learnt to use that thing yet?'

'That's because the skipper was half a degree off course.'

Hyde did not defend his flying. Any pilot who never gets more than half a degree off course is so far above average that what appeared to be badinage was actually praise.

Spirits and hopes were high. As they flew across France and into Germany they felt their high hopes justified. Flak, when they encountered it, was light and wild. Johnnie had reported an excited confusion on German radio. The Hun stood dazed by the new tactics, like a boxer out on his feet. The Germans shook their heads to clear their vision, but when they looked again the scene was as hazy as before.

'We've bowled 'em a googly this time,' said Joe. 'Every ball a wicket!'[4]

It was along the Rhine that they first noticed the fog; light, wispy stuff at first. Then steadily it thickened, flat and dull, blanketing everything.

'Sometimes I think they've got God on their side,' said Bill, peering over his bomb-sight at a grey sea of nothingness.

'Nonsense!' said Magnetic. 'It would never occur to God to support anyone but the British.' He meant it as humour, but it had a ring of shocked sincerity.

But it was obvious that the deterioration in the weather had disappointed them all. Everything had looked so right. The trip was going so well. The opposition was slight and disjointed. Vincent kept telling them *exactly* where they were; he couldn't resist it, he was so overjoyed at knowing it himself. With reduced opposition permitting them to mark accurately, PFF could have done an exact job. Altogether it could have been the perfect attack. But now a thin layer of fog had come to spoil it.

'Five minutes to TOT,' said Vincent. 'I know *exactly* where we are, so even if we have to bomb on ETA we'll still be spot-on.' He sounded optimistic but the crew could not hide their disappointment. Maybe all Gee-equipped aircraft would bomb accurately. But, with a little luck, every aircraft could have done so. It was such a wonderful opportunity – spoilt.

'Thah can't see nowt down thar,' Bill mumbled.

'Keep eyes sharp just t'same, lad,' Vincent answered him in studied Yorkshire. 'Markers be 'bout t'fall reet soon.'

Sullenly the men watched the sombre fog, swirling four miles below; beneath it Nürnberg was skulking, smugly safe. And then, like a torch switched on beneath a muddy pond, a red-brown glow appeared.

'Eeeh! Look!' cried Bill. 'Thah can see t'markers clear through it. Look! Thah's more an' all!'

The dull red glow was suddenly joined by grey-greens and then some misty yellow. Candle bombs through the fog! Bombs had begun to fall, and as the blasts rent jagged holes in the fog blanket, there were instants when the vivid markers shone through with greater brilliance in contrast with their fog-grey backdrop.

Six hundred bombers saw it, and every long black nose turned to the attack.

'Eeeeh! Luvly!' said Bill. 'We're tracking for dead centre, skip. Just hold her steady … steadeee … steadeee …'

It was to be a nine-minute attack: six hundred bombers carrying 2,300 tons of bombs. That was the plan, and now, remorselessly, that plan was becoming a fact. Within one minute the concentration of bombs on central Nürnberg had melted the fog away. Surrounding fog hid everything but the target. Like a blood-red cherry in a vast plate of porridge it clamoured for every eye's attention; from the heart of an uninviting mess it beckoned – the one choice morsel. And how each bomber relished it.

'Bombs gone!' said Bill, and Vincent checked the time: with ten seconds of his ETA. He patted the Gee box affectionately.

Almost at the instant of bombing – certainly not longer than half a second afterwards – Q-Queenie's lurch as her heavy bombs fell was shaken with a staccato shudder. Quickly the smell of cordite filled their oxygen-masks, pungent and frightening. Instantly every man tensed, wondering if Queenie had been hit.

Then in a flash, before they had time to decide what had happened or what to do, Joe's voice crashed in their ears: 'I got him! I got him!'

'You got what?' asked Hyde, not without irritation.

It was Yarpi's voice that spoke next, almost choked with excitement. 'He's blown up! Gee, man! He's blown up!'

'You bloody beaut!' cried Joe. 'You bloody beaut!'

Hyde spoke, terse and commanding. 'Stop shouting and tell me what's going on.'

'I got a Ju 88,' said Joe. 'He appeared as we were about to bomb.'

'Why didn't you give evasive action?'

'It would've spoilt our bombing-run. I had him covered. And when he turned in I gave him a quick burst.'

'He started burning, then suddenly blew up,' added Yarpi.

'You can still see him,' continued Joe. 'Low on our port beam. On fire.'

Hyde tipped Q-Queenie up on her left wingtip. A tiny comet

burnt below them, falling quickly down and away to port. As they watched, the tiny spark vanished; and an instant later a mushy explosion bubbled up out of the fog north of Nürnberg.

'Good shooting,' said Hyde a little coldly. 'But you should have told me it was there.'

'I thought it might throw Bill off, sir.'

'Okay. But you might try that once too often.' Then suddenly Hyde's tone changed.

'Say! What a night this is!' His voice was bubbling gaiety. 'Just look at that target!'

All this had happened within little more than one minute of bombing. Queenie had bombed at her own appointed time of H-plus-four. It was now just after H-plus-five; the attack was little more than half over. But already the inferno that was Nürnberg had melted the fog for miles around it. Flames and explosions overlapped and inspired each other in seething competition. It looked like the birth of a gaseous world whirling through fog-filled space. And still the bombs rained down; cascading fuel to stoke the flames of hell itself. Still they fell; 2,300 tons in nine minutes; over 250 tons per minute; almost five tons per second.

The RAF had brought them but, more important, they had delivered them. Each factory's quota had whistled almost straight down every tall chimney. Never before had they known such large-scale success. Targets had been hit before. Hit hard; even wiped out. MI5 had recently announced that, following the Remsheid raid, Germany had abandoned production of the feared He 113. But that was seventy aircraft raiding one factory successfully. Tonight the force was increased almost a thousand per cent, and with similar devastating accuracy they had plastered an entire factory area. Rotterdam, London, Coventry were avenged and more; against vital military targets, not useless, helpless civilians.[5]

The Hun was learning what it means to fight a powerful enemy. Gone were his days of easy victory over half-trained, ill-equipped troops. Having failed to conquer vulnerable Britain for the air, Germany now face the double indignity of airborne defeat herself, despite a much-vaunted defence system. Germany had invented the aerial blitzkrieg, now the Allies were perfecting it. The mad scientist was threatened by his own robots.

Looking back, the crew of Q-Queenie saw Nürnberg encircled by fire: a flaming doughnut frying in boiling fog. Why was there so little fire in the centre? Had the vortex completely burnt itself out? They would learn the frightening answer to that question very soon.[6]

Opposition continued light. The only fighter they saw was the one Joe had dealt with so summarily. The fluttering cover of window continued; a few strips from each aircraft every ten seconds. Johnnie repeated the glad news that German radio was confused and excited. Vincent, sunk in the huge, coloured maps of curving lines which translated his Gee-readings into latitude and longitude, watched delightedly their passage straight along the required track, with hardly a waver to left of right. And behind them fell, fluttering brightly, the silver window, littering the German countryside like giant confetti. But no festive confetti, this. To the Hun it was no harbinger of joy. It was, instead, a dreadful threat: a symbol of wedded might and precise destruction.

'Cop this,' said Joe, holding up the morning paper. 'It says 'Target Located by Radar. In last night's devastating attack on Nürnberg pilots located and marked the target by radar.' How d'ya like that? 'Pilots' they say. The pilot couldn't switch the set on, let alone use it. Don't these journalists know that a pilot is exactly one-seventh of the crew of a Lanc?'[7]

'One-eighth of a One-o-one squadron Lanc.' corrected Johnnie.

It was a not-uncommon grouch amongst aircrew: to the public at large there was only one man in the aircraft – the pilot. Journalists, far from correcting the idea, encouraged it. The big trouble was that some pilots (not usually the good ones) believed it.

'Some sprog pilot has written a book in which he says: 'And so, taken by and large, it is still the captain who looks after fifty percent of the navigation.' And as for the story that pilots make or mar accurate bombing … it's nonsense. It's true that a bad pilot can ruin a bombing-run, but a bad bomb-aimer still couldn't hit a target even with the best pilot in the world. It's true that a bad pilot can spoil good navigation, but at night a good pilot still knows less about where he is than the worst navigator.[8] It's true that a bad pilot can ruin a gunner's sight but even the best bomber pilot couldn't shoot a damned thing on his own.'

'Should the journalists confuse everybody by mentioning each man in turn, then?'

'Not at all. They could simply write 'the crew' instead of 'the pilot'. Everybody would understand and it would be much more accurate.

'But surely the pilot is the most important crew member?'

'Why? In a combat the gunner is the most important crew member. In finding the target the navigator is most important, and if the bombs miss the target they've all wasted their time so you can say the bomb-aimer's the most important. You might as well say the rudder bars are most important because if they stopped steering nobody could get anywhere.'

'But the pilot *is* captain.'

'Not always. I've know pilots who lost their captaincy and others who requested that their observer be made captain. The pilot is in the best position to be captain and so, usually, he is captain. But he's not in a position to navigate at all; that's why this pilot-turned-autobiographer is writing bullsh. He might live long enough to learn better. If he does I'll be he regrets the day he ever wrote such rubbish.'

'We've flown home three times with a dead navigator,' Joe said to Vincent. 'And once with a dead gunner. And we missed 'em. Other times, like Remsheid, we've lost the intercom. Not one person or one instrument can be allowed to go wrong or the whole system suffers, or even breaks down completely. A bad crew member, or just one loose nut, can kill a crew. Is a quarter-inch nut more important than I am, or than the pilot? Sometimes it is! So you see, this whole argument proves nothing.'

'Except that journalists and sprog pilots often write rot.'

'You might have to eat your words. This sprog pilot is called Leonard Cheshire, isn't he? If he's the same chap I've heard about, he's certainly lived long enough to learn better. It just shows how much experience teaches. A certain Leonard Cheshire, at twenty-five, is now the RAF's youngest Group Captain and he's won a DSO and a DFC. And he's still going strong. If we ever have to fly with a bad pilot I think we'll discover pretty quickly just how vital a reliable skipper is.'[9]

'And so is a reliable navigator and wide-awake gunners. And I still say newspapers shouldn't say 'pilot' when they mean 'crew'.

'Okay then! Write a letter to the editor and he'll think you're one of the chairborne troops from rear hindquarters.'

Wanting to change the subject, Bill turned to Joe and asked; 'What else does it say about Nürnberg?'

'Losses were very light; less than one percent. And it quotes a German report that civilians in central Nürnberg were trapped in a ring of fire and those who weren't burnt to death were suffocated because all the oxygen was burnt out of the air. Gosh! We could save a lot of bombs that way.'[10]

The armourer sergeant had joined the group earlier, and now he tapped Joe on the shoulder. 'Did you have a combat last night?'

It was Yarpi who replied; 'Did he have a combat! We shot down a Ju 88, man!'

'Must've been a mighty short combat,' said the armourer. 'You only fired nine rounds. Three rounds from one gun and two each from the others.'

'Yes. It was a short burst.'

'Just brrrp ... and he blew up, man,' added Yarpi.

The armourer shook his head almost in disbelief. 'That's a mighty fancy piece o'shootin', pardner,' he said. 'Even a half-second burst would be thirty-six rounds.'

Magnetic took the armourer by the arm and whispered in his ear confidentially; 'As a matter of fact he didn't fire those rounds at all. He took them out of the ammo-belts one at a time and *threw* them at the fighter. You know as well as I do that to fire a nine-round burst out of four guns is quite impossible.'

'My corporal says it *is* impossible.'

'Well, that *proves* it then.'

Something of the new elation that thrilled the Squadron could be felt in the surrounding villages. Although most of the locals divorced themselves from the disrupting aeroplanes and the rowdy youngsters who flew them, they could not disregard the Squadron altogether. When things were bad and losses heavy, the villagers said it was none of their business and no more than the RAF might expect, teaching schoolboys to fool around at hundreds of miles an hour. But deep in their hearts the villagers were sad and sympathetic. Now, when times were quite suddenly better, the villagers wondered aloud what devilry the new high spirits might be up to next, but in their hearts they rejoiced.

The villagers' loyalty was put to the test about this time, and passed with flying colours. The Luftwaffe raided Ludford, an attention the village would have escaped had it not been for 101 Squadron.

While Vincent, Johnnie, Bill and Magnetic were walking together from the mess of their barracks, there came a wail of sirens and, almost immediately, the growl of engines and the grumble of guns as a German aircraft swept low overhead. There was a scramble into the slit-trenches.

'The cheeky bastards,' said Magnetic. 'Raiding *us*!'

'Anyone see what it is?'

'There he is! Another Ju 88.'

'As it passed over them the men could see it quite distinctly against the moonlit sky.

'I can see now why we aren't flying tonight.'

From surrounding aerodromes, also being raided, came flashes of bombs and quick exchanges of gunfire. At this extremely low level, in fair visibility, the Junkers would be quite vulnerable to light flak. But nothing yet seemed to have been fired by Ludford's ground defences.

The Hun flew back over them again, guns roaring once more. No shells seemed to be landing nearby. Johnnie stuck his head out of the trench and shook his fist at the retreating aircraft. 'We'll get you for this. Wait till tomorrow night! We'll knock the ...'

Suddenly Johnnie turned and, with a shouted; 'Look out! Here he comes again!', dived back into the trench, hotly pursued by the sounds of firing.

There was comparative quiet for a minute. The men were already leaving their shelter. And then the bombs came. Six of them in a neat row. They sounded like only 500-pounders, but the earth trembled.

'Where did they hit?'

'I think they fell between Flying Control and the village.'

'Good. That's open field.'

Again the fighter was swooping over them, guns awake.

'He's got guts, this bastard. Why don't RAF Regiment shoot him down? They've been training for this chance for years. Now they're all in bed, I suppose. Or the corporal's got the key to the armoury.'

'Look! He's making a run on the clothing store. He must think it's a hangar.'

The fighter zoomed towards the store. Then, like lazy bubbles in a glass of beer, fire-balls flickered up from the ground. They seemed to pass right over the fighter, but as they appeared, he flicked down. A wingtip touched the ground and for three seconds the fields were filled with flames and noise. Then the aircraft was still, burning with a fierce crackle and the noise of exploding ammunition.

From all over the aerodrome faces watched the flames. The gunners cheered. The ground staff grinned. But the aircrew watched a little grimly. In that Junkers had been a crew; men like themselves – flyers – proud of their wings; confident of their skill. Now they were mashed to pulp, or maybe burning to death. It was almost as though it was a crew of their own in that inferno.

The feeling was not lessened next day when it was announced that the German navigator was only sixteen.[11]

While 101 Squadron were still dazzled by Gee and PFF, another new idea was put forward and once again the Air Vice-Marshal was at briefing to tell them about it.

'PFF,' he explained, 'is to be improved. Though most of their markers have been accurate some have fallen wide and attracted bombs which have been wasted. So tonight your attack will be directed by R/T. A master bomber will be sitting upstairs at about thirty thousand feet and he will tell you which markers to bomb and see that the whole area is plastered.'[12]

'It is terribly important that we do plaster the whole area. We're going to Peenemunde with six hundred heavies. It is the site of Hitler's secret weapon. We must get it. The safety of London and perhaps the very advent of the second front could depend on your success tonight.'[13]

H-H had news for them at this briefing, too. Since the German introduction of female radio operators, 101's Specials had not spoken to confuse German fighters but had been content to jam. Now H-H announced that 'some clot' had invented long-range radio with which German-speaking Waafs could broadcast to the German fighters *from England*.

'So if this succeeds there'll be no Waaf flyers.'

A moan went up from the aircrew.

It was an unusually short and undramatic trip. Peenemunde lay only a hop across to the shores of the Baltic. PFF found the target area with ease. There was little to see: no city, no factories, no bridges or railway marshalling yards – just countryside dotted with solid, blockhouse-like structures and a maze of roads and ramps of steel girders.

The area was heavily defended, both from the ground and in the air. But then, the area was heavily attacked, too. Good though the much-vaunted German defences that Goering proclaimed impregnable were, they could not stop all of six hundred bombers flown with determination and guarded by window and XYZ. The Germans did their damnedest but the attack succeeded. The PFF markers covered the entire target area. The master bomber directed the main force on to the best placed markers, then moved the attack from point to point until the whole site was mangled and smashed.

It did not look like a spectacular raid from above. There were bomb flashes and gun flashes but no great fires or explosions. It was simply a process whereby many 4,000-pound bombs smashed a lot of plant and equipment that had been built to withstand 2,000-pound bombs.

Hyde was called early next morning to the Wing Commander's office. H-H was there when he arrived.

'You chaps will parade at Buckingham Palace at eleven hundred hours on Thursday next,' the Wingco announced. 'You can take just forty-eight hours' special leave or, if you prefer, you can have your week's due leave and tack the forty-eight on to it. Which will you have?'

The Wingco was being pleasant enough, but Hyde noticed a certain heaviness – almost a sadness – about him.

'Two leaves are better than one, sir,' H-H said. 'I'd rather a forty-eight now and normal leave later.'

'What about you, Parke?'

Hyde thought a moment, heavy brow massive with wrinkles. 'I was going to say we'd take the lot, sir. But I suppose two leaves are better than one.'

'Well, make up your mind.'

'Two leaves, thank you sir. A forty-eight now and the remainder later.'

'Right. I'll have Orderly Room prepare your passes and take you all off the bloodsheet.'

It was the end of the interview. H-H was about to leave, but Hyde was worried by the Wing Commander's manner.

'Er, excuse me, sir, but any news of Peenemunde? Has Hitler still got a secret weapon to chuck at us?'

The Wingco frowned, then looked up brightly.

'No, he hasn't, Parke.' He smiled and added: 'We wrecked the joint. We won't see *that* secret weapon for a while.'

'Oh, good, sir! And it's one in the eye for your opposite number, Hans what's-his-name.'

The Wingco looked up quickly; all the sadness had returned. 'Hans Jeschonnek? Yes. Rather too much for him, I'm afraid. Having failed to defend Peenemunde so soon after our success against Nürnberg, he's committed suicide.' The Wingco looked into the distance. 'I'm going to miss him,' he said.[14]

— 6 —

'Squadron Leader Hyde, sir,' said Joe, eyes a-twinkle. 'if you had arranged for us to take leave at a time like this, I for one would've castrated you with a bread-knife.'

'You're durn right,' agreed Krink. 'After even a forty-eight we might return to find the war's over.'

'I know you chaps aren't serious,' Hyde laughed. 'And I do know you could do with some leave.'

'I can certainly use it,' said Bill.

'Maybe we're not absolutely serious, skip, but surely you don't think Germany can take much more punishment? At this rate we can just wipe the whole place out; city by city.'

'Germany might still fight on even if we did. But what is more likely is that Germany will find counters to our new tactics. Don't think I'm pessimistic. I've known the Hun longer than you chaps have and he doesn't take a beating lightly.'

Hyde threw a mischievous glance at Joe and added: 'Anyway, Command are playing safe; they're still posting new crews to the Squadron.'

'Don't remind me,' groaned Joe. 'Vincent's gone and lost his table-tennis title to some sprog officer. First time the title's left our mess in years.'

'He was far too good,' Vincent apologized, 'I could never hope to beat him.'

'Fair dinkum, skip, said Joe. 'I couldn't bear to watch the slaughter. You'd think Bill O'Reilly or Larwood[1] or somebody like that had blundered into a village match. It was murder. What a *tussle*: twenty-one-seven, twenty-one-three. Oooh!' Joe took his sport very seriously. It was as though the Allies had lost a great battle.

'Well,' laughed Hyde, 'he can recuperate from this grim but glorious defeat starting Wednesday morning. I'm catching the earliest train. I'll have a staff-car to the station, so anybody else who's coming on that train can have a lift. Okay?'

There was a general chorus of acceptance.

'Hey!' warned Hyde. 'It's only a little Hillman, it can't take the bloody lot of you.'

As it happened, all the Parke crew except Bill wanted to catch that first London train. And to make up for Bill, who had already left for Rotherham, H-H joined the party. They found another driver and with Krink's car 'formating loosely' on the Hillman staff car, the party arrived with plenty of time and noise at 'Grimtown steamworks'.

As they showed their passes at the barrier the ticket inspector spoke to Hyde. 'Is that your dog, sir?' Trotting confidently beside him was a little black scotty.

'He's not mine,' said Hyde.

'Whose is he, then? He can't travel without a ticket.'

The men looked blankly from the dog to the inspector and back at the dog again. 'Come on, now! Which one of you owns him?' The scotty stood so cockily beside them that they felt sheepish and guilty as they shook their heads and denied ownership.

'Then he can't come in here. No dogs without tickets.'

Scratching and whimpering, the dog ran along the barrier as the group walked away.

Immediately they settled in their carriage they heard an excited barking. The scotty had squeezed between the bars of the barrier and was rushing towards them as the train began to move.

''Ere! Grab that dog, Bert!', the ticket-collector yelled at a porter. 'It can't travel without a ticket.'

But the porter was too slow. Vincent swung open the door as the dog bounded alongside and with a leap it landed in the carriage. Unashamed, and none the worse for his dangerous athletics, the scotty looked at the men, panting through open mouth, red tongue wagging and black eyes gleaming.

'That was a true One-o-one squadron take-off you made,' Hyde addressed the dog.

The scotty licked its nose, closed its mouth and whimpered pertly in reply.

'He's the most airborne dog I've ever seen,' said Krink.

'He's a real RAF dog,' said Joe.

'What say we call him that, then?'

'Raff!'

'Right! Raff it is. Hey!' Vincent said, 'Hey, Raff! How do you like being a Raff dog?' Raff jumped on to Vincent's knee and licked his ear. It did not occur to any of them that he should not be, as from this moment, their very own dog. Had you asked them, they would have assured you it was not acquisition by theft. Theft? How preposterous! It was a sort of mutual legal adoption.

The wartime train that takes a soldier on leave is a magical thing. No matter if it be crowded or slow. Even if there is a bomb on the rails ahead and the train must be diverted; it is heading home, back to Mum and the family and the girlfriend. Even to the man from overseas – men like Joe and Krink and Johnnie, thousands of miles from home – the leave train is his brightest company.

As they rumbled south they passed an airfield where American Flying Fortresses were taking off for a daylight raid. One Fortress swooped so low over the train that they saw the face of the belly-gunner. Joe waved out of the window.[2]

'Fly, you bastards, fly!' he yelled happily.

'A pity they can't fly a bit further,' lamented H-H.

'And carry a decent load of bombs,' added Hyde.

High flying, plus the weight of a crew of eleven and many guns with the necessary ammunition, cut the Fortress bomb-capacity to less than half of a Lancaster's bomb-load. The RAF, as might be expected, had an uncomplimentary song about it; they sang it to the tune of 'John Brown's Body' and Magnetic launched into it now, quickly joined by the others.

'Flying firkin fortresses at forty thousand feet,

Crew and guns they've got on board enough to sink a fleet.

They're only bound for Calais so we know they won't retreat

With their single, teeny-weeny little bomb.

Flying firkin fortresses at forty thousand feet,

They've got the Norden bomb-sight and the Colonel's in
    the seat

They're flying swell formation but we really must repeat:

They've only got one teeny-weeny bomb!

They were only bombing Calais ...

They were only bombing Calais ...[3]

They sang on happily, quite without malice. Despite words that the uninitiated might think were insulting to Americans, Krink, the American in their midst, joined in lustily.

'Say,' interrupted Krink, 'that reminds me of a joke I heard about the USAAF ...' They all stopped singing and looked at Krink. 'Let me think ... I know it was about briefing ...'

'One of these days you'll announce a joke that you really remember.'

It was a Krynkiwski failing to either forget his jokes altogether or, even more annoying, to forget the tag-line. Now Krink was saved the embarrassment of trying vainly to remember by a voice in the next compartment saying, 'Tickets, please!'

'The inspector! What about Raff?'

'Here, Raff!' called Vincent. 'Under my greatcoat. Now stay there, boy. Stay still! Still!'

'Tickets, please,' called the inspector at their door. 'There are seats up in first class, sir,' said the inspector when he saw Hyde's pass.

'We're all friends. We're travelling together.'

'Very well, sir. 'Ere!' His explosion was reminiscent of the inspector at Grimsby as his eye fell on Raff peeping out from under Vincent's coat.

''Ere! Wotchoo got there?'

There was no point in attempting to hide Raff now.

'A dog, officer,' said Vincent, unable to think of any rank higher than 'officer' in railways terminology. 'His name's Raff. He's our mascot. He travels everywhere with us; even on raids. He barks when he sees a fighter coming.'

'Yeah? Well, I bark when I sees dogs in my compartments. He's gotta have a ticket and he's gotta travel in the van.'

'Oh, officer. He gets frightened in the van; he thinks they've taken him POW.'

'Well ... where's his ticket?'

'He travels,' announced Krink, 'on the difference between our three first-class tickets and the three third-class fares. Look, I'll show you …' Krink fished in his pocket and brought out a flask of brandy. 'Have a drink.' The inspector looked suspicious. But he also looked thirsty.

'What's this got to do with it?' he asked.

'Just go ahead. Have a drink,' said Krink, breezily.

'Or would you rather have Scotch?' asked Joe, producing another bottle. 'Scotch or brandy?'

'Well, brandy if it's all the same to you.'

'Sure it is. Go ahead. Have a brandy.'

The inspector drank a burning mouthful from Krink's flask.

Krink and Joe then raised their bottles to the inspector. 'Here's to you,' they said. The inspector flushed.

The bottles were passed around. Each man drank and each man seriously toasted the inspector. He stood, smiling self-consciously.

'Have another before you go,' said Krink. The man flushed again.

'Well, if you don't mind.'

They all protested extravagantly that they didn't mind a bit. The inspector finished his gulp, smiled again timidly, patted Raff on the head, and with a murmured 'Well, thanks,' left the compartment. Raff was as good as in London.

Hyde, Krink, Johnnie, Yarpi and Joe had all booked at the Regent Palace Hotel. When Krink heard it was right at Piccadilly he was delighted. 'Are we happy in the circus?' he asked affirmatively.

Magnetic set off, with no great show of enthusiasm, for his home in Lewisham, H-H left his address in Knightsbridge with Hyde but explained that he was going off immediately to see Barbara at Chiswick. Vincent still had a short train-trip to make; 'It's only half an hour in a slow train,' he explained. 'I'll take Raff with me; he'll enjoy the open spaces down at Horley. Surrey is neither London nor the country; and yet it's a little bit of both.'

They parted, agreeing to meet again in town that night.

Joe had suggested they meet at an old pub off Fleet Street, 'Noted', he said, 'for its international clientele.'

'Let's meet for drinks at Coger's,' Joe had said.

'Right-ho,' H-H had agreed. 'Make it Coger's.' But while Joe had pronounced Coger's to rhyme with Rodger's, H-H used the long 'o' as in flow: 'C-oh-dgers'.

'Come off it, sport,' said Joe. 'Pronounced 'Codger's'. It's an old Australian word for a chap or a bloke; we call him a 'codger' and we pronounce it 'Cod-ger's'.

H-H put on the look of an outraged Oxford Don, which he could well have been, and replied; 'Codger' may be an ancient and honourable Australian word. But since this pub – 'C-oh-dger's' – was named in the seventeenth century, before Australia was founded, I insist that the Australian vernacular cannot influence what Englishmen call it, which is, let me again assure you, 'C-oh-dger's'.

Joe smiled politely, bowed a little and replied: 'Your point, sir. We meet at C-oh-dger's.'[4]

When H-H met them there, however, it was only for a moment. Barbara Cunard was with him. H-H insisted on buying the first round and, while they drank it, announced: 'Barbara and I are getting married tomorrow. Three o'clock, after the investiture. We'd like you all to come.'

There was a babble of congratulations and acceptances.

'It's so good of you to accept on such short notice, and during your precious leave,' said Barbara.

'But right now we'd like you to excuse us,' said H-H. 'Would you mind? Bags of visits and organising, you know.'

H-H and Barbara finished their drinks and hurried out into the gathering blackout.

When they had gone, Joe said, 'You know, I've heard the English gentleman much maligned. But the few I've met are as likeable as anyone could wish. And folks can sneer about to-the-manner-born, but I've found they all have an easy correctness that's theirs alone.'

'You speak,' said Hyde, 'of the true English gentleman. It's the near or would-be gentleman who's a prig and a bore. I should know; we see enough of them strutting around Ireland.'

There followed a moment's silence, until Krink suddenly slapped his thigh. 'I've remembered that joke about the American's briefing,' he announced.

'The General's briefing 'em, you see: hundreds of Colonels and Majors with Mickey Mouse painted on the back of their flying-jackets. And he says: 'The operational height for this mission is forty thousand feet. But any man who goes in at thirty thousand feet gets a Purple Heart. And any man who goes in at twenty thousand feet ... I'll give him the DFM. And any man who goes in at ten thousand feet, godamnit, I'll give him a Congressional Medal of Honour. But, fellas, don't go in at five thousand feet, will you? Because sure as hell you'd get all tangled up with the RAF.'[5]

Krink was facing his crew-mates as he spoke and had not noticed a knot of American flyers behind him. One of them tapped him on the shoulder. 'Hey, laughter-boy,' he said. 'I dunno where you got the phoney accent or the corny gags. But let's drop it, eh? We got a few funny stories to tell, too, but we're too polite to blab 'em out in international company.'

Krink, far from being taken aback, answered quickly. 'Who's got a phoney accent? I was born right in the twin cities; St Paul's my home town.'

The American eyed the RAF uniform. 'Turned traitor, eh?'

Krink answered quietly: 'Traitor? How come? Last I heard we was both fighting for the same side.'

'Sure we are! Both on the same side; that is, I'm not so sure we're *both* fighting.'

There were six 101 Squadron men present, and four USAF. Now, each group was facing the other, tense.

'And which of us would you suggest might not be fighting?', Hyde asked.

'Read any good books lately?' said Vincent.

But the American was facing Hyde obviously with no intention of changing the subject. He shot a glance at Vincent and answered: 'Yes, I have. It was a book about the retreat from Dunkirk and Singapore and Java and I seem to remember it was called *How to Lose a War.*'

Everybody was being calm and quiet with such intensity that the situation seemed far more electric than if voices had been raised.

Vincent took a long sip of beer. A studied gesture; because

although it was long he certainly took no more than a sip.

'I've read one, too,' he said. 'A thing called *Queens Die Proudly* by an American called White. Have *you* read it?'[6]

'Not that I recall.'

'Then I'll tell you what it says about, for example, the battle of the Java Sea; I think I can quote. "The American Navy skirted the Jap back edge, firing on the run." That sounds rather a shameful retreat to me.'

'In that same battle,' put in Joe, 'HMAS *Perth* was still fighting when her decks were eighteen inches awash. She sunk a hundred and fifty thousand tons of Jap shipping before they got her and all this time your boys were full steam for Melbourne.'[7]

'This writer explained,' continued Vincent, 'that it was not American policy to dissipate their forces "in lost causes", adding that they "needed every man in Australia". Why defend Australia and not Java? And I don't think our cause ever was lost.'

'I didn't read that book. Anyway, that's the Navy.'

'Oh, he wrote lots about the Air Corps. Their entire bomber force was one squadron full of old Fortresses – you know the type, without rear turrets.'

'Those boys were heroes. They sure took a beating.'

'They certainly did; and to what effect? White writes of a force – I think it was eight bombers – setting off from Darwin to bomb Batavia. Half of them turned back but four did arrive, and there they bombed the Jap fleet. And do you know what they dropped? I quote: 'four, beautiful blue six-hundred-pounders'. What deadly effect their being blue might have I cannot imagine, though White thought it worth mentioning. But I *do* know just what damage a total of sixteen six-hundred-pounders would do to a fleet. The Nips would just polish the spot where they landed and it wouldn't even dent the armour-plate. Yet White paints such a picture of destruction that the eager American readers might think the Japanese Navy would be hard-pressed to put to sea again for months. Those flyers, as you said, were heroes. They had taken a beating. They had retreated for thousands of miles and they were still fighting. But that's not the way the story was written. The retreat was forgotten and little skirmishes were made to look like great victories. What's shameful about a retreat? I'm mighty glad some American Navy did survive the Java Sea encounter and later thrash the Japs in the Coral Sea. But get the idea that only the British retreat right out of your head. I seem to recall the evacuation of Manila was none too glorious.'

The American had subsided a little. 'But that was in the Pacific, right at the beginning.'

'The beginning? Hadn't the war been going on for two years by then?'

'Oh, *your* war had. I mean the United States' war.'

'You don't imagine that morally it wasn't just as much your war, do you? Except you were making no attempt at all to fight it then. 'All aid short of war', remember? And good luck to you; I'd rather stay out and make money than fight any day.'

'You're getting off the point,' said the American. 'What happened in the Pacific in those days isn't what's happening here now. The USAF in Britain is bigger than the RAF today. That's what started this: *who* is doing the fighting.'

'Shades of nineteen-nineteen,' murmured Magnetic. '*Who* won the war?'[8]

'Bigger? In what way?' Vincent refused to be sidetracked. 'How do you measure a bomber force? Not personnel, chum! You measure it by bombs. That's what does the damage: bombs. One Fortress, with a crew of eleven, carries less than half the load of a standard Lancaster – and special Lancasters are carrying up to four times the Fortress load with a crew of six. RAF ground crew averages three men per bomber against the USAF's fourteen.'

Vincent did some quick mental arithmetic. 'That means that the ordinary man on an RAF bomber squadron does the work of five Americans, measured in terms of bombs on the enemy ... and you note I say 'on the enemy', and not 'on Germany' because you've dropped precious few on Germany.'

Before the American could counter this thrust, Vincent asked him, 'When are you going to bomb Berlin?'

'Berlin's a mighty tough target. You guys skulk over there at night. We gotta go in daylight, remember. I'd like to see you fly to Berlin in daylight.'

'The RAF *have* bombed Berlin in daylight. In Mosquitoes. We broke up Hitler's anniversary party, remember?'[9]

Joe had been busting to have his say and at last he burst in. 'I trained in Canada and used to read US newspapers. And I hardly ever saw mention of the RAF. Plenty of 'Americans bomb Lille', then 'Allied Bombers Pound Berlin', but that the bombs on France were American and the bombs on Germany were British was carefully omitted – I'd even say that every attempt was made to make it read as though they *were* American bombs on Berlin. I was astounded to hear, when America had been in the war a year, that they had never once bombed Germany. The RAF raided Germany one day after war was declared. And we hadn't two years to get ready while our friends held our end up. But your papers don't tell the true story; no wonder Americans get a false picture. I see the same tendency in my own country – Australia. It's sheer national boastfulness and it's a sign of immaturity. But we're growing out of it lately; perhaps because we've lately listened to so many Yanks. Tell me, sport, did you read about the first defeat of the Japanese army at Milne Bay?'[10]

'Yes, I read about it.'

'Who fought *that* battle?'

'We did, I guess.'

'Well, guess again, mate. The only American force at Milne Bay was a solitary unit of anti-aircraft gunners who arrived on the last day. The rest of the 'Allies' were Australians; many of them the same chaps who held Tobruk with the Desert Rats while the Yanks were still giving 'all aid short of war.'

'Hey, man!' said Yarpi. 'It was the South Africans in Tobruk.'

Now the Empire was at war within itself.

Joe turned on Yarpi. 'What's that, sport? Though the South Africans were *in* Tobruk they didn't *hold* Tobruk. That was the last time it was surrounded and they capitulated in three weeks. The Aussies had held it for nine months and it never looked like falling.'[11]

Joe had introduced the first hostile note into the party and

Vincent chuckled pointedly as he said; 'I was with the Aussies in Crete and they were getting out of there pretty fast, Joe.'

'In Crete? Well, maybe they were. You can't hold an island without supply lines.'

'Maybe the same thing happened to the South Africans in Tobruk. I've heard it said that the real credit for the stand of Tobruk should go to the Royal Navy. They got supplies in and casualties out during that whole nine months.'

'I don't care *who* wins this war,' said Magnetic. 'America, Australia, even South Africa if it makes her happy – but I wish they'd win it *soon* and shoot Hitler and let's all go home.'

'There is one man I would like to discover,' said Johnnie. 'Not the man who wins the war but the man who begins it. Let us all hate him and hunt him out and destroy him and never again boast of how well we have killed.'

Every man turned and looked at Johnnie and there was a long moment's silence. Then Hyde thumped Johnnie's shoulder and, addressing the Americans, said; 'That was spoken by a German.'

'Let's put him in the Peace Delegation after the war.'

'If we do, Johnnie,' said Vincent, 'don't fall into the old British rut. The trouble with this country is that, after every war, we carefully disarm the people we fought *last* when the wise thing to do would be to disarm the people we shall probably fight *next*.'[12]

The discussion had known several tense moments – natural when many things so near to national pride had been broached – but the Americans, already eager to bury the hatchet, thawed completely when Hyde insisted on including them in the next round of drinks.[13]

It is never very long, when young men are out together, before somebody wants to eat. Joe announced that he 'could go a steak and eggs', and when Magnetic, the Londoner, said it was out of the question to procure steak in food rationed London, Joe assured him that 'Sloppy Mo, behind the Cheshire Cheese serves a bonzer steak – horse meat, of course – and fair rubber eggs'. Hyde asked the Americans to join them.

They declined politely, explaining that beefsteak, which was unheard of in RAF messes, was served 'with monotonous regularity at Base'.

At Sloppy Mo's they ordered Mexican soup which turned out to be a milky water with floating worms of red and green chilli. Joe ordered an entree 'to awaken our outraged palate'. When it came it was a slice of garlic sausage. 'This meal is going from bad to *wurst*,' said Vincent. But they enjoyed the steak of 'prime horse'. Surely this was food for heroes.

Raff was with Vincent when he met the others outside the Registry Office. Then H-H arrived, driven by Barbara in a sleek Riley.[14] The flyers were introduced to many other people who had been waiting nearby. The last introduction was when Barbara formally met Raff, then everybody trooped into the Registry Office where quite the most poised of that distinguished company was the nonchalant Raff. If his canine ear had caught the many titles during the introductions his perky manner did not reveal his awe.

Hyde acted as one of the witnesses of the quiet, drab little ceremony. Without choir, without music, without ritual, even without flowers, it was an unimpressive wedding indeed. Vincent saw a tear in Barbara's eye and was surprised; the ceremony was not moving. Or was she crying for the wedding she had dreamed of? No matter what the setting she could hardly have looked lovelier; in grosgrain suit of palest blue, accessories of sandy fawn and a fairy-light hat that did not more than pamper her pretty hair – she looked Venus enough for any Apollo.

The speakers at the reception, like the social writers, made their dramatic most of that morning's investiture, the wartime rush of impetuous youth, the courage and sacrifice of the wartime bride in facing the dangers and forgoing the pomp. They said, in short, everything most likely to embarrass and upset the bride and groom. They spoke of children and of heroes and of better worlds to live in; one even mentioned widows. H-H's mother vowed that that was unforgivable 'especially in the complete absence of French champagne'; yet the condemned couple, setting out on what had been made to appear a hazardous and gruelling ordeal, contrived to face it gaily, even, it seemed, with relish.

They left with the dusk to drive to Ludford in Barbara's Riley, the whereabouts of the night stop en route a furtive secret.

'As soon as it's dark,' said H-H, 'we'll find some spot beside the road where we can stop, strip off these clothes, and rid ourselves of every possible shred of confetti.'

'For one moment, darling, you gave me quite a thrill. But then your intentions were shown quite the opposite: decorum to the last.'

Fifty miles north they pulled into a charming country inn where H-H had booked a large room noted for the famous occupant two centuries before, and of its massive four-poster. Barbara wore slacks and sweater and was hatless; H-H wore unpressed flannels, duffel coat and cap and carried a small leather case. Neither their attire nor their manner could betray this as their wedding night to even the most intuitive inn-keeper; but was that not a smirk upon Mine Host's plump face?

The honeymoon door closed heavily behind them; they switched on the light and turned to kiss, then fell into each other's arms laughing. In their hair were handfuls of confetti.

— 7 —

'Are you Vincent Farlow?'

Even his pilot officer's uniform did not make the speaker look old enough to be in the service; his pink, beardless cheeks and boyish eagerness still smacked of the schoolroom. 'Because, if so, I believe you're the bounder I have to beat for the table-tennis title.'

'I was a week ago,' said Vincent. 'But not any more. I lost it to a F/O bomb-aimer called O'Brien.'

'Yes, I know. But O'Brien got the chop. Went missing Wednesday I was told. I'm all for retiring when you're at the peak but that's carrying it a bit far, what?'

He laughed shrilly. Vincent wondered if his boyish mind comprehended what he was joking about.

'So you're champ again, Farlow old thing.'

'Well, any time you like,' said Vincent, eager to end the conversation.

'Now?'

'If you wish.'

'Oh, topping! I'm flying second dickie tonight with that South African fellow Lieutenant Cahill; he's screening me, it's my first op. So we can just fit it in before bacon and eggs.'

Vincent looked at the pink cheeks and pubescent pimples and listened to the childish drivel.

'This creature is to be in charge of eight lives and more than L70,000 worth of aircraft', he reflected. 'And, who knows? He might do wonders. Perhaps he can fly like a swallow and the playing-fields of somewhere-or-other may have made him frightfully brave.'[1]

Something had certainly made the P/O a very good table-tennis player. He won the first game and was well on the way to winning the second when the Tannoy called new and earlier meal times and the game had to end straight away. But Vincent was so obviously beaten that he conceded the set and became ex-champion for the second time in a week.

The P/O was thrilled in every fibre of his body. 'Oh, this is ripping; quite my lucky day. Now for those bacon and eggs and my first op.'

He turned to Vincent and asked; 'Are you flying, too? I suppose not, being straight off leave.'

'I'm afraid we are,' said Vincent. 'Off leave one is supposed to be fit.'

'Oh, wizard! I'll see you over the Third Reich!'

'If this cloud clears.'

Vincent scowled at the sky. 'If it doesn't, neither of us'll see a damned thing.'

'Tonight's weather,' said the met officer, 'is likely to be tricky. We bomb beyond and land between two cold fronts. Visibility at take-off will be poor but you will fly quickly into good weather and over the target skies should be clear. Winds will be strong westerly – perhaps exceeding seventy mph – so you'll have a fast trip in and a slower trip home. As you pass through the first cold front en route home watch out for icing. But cloud-top wouldn't exceed twenty thousand except in isolated places so stay high and you'll keep above it. Forecast wind at twenty thousand over Nürnberg is two-eighty at sixty-five mph so bomb-aimers will have to be snappy. Don't waste time coming home because visibility will be deteriorating.'[2]

Hyde leant towards his crew and said, 'I prefer Wendy's briefings to this boy's. She always gives herself away if she thinks the weather's shocking. But this chap is so confident you don't know whether he's being careful about an average set-up or light-hearted about something bloody awful.'

'I wish we'd taken a week's leave instead of just a forty-eight. I don't like the look of this trip.'

'Who's the cloth-headed maniac who puts off-leave crews on the blood-sheet?'

'The Flight-Commander,' Hyde said, coldly.

The first part of the met forecast was accurate; visibility at take-off was poor indeed. Heavy rain in big drops flattened blindingly against the perspex and, to make matters worse, the wind was not straight down the runway. It was so strong that even a few degrees of cross-wind forced them to drift off the ground alarmingly. To take off in such conditions was bad but to do so with full bomb and petrol load was hair-raising.

Hyde felt clumsy tugging and struggling at the controls; was it because he had been away from aeroplanes for a while? Years of flying should accustom one to flying, but it was never so. After a few days away nothing seemed automatic any more; every action had to be thought out and made deliberately.

Or was it because he was in a strange aircraft? Q-Queenie had been shot up the night they went on leave and was still unserviceable. Tonight they were in V-Victor, an almost new aircraft; this was only her third trip. Well, she didn't leak, anyway. If she did it would have been apparent in *this* filthy rain. Hyde would hardly have thought it possible but the rain seemed to be getting worse. 'No wonder they put the time forward', he thought; 'another half-hour would make flying impossible.'

'Nav to skipper,' said the intercom. 'Terrific wind, skip. It's dead abeam and we've got seventeen degrees of drift.'

'What!'

'That's right, skip. Seventeen degrees. Alter course eight degrees starb'd to two-eleven.'

'But we're only at two thousand. What'll it be like at height?'

'I hate to think. I've checked with Gee four times. When we turn east with this wind behind us we will go too fast to maintain timing.'

'But we'll fly out of this weather when we turn east.'

'I doubt it. Winds have backed ninety degrees from the forecast, which means the system is further east than they expected, and moving faster. It makes good sense meteorologically. So we'll be in this weather almost to the target; and I hope it's only almost.'

'Okay, nav. But you'd better be right.'

Bill spoke and his voice was strained, almost a scream. 'We could still be on leave now.'

'Shut up!' Hyde was worried about Bill. Ever since the night his bombs had blown up that aircraft Bill's nerves had been deteriorating. Hyde was not going to let Bill infect the whole crew with his fears.

Outside, the world was liquid grey. Grey swirls of cloud and squalls of rain and chunks of hectic sky. Great cumulo-nimbus curls of cloud whirled about them, shocking and jolting the battling aircraft as rapids toss a slight canoe. The wild west wind was not a highway but a writhing, tossing road to war. They looked out upon it with startled eyes; some cursed, some trembled.

'Nav to skipper. Windspeed at sixteen thousand feet is ninety-two mph. We have a twenty-eight degree drift. Alter course now, thirteen degrees starb'd, to two-two-four true.'

'Surely that's impossible, nav!'

'Work it out yourself. Windspeed is more than half our airspeed while we're still climbing.'

'Are you *sure*, nav?'

'Positive.'

'Christ!'

It was difficult to estimate which prospect was blacker.

If Vincent were right then all the timing of this raid would be hopelessly out. Those aircraft without radar would arrive over the target perhaps an hour early and fly beyond it at astonishing ground speeds. At an airspeed of 230 mph, they would expect to cover the ground at 295 mph. But, in fact, they would be doing 330 mph, or more. It would be chaos.

It would destroy the precious concentration that was their defence over Goering's Germany. It would be tragedy.

And if Vincent were wrong? Then, instead of the force being an hour early, V-Victor would be an hour late. *They* would be the straggler marked down for easy destruction. It would be murder.

'Nav to skipper. Windspeed at eighteen thousand feet is a hundred and three mph. What about going down to sixteen thousand, skipper? Even throttled right back we'll still reach Nürnberg forty minutes early unless we dog-leg at twenty thousand feet.'

Hyde did not answer for a moment. When he did he spoke very calmly.

'Nav. Are you certain you are right?'

'Certain.'

'Gee couldn't be wrong?'

'No. Gee is either very wrong or dead right. And the synoptic situation makes sense. Our track runs dead straight from alteration to alteration. Gee is right.'

There was another pause while Hyde pondered.

'Nav. Check every figure and every fix you've plotted.'

'I have checked, skipper.'

'Well, check again! And are you sure you're using the correct Gee channel?'

'Yes, you clot! I couldn't plot the readings otherwise.'

Vincent was not being kind; Hyde's doubting his skill riled Vincent's vanity.

'Bomb-aimer,' called Hyde, 'go back and check the log and chart with the navigator. I'll carry on up to twenty thousand feet and if winds really are too strong then we'll come down a bit.'

Navigators do not like having their logs and charts checked. Especially by those who know less about navigation than themselves, such as bomb-aimers or pilots.

Hyde knew Vincent would not be pleased. But Hyde could not assume a remarkable situation were so until he had made every effort to disprove it and it had stood that test.

'Nav to skipper,' said Vincent smugly. 'Log and chart checked by bomb-aimer and self and found correct. New wind is a hundred and twelve mph and we're still not at full height.'

'Okay, nav. I'll take her right up to twenty thousand while you check windspeed there, though.'

'Well, let me know soon. I'll have to compute a different course depending which height we fly and we turn east in a few minutes.'

At 20,000 feet the wind-speed was 117 mph. With that tail wind they could have tracked into Germany, throttles wide, at over 400 mph. If only Met had known, and were sure the target would be clear, what a raid this might have been. What anguish to pursuing fighters, what speeds to leave the puzzled flak behind! They could have flown out of the cold front, bombed in clear skies, and popped back into the sheltering clouds again within a score of miles and half a dozen minutes.

But they had not known. Met's ignorance was a grievous fault and grievously must the flyers now answer it.

Hyde had decided. V-Victor would fly at 16,000 feet at their slowest speed – 115 mph – almost stalling speed. They arrived few minutes late over Beachy Head, yet would still have to dog-leg time away in order not to reach Nürnberg too early.

Wearily, resigned to God-alone-knew-what, they turned eastward for Germany.

Already the bomber force was scattered and baffled. Many lacked the tools to measure their plight and flew unheeding into chaos. Others, distrustful of themselves, refused to believe the things their instruments told them. Those who had measured, checked and swore that they were right still flew with the fear that the *might* be wrong; that such weather really *was* impossible.

So the force split into three: the unknowing in front, speeding further and further from safety; the unsure next, tortured by doubts of their actions and their future; and finally the few, the unhappy few who knew and staked their lives upon their knowing.

Spreading ever thinner and more vulnerable across Europe they straggled like leaves upon the breeze, powerless before their airy executioner – the wild west wind.

German radar pierced the widespread cloud of window and the shells came crashing up into the liberal target. Most XYZ aircraft, having Gee, were with the rearward forces so fighters homed upon the leaders unmolested. Gunners below had never known such a night. Usually the bombers came, remained in range some few minutes, then were gone. If one fell during those minutes the gunners cheered. Tonight their targets droned across their eager sights for an hour or more, and each few minutes claimed another victim.

Then, already past the target, the leading bombers flew out of the bad weather. Now for a pinpoint!

Gradually, one by one, they saw their error; discovered where they were. Many were slow to believe and blundered further from safety. Many died before they discovered; died fighting their way to a target they had gained and passed. Those who lived to learn turned, now, into the teeth of the wind that had beguiled them, a few to crash head-on with others puzzling still. The wind that had sent them hurtling over Germany now buffeted them back to keep them near to danger. Before, they had fluttered east at five miles a minute; now they battled back no faster than a car.

Some overshot Nürnberg by 150 miles. By the time they regained the target they were almost two hours late. It was hopeless. Suppose they survived the guns and fighters, what then? In four hours, still far from home, their petrol would run out and, if they lived, they would be taken prisoner.

'And all because the weather man was wrong', thought Hyde. 'Then wind, invisible wind, had played the Germans' game. O cruel west wind! How many men? How many hundred men this night had learnt to

... know

Thy voice, and suddenly grow grey with fear,
And tremble and despoil themselves: O, hear![3]

'Five minutes to TOT,' said Vincent.

'Can't see a bloody thing,' said Bill.

'Watch out for the markers,' ordered Hyde. 'They might show through this muck.'

Keen eyes stared into the night but saw nothing. Nothing but whirling mists and curling cloud. By the time correct TOT was reached, Nürnberg had been swallowed up by the cold front. All that indicated that Nürnberg was below them was the flak. Exultant, the gunners were making this an opportunity for revenge. V-Victor, now down-flung by the storm, was as suddenly hurled upwards by fierce flak.

'Can't see anything, skipper. Will we bomb on ETA?'

'I'm afraid we'll have to.'

'Bomb doors open.'

Vincent counted out the seconds, Bill pressed the tit, and V-Victor lurched with added lift as each weight dropped.

Their bomb-doors were just closing when a sparkling triangle of shells surrounded them. There was a gritty, crackling noise above the roar of engines and of wind, then two distinct thumps which made V-Victor shudder. Blast caught the empty, open bomb-bays and sent the aircraft reeking up to heaven, her vitals filled with the smoking stench of war.

Hyde felt fire strike into his thighs; as shrapnel bit into his buttocks his body lifted, flinging his feet from the rudder bars and wrenching the control column from his hands. He did not scream or cry out or make any sound; his mouth remained tight-clenched, as were his hand and eyes in pain. Then his harness pulled him back into his seat and once more, not knowing how, he was flying V-Victor.

The Lanc had leapt, startled, into the sky as if she meant to vault the clouds above her. When Hyde recovered after the first agonizing moments of his wounds he found V-Victor there, off-trim and straining up to the stars.

He did not think 'I have been hit, what of my wounds?' but, like a robot, saw a task before him and set about it urgently. V-Victor must be flown. What blood he lost would be but little – he hoped – compared to that which he would bring home, later to pound with passion and not pain through happier veins.

He tested the controls. Movements were sloppy and the trim was rough. Flying surfaces were in shreds somewhere and there was a great hole in the nose where cloud and cold came gushing in.

Hyde called over the crew on intercom and no one was hurt. Each had a little grouch; Bill was getting wet, Magnetic thought he could smell petrol, Vincent said some flak came through his desk and burnt a jagged hole in his protractor, Krink's oxygen pipe was severed but he guessed he could fix it with insulation tape. The gunners complained that the draught through the nose was freezing them but their guns seemed all right.

Nobody thought to ask the skipper how *he* was. Why should he be anything but fit? He was speaking to them, as normally as might be expected after such a shaking on such a night. He did not sound particularly worried. He was still flying V-Victor. He did not tell them of his wounds.

He would not have known how to speak of them had he chosen to; he did not really know himself. When he was first hit he had been numbed by the solidness of it. It did not feel like being pierced with sharpened steel but as though a hard, flat bat had whacked him. Solid force was its first impact. Then came the pain. Anti-aircraft shrapnel, when it hits, is red-hot. It burns as much as it gouges. Hyde's flesh and bones and nerves had clamoured with the agony of it. What simile can tell the woundless how wounds feel?

Then suddenly he had seen, with his tradesman's eye, his work in jeopardy. His mind flashed from his wounds to grapple with familiar things.

Now, with V-Victor back in trim and routines checked, with life a normal thing again he could take stock. How did he feel? Strange, yes; yet not incapable. His legs and thighs, where he had been hit, performed the little tasks he set them. The turning of a rudder bar caused him no special pain. Indeed, the pain was gone; all that remained was a shocked numbness. All he could feel that was strange was the warm, sticky ooze in which he sat. Perhaps his wounds were just a scratch. To mention them at all might earn men's scorn. No; it seemed more than that. But minds do fiendish things: imagine gaping wounds and gushing blood where baby cuts and little trickles might exist; minds kill the spirit fretting over wounds less mortal than cool fever. Hyde thrust these worries from his mind; decided that his wounds were slight and not to be considered, and gave his full attention to his work.

The night whirling about them, tossing them easily on its powerful way, had continued to rage. Their throttles were open now, straining against the storm. Hyde checked his petrol, checked his watch, cast a troubled glance over his shoulder looking for the dawn. If this weather strengthened, the day might find them still over Europe.

A cloud raced by, and for an instant they could see it was *one* cloud and not a cloud-filled sky. And then another, and soon they saw a star. Quickly the cold front cleared; within ten minutes they could see the world. Earth! Sky! Each set in its right place. How good it was to see these standards and know they were still fixed!

'How's the wind now, nav?'

'Three-five-two at eighty-five mph.'

'Isn't it dropping?'

'Not significantly.'

'Would the wind be much less if we went down, nav?', Hyde asked.

'The winds would, skip. But we'll hit that next front soon and there'll be icing below twelve thousand feet.'

'But we'll have to descend through it over England.'

'We'll probably be okay going straight down through it, it only occurs round about freezing-level, but if we fly in it for an hour it'll be our lot.'

Vincent added: 'She sounds pretty mushy; could she stand much ice?'[4]

'No, not much,' said Hyde. 'She's flat out now and only crawling. You're sure we'll ice-up if we descend?'

'I'm certain we will.'

'You'd better be right.'

'You said that once before.'

'Yes, you bloody Jonah, you. And I wish you hadn't been.'

'Sorry, skip. But even this wind is better than ice.'

The leading bombers in the race for home met the second cold front just west of the Rhine. Most of them, still wanting to trust the briefing forecast, had expected clear skies and lessening winds all the way to England. As they droned, exhausted, towards more friendly France, cloud rose like a cliff to bar their way. Some realized their danger quickly; realized the full threat of icing and frenziedly started to climb. Throttles full and nose thrust high they strove to out-climb ice before it smothered them.

Others saw the danger but either failed or refused to recognize it. Wind – fog – petrol – ice? Their choice of executioner! He could but kill them once; what did it matter? Resigned to face the nearest foe to hand, they flew straight on to meet the storm.

Of the two groups, the ones who chose to climb fared better. But even they fared ill.

The crew of V-Victor saw the cliff of cloud from four miles high, and still it seemed to tower above them. Hyde searched the far horizon for some gap and thought that he could see one. Even gaps in cumulo-nimbus can mean danger – danger from hailstones that hit swift-moving aircraft at hundreds of miles per hour, bullets of ice. But danger and this night were one, so Hyde turned V-Victor towards the misty pass. Vincent plotted the new course and estimated their ETA Ludford Magna.

'Nav to skipper. We're going to be ninety-four minutes late at Base.'

'Ninety-four minutes, check,' said Hyde. Then he asked: 'How will we be for petrol, engineer?'

'We'll have enough for twenty-six minutes.'

'Just pray we find somewhere to land.'

Hyde spoke with feeling. His crew noticed it but put it down to fear of weather. In fact it was more than that. Hyde felt himself growing weak and immeasurably tired. The flight home he had braced himself to endure. He rallied his spirit to stand as much as that. Then he saw the cloud ahead and his spirit quailed before it. Faint qualms were now becoming pressing doubts and soon true fear was nagging at his mind. To last the distance was ordeal enough. But this looming weather signalled battle; Hyde and V-Victor, both faint with wounds, would need to battle every inch of the way. The test was at hand and he feared that he would not endure it.

There were moments when he floated, detached from solid things. These moments he found himself enjoying and that was why he feared. For now the numbness was going and in its place pain was spreading from hips to knees.

'If I could only float,' thought Hyde in that calm, detached mind he had just discovered, 'if I could just fly with you, O wild west wind ...'⁵

'Nav to skipper. What's your course, skip? Off a bit, aren't you?'

Vincent's voice snapped him back. Hyde looked at his compass. He pulled Victor around, back towards the misty pass.

'Sorry, nav,' he said. 'I was watching the weather.'

Well might he watch. The cloud-tops lay beyond V-Victor's power. Hyde felt the tug of the first curled cloud and braced to meet the task. The threat he had feared to face now spurred his spirit. His mind was clear again and full of fight. The pain he felt he would use to goad his actions.

So much an enemy was weather, so ever-present, that the lesser enemy was almost forgotten. Yet, this other enemy, the Hun, had never been more deadly. The force was now his toy. He had targets far and wide, high and low. All semblance of concentration was lost. Suddenly the rocking, roaring storm would lighten into twinkles of steel and make men remember that there was still an Earth.

Hyde hardly knew the fight he fought. Time was no longer real. Perhaps he had flown through the storm for an hour, or perhaps it had been a day. One thing seemed certain: that it would never stop.

But it did.

With the coast of France the weather cleared. With the coast of France the guns were left behind. They had survived this dreadful night. With the coast of France the dawn came faint behind them, turning the tumbling clouds into a maze of beauty: deep chasms of purple, of darkest green and black: as clouds are seen only from above. The wind dropped down as if by magic. there was calm beyond belief. The soft sun rose out from the vanishing storm and they looked for England.

What they saw was mist. Flat, blank fog. Endless and complete. Hyde looked and trembled.

Vincent spoke. 'That's unlucky. Visibility behind a cold front is usually good.'

'Tonight nothing is good.'

The men gazed listlessly at the low, flat motionless layer. For a minute nobody spoke. 'I'll try to home you in on Gee,' said Vincent.

'Okay, nav.'

Hyde's voice was resigned; as flat as the fog. He could no longer feel. There was not pain or fear or even will to live. Vincent's voice droned on with constant directions. Hyde flew them like an automaton.

Other aircraft were flying port circuits above the hidden runways. How battered and wretched they looked! Some flew on three, or even two engines. Some had shattered perspex and jagged holes in their metal skin. The aircraft going in on radio beam[6] as they arrived was trailing smoke. They were over base and still all danger had not passed. Beam landings were never fun. And every aircraft was short of petrol. The air-to-ground radio buzzed with emergency calls. Flying-control was trying to sort them out into priority order and hurry them through the tedious drill of beam approach.

Lieutenant Cahill's voice was heard to say; 'Z-Zebra on two, wounded on board, request immediate landing and ambulance.'

Control called him straight in and he flew the long, slow, flat approach on beam then sank into the fog. Immediately there came a tiny twinkle of orange flame, then a mushroom of smoke billowed up through the flat fog-top.

There was a long silence on radio while the airborne crews flew around and around, looking and wondering. Then control announced; 'All Brylcreem aircraft divert to nearest beam approach 'dromes.'

That meant Z-Zebra's wreck was blocking the beam runway. The ether jammed with protests about fuel shortages and damaged aircraft. Hyde knew there was nothing Ludford could do.

'There must be general chaos down there for them to give such a loose diversion order,' said Magnetic.

'Want a course for Binbrook, skip?' asked Vincent. There was no reply. Magnetic glanced at Hyde and noticed how pale he was.

Vincent spoke again. 'Nav to skipper. Where do you want to land?'

'We'll land here.'

'But beam's busted.'

'Bring me in on Gee.'

There was a long pause. It was a strange order; given tonelessly and utterly without emotion.

'You want to land on a Gee homing?' Vincent asked, almost in disbelief.

'Yes.'

Doubt echoed in Vincent's voice but he replied; 'Homing on Gee, skip. Fly one-six-five true.'

Again they droned along the curving radar pulse. V-Victor sank into the fog. Gently they floated down ... and at the same time Hyde felt himself go floating up, up, up. Hyde's spirit could not be goaded by this passive fog. He longed for turmoil again. This nothingness was a vacuum, void of life. He yearned to plunge again into the wild west wind; to float and whirl and fly with it ...

O, lift me as a wave, a leaf, a cloud!
I fall upon the thorns of life! I bleed![7]

Then V-Victor struck; mushed down on her belly into soft meadow. They had got down; they had been lucky.

But not completely; just before she stopped, V-Victor hit a fence and slewed round, ripping her giant port wing apart like so much tinder.

'She's on fire!'

'Christ!'

'Fire! Out! Quick!'

The men tumbled from their places and rushed the exit while flames spread quickly up the crumpled wing, lapping at the fuselage.

Hyde felt the cabin heating up as he struggled weakly to undo his harness.

They leapt over each other out of the rear hatch (strangely near the ground with the wheels up) and each man landed running, running from the explosion which was sure to come.

They piled into a ditch beside a nearby road and looked back through the fog at the crackling, spluttering plane.

'Where's Hyde?', asked Magnetic.

The men looked around with sickly fear.

'He must be caught inside!' shrieked Bill, staring at the flames now engulfing the cabin.

'Perhaps he's hurt,' said Magnetic. 'He was looking terribly pale.'

Vincent clambered out of the ditch and ran towards V-Victor. The door was on the starboard, away from the fire. He flung himself up into the fuselage and coughed at the billows of smoke. He had not removed his helmet when he fled and fixed upon it were his goggles. He pulled them down to shield his eyes and peered forward.

Flames filled Hyde's cabin and Vincent could see them lapping around his body. Vincent groped forward and grabbed Hyde's arm. It was so hot he could not grip it. A yard away at his nav desk was his bag, and from this Vincent snatched his gauntlets.

Protected, now, from both heat and the fire itself, he grasped Hyde beneath the armpits and tugged. But Hyde's harness still bound him to his ticking pyre. Vincent grappled with the quick-release, fascinated to watch flames licking his own gauntlets and sickened by the smell of burning flesh.

The harness snapped free and Vincent pulled to hurry Hyde from the flames. But Hyde's left hand was set round the controls; held deep into the flames, hidden by fire. Vincent summoned all his fortitude and strength. With a mammoth effort he dragged Hyde from the seat and down the fuselage. At the doorway Magnetic met him.

Between them the two men carried the unconscious Hyde away. They laid him in the ditch, then stared in horror. His face and hands, unprotected from the fire, were gone. Those strong, capable hands that they had come to trust so much; the broad forehead and the powerful jaw were all just gore and bone, blackened with smoke; the face made ghastly by the grin of white-bared teeth.

Hyde's sightless, lidless eyes stared up at them.

'Has anyone gone for an ambulance?'

There was a roar as V-Victor blew up. The men dived into the ditch until the flaming fragments had ceased to fall.

'That ought to fetch them,' said Vincent.[8]

— 8 —

Squadron Report: Nürnberg
101 Sqn aircraft engaged: 28. Missing: 9. Damaged: 19.
Flight or Sqn Commanders missing: 0. Other aircrew missing: 71.
Flight or Sqn Commanders wounded: 1. Other aircrew wounded: 6.

Command Report
Total aircraft engaged: 413. Total missing: 96 (22.76%).
Squadron Commanders missing: 3. Wounded: 1.
Flight Commanders missing: 12. Wounded: 2.
Other aircrew missing: 665. Wounded: 231.
Aircraft lost over UK (not included in total missing): 67
Aircrew killed in UK (not included in total missing): 268
Total aircraft damaged repairable: 237.

Photo reconnaissance shows 26% of bombs landed in primary target area. Further 16% in secondary target area. Ball-bearing works, missed on previous successful raid, destroyed. To this extent the attack was a success, but this force was scattered by exceptional weather which was unforeseen, and encountered very heavy opposition due mainly to loss of concentration. Only thirteen aircraft (3.1%) returned undamaged. In the 96 aircraft lost over Europe plus the further 67 lost over UK on return, total casualties were 1,255 aircrew, including 949 killed. Many aircraft ditched, having run out of petrol, and Air-Sea Rescue were unable to meet the demand on their services.

This unfortunate raid teaches us two things:

Even with radar, window, PFF and XYZ, Bomber Command cannot operate in all weathers.

Some method of landing in fog, more reliable than radio-beam or radar homing, would have cut losses by 41%.[1]

Hyde was alive.

And he still had eyes.

His face was gone but doctors said they could build him another face. What worried the doctors was his left hand. To rebuild that, they said, they would need not a surgeon but a creator.

From nine wounds in his legs and buttocks they removed four and a quarter ounces of shrapnel.

'Nasty, of course,' the MO told the anxious crew. 'But none of it important. Pity about the flak. Without it he wouldn't have been burnt, and those burns are going to be terribly tricky.'

'Terribly tricky!', exclaimed Joe. 'This man is burnt till he looks like a gargoyle and you're upset because you might find it 'terribly tricky'!'

The MO sniffed and looked at Joe icily. 'As a matter of fact,' he said, 'it's your own fault. From what I can see, that hand was damaged *after* burning. Whoever pulled him out just wrenched him free. The fingers should have been unwound gently, one by one. We keep telling you chaps that how a burnt man is handled immediately after burning makes or mars successful treatment. And still you bring in cases that appal me. Surely you are taught first aid?'

'We can't all be Flight Lieutenant doctors, you know, and face the horrors of the operating theatre.'

The MO turned on his heel and walked away.

'I'm afraid you didn't make a firm friend there,' said Joe. 'He's the joker I saw about being sick. He as good as said that I was LMF.'[2]

'No doubt doctors meet more than their share of malingerers and become suspicious.'

'And have you noticed *which* medics become suspicious?' asked Joe pugnaciously. 'Never the experienced ones. Only the young upstarts just through exams. They read a few books and trudge behind some house physician for a while, then Air Ministry bung two rings round their sleeves and send 'em here. They know all about diseases and nothing about people. Hear this bloke talk about Hyde's burns. He won't treat Hyde. The big gen-boys will; and you won't hear *them* blaming somebody's foolishness.'

Vincent was looking upset. 'I did have to wrench him out,' he said. 'I suppose I am to blame.'

'Balls!' said Joe, growing more and more annoyed. 'I wonder how carefully our Flight Loo-bloody-tenant chum would've unwrapped them? If it had been him instead of you in there Hyde would've burnt to death. It would've saved him a 'terribly tricky' patient.'

'Take it easy, Joe.'

'But I get real wild inside.'

'Well, relax. You'll finish up flak-happy.'

Many of the squadron were more than a little flak-happy. Every crew had experienced trouble on the Nürnberg trip. Every aircraft was damaged. Everybody had lost good friends. Aircrew wounded had left their crewmates standing around incomplete and inactive. Lieutenant Cahill, with flak in a tyre, had ground-looped on touchdown, killing two of his crew and the pimple-faced second dickie, and breaking his own back. Cahill would be in plaster for many months. For a few days the squadron could not fly, and during that time Bomber Command operated without XYZ cover.[3]

It was a setback for both nerves and morale. It came as more of a shock following on recent successes.

An unusual casualty of the Nürnberg fiasco was Wendy Marlborough-Jones. Two aspects of this raid caused her pangs of conscience when awake, and dreams of horror while she slept.

That the whole tragedy should be caused by her department – meteorology – she felt as a personal failure. In her inner mind she felt she had foreseen the possibilities and done nothing about it. Of course her self-reproaches were foolish; what should it avail if one junior met officer, and female at that, cried 'Halt' to a dozen of Europe's best meteorologists?

A seemingly impossible situation had arisen and had been misjudged. It was unfortunate. But Wendy took it to heart like a mother who had lost her child.

All the affection she felt for Hyde now rekindled in sympathy for his hurt. She was a serious, tender-hearted woman living a sheltered life in the midst of hectic drama; she was too close to war not to absorb some of its horror, and that horror took the form of self-reproach.

How she envied Barbara! Barbara and H-H were the squadron lovebirds *par excellence*. Barbara had about her the air that only a passionate woman who is in love and revels in it can have. Wendy had heard H-H whisper to Barbara; 'I could navigate by the stars in your eyes', and for one breathless instant she imagined she did know the fires of love that put the sparkle there.

She had tea with Barbara one day when H-H was briefing to fly. Barbara's gaiety allowed no trace of worry or concern. The cottage was bestrewn with reminders that its occupants were lovers. In the bathroom, scrawled on H-H's shaving mirror in lipstick was the message; 'Very close, darling. Bib-n-Bub hate stubble trouble.'

When Wendy commented, Barbara laughed and said, 'See the beast's reply!' On her dressing table mirror, written in soap, was an answer so frank and intimate that it would have been vulgar had it not been so naively sweet.

Whenever H-H was flying Barbara would waken to the sound of the landing aircraft, and returning crews would see her parked outside de-briefing, waiting to drive H-H back to their cottage. For some time she grew to be a lovely symbol of fidelity and faith. Her carefree confidence did not permit of love that knew an ending.

Wendy wondered how such emotions could fail to feel the strain of war. Did Barbara never think, as she held her lover in her arms, that this kiss may be their last? Did she not count the hours he was away and know some fear, or dream she saw him die?

It seemed that she did not. Surely no woman who spent the night in fear could trip so gaily, smile so serenely, chatter so brightly the next morning! It was bad enough, one might think, for the wife in Rotherham or the mother in Kroonstad who heard the BBC announce: 'Last night Bomber Command attacked Düsseldorf. Sixteen aircraft are missing.' But to be on the squadron, in the battle as it were, to hear the petrol-load and watch the aircraft leave and then wait ... No wonder officialdom frowned on having wives living in the village. Yet Barbara did not seem to wane. The sight of her with H-H, indeed, did wonders for morale in people like Wendy, with far less to lose than they.[4]

When Hyde was moved into the burns ward of RAF hospital, Cosford[5], it was found that dermatitis had infected both his hands and face.

'Neuro-dermatitis,' the specialist said. 'A not unusual complication. Unfortunate, that's all. We can't treat it until we pacify these burns. It'll itch, but you'll have to ignore it. Whatever you do, don't scratch.'

While he was awake Hyde endured the itch. But when, despite his incomplete eyelids, he fell asleep, he clawed the maddening irritation with his bandaged hands. So then his hands were tied to the head of his iron bed and it was no longer possible to scratch.

'Ah, capital!', said the specialist a week or two later. 'Soon we'll be able to begin the first graft. We're going to make you a pretty boy again. And I *do* mean a pretty boy. Your new cheeks mightn't be like a baby's bottom, but they'll be genuine bottom all right; we'll use your own bottom for the job.'

'If the French ever offer me a Croix de Guerre,' said Hyde through thin, cracked lips, 'I'll tell General de Gaulle he can kiss my, er, cheek.' Hyde wanted to laugh but the prospect was too painful.[6]

'With your permission I'm going to attempt to mend your left hand, too,' said the specialist. 'Sinew might respond to a new idea I have. Are you game? There's nothing to lose.'

'Game if you are,' said Hyde.

'Good! We've got plenty of time. You're going to be here a long while.'

He went to move on, but paused to add; 'I won't be around tomorrow, so I'll wish you a merry Christmas.'

'Thank you, sir,' said Hyde. 'And here is your Christmas card.'

Hyde handed him a sheet of folded paper. Written on it in a painful hand, the specialist read; 'A Merry Eczema and a Happy Neuritis.'[7]

Following Nürnberg new timing tactics were introduced by Bomber Command. If winds varied significantly from the forecast, TOT could be put forward or back in order to preserve easy timing and not waste petrol. Each squadron was instructed to direct the best navigators to radio back to Base giving the actual winds. These winds were then averaged and forwarded to Group. If a TOT change were needed it was broadcast. In addition, averaged winds would be broadcast for the use of navigators without radar or for crews whose navigator might be wounded or dead.

Ludford needed somebody to plot the winds as they were wire-lessed back and average them. Vincent was an 'odd bod' navigator whose work seemed reliable so the job was given to him. He could also do the hack work around the navigation office and save the more valuable time of the nav leader. It was interesting work, and although nothing was said, he assumed it would take him off ops.

Working, as he was, with the squadron and base nav leaders, he came under their eye. As an example for new crews Vincent had stuck one of his own charts and logs to the nav section wall, and base nav leader asked him what the yellow arrows on it represented.

Vincent explained that they were the forecast winds at opera-tional height, and that by comparing them with the actual winds he had a quick guide to what the real weather situation was. From that he could more accurately compute future winds for each new leg of a trip. The base nav leader thought the idea good, and said he would submit it to Group.

Taking a leaf out of the nav leader's book the engineer leader recruited North in a similar role in the engines section, so Vincent and Magnetic found themselves drawn closer together by mutual staff duties. Bill and Yarpi hoped that they would receive similar invitations but they did not.

The sub-note on the operation report which said, 'Some method of landing in fog, more reliable than radio-beam or radar homing, would have cut losses by 41%', did not escape notice. It was said that Mr Churchill himself, appalled by the Nürnberg losses, had ordered a speeding-up of investigations into fog dispersal. At last something had materialised; something called FIDO.[8]

Ludford Magna, as Group's highest aerodrome (and therefore where fog would usually be thinnest) was chosen to have FIDO installed.

Two heavy pipelines were laid outside the main runway, with two smaller pipes at each end. This enclosed the entire runway in a petrol-pipe box. Small valves, like those on lawn-sprinklers, were set in these pipes at intervals; through them squirted jets of petrol which were then lit. The two miles of pipes burned thousands of gallons of petrol an hour but the heat created was immense, and either dissolved the fog around it or caused the fog cloud to lift bodily into the air.

In the gap, sandwiched between earth and cloud, aircraft could land visually. It cost the mint to run FIDO, but those sixty-seven aircraft and 268 aircrew lost over the UK following Nürnberg had a paper value of about L5,494,000, so FIDO could still pay dividends.[9]

Its first application had an unfortunate sequel.

Fog landing on FIDO was progressing successfully with aircraft from all of 1 Group landing at Ludford, when one Lanc made its approach with flak-holed tanks leaking petrol. The FIDO flames ignited the stream of petrol from the aircraft, flames climbed the rope of fuel tying the plane to FIDO's fire ring, and the Lanc blew up, killing all its crew.

Later the same thing happened again and another crew died. So FIDO was modified and the end bars removed (they had made the approach bumpy anyway) and thus the risk of flying directly over fire was averted. The 'method of landing in fog' had arrived.[10]

Lieutenant Cahill was out of hospital, and he and Krink were celebrating. They had discovered that great amusement capital can be made from a plaster-encrusted torso.

One lark was to walk into people. They reel back as though hit with a brick wall.

Another lark was to ask strange girls to dance, then watch the expression on their faces.

If a girl refused to pay any attention to his unusual thickness and solidness, Cahill would offer to show her his etchings and, before she could refuse, unbutton his shirt and show the much-decorated plaster. There were signatures galore, verses of various and dubious origin, sketches of widely differing topics and catering for widely differing tastes.

But the best lark of all was to entice fellows to punch his stomach. 'Go ahead,' he would say. 'Punch. Hard as you like.' One victim swore he broke a knuckle and another really did dislocate his thumb.

'Breaking your back,' said Cahill, 'is about the most fun you can have.'

'He's not even letting it upset his love life,' announced Krink to Vincent. 'By the way, how is Blondie standing the strain?'

Cahill looked hard at Krink. 'Oh, she was madly dramatic at first. Heavy pauses between lines, you know. But then I worked her over gently and she realised all was not lost.'

'But can you really cope in that rig?'

'Oh, but definitely! She's the sufferer; she's black and blue from knees to navel.'

'Oh, my shattered hip!'

'She's a bit up-stage about it lately. Time for a quick change, I'd say. Have you finished with half-pint, yet, Krink? She interests me.'

'Do you always pirate Krink's cast-off women?,' asked Vincent.

'I run my casting-eye over them,' admitted Cahill. 'If they fit the role I let them try the part. Usually understudy first. But as a star Blondie is slipping. What say about half-pint, Krink?'

'You take her. She's too fond of postamble for me anyway.'

'Postamble?'

'Yeah. She wants to talk when I want to sleep. The opposite of preamble.'

'Oh, I don't mind that. As long as she's not shy in the boudoir scene.'

'The boudoir is her natural setting.'

'Well, that's settled. Oh, and by the way, I'm always seeking new talent. Make the next one tall and dark with perfumed hair and a languid voice – Russian spy type.'

'And then you'll take her over, too?', laughed Vincent.

'When I've finished,' said Krink.

'Certainly,' said Cahill. 'She plays the Krynkiwski circuit first, then I run her in the provinces.'

'The scavenger for cast-off women,' said Vincent. 'We should call you 'Jackal'.'

'Careful. Krynkiwski here is my only talent scout. Though sometimes his auditions appear a trifle thorough.' Cahill frowned admonishingly at Krink.

'Now then, Jackal,' said Krink, 'I find 'em, feel 'em and fondle 'em, and you don't figure until I forget 'em.'

'Of course, dear boy. Strictly West End before they play the Cahill circuit.'

'The Jackal circuit.'

'Please, please, less of this dirty dialogue.'

Cahill could scoff, but 'Jackal' he was thereafter.

There was a real drama coming to a showdown at this time; a big one. The Allies were massing for the Second Front.

Over England droned formations of gliders and troop-carriers. Ports were clogging with landing barges. Portable harbours were being assembled. Tanks and heavy guns were rumbling coast-wards. Across the Channel the Hun was hurriedly piling defence upon defence, moving his forces west until it seemed the two opposing armies could overhear each other's plans, while each side's armourers

With busy hammers closing rivets up,
Gave dreadful note of preparation
for the hugest battle Man had ever known.[11]

Bombers pounded Hitler's defences; railways, factories, stores; smashed them faster than they were produced until every day a weaker – not a stronger – Hitler barred the Allies' way. Bomber Command was flying more often and with more reliable success than they had ever done before.[12]

But not without cost. The Germans moved defences west, seeming to give anti-aircraft defences priority. They had grasped that, for them and for Bomber Command, the invasion had begun; round one was being fought in the air. When the next battle came, whichever side had lost round one would face a sorry future.

Throughout all this time Hyde was in hospital and his crew were taking little part in the fray. Vincent and Magnetic discovered that, contrary to their beliefs, they were not off ops but still flew occasionally as odd bods, as did their crewmates. Actually, none of them was doing very much work, but although they led an easy life at this time it was not a satisfying one.

Then came D-Day! And 101 Squadron were flying a very special mission. This vital day was the only time the squadron flew without bombs. Today they had more important work to do than to bomb. Today they were to strike the German dumb: their function was solely XYZ.

All communication within the German defences was by radio telephone: pillbox to pillbox, tank to tank and pillbox to tank. Just as the 101 Squadron Specials were able to prevent German messages reaching the Luftwaffe, so could they now jam the orders for the defence of Hitler's Europe. A vital role and one which they must maintain all that long, tumultuous day. That was why they did not carry bombs; all spare weight was taken up with extra petrol so they could stay airborne as long as possible.

Every squadron flew that whole day long. More than 11,000 air sorties were completed in nineteen hours.

Before the invasion was launched, while other squadrons were hitting the defences and two special forces were inching their way across the Channel, dropping window from low-level so that each force would appear on the German radar screens as an invasion fleet, 101 Squadron aircraft were setting off singly to patrol above the invasion beaches.

Throughout the day each aircraft was to operate separately, flying up and down the coast over the invasion area, jamming every German message they heard. They carried extra ammunition because fighter attacks were likely; they carried extra food because there would be no returning for a meal for sixteen to eighteen hours.[13]

Vincent and Joe were both flying as odd bods with a new Canadian skipper in S-Sugar. They were pleased to be in Sugar – she had completed the most aircraft on 101 Squadron. This was her eighty-ninth trip; her life, it seemed, was charmed beyond reach of statistics which insisted she should have been lost at least four times by now.[14]

Vincent was secretly pleased to have Joe in the rear turret. Ever since Joe had blown up the Ju 88 with nine rounds, squadron respect for his dead-eye shooting had been high. Today, they might need it. To be one of many bombers and encounter a fighter was bad enough. But to be alone – just you and a fighter – was infinitely worse, especially in daylight. In theory the fighter had it all his way. Joe knew it, and kept his keen eyes scanning the hostile horizon.

H-H was flying with them as Special, and all that long day he toyed with German radio. He was delighted to hear dramatic messages, vital and urgent commands, and snap them off when they had hardly begun, jamming them for ten seconds until the Hun was lost. Orders to fire, to advance, withdraw, assist, cover … every military urgency he stifled, and the German consternation he well and gleefully imagined. With twenty-seven other men doing as he did, German communications must be wild confusion, he thought.

Occasionally they were attacked by flak. The first bursts never hit them and they were always able to outsmart subsequent bursts. It was only if the first burst got them that they need worry …

To escape flak as much as possible, and to amuse themselves, they climbed to maximum height. As their petrol load went down, Sugar went up, higher and higher until they passed the specification ceiling and were tip-toe at 26,000 feet. It was terribly cold, and even with oxygen taps full on their fingernails were purple from lack of oxygen.

Much of the day they could see only cloud below. Hour after hour they flew and they were very bored. Occasionally they would glimpse the battle through a gap in the clouds, and below them would stretch the spectacle of battle. On land it looked like just another layer of cloud: vast black clouds of smoke, with tiny fires twinkling here and there. But over the wind-foamed sea came the endless armada that followed, hour after hour, bearing a million soldiers; land-fighters turned sailor for a day.

H-H was growing exhausted but still he laboured with his sets.

Was he only imagining that as he grew more tired the messages grew thicker? At dawn he had been forced to search for messages to jam, but now the ether buzzed with them and many were getting through.

With nightfall they ate the last of the sandwiches and drank the last of the coffee. They had been awake since midnight and flying since 4 am and tiredness and boredom worried them more than hunger. Nevertheless they ate for lack of anything else to do – only H-H was busy – as much as for nourishment.

Now the battle was the flickering of a million fireflies. It looked like the birth of a universe seen from space, with now and then a brilliant galaxy exploding momently and falling away into nothingness.

Vincent computed endless courses to cover and re-cover the same dull few miles. The engineer eked out their petrol to keep them in the air another instant, and the gunners forced their tired, aching eyes to continue searching.

At length they turned for home. They were the only aircraft over base so they came straight in and landed. They had been airborne for eighteen hours and forty-two minutes.

Debriefing room was almost empty. Two aircraft had returned during the day; one with engine trouble and the other damaged by flak. Two more had landed about half an hour before and their crews were now asleep. Three crews including their own were now being debriefed. They were annoyed to be back so early because they felt sure that their petrol-consumption rate was very low and that they would be one of the last.

Tired as they were, they decided to wait for the other crews. They put an extra tot of rum in their coffee to help keep awake and settled down in armchairs to wait.

After twenty minutes there was still not another plane back; not even a drone in the sky of an approaching Lanc, and the engineer expressed amazement that anybody could have made his petrol last so long.

Ten minutes later he said he defied anybody to keep airborne for another five minutes and if they weren't back then – well, they just weren't coming back.

Then suddenly they all stared at each other.

Could it be?

Were they the last?

The engines leader and the Squadron Commander were talking gravely in one corner. The intelligence officers were chatting together, trying to appear gay while they waited for another twenty-one crews.

They waited another half an hour. Then, at a word from the CO, they packed up and went to bed.

Twenty-eight had gone out. Seven had come back. The theory put forward in explanation was simple. If a bomber was attacked by fighters in daylight, it was destroyed. Those who had been attacked were lost; those who returned had been lucky enough not to encounter a fighter. Of 101 Squadron's aircrew strength of 244 men, 168 were lost in eighteen hours. They remembered again the hazards of breaking radio silence.

We attract fighters on to ourselves.[15]

'That means you're champ again, mate,' Joe said to Vincent, sadly. 'It seems you did fix a jinx when you arranged that title match.'

'Nonsense! he was flying on an unlucky trip and there was every likelihood of his being killed. Nürnberg and D-Day – you can't call those ordinary ops ...'

'Jinx or no jinx,' said Vincent, 'I don't like it. Even *I'm* getting scared of this championship now.'

The squadron had been stood down. With less than one flight left they could not fly as a squadron. Two hundred new aircrew had to be posted and trained, including two flight commanders and two section leaders.

Vincent was summoned by the Squadron Commander. He could not imagine why and entered with some misgivings.

'Farlow,' said the Squadron Commander, 'do you think you could handle the job of nav leader?'

Vincent was surprised but answered quickly, 'Yes, sir.'

'Base nav officer suggested you. It'll be worth your commission. Indeed, you'll probably do a quick jump from flight sergeant to flight lieutenant.'

'Yessir.'

'You have to apply. Here are the forms. Fill them in and I'll give you your first interview now. Can't see your Flight Commander because you haven't got one. Don't worry about the job but have a good crack at it. If you can't make it we'll leave you assistant nav leader and I think you've won your commission anyway.'

Within a hundred seconds Vincent was outside again, dazed but elated.

The new aircrew started arriving. Walking into the mess was like going into a strange club. The faces were all new and the atmosphere did not feel natural or relaxed. The fifty-odd veterans of the old 101 were outnumbered and engulfed. It had become a squadron of sprogs.

These new chaps did not know the squadron traditions and there were too few veterans for the old order to prevail. Vincent even saw one crew shoo Raff from the mess. His blood boiled; Raff had become an institution, these new bods did not even know his name and now they tried to exclude him from the mess ...

Settling down to the tasks of nav leader was doubly, trebly difficult, too. Because of the sudden rush of new crews, vast training programmes had to be flown. New crews generally learn much during their off-hours just speaking to the experienced crews. But now the experienced crews were few, and they tended to stick together, like an oppressed minority. None of this off-duty learning was being done. The squadron had turned into another Training Comand station with pupils and instructors, complete with the gulf that goes between.

In addition, Vincent's commission was not through and would not come through until the red tape unwound itself. He wore flight sergeant rank and had to tell officers what to do. His experience and his status as nav leader put him correctly above his own section, but still his position was delicate.

It was almost a month before the squadron flew on ops again. And when they did they flew to a changed war.[16]

They took off in daylight, bombed just across the Channel in the dusk and hurried home to land within four hours. No losses.

It was anti-climactic in the extreme.

Next trip was another daylight trip; to an airfield in Holland. Four hours thirty. Again no losses; but one clot pranged on landing and his bomb aimer broke his ankle.

Many of these sprogs did not fly well. Indeed, flying accidents became the major hazard. One attempted economy was changed, by this indifferent flying, into an expensive loss. Poor target visibility often frustrated close-support attacks and returning bombers would dump their bomb-loads in the Channel.[17]

Upset by this waste, Command ordered one force returning from Le Havre to land with bombs. The load was all 1,000 pounders, very stable bombs, and should have caused no anxiety.

The first pilot returning to Ludford, however, forgot to allow for the extra 16,000 pounds when landing. He touched down half-way along the runway. Normally this would have been safe but, with an extra eight tons to hold, the Lancaster's brakes could not counteract this bad flying.

The bomber was still doing 50 mph when it ran out of runway, went through the fence, over a road and into a ditch and crashed.

Nothing exploded and nobody was hurt.

That crew had scarcely climbed from the wreck when another bomb-filled Lancaster repeated the stupidity.

The second bomber, with another 16,000 pounds of bombs, crashed onto the wreckage of the first.

Nothing exploded and nobody was hurt.

Sheer luck had outweighed sheer folly. Had these crews died as they richly deserved to, Le Havre would have been 101's costliest raid since D-Day. Thus had flying changed.

For every one trip after the old, hard style, there were six or eight 'trifling little daylights'. Men who had previously not flown one operational hour were, within a month, almost tour-expired veterans swanking about full of bravado.

'Full of piss and wind, more like it,' said Joe, and he spoke for all the old lags to whom this new war in the air was stranger than it appeared to the novices.

'Cop this crew,' Joe said one day. 'Twenty-six ops in thirty-five days – another four and they'll have finished a tour inside six weeks, whereas las year it would've taken nine months. And they haven't flown one *real* trip at all.'

'They're winning the war,' Vincent pointed out. 'Look at Europe.'

'Nonsense! *We* won that war ... in the months before D-Day!'

'Remember I said that once? Some more facts came to light the other day. Sir John Baldwin announced in the House that there were more casualties – killed and missing – in the RAF from D-Day to D-Day plus 3, than the total combined casualties of the British and land forces in Normandy.'[18]

'Is that fair dinkum?'

'Dead accurate. His very words. Europe *was* invaded from the air. Not only before D-Day but on D-Day itself.'

Occasionally there came a long night trip. 'Almost a good old-fashioned op,' the old lags would say with morbid relish. It could never be quite the same again because France was gone and German defences disrupted. They would fly and meet comparatively light opposition, and then the new crews would return, pale and shaken, saying, 'We see what you mean.'

But they had seen only half; ops were getting easy.

'Now watch the chairborne troops from rear hindquarters come running on to ops,' Magnetic said. 'Those poor devils who'll tell you they've been struggling to get a release from the Ministry since 1939. Watch 'em now it's easy. They'll all suddenly get those releases and come rushing in now they think it's safe, all squabbling like hell to wangle themselves a DFC so they can prove it wasn't the civvies who won the war.'

'I say let them come,' said Vincent. 'They'll also wangle us their fancy afternoon teas a la Whitehall.'

Part Two

Chiltern

— 1 —

Acting Squadron Leader Matthew Thomas A'Becket Chiltern arrived as the new B Flight Commander during September, 1944.[1] He had been commissioned in 1937 soon after leaving Grammar School. During his seven years in the RAF he had flown practically every aircraft type known, was recognised as a clever pilot and thorough administrator with sound knowledge of regulations and service etiquette.

He had flown on goodwill missions to India, Australia and the United States and behaved impeccably. His log-book, written in fine backhand, showed that he had a total of 2,472 flying hours to his credit and he had never aimed bomb or bullet in anger.

The Ministry and Training Command, when their turn came, had both been sorry to lose him. He had fitted in there so well. Squadron Leader Matthew Chiltern was a stern man but fair and his superiors said he had courage. Moreover, he was a good man: he said his prayers every night.

He stopped the staff car in the village of Ludford Magna and sat, tight-lipped, while a sergeant struggled to remove a large steel trunk from the back seat. When his struggles had succeeded and the sergeant stood, panting but at attention beside the car, the Squadron Leader said; 'Find the B Flight officers' quarters and leave that trunk with the NCO i/c, and impress upon him that it is mine.'

'Yessir,' said the sergeant, and saluted.

'Oh, and sergeant!', the Squadron Leader called as the lad turned away carrying the heavy trunk.

'Yessir?'

'After that, report to me at my flight office. I might want you for something. It's this way, I believe, about a mile if you walk over the fields.'

The sergeant said, 'Yessir', and saluted again, then trudged off unhappily as the staff car drove away.

Joe, who had seen and heard the whole incident from where he stood at the bus stop, wandered over and said to the sergeant, 'Would you like a hand with the trunk, mate?'

The sergeant looked fearfully at the crown on Joe's arm and said, 'No, thank-you, flight.'

'Come off it,' said Joe. 'That's too heavy for one. And I can show you where B Flight is.'

The sergeant thanked him with embarrassment, then Joe broached the topic that had prompted his interference.

'Who's the la-de-dah dandy?'

'Squadron Leader Chiltern, the new B Flight Comander.'

'How come he orders you around like a batman?'

'I suppose he's entitled to. He's my skipper.'

Joe dropped his end of the trunk. 'He's your *what*?'

'My skipper.'

'But he called you 'sergeant', and you called him 'sir' and flung salutes like you was mountin' guard.'[2]

'Oh, always! He insists. He's very proper. A great disciplinarian.'

'You praise him, but do you like him?'

'Well ... No, not really. But he's a fine officer.'

'Balls! Fine officers are liked by their men. He seems to think this is the Lord Mayor's Show.[3] Has anybody told him there's a war on?'

'Oh, I'm sure he knows. Squadron Leader Chiltern tells me he's been terribly conscious of the war ever since it started. He's tried again and again to get on to ops, he says.'

'You mean all that – and a sprog, too?'

The sergeant looked shocked. 'A sprog? Well ... Yes, in the strictest sense I suppose Squadron Leader Chiltern is a sprog.'

'And that's our new flight commander?'

'He says so.'

'Then gord help us,' said Joe, and picked up the trunk again.

Vincent's first contact with Squadron Leader Chiltern was through his navigator, Sergeant Wall. Wall's navigation on their first training flight had been indifferent at best. One obvious mistake Vincent mentioned.

'You were told to climb to height between points B and D, yet you reached height before C. Why?'

'Squadron Leader Chiltern always tends to climb quickly. He

was instructing on fighters for years; probably he got the habit there.'

'But you must tell him what rate to climb.'

'I did.'

'You mean you told him one rate and he flew another?'

'Yes. He insists on prerogative.'

'You are in charge of navigation, Wall. Tell your pilot what to do and make sure he does it.'

Wall looked hesitant. 'All right. I'll *tell* him.'

Wall was not the only member of Chiltern's crew who displeased his section-leader. The engineer failed to follow squadron method and excused himself by saying he had done his job the way his skipper had insisted he do it. The bomb aimer's figures showed wide misses and he mentioned respectfully that his directions were not always followed promptly enough.

The whole crew, with the exception of the pilot, seemed under-confident and ill-trained. Flight Lieutenant Marshall, the sigs leader, said to Vincent, 'It is as though they had come straight off course, without operational training at all. They reek of Training Command.'[4]

Every crew has to undergo further training on posting to a squadron; each crew member is assessed individually, then the worth of the crew as a whole is considered and their probable worth and reliability discussed by flight commanders and section leaders in conference with the Squadron Commander.

Squadron Leader Chiltern therefore suffered the embarrass-ment of being present to hear his own crew left off the Battle Order for weeks on end. Then they were shifted off the 'In Preparation' list and put into the 'Unsatisfactory standard attained. Require special training' category. Squadron Leader Chiltern was *livid*.

Squadron Leader Chiltern felt victimised but he was too proper to say so. The standard of his own flying was obviously very high so he felt let down by his crew. Every pilot on the squadron agreed that Chiltern's flying looked excellent; his landings were a picture straight from the text-book gallery. He repeatedly requested permission to start flying operations without further training but was as often refused.

'I fully appreciate your anxiety to get on to ops,' the Squadron Commander would say. 'But if you crew flew over Germany as they have been flying over England you would all be killed. And you aren't much use to me dead.'

Following further intensive training which achieved nothing, the Squadron Commander gave much time at the next conference to discussing the future of the Chiltern crew.

'Normally, Mr Chiltern,' he said, 'you would be sent on ops and almost certainly killed. Believe me, I am doing you a favour. But I like crews to start right. More so in your case, since flight commanders may have to lead formations in the near future now we're flying so much in daylight.[5] But as you yourself are obviously up to scratch, and since you are already functionally established here as a flight commander, I am returning your crew to OTU. A predecessor of yours, Squadron Leader Parke, has left a crew here and I'll arrange for you to have them. They aren't strictly ready for a second tour but in fact they've had a long rest and should welcome some more ops by now.'

He turned to Vincent. 'What do you feel about that, Mr Farlow?'

Vincent's heart had leapt as the suggestion was made. He had disliked Chiltern even before he had met him and actual contact had strengthened the opinions he had gained through Wall. Chiltern obviously resented Vincent's rank, too; he had noticed Chiltern's eyebrows pucker just now when the Squadron Commander had called him 'Mister Farlow' out of deference to his position instead of simply 'Farlow' as his flight sergeant rank demanded.

Nobody welcomed a return to ops but this aspect of the move worried Vincent less than the dislike he felt for Chiltern himself. There was little, however, that he could say. He had not the right to refuse to fly at all, and to agree to fly but not with Chiltern would be to insult the Squadron Leader sorely.

'I can't speak for the whole crew, sir,' he said, 'but I'm quite agreeable.'

After the conference the Squadron Commander had a private word with Vincent. 'I'm sorry about this, but your Commission papers have been returned. I explained there was no flight

commander to interview you at the time but evidently that won't
do. Squadron Leader Chiltern is your flight commander now. Have
him fill these out and I'll try to rush it through.'

Vincent had not expected Squadron Leader Chiltern to be
particularly pleasant but he had not been prepared for the antag-
onism he encountered when what should have been the pure
formality of the commissioning interview took place.

'Why are they promoting, or thinking of promoting, a flight
sergeant to a flight lieutenant, Farlow? Isn't there a flight lieutenant
navigator recently arrived on the squadron?'

'Yessir, there is.'

'Why not give him the job?'

Vincent was about to explode that the man was a sprog, but
thought better of it and said, instead, 'I don't know, sir.'

'You paused, Farlow. Were you about to say it is because he lacks
experience?'

'Yessir, I was.'

'Then you would also say I lack experience?'

'Of operations, yessir.'

'I see why you have been so long an NCO, Farlow, if you always
tell your interviewing officers you consider them unfit for the positions they fill.'

'I didn't say that, sir.'

'Don't imagine, Farlow, that in these interviews we analyse the
actual answers; we try to get to the root of the man himself.'

'Yessir.'

'This flight lieutenant navigator has been instructing in Canada
for three years. He probably taught you to fly. Does the pupil now
know more than the master?'

'It is possible that the pupil will know more of actual operations,
sir, just as the instructor would know more of instructing.'

'So the teacher knows only how to teach?'

'I said it was possible, sir.'

'But I ask *is* it possible?'

'Of the world's many male obstetricians, sir, not one could have
a baby.'

'You reveal your level admirably, Farlow. I don't think we need continue this interview.'

Vincent paused, then decided to stick to his guns.

'But surely this interview has been most irregular, sir. All you asked me was why another man should not be put into a post that the Squadron Commander has given me.'

'He has told me it is on condition that you make the grade.'

'Yessir. But at the job itself. This commission business is a prerequisite. He suggested it.'

'This form, Farlow,' said Chiltern coldly, waving it at him, 'is an application from you begging a commission.'

'Surely it is a mere formality, sir.'

'One does not approach one's king and ask for a great privilege, Farlow, regarding it as 'a mere formality'.'

'No, sir, but ...'

'The more you say, Farlow, the more you damn yourself.'

'But, sir ...'

'That will be all, Farlow.'

Vincent said, 'Yessir', saluted, turned about and walked to the door.

He twisted the knob but then half-turned back to speak.

Then he changed his mind and walked out.

None of the crew would refuse to fly another tour, but none of them welcomed Chiltern for a skipper. Joe told of his experience with Chiltern's bag-carrying sergeant and said; 'If Chiltern was burning to death I wouldn't do him the honour of pissing on him.'

As a crew they flew one training flight together and were put straight on the Battle Order. The old crew were fully trained and that Chiltern himself should need further training was more than anybody, even the Squadron Commander, liked to suggest. The only change in the old crew was in their Special. Johnnie, who had been screened,[6] was replaced by the oily Willy Schydt, still very much a sergeant.

At the briefing for Squadron Leader Matthew Thomas A'Becket Chiltern's first operation of his long service career the atmosphere was so electric that the men almost forgot their own tensions and rekindled the squadron enthusiasm. The war in the air was going well. The Squadron Commander told them they must now make a terrific effort to keep the Hun disorganised and stop his reinforcements reaching the front, and that if they did, the war would be 'over by Christmas'.

Tonight's target was Cologne: the railway yards and bridges.

'We have to get across the Rhine,' said the Squadron Commander. 'Our armies have reached it here and there and been forced to stop. Behind the Rhine Hitler will try to make a stand. We must stop him. His armies are in flight now. We must keep them that way. So remember, on this charge cry; 'England, Bomber Harris and Christmas turkey at home!'[7]

This news did not particularly please two of the men who heard it. One of those men was Sergeant Schydt and the other was Squadron Leader Chiltern. Each was thinking that the race was near its end and he had left his run too late. That was why Schydt decided to act immediately and why, too, when he approached Squadron Leader Chiltern about his commission in the dressing-room that Chiltern's mood was so much worse than usual. He was positively rude to Schydt instead of just his usual unpleasant self.

On their training flight, Vincent had suspected why Wall had never navigated successfully. En route to Cologne he confirmed it. He was watching his compass repeater carefully and checking the ASI and altimeter. Then he spoke:

'Nav to skipper. Will you watch your course, please? You are four degrees off. And we're climbing too quickly. We should not reach height until five degrees East.'

There was a little gasp before Chiltern replied, 'I like to climb quickly, navigator.'

'So the Germans can pick you up on radar and get their fighters into the air? We should not reach height before five degrees East.'

'There is no need for you to explain tactics to me, navigator.'

'But there is a need for you to fly my courses and airspeeds. Otherwise I can't navigate.'

'The discovery that you could not navigate would not surprise me. I have had qualified navigators before who could not navigate.'

The crew sat stunned. From here on, it seemed, they would have to fight not only the enemy but each other. It was something none of them believed could happen. Not a word was said. As they droned towards the Ruhr their very aircraft seemed sullen.

Some things were new since they had flown regularly before. Joe and Yarpi wore electrically heated suits and gloves. 'This suit,' Joe said when he tried it, 'is the only perfect climate outside bed.'

Vincent was experiencing heavy German jamming on Gee. Theoretically radar could not be jammed, but the Hun simply transmitted so much false radar, termed 'grass', that it became increasingly difficult as they flew towards Germany to distinguish the correct blip from the false ones.

Schydt was silently jamming and every voice he throttled was a German voice; the Specials no longer spoke themselves, nor were the long-range radios speaking from England.

Vincent tried to average and plot the actual courses that Chiltern flew. He prayed for the day when their Lanc would be fitted with an air position indicator: a machine which automatically computed air position from the readings of the compass and ASI. This machine plotted the actual course the skipper flew and not the one his navigator asked him to fly. Evidently Vincent's experience with Chiltern was not a unique one between pilots and navigators.

The run into the target amazed them all. They had to keep reminding themselves; 'this is the Ruhr, this is the Ruhr.' It did not look like a Ruhr target any more. This was once an aerial hell. So far, tonight, it seemed only an average target.

As they were about to turn in to the target, though, predicted flak came on to them very suddenly. It was close and the next burst would be closer. They had three seconds to see the first bursts, judge the situation, give the order and be out of range before that next burst came. Bill said calmly, 'Dive port, go.'

'Why?' asked Chiltern.

Vincent's reaction to Bill's order had been to grab at his equipment to stop it flying off his desk as the aircraft fell away port faster than gravity. Instead of violent action, as his microphone had been switched on to give the new course into the target, at Chiltern's unbelievable reply he cried, foolishly, 'Christ!'.

The flak answered for Bill. It sprinkled the sky nearer their port beam.

'Because we are being predicted by flak,' said Bill.

'Very well,' said Chiltern. 'Diving port.' And he dropped the nose gently and flew a timid turn. Everyone was surprised when the next burst managed to get above them and they were safe.

When they were back on course, tracking for Cologne with three minutes to TOT, Chiltern began a little lecture.

'Bomb aimer,' he said. 'always announce yourself before you speak. I must know who is talking so I can appraise what you can see and decide what weight to place on your advice.'

'Yes, skipper.'

'And navigator! I did recognise your voice and I must say I disapprove heartily of your outburst. Not only does it betray a lack of confidence in my own decision, it also shows an alarming lack of respect for sacred things. Neither of these things will I tolerate in my crew. I hope that is absolutely clear and that I shall not have to mention it again.'

'Yessir. Sorry, sir.'

'Very well. We shall forget it. With this warning: I dislike profanity intensely. It is unnecessary. Should I hear it from any of my own crew, in the air or even off duty, I shall be seriously displeased.'

'Yessir.'

'Left ten degrees,' Bill interjected. 'Bomb doors open.'

'Bomb aimer! I have just finished telling you always to announce yourself.'

'Sorry, sir,' said Bill hurriedly. 'But we'll overshoot. Left twenty degrees.'

Slowly the aircraft turned on. Bill's orders were hurried and garbled and were soon wild with near-panic.

'Skipper! Left! Hard! Quickly!'

'This is a bad approach, bomb aimer. We shall go around again. Turning off.'

Chiltern took them miles back and ran in again. Fortunately

they had been timed near the start of the attack and there were still a few bombers around them when they made their second run.

'Even then,' Bill said after they had landed, 'it was a rotten bombing run. I'd say 'five left', and by the time he had thought out whether or not he could find it in his captaincy prerogative to follow my advice the correct alteration was about fifteen.'[8]

'And he wouldn't put in supercharger when we should,' added Magnetic. 'And that spluttering when we touched down was because he insists on handling the throttles himself.'

'I thought his landing was good.'

'I'll grant that he flies beautifully. He's a perfect pilot but a dreadful skipper.'

'Well, he's ours whether we like it or not.'

'We've certainly got a lot to teach him,' said Vincent.

'You'd hardly believe that he and Hyde could belong to the same air force; when you told Hyde 'dive-port-go' either the aircraft fell port or the stick came away in his hand. Gee, I wish we could've had Hyde back.' As Joe said this he looked around wistfully at the others; nostalgia showed in every face.

Two men who had said nothing were Yarpi and Schydt. All Yarpi's old fears had returned tenfold. What good had come of a rest on the squadron? At any time during this rest he had been ready to fly. That he had flown little seemed unimportant. True rest – security from fear; certainty that for a week or a month his life was his own – he had not known. He looked like a hunted thing. Schydt, on the other thing, looked full of Teutonic hate, as though he had been tricked into turning traitor and now he was set on revenge.

Again the war was changing. The era of 'quiet little daylights' had passed. There were two reasons for this. First, the German armies were no longer making stubborn stands as they had at Caen, and close-support attacks were not necessary.[9]

Secondly, winter was coming with its long nights, giving more scope for deep penetration. Railways, factories and stores became the targets again.

It was not surprising, then, that their next target should be a tough one: the Dortmund-Ems Canal where it crossed the Ems river near Munster. It was a vulnerable point, heavily defended, and it would be difficult to find.[10]

Fortunately, PFF now had another radar air to navigation and bombing, a cumbersome and expensive gadget called H2S, which both transmitted and received its own signal and therefore had unlimited range.[11] A clumsy H2S cupola sticking out below the fuselage caused it to be named 'the airborne udder'.

Vincent prepared his flight plan with misgivings; to find this target they would need to fly better than vague courses and approximate airspeeds.

They never did reach that target. Indeed, they failed even to take off. Their aircraft, N-Nuts, was unserviceable. During his pre-take-off check Chiltern found a 700 rpm drop on one magneto. They did not fly.

Chiltern ordered them out of the aircraft and back to his flight office. There they stood before him while he sat upright at his desk and said in that 'let's-get-straight-down-to-brass-tacks' way of his that they were to know so well; 'Tonight my aircraft was sabotaged. This is most damaging to my service reputation. You are civilians; to you it does not matter, it simply saves you the inconvenience of flying to war tonight. But the Royal Air Force is my career. I will know the culprit.'

He turned to Vincent. 'Farlow, in my position, whom would you suspect?'

Vincent stood stunned. Then he felt vast hate for this insufferable paragon. His mind rebelled as such insolence of authority.

'I know these *civilians* well, sir. I have been to war with them all. Had I found a fault in my aircraft, and had I been tempted to attribute it to sabotage I would suspect myself.'

'You suggest that I sabotaged N-Nuts?' asked Chiltern, purposely putting the unpleasant interpretation on Vincent's answer.

'No, sir. That is as preposterous as the idea that I or North or Trinket would sabotage N-Nuts. I mean that I would doubt my suspicion of sabotage.'

'Farlow, how many hours have you flown?'

'About eight hundred, sir.'

'I have flown two thousand five hundred, and what may be a suspicion to you is a certainty to me.'

Chiltern never let a point pass. He seemed to list things in his mind and bring them out again when he thought they would be most unnerving. He tried this trick now. 'You said you had been to war with all these civilians, and I believe you stressed the word, and you named North and Trinket and yourself as being as trustworthy as I. Why did you not name Krynkiwski or van Rijn or Schydt? And incidentally, I was not aware that you had 'been to war' as you dramatically choose to put it, with Schydt until last night. Had you?'

'I had not flown with him before, sir, but I have known him well.'

'How well?'

'Quite well.'

'What is his Christian name and where is his home town in Germany?'

'I ... er, I don't know, sir.'

'Ah! You see! You vouch for men – even for members of an enemy nation – and then we discover you hardly know them. His Christian name is Wilhelm and he comes from Munster which, virtually, was tonight's target. Is that not so, Schydt?'

'Yes, sir.'

Squadron Leader Chiltern leaned back in his chair and looked keenly at each man in turn. Then he said, giving weight and import to every word, 'I could check N-Nuts for fingerprints and doubt-less learn to my own satisfaction who was the culprit. But each of you has a right in my aircraft and that alone could not convict you. Anyway, I believe I know who is guilty. This chat is to acquaint you all, and that guilty man in particular, with the fact that I am not a fool. I know much more about each one of you than you may like to think – and I have not always been pleased with your various qualities either social or military – so be careful. Mend your ways. Mine is going to be the most efficient crew on this squadron for one reason alone: I am going to make it so. Any man who tries to stop me I shall remove.'

He looked again at Vincent. 'And when I say 'efficient', Farlow, I do not mean that I will draw little yellow arrows on pieces of paper. What is this nonsense you've been spouting to the Commanding Officer?'

'It's a visual met wind check, sir.'

'Delightful! We now check invisible wind visually. And what purpose, pray, other than that the colour is popular for rowdy sports cars and window boxes, does its being yellow serve? I would have expected *you* to choose BEM pink.'

Vincent answered in the same precise tone. 'It is yellow, sir, so that it will not be confused with the dark blue of the outward track, the green of the homeward track, the red of the flak areas and the light blue of the searchlight areas. And a BEM is red. Mine looks pink because it is faded; I have been wearing it a long time.'

It was not quite the note on which Chiltern had planned this interview to end. However he had nothing more to say and dismissed them curtly.

The men hurried from Chiltern's office, then stopped in an outraged group to discuss this new insult; all except Schydt who crisply bade them good-night and left.

'This guy,' said Krink, 'reminds me of the picture in my history book of the Englishman who provoked the War of American Independence; fleshy, flabby face, watery eyes, small teeth and a chin like a downhearted chicken. Only that guy wore a wig while this gink should wear a wig back-to-front so we wouldn't see his fish-face or curly horse-hair.'[12]

'His crew will be the most efficient because he makes it so,' mimicked Joe. 'I believe he honestly thinks he could fly better alone. It's only the civvy pilots who need a crew and Squadron-Christ-Almighty-Leader Chiltern carries one too so as not to embarrass them. Him and his two thousand hours.'

'Remember once discussing whether pilots were all-important?' asked Magnetic. 'This bloke might make us appreciate a good captain next time we meet one.'

'He'll learn,' said Vincent. 'He might become a wizard. If only he'll grasp that it's not the hours you've got in, but what you've got in those hours.'[13]

— 2 —

The Squadron Commander had sent for Vincent.

'I have two things to tell you, Mr Farlow,' he said.

'First is that I think you have come up to scratch in this nav leader job, and second that Squadron Leader Chiltern hasn't given you a very favourable commissioning report. Have you rubbed him up the wrong way?'

'Not intentionally, sir. Though I do find him difficult.'

'Really? I find him charming and efficient.'

'Will his unfavourable report squash my promotion, sir?'

'Well, yes. That is, theoretically. But since Base put you up and I had already decided that you were doing well I'm going to force it through. It's not very satisfactory having you in the sergeant's mess, either, so I am allowing you to put up Pilot Officer rank straight away and to move into our mess. All right?'

'Yes, sir! Thank you, sir!'

'Oh, and just to please Squadron Leader Chiltern, put up a new piece of BEM ribbon, will you? He thinks your old one looks scruffy. He also asked me how you won it. I had to admit I didn't know. How did you win it, Mr Farlow?'

'It was a bit of a fiddle between Crete and Cairo, sir.'

'I see. I had heard of people fiddling themselves gongs but you're the first one I've met who admitted it. I would have thought that sergeants lacked sufficient influence. That's all, then. See me in the mess tonight and I'll buy you a drink.'[1]

'Thank you, sir.'

As P/O Farlow, a new spring in his step, left Squadron HQ, he thought to himself; 'And that, despite Mr Chiltern, is that.'

It made him feel rather warm and smug.

'It'll mean leaving Magnetic and Joe and Johnnie and the chaps, though …'

That thought made him, in turn, a little sad.

Bomber Command was raiding Germany during daylight, in force, for the first time. The target was Emmerich where German army forces were massed in a forest. Bombers carried incendiary bombs; tactics were to set the forest on fire. Chiltern and his crew were flying.[2]

The German army, they were growing to know, had heavy and well-trained anti-aircraft defences. Even the veterans were alarmed when they saw the barrage of flak over the target. Chiltern showed absolutely no fear.

At night exploding flak showed one momentary twinkle and then was gone. By day, flak had to be very near for aircrews to see the flash because at all but critical ranges it showed as a puff of smoke which hung in the air where it burst. Over Emmerich it was impossible to see through; literally impossible to see through the black cloud of bursting flak. At the sight of it their respect for Americans rose considerably.

N-Nuts was at the lowest level of the attacking bombers, and what proved even more alarming than the flak was the hail of bombs through which they flew when the aircraft above released their loads. A single Lancaster can carry 3,500 incendiaries; flying beneath several hundred aircraft releasing such loads was obviously dangerous. Yet the danger had to be actually seen to be realised; the sky seemed full of twisting, flashing, four-pound incendiary bombs. Many of the officers above were alarmed at this sight, normally hidden by darkness. Indeed, such an outcry resulted that never again did Bomber Command put incendiaries in higher-level bombers.

Chiltern turned rather tight as they headed for home so they found themselves flying on the edge of the gaggle. Vincent quickly computed an alteration.

'Nav to skipper. Six degrees starb'd to two-eight-four true.'

'Why, navigator?'

'Oh, God!', thought Vincent, but said; 'Because we are port of track and this course will converge on the next turning-point.'

'How far are we port of track, navigator?'

'Three miles. Far enough from the mob to be jumped by fighters.'

'Thank-you, navigator. But I shall continue to fly as we are. It is too tiring flying in the slipstreams of a close gaggle.'[3]

Then he added; 'Skipper to gunners. Be alert for fighters.'

Vincent had never had a pilot refuse to fly his courses before, and the experience left him dumb. He knew his rights in the case; he could actually put Chiltern on a charge for refusing a legal command but in fact such charges were only upheld where trouble resulted from a captain having deliberately failed to follow specialist advice. It was one time when a sergeant could give an order to an Air Marshal and enforce punishment were the order disobeyed. Vincent almost hoped they would be attacked, just to prove his point, but they were not.

At debriefing, however, Vincent did raise the subject with Chiltern. In his friendliest voice, and with a smile, he said; 'I would like you to know, sir, that if I ever give an order which you disobey, and we encounter trouble as a result, I shall put you on a charge the minute we land.'

'But, my dear fellow, of course!', Chiltern replied. 'It would be the only correct thing you could do.'

Vincent said to the others afterwards; 'You know, in a way, I'm getting to like the bastard. He *is* brave, he *can* fly, and his disinterested passion for regulations amounts to *true love*.'

'It's just that he can't help being a bastard,' said Joe.

'I'm more afraid with this man on an easy trip than I was with Hyde on our toughest night,' said Bill.

'With all humility,' said Magnetic, 'I must agree. I have already resigned myself to the fact that this maniac is going to kill us. We shall die immaculate, text-book deaths, but die we surely shall.'

Chiltern was winning unpopularity elsewhere, too. One young pilot, a sprog named Hardy, was taking off to fly his first op on Emmerich and removed the flap too early, so that his Lancaster lost lift and mushed into a field beyond the runway. Fortunately none of the bombs exploded and nothing caught fire so nobody was seriously hurt. It was an expensive mistake that most flight commanders would reprimand officially, then dismiss as 'just one of those things'. But not Squadron Leader Chiltern.

'Tell me what happened, Hardy,' he insisted.

'I had never taken off with a bomb load before, sir,' said the unhappy Hardy. 'I selected flaps-up same as usual and she just sank into the ground.'

'*She* sank into the ground, Hardy?'

'I mean the aircraft, sir.'

'I fully realise you mean the aircraft, Hardy.'

All of Squadron Leader Chiltern's unpleasant interview manner had returned. 'But you imply that the *aircraft* is responsible and not your bad flying.'

'I've always taken off like that, sir. It was the bomb load, sir,' said Hardy, illogically. Chiltern's manner had rattled this underconfident sprog as it so often had with his pupils.

'Now we are blaming the bomb load. Everything is at fault, one would gather, Hardy, but the pilot. I believe the antithesis.'

'The what, sir?'

'The direct opposite, Hardy. What height were you when you selected flaps off?'

'About fifty feet, sir.'

'And what was your ASI reading?'

'About one-thirty, sir.'

'You are lying, Mr Hardy. Your speed was nearer one-six-five and your height was nearer zero. You were taking off to the mess. Boastful flying, Mr Hardy. Since you are so fond of showing the mess how well you can take off, Hardy, you will fly circuits and bumps, with your full crew, two hours each morning and afternoon for the next week. I hope this will improve your take-offs, Hardy, and show you that the mess can be a very unsympathetic audience. That is all, Mr Hardy.'

There was no greater indignity than to be obliged to practise take-offs and landings – the learner's first task – at an operational squadron. Nor would this punishment enhance Hardy's reputation in the eyes of his crew. It was an unwise, unkind and unnecessary punishment. The very unkindness of it was what Chiltern wanted.

'I will not have mistakes in my flight,' he told his pilots. 'This flight will be the most efficient flight in Bomber Command – because I am going to make it so.'

He was therefore more annoyed than usual when their own next operation was frustrated. Chiltern was watching his crew very intently as they stood around the aircraft awaiting take-off time.

Joe was unable, therefore, to hide the fact that he suddenly felt sick. He explained that it had happened before but Chiltern insisted that he see the MO again.

'Not now. Nothing must prevent our flying. But be on sick parade tomorrow.'

They would land after three am and sick parade was at 0800 so Joe greeted that order very coldly.

When Chiltern did his pre-take-off checks, however, he discovered faulty hydraulics. The bomb-doors could not be closed. An oil leak was discovered and by the time it was repaired they were too late to take off.

There followed another extremely unpleasant verbal investigation in the flight office during which Schuydt was bombarded with questions and, white with rage, refused to answer with anything but monosyllables.

Matters were not improved when the MO decided to put Joe into hospital for some tests and a few days of special diet. Squadron Leader Chiltern, having at last reached a squadron, was now eager to fly ops all the time and he gave himself another gunner and they were back on the Battle Order that night. The new gunner was a timid, reserved eighteen-year-old from Blackpool. His name was Smiff[4] and he had flown four ops.

'It's only a couple of days before Joe's okay again,' Bill complained. 'You'd think Chiltern could wait that long.'

They saw Joe in hospital and told him that he'd be missing a trip or two. Joe would have to make up these trips after his crew was screened.

'Not very considerate, I'm afraid,' said Magnetic.

'You've got as much chance of experiencing consideration at that bastard's hands,' said Joe vehemently, 'as you have of ramming two pounds of melted butter up a wild-cat's arse with a red hot gimlet.'

Joe glared around the ward.

'That, by the way,' he said, 'is the treatment I'm getting in here. Rather, that's what it feels like. And the tucker! All liquid goo that looks like jellyfish with cats' eyes in it.'

He peeped furtively around. 'And all a waste of time. This MO is wet. D'ya know what he's been doing all day today? Slobbering soothing condolences all over P/O Hardy's wife. He went missing last night. She was staying in the village and she tried to kill herself. Wendy and Barbara were sitting with her first but they aren't good enough for old Doctor Jellyfish; he has to butt in every two minutes and now he's brought Mrs Marshall, the signals leader's wife along. He says the older influence is needed. If he does as much for Mrs Hardy as he's doing for me she needn't have slashed her wrist; she'll die anyway.'

Wendy and Barbara and Molly Marshal were being as kind as it is possible to be to a young girl who has lost her husband. But what *can* one do? The MO dared not give her stronger sedatives than he had done and yet she had hardly dozed, and now she lay staring wild-eyed at the ceiling. Occasionally she would turn suddenly and look at one of them and talk like a mad woman.

'Do you know why I came up to see him?', she asked Barbara.

Barbara shook her head.

Mrs Hardy laughed loudly and the sound was hideous. 'I came to tell him we are going to have a baby.'

She laughed again; a piercing laugh that ended in a scream.

'If only she would cry,' thought Wendy.

'... And all day he was flying around in circles practising landings.' She stared at them again.

'Yes! *Practising* to be killed!' She thrashed her head from side to side and writhed as much as the restraining straps would let her.

'The day before, he had crashed. I saw it. I saw it and I knew he was crashing with tons of bombs right next to him. I hid my face and waited for the explosion. Can you think how I felt as I waited for the explosion?'

Then her voice was strangely quiet and sane. 'When I looked up I saw him getting out. Alive. Climbing from the wreckage as though he were a god. I rushed out and he came up to me and he was white.'

She was talking to the ceiling now, not looking at any of them.

'He had almost been killed – and then they punished him.'

'Gently, dear,' said Molly Marshall. 'You're having his baby. He was glad about that, wasn't he?'

'I won't have his baby!', she shrieked. 'I won't have any babies. I won't have babies to be sent to war and killed. I won't, I won't ...'

They had to hold her head still. When she stopped struggling, Molly Marshall said, 'He's quite probably safe and sound. He'll turn up, you'll see.'

The girl looked at the older woman and though there was hatred in her eyes it was not hatred of the woman she saw.

'You cannot comfort me,' she said. 'You cannot even feel as I feel. Is your husband dead? Are you a widow at twenty and having a baby? You're Mrs Marshall, aren't you? Your husband has finished his flying. He's safe. Even had you ever loved as I love, you could not comfort me. You can't understand. None of you can understand. None of you, none of you ...'

'I understand,' said Barbara. 'Believe me, I love as I am sure you love, and I understand.'

The girl turned and looked at her.

'You do?'

'Yes, I do. But if ever my husband were killed I would not rave and shout. I feel that would cheapen my love. And you wouldn't want that to happen, would you?'

'What would you do?'

Barbara thought a long moment.

'I would do nothing to destroy the sweetness of my love,' she said at length. 'It might kill me to stay silent; but I would let nothing hurt that memory.'

It was announced that the Squadron Commander was to come off ops. That finished his third tour. He had flown bravely and well, as could be expected of a permanent RAF officer. He had led his men with sensible devotion to both themselves and the job they all had to do.

Everybody was delighted when it was also announced that he had been awarded a DSO. He already had a DFC.

A place was always reserved on the mantelpiece, near his traditional spot by the fire, for the Squadron Commander's beer tankard. If any other officer was warming himself there when the Squadron Commander came into the ante-room, then that officer simply had to move. Tonight the only person moving regularly into the Squadron Commander's spot was the bar steward. Things had all the earmarks of developing into a party; the kind of party they all liked best – the party nobody had organised.

Vincent, a very new member of the mess, was keeping in one corner of the bar; a little room removed from the ante-room itself. He was waiting for Wendy, but did not know she was with Mrs Hardy. Vincent had seen a lot of Wendy during his few hours as an officer. To be in the same mess and on a level standing with Wendy was one of the things that pleased him most about being commissioned. In theory officers are not allowed to be friendly with other ranks, and to Waaf officers this rule was usually strictly applied by the Waaf Queen Bee, even on a squadron.

He had asked her to join him for a drink and she had said she would. It was not a serious date; simply a suggested meeting, but he had expected her to be here. For him it was important. And she had not come; not even bothered to phone. Wendy, had he known it, would gladly have had his company. She wanted to tell Vincent how helpless and out-of-her-depth she felt with poor Mrs Hardy. Vincent, Wendy thought, would understand how she felt.

Vincent was wondering whether to have another drink or go back to his room when Flight Lieutenant Marshall and H-H came into the bar.

'It's bloody amazing,' Marshall was saying. 'He knows all the old lags. Even barged up to the CO and banged him on the back and called him 'Cluster'. We only named the CO that last year, so he can't be an old, old crony.'

'And nobody recognises him?' asked H-H.

'Nobody! Here, you have a look.' Marshall drew back the curtain and looked around the room.

'There he is. The tall Flight Lieutenant with the blond hair. Do you know him?'

H-H looked.

'No,' he said. 'You say he knew you and the Gaffer?'

Vincent stole a look, too. The newcomer meant nothing to him.

'Recognised us yards away,' said Marshall. 'And he asked

Anderson if they had had a boy as desired and that was only born last month. I tell you it gives me the creeps – he must be psychic. I swear I've never met the man.'

Vincent drew the curtains again to watch. The stranger was nearer now, talking to Buckley, who had returned to ops after his crash and was now almost tour-expired. The stranger was indicating Buckley's second ring.

'Flight Lieutenant Buckley,' the strange voice said. 'I didn't think you'd ever ...'

That was all Vincent heard. All the actual words. He was looking at the stranger. He *was* a stranger, but his voice ...

Then Vincent looked at the eyes and the teeth, and quickly his glance fell to the left hand ...

'Hyde, you scoundrel!' Vincent yelled from the bar, and rushed out and embraced his old skipper. 'Hyde! I might have guessed *you'd* try a trick like this.'

The two men actually embraced and Vincent was afraid there were tears in his eyes. Suddenly they realised they were embracing and Hyde threw him away.

'Quite a welcome,' he roared. 'But do it properly!'

He pointed to his cheek. 'Here, kiss my arse!'

At that there were wild roars. Parke's old tankard had been found and every one of the old gang were milling around shaking his hands.

The Squadron Commander had joined the group and now he led Hyde back to the sacred section of fireplace.

'Yes,' he said. 'We still have Q-Queenie. And of course you can have her back.'

'Good old Queenie,' said Hyde, his eyes sparkling.

'And I must see what we can do about this.' He pointed at Hyde's rank. Squadron Leader had been his acting rank, relinquished when he was wounded.

'Can't give you a flight right away. And I'm afraid you, shall we say locum, has taken over your crew. You must meet him.'

He glanced around the room. 'Where is Squadron Leader Chiltern, Farlow?'

'Not here, sir. He's seldom in the mess. He doesn't drink.'

'Then he's not my locum.'

'But, by God, we're looking for a new Squadron Commander. If I thought they'd listen to me I'd put your name up. I'll see the Air Vice-Marshal tomorrow ...'

Hyde's appearance was completely changed. His face, once rugged and mobile, was now smooth, pale and impassive. He would never have to shave again. He wore a wig – he had chosen a blond one to replace his normal dark hair simply out of devilment – and the doctors said his own hair would grow again in time. He was utterly different and yet, after the first moment of strangeness, he was exactly the same. His eyelids would not bear scrutiny and people knowing his story could see the fine, pale scars running here and there around his face. His lips moved less than normal even when he laughed, but all-in-all it was a fine job. He could face the world. More important, the world could face him and not shudder.[5]

His hands? There lay the question-mark. Both hands looked strange because neither of them grew any hair. His right hand would be all right, he said. It was still tender, but functionally perfect. His left hand, he explained, was wonderful, really, when one considered that it was thought originally that he would never use it again. There were two scars down the side of each finger. It made them appear square, like thin blueish boxes. The fingernails were shrivelled and triangular, curling forward to a claw-like point that tended to grow down over the tips of his fingers. His left hand was not pretty; it looked like the hand of a werewolf.

'But I can use it!', he had said brightly. Then, painfully, he had flexed the pantomime fingers: slowly, with difficulty, and obviously it cost great effort. Even then his fist had not closed. Vincent noticed, too, that these fingers never quite straightened but remained hooked and unrelaxed; this hand, one felt, would never rest again.

'I have changed, though,' Hyde admitted seriously to Vincent when they were alone the next morning. 'My mind thinks differently now. And it thinks the same things over and over. You've heard me mention Aubrey? He was one of my navs before you;

he was killed.' Hyde was speaking quietly, eyes set on distance, as though he spoke his thoughts.

'Aubrey's head was blown off. You know the set-up in the Halifax – nav in front?[6] Well, his head lay on the floor in front of me. And when I banked, it would roll across the floor, first one way and then another. And, do you know, it didn't worry me. Not at the time. Do you know what I thought when I saw that head, my friend's head, rolling around the floor at my feet? I checked my turn-and-bank indicator. I thought, 'If I were flying a perfect turn, then gravity should be straight down and that head should not roll.'

I used that head to teach me how to fly. To me, then, it was not my navigator's head but another instrument. Can you believe that?'

Vincent said nothing. He looked sympathetically at his friend as Hyde continued.

'But now I see it as a head.' Hyde closed his eyes and hit his forehead with his clenched right hand. 'All the time I see it as a head. Aubrey's head with open eyes and mouth about to speak …'

Vincent thought; 'Yes, Hyde. You're right; you have changed. You've had enough of war. And then – fatal combination – you've had enough time to think.'

Vincent spoke what leapt to his mind. 'Are they putting you back on ops?'

'I don't know. They said at first I would never fly again. I determined to beat that. They suggested that I should take my discharge: go home. I protested and they agreed to let me come here and if I could convince the squadron they should take me on again then the medical boys would okay it. So here I am. I want to fly. Yet, in a way, I fear to fly. I guess I've lost my nerve. I had hoped to get my old crew back; being with you chaps – links with my confident days – I felt I'd regain the old zest. I don't suppose that's possible.'

Again Vincent did not reply. He wanted to fly with Hyde. Yet he feared to fly with Hyde; he feared that Hyde would never again be fit to fly.

'But, tell me,' Hyde said with sudden brightness. 'What's the news with you? Explain your commission! A bad type like you – an officer!'

Vincent told Hyde that he was nav leader and awaiting Flight Lieutenant rank. He told the sad, grand story of 101 and D-Day. Of his wind idea. Of Chiltern and of Schydt.

'... and finally, I've *really* lost my table-tennis title. Flight Lieutenant Marshall has played me a few games, mastered my tricks, challenged me, and won. And he never leaves the ground so there'll be no German interference this time. I'm really the ex-champ ...'

They did not have time to talk again. Hyde was going on leave as soon as he saw the squadron authorities and, anyway, Vincent was called on the next battle order.

It was another night trip. Target: Saarbrücken.[7] Flying with Chiltern, they found, was becoming no less unnerving. Over the target they encountered predicted flak. Window was preventing radar flak-prediction, so the German defences were forced to fire at the area through which the bombers were flying and hope to hit something.

Barrage flak had a special paragraph in the text-book. It was not aimed at any particular aircraft, the book explained, and therefore evasive action was pointless. If one weaved there was as much chance of weaving into a shell as weaving away from one. So, said the text-book, in barrage flak, drop your nose a little, jam on extra throttle, and fly fast and straight. The quickest way through was the safest way out.

Squadron Leader Chiltern had read the text-book, hallowed it and determined to put it into action complete to the last full-stop and footnote.

There was one aspect of barrage flak, however, which was quite familiar to experienced aircrew but not mentioned in the text-book, and therefore either unknown or unacceptable to Squadron Leader Chiltern. Even within barrage flak one might encounter an accurate, fixed gun, pumping sixteen shells a minute into one particular spot in the sky. About every three seconds it would throw a shell into exactly the same place. If one's aircraft were heading exactly for that spot it was obviously sheerest folly to continue flying straight. Even the authors of the text-book must admit that. They had never said so, but surely they expected men to interpret their wisdom and apply it to practice.

Squadron Leader Chiltern no more interpreted or allowed interpretation of text-books than he would of the Ten Commandments. A text-book drill was no less holy than an order.

Bill saw the fixed flak exploding dead ahead and ordered: 'Bomb aimer to skipper. Flak ahead. Alter course twenty degrees starb'd.'

'Why, bomb aimer?'

'There's a fixed gun. We're tracking straight into it.'

'But this is barrage flak, not predicted.'

Bill's answer was rising in semitones of panic. 'But look at it. Dead ahead! We'll fly straight into it. Starb'd! Starb'd – quick!'

Squadron Leader Chiltern ploughed straight on …

It could have been worse.

It might have got them right in the bomb bay.

As it was, one burst went about fifty feet in front of them and the next one was too far behind to do more than rock them around the sky.

Bill's panic hit a top G-sharp. 'I've been hit! My arm! I've been hit!'

'Will you be able to bomb, bomb aimer?', asked Chiltern.

Bill's answer was to shriek again; 'My arm! Oh, Jesus! My arm!'

'Attend to the bomb aimer, engineer,' said Chiltern, exasperation edging his voice. 'Navigator. Do you remember how to bomb?'

'I think so, skipper.'

'Come forward and take over, will you? I've over-shot now. We'll have to go round again.'

Bill's wound looked bloody but superficial. Magnetic slipped the escape knife out of his flying boot and cut away the battle-dress sleeve, then applied a dressing from the first aid pack. Bill was already suffering from shock far more severe than the wound warranted, so Magnetic dragged him amidships and propped him against the main spar. All other Lancasters have a rest position amidships – 'dead man's bunk' – but in 101 aircraft the space was filled with the Special and his equipment.

Not on intercom now, Magnetic shouted in Bill's ear, asking if it pained him.

Bill did not answer; simply stared at his arm and the blood all over his clothes and gibbered hysterically.

'Oh, well,' thought Magnetic, 'this won't do you any harm'; and he took from the first aid pack a thing like a tiny tube of toothpaste with a long sheath over the stopper. He unscrewed this sheath; under it was a hypodermic needle. He broke the seal, then jabbed the needle into Bill's forearm. From the tiny tube he squeezed half the contents: a quarter grain – twice a normal dose.

'There,' said Magnetic. 'That should keep you happy.'

He connected Bill's oxygen pipe to a spare point. 'And keep that thing on,' he yelled to the already sleepy Bill. Wounded men had been known to die because, in their semi-consciousness, they had pulled off their oxygen masks.

Magnetic was feeling the lack of oxygen himself when he returned to his position and plugged in. He took several deep breaths and said; 'Engineer to skipper. He'll be okay. I've given him morphia.'

He looked around. They had already bombed and were heading home.

Magnetic had been surprised by his own calmness. Not only in dealing with Bill, but as they had tracked up into the flak that this fool had refused to avoid and that Magnetic had known must hit them.

He knew why he was calm. He had told the others about it, but he had not been sure that it was true. Now he knew it was true. He had quite resigned himself to being killed. They had encountered more trouble during a few trips with Squadron Leader Chiltern than one would normally expect on a whole tour with a pilot showing less courage but more sense. The paradox was that all Chiltern's devotion to duty, all his correctness, was not achieving good bombing. All it would do, all it could do, was kill them.

Perhaps Bill was lucky. Perhaps, through this wound, he would escape.

When they returned to Ludford their own news of a wounded bomb aimer was a small item by comparison with the news of squadron events while they had been flying.

Pilot Officer Hardy had arrived back, with three of his crew. They had crashed not far behind the German lines and had hidden until the Allied advance swept past them. Their other crewmates were either wounded or taken prisoner. As far as Hardy knew they were all safe.

Flight Lieutenant Marshall, driving back from Louth with his wife, had misjudged a turning and run off the road into a tree. He had been killed. His wife was in hospital next to Mrs Hardy. Molly Marshall was not badly hurt. She was perfectly conscious and Mrs Hardy was trying to comfort her.

The CO came up to Vincent and spoke to him. 'You've heard about Mr Marshall?'

'Yessir.'

'It's just crazy coincidence, I know. But I'm going to stop these table-tennis title games. I have to, Farlow. It'll be upsetting morale. In wartime people become superstitious too easily.'

— 3 —

Smiff was sitting outside the flight office in the pale autumn sunshine, writing to a girl called Thelma. Perhaps 'named' Thelma would be more accurate. By all her friends and relations, including Smiff, she was called 'Felma'.

Few boys of eighteen write good love letters. Especially boys as dull as Smiff and as shaken as Smiff was after the Saarbrücken trip.

'Thelma, my sugar,' he wrote. 'Your very welcome letter with news of your seeing Mum and the girls to hand for which I say thank you. But not just thank you – thank you with all my heart oh my darling. It brings you so close to me. Your letter, I mean. But, dearest sugar, you are always close to me. Oh that you were closer to me now.

'When I say dearest sugar I do not mean dear as in the money meaning of the word. I mean sweetest.

Sweeter than sugar is Thelma to me
Sweeter than honey from the bee.

Collecting honey on his trips
Around flowers, like her rosebud lips.

Oh sweetest, that those lips could say
Come to me forever and a day.
Living forever side by side
Me the bridegroom, you the bride.

But war is upon us. Sugar's on ration.
Quiet, inside me, o'erwhelming passion!
You will be mine when warring is up.
I shall have sugar – three spoons to the cup.

'I am glad your brother Harry could use my old suits. By the time the war is over I would have grown out of them anyway. That's the pity of having all sisters: I have no little brothers for hand-me-downs.

'Oh my darling after the war it will be wonderful. To be forever safe in your arms. I don't mind telling you my sweet, because you will understand it, that war frightens me. Last night I flew to Saarbrücken and we were shot up and my bomb aimer was wounded and the crew blamed the pilot who they said was silly but is very good. He comes from Rotherham. I mean the bomb aimer. He is not hurt but it sounded dreadful.

'I thought of you and that it might be me and then I was afraid for us both because the shells come up and me sitting like I do you know what they might hit. I fear to be crippled more than anything. More than being killed but not a nice subject so enough of that.

'Today the sun is bright but it is getting cold. The nights grow longer and that means flying. Back on to flying again but I will not talk of that but happy things. I shall talk of …'

And there Smiff was stuck, staring across the aerodrome, sucking his pencil.

Bill had taken his courage in both hands and broached recategorisation to the MO. His wound looked slight now it was dressed and stitched. It would only keep him in hospital for a week or so. But he felt that his nerves needed attention.

'We'll have you back in the air this month, Graham,' the MO said.

'I'd like to talk to you about that, sir,' said Bill.

'How do you mean?'

'I don't know that I'm fit to return to ops, sir.'

'Nonsense!' the MO said brightly. 'This will heal perfectly.'

'Not my arm, sir,' said Bill, and added, with an effort, 'I feel mentally shot about more than physically, sir.'

'Only natural, dear boy. Most upsetting experience. Don't let it worry you.'

'But before this happened, sir.' Bill was not going to be brushed aside now. 'My nerves are so bad I can't sleep and I can't do my work properly and I feel that I'm going mad. I should not have agreed to fly another tour. I need a rest.'

'You've just had a rest.'

'More than a rest, then. I want to come off ops.'

'Off ops – for good?' The MO took a long look at Bill with cold, appraising eyes. Gone, now, was his breezy manner.

'Graham,' he said, 'how old are you?'

Bill paused.

'Your real age.'

'Thirty-six.'

'I thought so. Top age-limit is thirty-two so you put your age back to get into aircrew. An old man striving to share young men's glory. Hoping, I suppose, that you could simultaneously hide behind an old man's immunity from action. Well, you can't. Now now the RAF have had the trouble and expense of training you. Why do you think we set a thirty-two age limit? To keep valuable men out? No! We *want* fliers. Thirty-two isn't too young, it's too old. You and your type are a problem to yourselves, a nuisance to the air force and a menace to your crewmates. It's too late now to plead age and the nerves age brings. I will not recategorise you. You can go LMF or go on flying. I knew your nerves were bad when I saw your morphia label for such a slight wound. Other men would have carried on working. Don't look to me to save your neck. I am going to forget this matter was ever mentioned. I suggest you do the same. If you find you can't stick it, see the Squadron Commander and tell him officially. At least have the guts to quit like a man.'[1]

During the next hour Bill decided that he would quit, and then changed his mind. Then he changed his mind again and again a dozen times. The MO had hit the nail right on the head: which course called for greater courage, to go on flying or be branded 'Lacking Moral Fibre' – officially? In his heart he didn't feel ashamed. Normally he could have taken it. But there had been too much. Aubrey, Dudley, then blowing up that other kite ... And now, Chiltern.

Chiltern put the cap on it.

Squadron Leader Chiltern refused to let the fact that two of his crew were in hospital hold him up for a day. He applied for a spare bomb aimer and the only one available was a lanky, lean Australian called 'Snow'. His name was Fry and he had very fair hair.

'This bloody Chiltern's a bit of a bastard, ain't he?', Snow asked the others as they dressed.

'Bit hot on regulations.'

'Bugger regulations, I say.'

'Well, not generally. Regulations are essential and usually wise. But they have to be followed sensibly, which is just what Chiltern doesn't do.'

'Follows bloody regulations for regu-bloody-lations' sake, eh?'

'Yes,' smiled Vincent. 'Some of his regulation-following of late has been a bit bloody.'

'What I'd call a typical bloody Pommy officer. I can't stand these pongo bastards.'

'Surely you meet rather a lot of them in the RAF?'

'Oh, not just Englishmen!' protested Snow. 'When I call _you_ a Pommy bastard, sir, that's meant friendly. But a Pommy bloody officer is different; that's a bloody pongo Chiltern bastard.'

Reviewing this conversation later with Magnetic, Vincent said; 'I had not expected 'Chiltern' to be made an English adjective quite so soon. Even the word 'Byronic' was little used before his death.'

'I can just imagine Mr Chiltern's reaction to Snow's speech if he insists on leaving in the swear-words.'

'Leaving them in? If he takes them out he will be mute. I don't believe he honestly realises he *is* swearing. He just drops a 'bloody' into every pause as other people do an 'er'.'

'He must be a more highly developed Australian type than Joe.'

'Poor old Joe,' said Vincent. 'He's fretting about missing these trips. The old crew's looking a bit sick, isn't it? What with a new skipper and Special and rear gunner and now a bomb aimer. There's only Krink and Yarpi and us left.'

'I could almost feel fond of Yarpi for still being with us.'

'He's all right really. Just a bit young.'

'A bit young? I hope he lives to be a lot older.'

'Eh? Oh yes, I see what you mean.'

When they arrived at the aircraft Chiltern was already there. He called them together.

'My radio telephone was switched on,' he announced. 'Has anybody here been in that aircraft this afternoon?'

'I have, sir,' said Schydt.

Chiltern swooped on him. 'Why?'

'To check my radio, sir.'

'You can't check your radio with engines off. Don't lie!'

'I do not lie, sir,' said Schydt, stressing each word. 'A gain control was making poor contact last time we flew. I was checking that it was all right now.'

'Why didn't you report it and have the ground crew fix it?'

'I did, sir. And they have. I only wanted to check it.'

Chiltern stood, silent and glaring. There was nothing more he could say. But he found a threatening note to introduce. 'For your sake, Schydt, I hope that everything is correct when I run her up.'

Chiltern intended to keep Schydt in sight until it was time to take off. Schydt sensed this and charged Chiltern with it.

'You suspect me, don't you, sir?', he asked.

'A less honest man than I would deny it,' said Chiltern. 'But I will not deny it. Yes, Schydt, I suspect you.'

'Because I am a German?'

'Were I on a Luftwaffe aerodrome they could rightly suspect me.'

'But I hate Hitler as much as you do, sir. Perhaps more.'

'Hating Hitler has nothing to do with it, Schydt. You are a German and we are at war with your homeland. We are enemies now as we have been before. If there is cause for distrust – and you must agree that sabotage gives such cause – then you are naturally the person to be suspected and investigated first.'

Schydt looked down at the wet, cold tarmac. 'They warned me it would be so,' he said.

'Who warned me?'

'My friends. My German friends. Before I joined the RAF. They said the British would never forget that I was a German; that I would be suspected and refused promotion and given a dirty deal. And it is all true.'

'How on earth do you mean?'

'I have twice been refused for a commission. Not only refused but curtly and bluntly sent away. All we Specials are receiving a dirty deal. We fly only the hard trips. We do not fly to Le Havre or Caen. We attack only the big cities.'

'But it's pointless your flying in daylight. What use is radio-jamming when fighters can *see* us?'

'Oh, I understand that. But still we fly only the dangerous missions. And now we are suspected. What they said is true.'

'If it is true you have only yourself to blame,' snapped Chiltern. 'Distinguished service will win you promotion, and surely you will not be suspected if nothing suspicious happens, and surely you must expect to fly where you are sent. You are perfectly well treated, and let me hear nothing more to the contrary.'

And Squadron Leader Chiltern walked away.

Schydt stood, trailing his toe backwards and forwards through a shiny black puddle. 'But I told them,' he said softly. 'I told them there would always be a way out ...'

Their target was Dortmund. They were to bomb from the south-west, then go out north to clear the Ruhr before turning for home. This route took them near Munster. Tonight, again, Schydt would be close to his birthplace.

They were told at briefing that many transient German army units were stuck in Dortmund. Withdrawn from the eastern front they were now stranded by chaotic transport within Germany. It was a good chance for the RAF to hit Dortmund and the army reserves at the same time. They had been warned, however, to expect opposition from the army as well as Dortmund's normally formidable ground defences.

The first sight of the target strengthened their fears. Vincent had just handed over to Snow for the bombing run. Snow's first action on receiving command was to observe: 'Jesus-Christ-all-bloody-mighty! Look at that firkin flak!'

A silence so intense and all-consuming followed this remarkable outburst that it filled N-Nuts more completely than would a great explosion. Every man except Snow strained to hear the click as a microphone switched on and the precise reprimand that would follow. But not a word was said; not a sound came out.

'A firkin forest of bloody flak, it is,' said the blissfully unaware Snow, then added, 'Left ten, skipper.'

Perhaps the profanity had frozen Chiltern to the controls, or perhaps he was simply taking his usual time thinking about the order. Whatever the cause, his delay displeased Snow.

'Left bloody ten, sport!' snapped Snow, 'Get your greasy finger out.'[2]

This time N-Nuts swung left and Snow had nothing more to say for a few seconds except to toss in the lighthearted remark; 'If you bloody-well let the wheels down we'd land the bastard on this firkin flak.'

Then, again, Snow added a direction. 'Left, left.'

The next instant their eardrums were shattered with a roar.

'If you don't bloody-well fly the bloody aircraft where I tell you I can't bomb the bloody target you bloody fool!'

And then it shouted even louder; 'Turn the bastard left!'

As N-Nuts came quickly on to course, Snow added a little more quietly; 'And bloody listen and smarten up or you'll root this bombing run.'

There was silence a while, then; 'Right a bit. Bit more! That's nice, skip. Hold the bastard. Fraction left. Oh, bloody lovely! We're smack centre. *Bombs gone!* Bloody good work, skip. Christ! I thought you'd rooted it for a bloody moment, though. Now let's piss off out of this bloody flak.'[3]

Vincent gave the new course and Chiltern turned port. Still they waited for his reprimand but still it did not come. Chiltern had realised that Snow, if chided, would laugh him to scorn. They flew in silence. This was the short leg of the Ruhr – up towards Munster.

They were surprised to hear Krink's voice on the intercom.

'W/op to mid upper. What's the Special doing, Yarpi?'

'I can't see. Just a minute, man.'

There was a short pause; from the mid upper turret it was necessary to bend double to see inside the aircraft.

'Christ! He's baling out! He's cutting the door open!'

Fuselage doors in the Lancaster have handles on the outside only. To release the latch from inside, the catch must be cut away with a small axe kept near the door.

'Stop him,' ordered Chiltern crisply. He had grasped the situation instantly.

'Mid upper, stop him! Quickly!'

Schydt had almost cut through the latch when he saw Yarpi climbing out of his turret. Guessing that he had been discovered, Schydt lunged harder and faster at the door.

'Skipper to rear gunner,' said Chiltern urgently. 'If Schydt gets out, shoot him. Do you hear? That Hun must not reach Germany alive.'

Smiff did not answer.

'Do you hear me, rear gunner?'

'Yessir.'

'Shoot Schydt if he escapes. Do you understand?'

'Yes, sir,' said Smiff, indecision and disbelief muffling his voice.

Yarpi scrambled from his turret and rushed at Schydt. He caught the hand holding the axe and pinned Schydt against the stringers of the fuselage. But Schydt was the stronger man. He pressed the axe under Yarpi's chin.

'I don't want to kill you,' Schydt said. 'But I will if I must.'

With an effort he flung Yarpi from him. Yarpi fell backwards, sprawled over the Elsan and saw Schydt hurl himself against the door.

The latch gave.

Schydt forced himself out against the slipstream with his shoulder. At the same moment Yarpi rushed to stop him, clutching at Schydt's disappearing body.

Gripping his fingers into Schydt's parachute harness, the weight of Schydt's flying body immediately pulled him from Yarpi's grasp.

Yarpi was left holding the metal D-ring. He had pulled the rip-cord; he had only succeeded in opening Schydt's parachute for him.

Smiff sat stunned by Chiltern's order. He was to shoot one of his own crewmates. He could not believe that this was why he had been set to air gunnery school. To shoot his own crew!

He decided that he could not do it. If Schydt got out he would fire a burst away from him and say he thought it had got him. Chiltern would never know. He could not bring himself to shoot a man he knew; not even a German deserting the squadron. He decided not to announce Schydt's fall from N-Nuts but to wait a second, then fire a long burst, and say he thought he had got him.

When Schydt's body whipped past him under the tailplane, an involuntary cry betrayed Smiff's intentions.

'There he goes!', cried Smiff.

'Shoot him,' snapped Chiltern.

For an instant the guns were silent and again Chiltern ordered; 'Shoot him!'

Then Smiff fired; away from the falling body still clearly visible behind. Smiff looked again. Why was Schydt still in sight? He should fall behind at three miles a minute, yet he was still there.

Then Smiff saw.

'Sir! He's caught! His parachute is caught in the fin.'

'Yes,' said Chiltern. 'I can feel the drag. Now take your time, aim carefully and shoot him off.'

'But, sir ...'

'Shoot him off, Smith.'

Schydt's parachute was firmly caught in the tailplane of N-Nuts. Schydt, at the end of the strong silken parachute cords, was flapping wildly up and down as the 200 mph wind lashed his clothes and body. His flying boots had been torn from his feet as the slack cords tightened and jolted him behind the plane. The harness had cut into his crutch and pain stabbed through his abdomen.

Still Smiff delayed. Now he would have to shoot his crewmate. He thought he could catch glimpses of Schydt's face in the darkness and it seemed misshapen, grotesque with fear.

'Why don't you fire, Smith?'

There was no way out now. Nothing could save Schydt. If he tore free, his parachute would be so damaged he could never descend safely. If he did not fall free he would be dragged for four hundred miles behind N-Nuts to die of cold, or suffocate from lack of oxygen or, if he survived all these, to be battered to pieces behind them when they landed.

It would be a kindness to shoot him.

'Yes,' thought Smiff, 'I would *thank* a man for killing me if I were dying in agony. To shoot him now would be kindness.'

'Why don't you fire, Smith?' said Chiltern again, impatiently. 'Shoot him off before he blows off.'

'Yessir,' said Smiff.

Determinedly Smiff ground his teeth. He would make himself do it. He turned his guns on the hurtling, spinning body in space. It flapped up and down and around his sights. He could not get a bead on it. The sustained effort was snapping Smiff's nerves. He decided not to try to follow Schydt's crazy orbits with his guns. He aimed at the middle of the parachute's swaying, swooping path, grit his teeth till the gums hurt, then fired.

Schydt saw the rear guns firing.

But nothing hit him.

He was still flapping stupidly up and down and spinning crazily around in this maddening rush of freezing wind. One instant his face caught the slipstream full force and dragged his mouth open, blowing his cheeks out and driving the breath from his lungs. Wind caught under his eyelids and he thought his eyes would be blown from their sockets. And still he flapped insanely up and down and spun round and round, tortured by hurricanes of cold and held in his silken web.

Smiff fired a long burst.

Then he stared behind. The body was still there, still flapping and spinning. He thought he saw Schydt's wide eyes staring at him.

He fired again; fired so that the blinding tracer would obliterate the hideous scene which dragged itself behind them.

'That will be enough, Smith,' said Chiltern.

'He's still there, sir.'

'I know. I can feel it.'

Smiff started. Squadron Leader Chiltern had said 'it'. And now that was all it was. It was not a man any more. It was not his crew-mate Schydt. It was an 'it'. A dead, mangled, bloody, horrid thing they were dragging along behind them, still waving up and down and spinning like a scarlet-feathered fly over rapid waters; carrion bait for the flying-fish of war.

'I had hoped the bullets would knock him off,' said Chiltern calmly. 'It might damage the plane, dragging that around. I hope we lose it before we land.'

Chiltern's hopes were vain. All the way to Ludford Magna the grotesque mass of flapping, spinning flesh and wildly waving limbs followed them.

'I'll land well down the runway,' said Chiltern to Magnetic as they approached. 'I don't want this thing catching around wires or fouling a fence.'

As they touched down, Smiff hid his face in his hands.

Still the shuddering, bouncing jolts against the tailplane reached his senses and in his mind he saw the body bouncing shapelessly behind them.

They stopped at the end of the runway and jumped down from the battered door. Magnetic and Yarpi were first to reach the body. They looked at it and turned it over. The fascination of the thing was too strong for Smiff. As he approached them Yarpi looked up and said; 'You missed! There isn't a bullet hole in him!'

'Poor devil,' said Magnetic. 'I wonder how long he lived.'

Smiff had instantly wondered the same thing. Perhaps he had been killed as they landed? He went to touch the body.

But he dared not. It might still be warm.

Squadron Leader Chiltern was inspecting the damaged tailplane and lamenting Schydt's parting gesture on behalf of his fatherland when Smiff came back and told him Schydt was dead but had not been shot.

Chiltern did not reply.

Chiltern did not speak a word in the crew bus. At debriefing he spoke only to the interrogation officer and then his words were few and toneless. As they drove back to the mess where a meal awaited anyone with the stomach to eat it, he was still silent.

They arrived at the sergeant's mess and the NCO's got out.

When they were gone, Chiltern turned to Krink and Vincent.

'Honestly,' he said, 'I was seriously thinking of baling out rather than remain with such iniquity.'

For a moment Vincent was puzzled.

Then he realised and his mind staggered.

'After all that has happened tonight,' he thought, 'what upsets Chiltern is the memory of Snow swearing.'[4]

— 4 —

Paps was one of those girls who make excellent tea. In fact, the most enjoyable cup of tea on the squadron was to be had in the met office when Paps was on duty. Vincent, Magnetic, Joe and a few others called regularly at met for morning tea and it was the boys who brought the food: biscuits and cakes, mostly. Joe's food parcels from Australia had provided many excellent feasts. It was the crumbs of these feasts that brought the mice.

A few mice had been caught in mouse-traps. Still fewer had been tempted with poison baits. Those surviving mice now carefully avoided traps and poison alike and seemed to be teaching their fast-multiplying progeny the tricks of survival. Mice seemed destined to gain the upper hand throughout the flying control block.

Then Vincent thought of catching them in kerosene tins. He would balance a piece of paper across the top of an empty kerosene tin and place some bait in the middle. The paper was folded so that it would support the weight of the bait and just a little more, but when a mouse walked out along it, it would collapse and down would come paper, bait, mouse and all. This not only worked successfully, but it continued to work nightly with each of four kerosene tins.

'So unless the mice can breed at a rate of five a day, we must obliterate them,' said Vincent triumphantly.

There arose, however, the problem of disposing of the live mouse that would be jumping up and down in the bottom of the tin the next morning. This seemingly simple job had led to riotous scenes in the met office the first time it had to be done.

Joe tried to kill the mouse by hitting it with a broom handle, but a wildly jumping mouse proved too small a target even to a hawk-eyed gunner at a range of one yard.

So Joe decided to put his foot into the tin and crush the mouse with his steel-encrusted heel. This, it was thought, would be effective if bloody, and caused Paps to exclaim; 'Oh, the poor little mousie!'

Paps had called the mouse a name when it had eaten a hole in an all-too-hard-to-get cream biscuit and that name was far less lady-like than 'poor little mousie'.

Undaunted, however, Joe stamped his foot into the tin.

Either Joe's hawk-eye aim was off that morning or the mouse saw the steel heel descending upon it and dodged. Whichever the case, Joe missed.

The mouse, quick to grasp its opportunity of escape, ran straight up Joe's leg. Joe instantly yelled a word that sounded vaguely like a Canadian lumberjack's cry of 'Timber!', and started kicking his leg in the air.

The mouse was flung from Joe's trousers and landed in the middle of the met office floor. The girls leapt up screaming, and ran around and around the room, the mouse chased them or so it seemed, and the sergeants, emitting lusty war-cries, chased the mouse.

Two of the other kerosene tins were upset, releasing another two mice, and pandemonium reigned until the last mouse had escaped through cracks in the skirting.

The met officer observed that things had come to a pretty pass when a station of nearly two thousand people of war, with bombs enough to blow up half Lincolnshire was thrown into confusion by a mouse which was then able to escape unscathed.

Magnetic had later thought of an effective mouse-disposal method. It was vaguely vulgar but simple and effective. He simply took the tin, emptied the contents – bait, mouse and all – into the lavatory block and pulled the chain. It became each morning's first job. This, however, was kept secret from the tender-hearted Waafs.

One day while Vincent and Magnetic were sipping morning tea and eating cakes sent by Mrs Marlborough-Jones, there came a scream from outside and Paps rushed in, pale-faced and clutching her pants.

'There's a Thing!' she screamed, pointing behind her as if a dragon came on her heels. 'All wet and jumping! I was sitting and it jumped up and *touched* me!'

Magnetic guessed the trouble. He looked in and there, swimming manfully, was the mouse. It had survived the first deluge.

Magnetic flushed the pan again and this time the mouse did not resurface.

'What was it, Saint George?' asked Wendy when Magnetic returned. Paps was incapable of speaking.

'I didn't see a thing,' lied Magnetic, eager to avoid so delicate an explanation.

That was the morning they had watched Hyde, officially returned to the squadron as the B Flight second-in-command, flying familiarisation circuits in Queenie.

It was painful to see. Time and again Hyde could not settle her down but came in too high and too fast and had to overshoot and go around again. Even that manoeuvre proved almost too much for him on one occasion when he throttled forward but was so slow in taking up flap that he sogged down to within a few feet of the runway.

When he did land, poor old Queenie bounced and shuddered so much that the onlookers expected her tyres to burst or her wings to shake off.

'Has Hyde lost his nerve, do you think?'

'Maybe his hands aren't sensitive enough.'

'Nonsense. He hasn't flown for ages. He'll be okay after some practice.'

Hyde mentioned his floppy landings to Vincent while they drank a pre-lunch beer in the mess. Hyde walked over to Vincent in company with the still-in-plaster and still grounded Lieutenant Cahill. They both looked so sad and serious that Vincent, in an effort to lighten their mood, greeted them with, 'Ha! It's Doctor Jackal and Mr Hyde!'

'Jekyll and Hyde I might well be,' said Hyde. 'One me knows how to fly as automatically as I know how to breathe. But the other me just won't relax; won't do what my mind orders.'

'We'll try again this afternoon,' said Jackal. 'Have a drink now and try and relax.'

'Were you flying screen?' Vincent asked Jackal, surprised.

'Yes. Chiltern said Hyde shouldn't really need a screen at all. He just cast me as understudy to keep me out of mischief.'

'I'll take her alone this afternoon,' said Hyde. 'I might be less nervous without a screen. Perhaps Chiltern is right. And he said he wants me operational quickly.'

'Chiltern!' exclaimed Vincent. 'He can't teach you a thing, Hyde. He hasn't as much know-how in his whole body as you have in your little finger.'

'This one?', asked Hyde bitterly, holding up the twisted little claw of his left hand. 'I'm afraid this is proof against mere know-how.'

Vincent did not enjoy that lunch.

Seasonal autumn thunderstorms lashed Ludford Magna that afternoon, but Hyde flew circuits and bumps in the bright intervals. The storms grew so frequent and the bright intervals so short, however, that Hyde decided to land and call it a day.

A black, heavy cumulo-nimbus cloud hung threateningly near as he made his final approach. It was quite a good approach, but so slow that he was virtually committed to it when the squall hit him. When Queenie was twenty feet above the ground she was heading into wind straight down the runway.

Before she was one foot lower, a side-current curled out of the menacing cloud in a way that only mariners and aviators know, and set her drifting across the runway quite alarmingly, flicking her windward wing high.

It was a tricky moment, but one any pilot should have been able to meet. Hyde should either have overshot despite his low speed, or kicked his rudder to correct Queenie's drift. But it had to be a split-second decision.

In that split second Hyde tried to hold Queenie straight and land on the runway despite the cross-wind and drift. Queenie's wing and tail tilted, one wheel hit the ground with a shuddering jar, not in the direction that the wheel was pointing, but at a drift-angle of twenty degrees. The olio-leg groaned, then snapped, the stabbing wingtip dug into the turf and Queenie ground-looped crazily, vaulting up on her nose and spinning over. Then she flopped clumsily back onto her belly, propellers buckling to a halt in the soft earth.

One of the company was wounded and the wound was mortal. The victim was Queenie; she had broken her back.

They pushed her over to the dump with a bulldozer and crushed her in with all the other aircraft that would never fly again.

Vincent had seen the crash. So had Magnetic. They knew, without exchanging a word, what that death at his hands would mean to Hyde.

Vincent was winning the paradoxical reputation amongst his navigators of an easy-going tyrant. He was not particularly worried about their punctuality on non-flying days. He seldom raised any objections about high-spirited rags in the section. If a man had missed breakfast Vincent would usually allow him to cycle to the nearby farm where bacon and eggs were served in the parlour. In fact, only two things seemed to concern him; one was that men must always be ready and fit for duty and the other was that, while they were flying, they must work hard.

The ex-instructor navigator, Flight Lieutenant Slade, deplored Vincent's laxness. Slade was an excellent navigator: fast, neat and accurate. But he thought that the easy-going squadron atmosphere compared ill with Training Command discipline. He had mentioned this to Chiltern, and Chiltern had considered it one of the strong points in Slade's favour.

Slade knew that Chiltern had recommended him for the post of nav leader. It is possible that this prompted Slade to ignore Vincent's warning – perhaps Slade read insult into Vincent's claim that even excellent navigators could be lazy and therefore dangerous.

Slade's crew were coming home from a night raid. They were heading south-west out of Germany. At the Allied front line they were to fly dead west then, at the French coast, alter course north for Base. Slade computed the course from the front line and, most unfortunately, read the required track from his flight plan for the north leg instead of the west leg.

Consequently, he hit the front line on track but then flew away from the force, headed back into occupied Europe on his own. One radar fix, taken in forty seconds, would have shown him his error. But Slade did not usually make mistakes and he did not check. Twenty minutes later they flew into flak over Utrecht, were badly shot up, and were lucky to get home. As it was, both their gunners were killed.

'You altered course and did not check for twenty minutes, Mr Slade,' said Vincent. 'Why? Wasn't your equipment working?'

'It was working,' said Slade. 'I just didn't bother, I'm afraid. We had crossed the front line, we were tired after the long trip, and I relaxed. I'm sorry.'

'It is unfortunate that it should be you, Mr Slade,' said Vincent. 'But I would do the same no matter who it was. I am putting you up for court martial. You have virtually killed two men.'

The Squadron Commander, when Vincent put the matter before him, took Vincent aside.

'You are quite right, you know,' he said. 'Slade deserves a court martial. But I'm not going to do it and I'll tell you why. At Arnhem we have just suffered a more important defeat than you may know. That airborne landing was to have got us across the Rhine before the German army regrouped. To have won at Arnhem would have meant winning the war in Europe before winter. The Germans, poor fools, don't realise that they have done themselves the greatest disservice; somebody must occupy Germany and if we don't the

Russians will and Germany will suffer far worse at their hands than they might at ours.[1] But that's an aside. Our chaps have been flying a lot lately; flying hard and flying well. We told them that if they did their job the war would be over by Christmas. Well, they have done their job, splendidly, but Arnhem has failed and the war will drag on for perhaps another year.

We must guard against loss of morale on the squadron and nothing attacks morale like a court martial. Slade might deserve it, but the squadron doesn't deserve the setback. Send Slade to me and I'll give him a private trial that might mend his ways. You do understand, don't you, Farlow? I agree with the serious view you take of this but I must do what's best for One-o-one Squadron, that is the vital thing.'

As Vincent walked out of the Squadron Commander's office he felt humble for the littleness of his outlook that he had thought so liberal.

They took off at six-thirty am for Duisburg. Magnetic's commission had just come through but he had not had time to change the rank on his uniform.

Hyde was flying this trip too. His first since Nürnberg. His old crew felt a warm glow of pride but around the edges gnawed the chill of the thought that this Hyde was only a shadow of the flyer that the other Hyde had been.

The crews did not know it but this was to be a great day for Bomber Command. Flying with the force were four war correspondents. They had been told that Duisburg, Germany's greatest inland port, and now only thirty miles behind the front line, was to be bombed off the map.

It was barely a week since they had raided Germany in force during daylight for the first time. Now they headed for the Ruhr in daylight. Above them the Luftwaffe were diverted and drawn into combat by the fighter escort. Only occasionally did a Me 109 or FW 190 break through to attack the main force, and when it did the Lancasters and Halifaxes took wild evasive action and fired off Very lights which brought protecting Mustangs screaming from the sky to take the fight off their hands.[2]

For some, the belligerent flyers of Bomber Command, this was a far more satisfactory war. Because they no longer had the darkness to overcome, much of the old skill was wasted; but with daylight the battle came into the open. For the man who preferred bullets to brains, who liked to see his enemy and fight him face to face rather than outsmart him with cunning and lose him in the night; for that man these major daylight raids on Germany were a welcome change from the fly-by-night raids that ran the German gauntlet but never came to grips.

Almost a thousand heavy bombers swept into the Ruhr for the first Duisburg attack. The punishment they took seemed only fair in exchange for the blow they dealt. In daylight their bombs were not vague flashes in a black sea, but sticks of bubble-bursting explosions[3] amongst wharves, barges and railways. The men could see their vicious handiwork and such is the hate that war creates, the men delighted in it.

In four bombers flew the four war correspondents, utterly ill at ease and lost, yet trying to understand it all. Trying, in a few airborne hours, emotion-packed and fearful, to grasp a way of life and reveal it to the world. Trying to see everything. Understanding so little of what they saw. Not knowing which voice came from where. Asking questions. Getting in the way.

Nobody liked flying with war correspondents. And everybody knew that the story they told could never be the true story because no crew flies normally with the consciousness that every word, every action, every motion is being recorded, sifted, analysed and rehashed in a form designed to impress Mum and the kids. But those war correspondents knew something that very few of the aircrew knew; that within hours they would be back in the air, headed for Duisburg again.

Snow and Smiff were surprised, and Squadron Leader Chiltern was annoyed, that Vincent, Magnetic, Krink and Yarpi rushed away the moment they landed to ask Hyde how he had fared.

They found him nervous but elated. He admitted, now they had landed, that he had not welcomed the prospect of the Ruhr by day and added that, as Joe put it later, having broken his duck in his second innings made him feel a lot better. It was obvious from his manner, however, that he still found the wicket sticky.

The second attack on Duisburg was by night and proved a routine Ruhr attack. The target was still blazing conveniently after the day raid so they found it with ease. They bombed the edges of the fires, where the firefighters would be. Aircrew had a firm dislike for the men who carefully put out the fires they had gone to so much trouble to light. And they bombed the dark patches which were not yet ablaze.

At the second thousand bombers turned away the target was as brightly lit as it had been when they arrived that morning and the sun itself had shown the way. Duisburg was 'on fire from end to end', the surviving journalist wrote.

Of the four war correspondents, only one survived the double raid. Unwillingly he found he had a scoop. Had the other journalists got in the way or asked one question too many at a vital moment? Or was it another fantastic war coincidence; a gruesome prank?[4]

One came back and, awe dripping from his pen, wrote;

In 18 hours Bomber Command sent out more than 2,600 aircraft and dropped more than 10,000 tons of bombs, including 500, 000 incendiaries, *far more than the Germans dropped on London during the whole of the Blitz.*[5]

No Londoner could believe it possible.

Most of the aircrews in the first raid on Duisburg did not fly on the second. They were therefore fresh to fly the next night. But they wanted XYZ cover – so 101 were obliged to fly again.

The target was Wilhelmshaven and it was a dusk takeoff for a night raid. Even the calmest men were tired and on edge, and at briefing, Magnetic noticed that Hyde seemed exhausted. His hands were shaking and one corner of his mouth twitched when he spoke. It would have been both kind and wise to lighten his re-initiation, but war is impersonal and the cog must not complain when the war machine is geared high.

As they set out over the North Sea Vincent was cursing his Gee box. On a trip with two long sea legs, Gee had broken down. He reported 'no radar' to Chiltern, adding the suggestion that to fly courses more carefully than usual would be a safe move. Over water without radar they could rely only on the stars. It was going to be a night of hard work, so Vincent settled down to force his tired brain and flagging body into sparkling action. It would not be a long trip: six hours at most. He felt that he could keep it up if Chiltern would co-operate.

With the coming of radar, too many navigators had put star navigation behind them. When it was needed in such an emergency as this they then found themselves rusty. Vincent, however, had done so much astro-navigation during pre-radar days that there was little chance of his forgetting, and in addition he had continued taking and plotting sextant shots to keep his hand in, so now he fell quickly into the old routine.

They were to cross the coast-in between two of the smaller Frisian Islands. All the Frisians were heavily defended. This land-fall would be Vincent's first check on how accurate his astro was proving. If it was right, they would pass between the defences; if not, they might fly straight into them. That was assuming that Chiltern flew at the correct course and airspeed which, Vincent noted with relief, he seemed to be doing.

Two minutes before ETA coast, Magnetic reported flak on the port bow. It seemed that their groundspeed was right. Then came flak away to starboard. They evidently were tracking between islands. They prayed that they were between the right ones.

Their track led south of Wilhelmshaven, then turned sharp north. If they were already north of track they would fly over the target before the attack opened; if south, they would arrive after the attack finished. Vincent gave the order to turn north to where they all hoped the target lay. In a few seconds the first colour markers would fall and then they would know.

'Markers going down ten starb'd!' said Magnetic suddenly. 'Good show, nav.'

They all breathed again.

They bombed half a minute early.

The target acted as a perfect fix, giving Vincent a wind to

compute with and a point from which to start a new air plot. After the turmoil of Duisburg earlier in the day, Wilhelmshaven seemed a quiet target and they turned for home confidently.

'We've crossed the coast-out,' Vincent announced after a short time, and everybody relaxed, already relishing the sleep that must soon be theirs.

Twenty minutes later, when they should have been seventy miles at sea, Vincent was shattered to hear Yarpi announce; 'Flak on the starb'd quarter up.'

'But there *can't* be!'

'It's flak all right, nav.'

'Navigator,' said Chiltern. 'If we're still over land, where have we bombed?'

'I don't know, sir. I'll check and let you know.'

Vincent double-checked every line in his chart and every figure in his log. Then he checked his astro plotting and computation. Everything was right. He wondered if a gale had sprung up since the target. But figures proved that wind that strong simply could not be. The fact remained that if they were still over land they could not possibly have been over Wilhelmshaven at TOT. Yet they had bombed with the attack, not on their own. If they were still over Europe, how would that influence ETA England? It was a navigational picture of some contemporary school too obscure for Vincent to interpret. It seemed to fit no known pattern, and Chiltern kept pressing him for the explanation.

It came after a few puzzling moments that had dragged like hours. A radio voice, possibly the Master Bomber's, announced; 'All Drummer aircraft beware flak ship at 53.21 north, 04.09 east.'

A flak ship. Why had they not realised that? It could be nothing else. Perhaps three ops in thirty-six hours had stunned their minds.

It was fortunate that their ETA England was not in doubt because there was no coast to be seen when they reached it. Fog had been predicted by met and fog there was. But fog was no longer the threat it had been at the time of Nürnberg when Hyde had been burnt. FIDO could bark and frighten fog from the 'drome. They found base and called up for instructions for landing by firelight.

Hyde's emotions were mixed as he approached Ludford above the swirling mists. He had been told what to expect and now, seeing it for the first time, fear of his old enemy jousted with rejoicing to win control of his thoughts.

The fog lay flat and dark, but just above Ludford, lifted by the soaring heat surrounding the runway, a mushroom of fog billowed high into the sky. Around this cloudy column the many aircraft circled, waiting to be called down into the fog through which they would burst suddenly to see the firelit runway. Tonight's only complication was a slight cross-wind; only one runway had FIDO, and this runway had to be used no matter where the wind blew. Fog, and drift on landing: two bitter memories dogged Hyde's exhausted mind. He waited to hear his order to land, excitement and terror turning his brain into a battlefield.

When the order came he was starting the down-wind leg; he would have to fly right around the aerodrome to the point of approach. As he flew slowly around, skimming the fog top, the thousand nightmares he had dreamed since Nürnberg revived in his mind.

Slowly his aircraft seemed to drag around to the approach point.

Should he come down at the edge of the mushroom?

No.

That would be too close.

But the further back he went, the more likely he was to descend into the distant fog, unbroken by the fires.

Hyde slid down into the fog, straining forward for his first fiery glimpse of FIDO.

It burst dazzlingly upon him. What joy to see dread fog defeated!

Quickly he saw that he was not in position. He had cut the corner; he should be further back. Would it be wise to overshoot?

Hyde appraised his height and speed and likely point of touch-down. This was the long runway. He could sideslip into position, land a third of the way down the tarmac and still stop with room to spare. He tipped his starboard wing and slid down across the bumpy air over the FIDO strip.[6]

He was still a hundred feet high but lining up well when the petrol drip, from tanks he did not know had been damaged by the flak ship, trailed through FIDO's flames. A climbing chain of fire, fading and flashing like a rope of brilliant jewels, curved up behind the new Q-Queenie.

Twice, slipstream almost cut the spluttering wick in two, but fire sensed an old companion and would not loose its hold.

For an instant the fire disappeared under the wing as if the climber shirked the highest summit.

Then Queenie blew up and fell in a brilliant shower of fragments.

Hyde, fire and fog had kept an old appointment.

FIDO, made to save him, became his murderer.

— 5 —

'That's the end of the kitty,' said Vincent. He raised his glass to the men about him. 'So for the last time – here's to Hyde.'

'To Hyde.'

'To Hyde.'

Many messes had what was called a 'chop fund'. Into this fund each man put one pound, and that pound was spent to drink him farewell whenever a member 'got the chop'. It was a less brutal and more functional practice than most outsiders who heard of it imagined.

It was an inescapable fact that hardly a week could pass without most aircrew on an operational squadron losing one of their friends. This friend might be the chap who slept in the next bed or took out your girlfriend's sister. He might be a new, casual friend or he might be a great friend of long standing. Perhaps it was fortunate that most of the closest friends were killed together.

No matter how recent or how dear a friend he may have been, however, it was obvious that his ghost must not be permitted to linger and torment the minds of the living. Only the utterly callous can gainsay death, and people who do are seldom pleasant folk to know, and never desirable. Yet it was also true that preoccupation with death would quickly unhinge minds that must constantly encounter it. Men should mourn their friends, but they must not go on mourning, piling grief upon grief, lamenting more and ever more dead comrades. That way madness lies: a madness that in war is suicide.

So necessity invented compromise. The close friends of a dead man would draw his pound from the chop fund and lament, drinking his health in the next world, for as long as the pound lasted. After that his name was never mentioned again. In theory, if somebody then said, 'What will you always remember about Jack?', his friends should answer; 'Jack? Who's Jack?'

The theory sounds brutal. In fact is seldom was brutal, and it worked. That was the big thing: it worked. It kept the dead at a decent distance and kept the living sane.

When Vincent put down his empty glass he should not have mentioned Hyde again. Hyde was dead. They had mourned him. Now he must vanish. But Hyde had been a great friend indeed; to some he had seemed a great man. Vincent could not force his mind to forget so overwhelming a memory; he could not snip off his thoughts: one yard of sorrow and not an inch more. Vincent spoke again of Hyde; 'It was all so bloody useless. So pointless! They should never have sent him back on ops.'

'He came back at an ill-fated moment,' said H-H.

'Duisburg, Duisburg, Wilhelmshaven,' said Johnnie. 'In thirty-six hours.'

'He wasn't ready for that pace,' added Krink.

'And then fog.'

'Nürnberg all over again.'

'At least the Germans didn't get him. The Hun never lived who could beat Hyde.'

'That's just what infuriates me,' said Vincent. 'It wasn't even the enemy he was fighting that killed him. I would accept it if he'd died gloriously. If he had died fighting the way we've seen him fight I could cheer and know his Irish spirit would out-shout me. But FIDO killed him. Stupidly. Killed him from behind. The whole story of his return is pitiful. His first day back in the air he wrecked Queenie, just as stupidly and wastefully. They should have taken him off flying then.'

'And how would he have liked that?' asked Jackal. 'My bet is that he would've refused any job but ops.'

'I don't think so,' said Vincent softly. 'Not from some of the doubts he expressed to me. He had changed and he knew it.'

For a few minutes nobody spoke. The unhappy men went on staring at their empty glasses. Suddenly Krink snapped them back. 'Hey, cheer up. This is a farewell drink to Hyde. If he could see us now he'd think we'd lost the war. Make it a party: a farewell party. Let's all put a quid in and give Hyde a farewell party.'

'Isn't that a bit, er, disrespectful?'

'Drinking? Hyde never thought drinking was disrespectful. I sure hope no sentimental slob makes air-films after the war with unhappy endings. The sight of you mugs would make Hyde feel like hell, let alone a whole damp-eyed audience. It infuriates when a book or play or film ends with a they-died-that-we-might-live note. I'm sure real heroes don't want gentlemen in England now abed to feel themselves accursed they were not here.'

'Half their rotten luck,' said Bill, and threw his pound on the counter.

Vincent threw his pound on the pile, saying, 'So many big names have got the chop foolishly. Gibson flew into a hill. Cain pranged showing off; slow roll at zero feet. Bader tackled six Huns on his own and of course they got him. Finucane stopped one stray rifle-shot in a petrol lead and ditched. And what were his last words? 'This is it, chaps!'. Not, 'now I die gloriously', or 'tell them I'm a hero', or 'long live democracy', but simply 'this is it'. *He* didn't make a song and dance. Why should *we*? Or why should some tear-jerking script writer? Hyde's in good company for a farewell party.'[1]

Vincent piled all the notes into a pyramid and leant forward.

'Barman! Fill these up again. And stick around ...'

Had Joe been there he would have summed it up with, 'Grog's the shot.'

Squadron Leader Chiltern, *after* investigating her social and financial position, decided that he approved of Section Officer Wendy Marlborough-Jones. To him, that made it obvious that he should court her and it should follow as night the day that Wendy would succumb. He was an honourable man and an ambitious officer; he had dignity, breeding and a future, he assured her. What more could she ask? They had everything in common and, he said, shared a respectable mutual attraction.

'But it's more mutual for you than it is for me,' thought Wendy. It might have saved further ado had she spoken her thought aloud. Chiltern would have read into such a rebuff stark stupidity on Wendy's part, which would instantly have disqualified her as a possible Mrs Chiltern.

Instead, Wendy had remained silent in apparent agreement and Chiltern assumed he had advanced one more step towards winning her acceptance.

Within a few days of arriving at 101, Chiltern had noted and approved Wendy's appearance and behaviour. Although he would have strenuously denied that there was anything carnal in his approval of her, he did admit frankly enough to himself that a beautiful and shapely wife, all other things being equal, was better than an ugly, angular one. Had not a wife often furthered her husband's ambitions with her charm and beauty? Besides, handsome stock breeds better.

He had been prepared to approve of Wendy even before investigating her suitability; prepared, indeed, to overlook it should some trifling point come to light of which he did not approve. Provided, of course, it was a point he could avoid or alter to fit his rigid standards. He was delighted, therefore, when her record and background proved exemplary. The additional discovery that her mother's family, though almost vulgarly wealthy, had never stooped to commerce and that one of her uncles was an Air Commodore, quite won his heart and kindled within him a feeling nearer to love than he had ever experienced before.

This did not, however, prevent him from decrying love. 'Popular love in our day,' he said, 'is both frivolous and dangerous. It is no longer God's love at all. Marriage should be based on respect and compatibility with unquestioning acceptance of the church's bonds. Marriage is a contract and a dedication, forever, for better or worse, whether it bring joy or misery. If modern couples would accept that,' Chiltern dictated, 'divorces would never happen.'

'Neither,' thought Wendy, 'would marriages.' But once again she did not speak her thoughts.

Chiltern's attentions bewildered Wendy; they left her questioning herself. She admired Chiltern. He was an honest, clean, honourable gentleman. He was many of the things she had told herself a suitor should be. Why, then, did she feel driven to oppose his arguments? Why, when he decried what he called 'Hollywood love' and spoke with scorn of any woman who would let the prospect of sexual enjoyment influence her choice of a husband, why, at such times, did her woman's blood boil and her copper eyes spark with distaste?

Chiltern was saying, clearly and coldly, many things that she felt she had believed before. She wanted to understand her feelings but had never expressed them lucidly, even to herself. Now she heard her feelings defined and realised that these were emotions which she had been taught to accept before she was old enough to understand them. Seeing them exposed and bare, her warm heart rejected them as cold, hard, ruthless. Could it be that her feelings were really stronger than her teachings? Chiltern, striving to achieve the opposite, had softened Wendy's attitude to the warmer emotions.

That had set Wendy looking for the real thing and, upon his return, she had looked to Hyde. In his new, more serious mood Hyde, who had always found Wendy herself attractive, then found her company more agreeable than ever before. Wendy, barely experienced enough to understand her own emotions, responded to the fundamental mother and nurse in her and wondered if this was love.

When Hyde was killed she felt sad and at a loss. But she was surprised that her sorrow was not deeper. She was sorry but her mind was not filled with it; she had to remind herself to keep being sorry or other thoughts would creep in. Was it that she was shallow or was it that she had never loved Hyde at all?

Or did she, perhaps, really love Chiltern? She tried to imagine how she would feel if Chiltern were lost. She reflected disinterestedly for a moment without any heartfelt response, then her mind stopped in an instant of panic as she realised that if Chiltern went, so would his crew – Hyde's crew.

That thought stopped her heart beating and left her spine cold-tingling. Vincent and Magnetic, Johnnie and Joe: these she knew she would miss. She had been testing herself to see if she had loved Hyde, or if she loved Chiltern. What she discovered seemed to have nothing to do with love at all. Yet she knew it was the most intense emotion she had ever experienced.

It did not matter whether or not she could trust these wonderings; they were soon to face the real test.

The target was the German village of Groninberg[2] where the Allies were still west of the Rhine. Powerful and efficient German forces could not be dislodged so Bomber Command were called in to help make the village less tenable.

At Ludford it was one of those daylight rush targets. The army never liked to call on the air force and once again they had left their call till the last minute. Briefing was rough and rapid. It was obvious that Intelligence knew little about the area except that the German army thereabouts was being altogether too stubborn and would not take 'retreat' for an order. It was brave of them because with the Rhine at their back, hurried retreat was not possible, and to lose one minor battle would mean capture or annihilation.

Bomber Command had no objection to that.

It was given as a close-support attack. The bomb-line (on the Allied side of which no bombs must fall) was only six hundred yards from the target. That meant an easy half-minute dash from friendly territory, then a fast about-turn and peaceful homeward flight.

The crews were surprised, therefore, to meet heavy flak twenty-five miles west of the target. Operational height was 9000 feet, visibility was perfect, so the German army gunners, always better shots than their civil counterpart, spoke terse defiance with every gun.

The Allied armies had either misplaced the bomb-line purposely to make sure no bombs fell near them, or else they had called the attack too late to stop a threatened German advance and the line had moved since briefing.

Perhaps some truth lay in both alternatives, and perhaps the target itself was already bare of German troops. But orders are orders and the bombers flew on towards Groninberg.

German army gunners wasted few shells. RAF crews had come to respect them as intelligent fighters. They did not maintain long, abortive chases across the sky. If three bursts failed to get a bomber they had selected, then they would move their sights to another. And they always tried with more likely success to make the first burst of each attack – the one bombers cannot see and therefore cannot evade – a crippling one. When flying over the German army, more than at any other time, the race was to the swift.

What Bill was thinking as they flew into the flak nobody knew. It was his first trip since he had been wounded, yet his voice sounded quite calm. A three-gun burst, which Chiltern must have seen, exploded near enough to their port bow to rock N-Nuts off course.

Crisply Bill ordered, 'Dive port, go!'

Chiltern should have already started to 'go' before Bill spoke; certainly if he wanted to discuss how the order had been given or its wisdom he should have acted first and discussed it later.

Instead, in his most exasperated, raised-eyebrows tone of voice, Chiltern said, 'Really, bomb aimer ...' when the next triangle of shells hit them and N-Nuts fluttered from the sky, wounded and on fire.

Seen from a distance, flak bursts appear as simultaneous explosions. For the men in N-Nuts, however, there were two distinct thumps; two direct hits a fraction of a second apart. There was no mighty, roaring explosion. Instead they heard two sharp cracks, felt the jabbing blast in their ears and then the sway and bump as N-Nuts seemed to bounce off something solid.

Two shells were bursting together; one just behind the port outer, the other on the port of the rear turret, instantly followed by a third which hit the starboard fuselage behind the Special's position. Being daylight, the Special was lucky to be absent; his chair was shot to pieces.

The port outer engine puffed a cloud of steel-blue smoke and stopped dead. The rear turret tumbled in on top of Smiff, crushing his legs under his guns. The mid-upper turret shattered, showering hundreds of splinters of perspex over Yarpi, pricking his face and hands with dozens of tiny cuts.

Chiltern continued to admonish Bill after N-Nuts was hit, but nothing was heard; intercom was smashed. N-Nuts immediately filled with stinking smoke and rapidly lost height. Then Krink and Vincent saw the fire.

Flames criss-crossed the entrance to the rear turret as if it were a mystic cave whose secrets the Gods had entrusted fire to hide from human eyes. Oil, spraying from the burst hydraulics pipes which powered the turret, was burning in mid-air, tangling its flaming net to trap the wounded Smiff and thwart his rescuers.

Yarpi, his face black with cordite smoke and streaked with blood from his pin-cushion cuts, climbed down from his turret, groped in the smoke and fire for his parachute, then half-shuffled, half-stumbled forward.

Krink and Vincent rose from their seats together; Krink stood there undecided. Vincent moved aft to fight the fire.

Yarpi stopped him at the main spar, shouting, 'Bale out, man, she's had it. Bale out, man!'

All this happened within five seconds and, as Vincent looked, wide-eyed, while the fire spread aft, he inclined to accept Yarpi's advice. If he thought of Smiff at all it was to assume that he would step from the flames any moment and bale out with them.

Krink and Vincent picked up their parachutes and turned forward, but as Krink clipped the 'chute to his harness he saw that sparks had burnt through the cover and the silk was smouldering.

They had once seen a man bale out with his parachute on fire. It had opened as it should, and in the lovely white spread of silk one could have missed the red-rimmed hole that threw out tell-tale sparks. Then the hole had blossomed like a crimson bud, fanned by the wind spilling through it like invisible life-blood. The bud had flourished into a giant flower, and still it grew and through it the billowing air escaped. Faster and faster its screaming burden had fallen, begging the dead cloth to hold and the live fire be gone until he was plunging down, silken cords streaming behind him like a comet's tail.

The ghastly memory flashed through all three minds as quickly as a dancing spark. Then Krink dived behind the Special's radio. Krink produced the spare parachute with a smile which could accept any trouble Fate might offer, and the three men moved again – forward, away from the fire and towards the escape hatch.

Stumbling forward down the rocking, still sloping aircraft, Vincent saw Bill's head looking back at them; looking *up* from the diving nose as he stood not so much on the floor as on the inside of the nose itself. Bill's expression was not one of quiet calm but neither was it one of panic. He saw them stumbling forward with parachutes fixed, looked beyond them at the fire, then looked back at Vincent again questioningly.

In Vincent's mind there was only one thing to do – bale out – and he indicated this to Bill by pointing down and miming to jump. With commendable alacrity, Bill spun around, jettisoned the escape hatch which comprised the entire floor of his bomb-aiming compartment, and tumbled out, knees up and head down in fine text-book style.

By this time – it was now ten seconds after being hit – the three men were grouped beside Chiltern, who was still grappling with the controls. They could not pass because Magnetic stood in the way, trying to quiet the port inner which had a runaway throttle. When Chiltern saw them standing there a bored, oh-what-is-it-*now?* expression crossed his face and he shouted, 'Why are you still here?'

'She's on fire', yelled Vincent.

'She's all right,' Chiltern yelled back. 'She's still flying.'

'The bomb bay's on fire. She'll blow up.'

'Go back. Put it out. She's still flying.'

'The fire …'

'Put it out.'

'The bombs …'

'Jettison. I can fly back. What's a course for Juvincourt?'

Juvincourt was a RAF emergency field in France. Then Chiltern must have realised that Vincent could not simultaneously fight the fire, drop the bombs and plot a course because he added, 'Never mind the course. I'll fly a reciprocal. You jettison, the others fight the fire.'

Shouting above the gale that whistled through the open escape hatch left Chiltern parched and panting. He returned to the seemingly impossible job of keeping N-Nuts in the air. Hesitantly, the others returned to their tasks.

Smiff had never had a chance. He watched uncomprehendingly when his turret was blown sideways on to his legs. Automatically he turned the control to move the guns off him, but all that moved was a jet of oil from the broken hydraulics and, as it splashed across him he watched it catch fire.

He tried to move his legs and found that the right one moved easily. Then Smiff noticed that the right foot was still crushed under the guns and, when he looked again, he saw that the leg was severed above the knee. He thought; 'That could be the only explanation.'

He admonished his mind for thinking so logically and coldly at such a time, but it refused to change its tune. Smiff knew he should be swamped with terror and pain and horror and panic but all his mind would do was reiterate the logic that if his foot was trapped and his leg could move, then somewhere between they *must* be severed.

Smiff tried to move his left leg but it was jammed. His calm, infuriating mind now wondered if it was better to still have the leg and be trapped by it in the burning turret or if it would have been better to have lost that leg, too.

Then Smiff realised that he was still holding the turret control and that burning oil was spraying over his clothing. If he stopped doing that, he should feel better. He released the control and the oil stopped, but he did not feel any better. He grew annoyed, then bitterly disappointed because stopping the oil did not stop the heat and he started to cry. That was about the time Chiltern sent the others back to fight the fire.

N-Nuts had lost a mile in height, which meant she was down to about 4000 feet, when Vincent came forward to drop the bombs. The bomb doors would not open because of the lost hydraulics pressure, but he decided to loose the bombs anyway and let their weight force open the bomb bays.

To descend into the bombing hatch was hair-raising; Bill had taken the entire floor of the bomb-aiming compartment with him when he baled out. Vincent tried standing astride the gaping hatch, feet forced against the fuselage walls, but almost slipped through and his heart skipped.

He decided to try it a different way. He had Magnetic lie on the step above and support him with an arm through his parachute harness while he dangled over 4000 feet of nothing, selected the bomb stations and pressed the tit. The release arm swung correctly around, making its contacts, but no bumping and shuddering came to gladden them. The bombs had not gone. His terrifying dangling had been wasted. Vincent reported this to Chiltern and said that he would release the bombs by hand.

When Vincent had told Chiltern that there was fire in the bomb bays he had not known for certain that there was. Now he found it was true. All the bombs were on 'safe', but the 4000 cookie was a dangerous, unreliable bomb at all times, and he decided to drop that first.

Above each bomb station was a manual trip-lever. With difficulty Vincent forced the flame-hot lever and felt the two-ton bomb trundle its way through the spring-loaded doors. He was surprised to see that Krink, instead of fighting the fire, was fiddling with his smashed radio and that Yarpi was just standing there, staring at the flames.

He went to Yarpi to tell him to help release the other bombs, the thousand pounders, but Yarpi could only point at the fire and say, 'Smiff'.

'Oh, God! Is he still in there?'

Vincent was amazed that so much could happen as to fill their minds with things so near and so vital that a comrade ten yards away should be forgotten. Yarpi had been unable to approach nearer than the still-dancing flames because he had no gauntlets and goggles; it seemed unbelievable but despite Nürnberg Vincent was still the only one in the crew, and very nearly the entire squadron, who always carried them.

Vincent wondered if Krink and Yarpi could see through smoke without goggles. Perhaps that was why they stood helplessly by.

Shielding his face from the flames with his left arm he turned the turret manually until he could open the door and reach in. His mind, as fire closed and menaced around him, shrieked two things at him; 'You must not damage his hands!' and 'Get out – your helmet is burning off!'.

The leather helmet, shrinking with the heat, was tightening around his skull, shrinking and sizzling until it felt one with his scorching scalp.

At first Vincent was too absorbed with the task of extricating Smiff to look at the man himself. Vincent caught Smiff under the armpits and tried to pull him free. Not until he realised Smiff was caught there did he examine the mangled, burning boy more closely.

Smiff turned his face towards Vincent, and the sight of it made Vincent ill. Despite the fire, he stood there and was sick, literally sick. The sightless eyes with eyeballs burst and dribbling, the inch-wide nostrils running red-brown blood, the shapeless, lipless hole that tried to speak, the mangled foot crushed in red-hot guns, the stump that bubbled as it bled and the whole, tortured, writhing body sickened him.

That reek of burning flesh which Vincent would never forget, and the painful swaying of the shapeless face, back and forth in slow arcs of agony showed that Smiff could never survive.

Vincent stepped back from the turret.

Beside the rear exit the emergency axe was clipped in its bracket. Unhurriedly and determinedly Vincent took it down.

Then he stepped back into the fire. His heart was racing but his brain was suddenly as clear and hard as a diamond; he had never been more sure that what he was about to do was right.

He took the axe in both hands, raised it a foot and chopped it powerfully into Smiff's skull.

When he walked back from the fire and into the fuselage, Yarpi was still staring at the flames and wringing his hands and Krink was still tinkering with the radio. Vincent wondered how long it was since they had been hit and glanced at his watch. From six minutes before TOT to 1558 – it must have been four minutes ago.

Could all this have happened in four minutes? It seemed impossible. He wondered if his watch had stopped from the heat but the second-hand was still moving.

He had caused one man to bale out over Germany, had himself dangled above a mile of empty sky, then dropped a two ton bomb he knew not where, stood in fire and tried to rescue a man, then finished up killing him. In four minutes!

While he thought this he had hurried to bring the other extinguisher, and now he and Magnetic were fighting back the flames – away from the bomb bays. Although the remaining bombs were stable thousand pounders, too much heat could upset them. Already the point-five shells were exploding in the ammunition trays. He wondered what could burn in the rear of the metal aircraft. Then he looked more closely and saw that the very *metal* was alight.

Suddenly he realised. For lightness, aircraft alloys contain magnesium; the same substance of which incendiary bombs are made. 'We wonder why she burns!' he mused, 'yet N-Nuts *is* a fire bomb.'

When the extinguishers were finished the fire revived. They had hustled Yarpi into helping them and the three of them beat at the flames with Smiff's singed parachute which had been protected in its tin rack, but the draught from the missing front hatch kept fanning the flames.

Vincent thought again of his navigation and returned to his desk. He checked Gee. What luck – it still worked! He took two readings and plotted them, frowned and checked. His gauntlets impeded him so he started removing them but the fire had stuck the leather to his skin so he decided to leave them on.

Again he took a Gee fix and plotted it. He could not believe what he saw. They were exactly two miles from where they had been hit and were flying around the spot in circles.

He went forward and checked Chiltern's compass repeater. It was not working. Then he remembered that the master compass in the rear would be upset by the fire. Chiltern must be using the old pilot compass. Vincent saw that he was and that they were flying a westerly course. It was now 1601 – surely they must be at least fifteen miles from where they were hit and back over Allied territory ...

Then Vincent noticed the sun. It was wandering steadily across their bow. And all the while their compass pointed stalwartly to starboard. Vincent realised suddenly what was happening. Fire at one end of a complete metal skin was turning N-Nuts into a giant solenoid magnet. The compass was following the current around and around and Chiltern was carefully chasing it – flying in circles above the guns that had hit them. Why they did not fire again and end his misery Vincent could not imagine. It all sounded impossible, but Vincent had heard of it happening before and it was certainly happening to N-Nuts now.

Chiltern was stubborn in his protection of the compass until Vincent succeeded in convincing him that if the compass needle really were pointing north, then the sun was lying nor' nor'east. They had been shouting unpleasantly at each other, each certain that the other was a fool and each only aware that the *other* looked wild-eyed, exhausted and half-mad.

Chiltern hated to admit that he must be directed by this screaming, panic-stricken boy with white, swollen eyes, blackened face, grey, cracked lips and wearing gauntlets.

'Why on earth gauntlets?', Chiltern reflected; 'is it because this draught is cold?'

Eventually Chiltern consoled himself with the belief that it was not a choice between the conflicting wisdom of Squadron Leader Chiltern and Pilot Officer Farlow but between the sun itself and his compass. He believed the sun.

'Put the sun on your port bow and keep it there,' Vincent shouted into the gale.

'Bearing three-one-five relative,' Chiltern shouted back. It was exactly the same thing but Chiltern hoped it seemed that he had had the last word.

The altimeter had caught Vincent's eye – it showed 1,100 feet. They could never reach home. With luck they could make the Allied lines ...

Vincent returned to his desk to plot a course for Juvincourt, though God alone knew how they could steer it without an astro compass. They had learnt to use these complicated but excellent gadgets during training but were not even issued with them on ops.

While he worked he found himself cursing Chiltern's stubborn stupidity. Then his thoughts changed. He realised that they had Chiltern's stubbornness to thank that they were not all prisoners of war by now. When Chiltern had ordered them back to fight the fire Vincent thought the decision was wrong and would almost certainly cost their lives. But Chiltern *had* kept N-Nuts in the air even though she was flying like a Heath Robinson kitchen sink. Chiltern had also done his best to spoil everything by circling the German guns.

'But I guess he has other things on his mind.'

Chiltern had. Plenty. Chiltern was an excellent pilot. He himself knew this and his fellow officers knew it. But now he intended to prove it more effectively than ever before. This was an excellent opportunity to get something practical written into his records that would assist his entire future. Not twenty men in the whole of Bomber Command could have kept N-Nuts aloft. Chiltern knew it and now he determined to prove it.

The port outer had seized the instant they were hit and the port inner, in fine pitch, had slipped wide open and stuck there. That meant one propellor would remain not only still but dragging, while the other would race at maximum revs until the engine cracked under the strain, yet still it would not give full power because, in fine pitch, it lacked coarse air to grip.

Also in that instant, the port fin (the Lancaster has two 'rudders') was blown off its upper hinge and much of its control surface shredded. N-Nuts fell into a dive and, with only half control of one fin and its stickiness tightening his rudder bar, Chiltern had succeeded wonderfully in keeping her from falling into a fatal spin.

Within a minute the port inner was overheating so seriously that Chiltern knew its cooling system was broken. He could not throttle back; he could not feather. He had held N-Nuts poised for the moment the port inner would seize, its overheated pistons first melting and then welding into one block of metal. When that instant came it could not catch him unready.

N-Nuts shuddered and slewed around. By the time Chiltern had forced the grating rudder bar to correct that, N-Nuts was waffling mushily near to stalling speed. More throttle on the starboard engines swung N-Nuts to port, adding to the drag of the dead port engines and dragging fin. Even with full starboard trim, N-Nuts still swung to port and Chiltern had to hold right rudder to keep on course.

It was then that he sent Magnetic back to help fight the fire. Many a pilot and engineer could not have met this concentration of hazards; Chiltern felt confident he could handle it alone. He had not failed to notice a worrying rise in cylinder-head temperature on the starboard outer gauges but Magnetic's presence could not remedy that ...

Then that fool navigator in gauntlets came up and started asking him if he had noticed what the sun was doing! Chiltern wished he had let them bale out – all of them – and flown N-Nuts home alone. '*That* would be something for the record.'

By the time Vincent had computed a course for Juvincourt and converted it to a relative sun-bearing the time was 1606 – they had been hit twelve minutes ago. He wrote the course on a slip of paper and handed it to Chiltern, at the same time offering him a piece of chocolate. Vincent had noticed that his skipper's mouth was dry.

'This will help,' Vincent shouted.

Chiltern merely looked from chocolate to navigator, grim martyrdom in his expression, and shook his head. To himself, Vincent said, 'Oh, damn the man! I simply won't try to be friendly,' and ate the chocolate himself.

'Can you get any more bombs off?', Chiltern yelled. He was growing quickly less sure of N-Nuts' ability to reach safety. When the cookie had gone N-Nuts actually climbed a little. Since then she had mushed lower and lower and the controls grew more soggy every minute. Chiltern knew that the pneumatics and hydraulics were gone, that his controls were being further impeded as the still-burning tail sagged on to them, that he was losing lift and losing power and suddenly he feared his superiors might never see N-Nuts and the wonderful job he was doing.

Vincent had just replied, 'I'll see,' when N-Nuts lurched wildly port, dropped a wingtip and stalled. The port fin had torn in half. Chiltern yelled, 'Crash positions!' and started a new struggle with his haywire controls. N-Nuts was diving and curling around port and trying to flick on to her back. Chiltern actually crossed his hands around the column to grind the ailerons full force against the spin and still she only just flew straight.

Chiltern's expert eye had selected a field for their forced landing. Surrounded by forest, it was big enough if they hit slowly with their wheels up.

As Magnetic came forward to his crash position beside his skipper, he leant a hand on Vincent's desk. The hand was bleeding and one drop of blood splashed across Vincent's chart.

'Careful, you untidy oaf!,' yelled Vincent, and Magnetic noticed that Vincent was really upset.

'We are about to crash,' Magnetic thought, 'God knows where or how successfully or if the nine thousand-pounders on board will explode, and our meticulous navigator is upset about a smudge on his precious plot.'

Though many navigators turned in charts that looked as though they had been used to carry fish and chips to a football match in the rain, Vincent's charts were kept map-room fresh and his fastidious-ness would not even *die* hard.

The emergency CO_2 bottle had pushed on flap and N-Nuts swuffled unsteadily down towards the clearing. The changed flying attitude caused the fluttering fin to lock hard port and the nose fell with the drop in speed. Chiltern switched both his heels behind the starboard rudder, braced his wrists behind the right-locked column and pulled his hardest.

It was not quite enough. N-Nuts' tail wheel caught in a sapling at the edge of the clearing and the whole weakened tail unit, together with many feet of fuselage, ripped off.

Facing backwards in the crash positions the crew saw Smiff's body dangle from the broken turret that now released it and then go tumbling along behind them, mixed up with three thousand-pounders which had also shaken loose and were rolling erratically along the turf.

N-Nuts fluttered on, tipping on her nose. Ten feet higher and she may have crashed headlong. Instead, she struck the ground with her forward belly.

There was a noise like a thousand snares dragging slowly across a mammoth drum, then N-Nuts stopped.

Magnetic, who was standing when she hit, had twisted his ankle.

Part Three

The Jackal

Fire follows a crash all too often. N-Nuts was already on fire before she crashed so the risk was great. Her burning tail, however, was torn off by the sapling and when she settled she showed no signs of bursting into flames.

Feeling sure that they were behind the lines, Squadron Leader Chiltern therefore ordered Magnetic to set her alight. Her equipment might interest the Germans if they found her.

Some say it is because aeroplanes can be as perverse as women that aviators call an aircraft 'she'; certainly N-Nuts was as perverse in death as any Marie Antoinette could be. Twice Magnetic set N-Nuts alight; twice she went out again. Ten minutes before, her very metal had been aflame and all their efforts could not extinguish it. Now, with tinder lit around her petrol-sodden engines and coaxed with every warmth, she shook her head and crossed her legs and froze the fires out. It was not until Magnetic slashed a fuel lead, tied it to an opened parachute and then lit the petrol-soaked silk that N-Nuts melted.

By then Chiltern had hurried the others away. Shocked at the sight of N-Nuts after they crashed, despite the damage crashing had caused, he could see how weak she must have been while he was still flying her, and why lesser men, or less foolhardy men, might have baled out. Commendably cool despite the shudder it caused him, he ordered the crew to separate.

'We have little chance of escape as a group,' he said. 'And each of you remember that to escape is your duty. Singly, at least some of us should get through to the Allied lines.'

Yarpi quaked at the prospect of attempting escape alone; shivering and muttering, obviously his nerve had gone. 'You come with me,' Chiltern said bravely. 'The rest of you get cracking.'

Vincent waited an instant for Chiltern to wish them luck. But the skipper had missed his cue, so Vincent said, 'Good luck, sir.'

'We need skill, Farlow, not luck,' Chiltern answered.

Magnetic waited until N-Nuts was irretrievably afire, then followed them westward into the forest.

'Man is what he eats.'

Not a very romantic notion but then Man – the animal Man – is not a very romantic creature. He tries to laud his spirit and forgets that, in his body, he is not superior but actually inferior to most other animals. For all his dreams of mind, of *homo sapiens*, the articulate, rational being, Man's body rules him.

It is possible to forget it for long stretches at a time. While life goes smoothly on, while the body's needs are met efficiently and without disquieting clashes with brute fact, the body is silenced and the mind is left to contemplate itself and marvel at its loftiness.

But if the body's needs are not met, what then? The body cries out and the body shall be served. The mind becomes a twisted knot of cunning and Man, sacred Man, will hunt and kill and steal and live worse than the wild creatures to preserve his life, his possessions or even his little comfort.

Vincent had walked home from an aeroplane ride before and he did not welcome this reunion with escape. He remembered, for example, what walking a hundred miles in flying boots can do to a man's feet.

Fortunately, this time he was wearing new issue escape boots. Nothing was so apt to betray an escaping aviator as his clumsy, calf-high, wool-lined flying boots. First they wore his feet, literally, to the bone and then they clamoured for his captor's attention. So the RAF made a new flying boot; really a fleece-lined shoe with wool-lined leggings attached. Inside the right legging was a knife. Vincent took out the knife, cut the leggings off where they joined the shoes, tore off his observer's wing and BEM ribbon, and buried them.

What was left would pass muster for normal walking shoes. Clipped into his pocket was a pencil. He removed it, slipped the clip off the pencil and balanced it on the pencil point. The clip swung backwards and forwards, then settled on north. It was a secret compass.[1]

Vincent struck south-west into the forest. He hurried. Soon it would be sunset and if he could avoid capture until it was dark he could leave the tell-tale aircraft far behind by morning.

He did not eat at all that night. Emergency rations should be kept until hunger demanded. He had discovered that before, too, the hard way. He wondered if anyone had thought to bring the rations stored in the Special's position. How seldom, in an emergency, one remembered everything. He came to the end of the forest at about midnight and found himself in freshly reaped fields. Away to the north there was heavy gunfire.

Later in the night he saw gunfire ahead and knew for certain they were behind German lines. At dawn he identified his position on his escape map; he was twenty-six miles south-west of Groninberg, yesterday's target. He had tried to judge his distance from the nearest gunfire and, using the speed of sound as a five-seconds-to-the-mile yardstick, estimated that he was still thirty miles from the Allied lines.

Twenty-six plus thirty – the six-hundred-yard bomb line had been rather inaccurate at briefing.

His gauntlets were still on his hands where the fire had welded them. He found a stream and tried to bathe them off. Easing the leather off his left palm, underneath he saw that the skin was tearing away, leaving the tender flesh raw and bleeding. He decided to leave his gauntlets on and hoped the tanned leather would not poison the burns.

It was essential that he remove his helmet, though it, too, was stuck to his skin. With the weather turning cold his gloves would not arouse suspicion but an aviator's helmet ... He soaked it off as gently as he could, but still the skin tore off his forehead, also pulling out large tufts of hair. He bathed these annoying wounds, applied some ointment from his emergency kit, then plastered his head and face with mud. A dirty man looks less suspicious than a wounded man. He also rubbed mud over his rank markings; while he wore his rank, he was in uniform and could not be shot as a spy, but the less conspicuous he was the better.

He allowed himself a small drink of water, one milk tablet, one butterscotch and one vitamin tablet, then hid himself in a hedge where he prepared to spend the daylight hours. Presently he fell asleep.

War at least gives most men a dog-like ability to sleep whenever and wherever the opportunity offers. It exhausts them physically and that helps. But oddly enough it frees them from sleep's great enemy – worry. With such huge issues at stake, issues over which the individual has no control, life's little worries fade into insignificance. A man flying to Berlin might worry about that noise in the gearbox of his little Austin, or whether his girl is out with a sailor, or how he can explain to the stores sergeant that iron-burn through his best blue, but he is not likely to worry about being killed. Perhaps worry is a purely social thing, or perhaps worry itself is too wise to take great issues seriously. Men who did worry about death went mad. Vincent, alert to the danger he was in, could dismiss it while he slept like a pregnant bear.

It was mid-afternoon when he awoke to the sound of heavy transport grinding past. He saw, on a road less than a mile north, big German trucks heading west. Two thoughts struck him: first, 'I must head further south tonight' and, secondly, 'what a perfect target'.

Patrolling fighters soon had the same idea. Rocket-carrying Typhoons zoomed out of the sky; Vincent watched the Huns scatter as rockets and cannon shells burst amongst them. Vincent had heard that a Typhoon's load of eight rockets had the same hitting power as a broadside from a cruiser. Now, hearing them on the ground, he believed it.[2]

After this excitement he realised that he was very hungry. He ate two more milk tablets and a vitamin pill and then sucked slowly at another butterscotch. Tonight he must steal some food – real food with some bulk in it.

Impatiently, trying to doze so he would forget his hunger and also gain strength for that night's trek, he awaited sunset. Before it was quite dark, he slipped back to the creek for a drink. As he leant his weight on his hands to reach the water he realised how stiffly his burnt hands had set in the gauntlets while he slept. He plunged them into the cold water and after a while they seemed softer; he was not sure whether the water really had loosened them or if the cold had merely numbed them.

His progress was slow that night. It began badly when he climbed a hill and rechecked by sound how far he now was from the front. It took an extra half minute after the flash for the sound of gunfire to reach him. The Germans had advanced between five and ten miles that day.

Occasionally he was forced to hide from German troops. Once he came across a party cooking in the open. He tried to think of a way to steal some of their food but as he came near, a German suddenly appeared down a path carrying branches of firewood. Vincent was certain he had been seen though the German raised no alarm. The fright of it kept him clear of camps that second night.

The next day he was so hungry he could not sleep, and desperate plans for getting food kept passing through his mind. There was no stock at all in the area, no cows to be milked, no chickens to be killed, not even a cat or a dog.

In one field some of the wheat harvest had not been taken in. It was cut, but wheat stalks lay about, still uncollected. He risked discovery to grovel amongst the stubble, collecting a few grains of wheat. It was dirty, so first he washed it in a creek. As soon as it was wet the wheat started to swell, and too late Vincent remembered when he was a boy and had kept pet pigeons that if they ate wet wheat it killed them.

He wondered if he should risk it. At first he picked out the grains that seemed to be dry, often dropping them into the dirt again as they fell from his clumsy, gloved fingers. One by one, without actually deciding that he would or would not eat the wet wheat, he chose the grains until they were all gone. They tasted dry and powdery and stuck around his tongue and teeth. He wanted a drink to wash them down but feared that more water might upset him. Soon he felt the swollen grains heavy in his stomach; gripe attacked him and he was sick.

That morning he kept walking. It was fortunate that a creek ran south-west and he could follow it and keep out of sight. Presently he saw a farm house near the creek, and in the garden were fruit trees. Scarcely bothering to see if people were about he scrambled up the bank and headed for the little orchard.

Before he had reached it, however, he saw that all the fruit was picked. But under one of the trees he saw a cot and, when he went closer, he saw there was a baby in the cot. He did not feel surprise that a baby should be put out to sleep in the sun so near a battlefield, he merely thought, and the very thought horrified him, 'I could eat a baby.'

He crept near and stood behind a tree where he could see it and then he noticed: it was eating!

In one hand the baby held a half-chewed rusk and in the other a biscuit which it now held to its dribbling mouth. Defying the danger, Vincent walked up to the cot. He took the child's two hands in his and waved them up and down, saying softly, 'Diddums ickle fella give ums rusk to uncle?'

Then he retreated quickly behind the tree again, bearing the soggy rusk and biscuit with him, together with another untouched biscuit he had found lying in the cot. He forced himself to eat them slowly, then went back to the creek and drank. Nearby he found a haystack and went to sleep.

When he woke it was dark. He was very cold and then he realised it was raining. His first thought was of his hunger. This was his third night since the crash and all he had eaten was his emergency pack (the size of a tin of fifty cigarettes, it was designed to sustain a man for one day), a few grains of wet wheat and the biscuits from his adopted nephew. That reminded him of the nearby farmhouse, and he wondered if he might steal more safely now it was dark.

He walked near the house, then right around it. Although the windows were blacked out he could see there was light in one room. He decided to wait until all the lights went out.

During his wait he discovered something precious: the garbage bin. He picked it up and ran with it into the orchard and scattered its contents over the muddy ground. Like a madman he grubbed through papers, bottles, tins and refuse, seeming to smell out any scrap of food there was. Rationed Germany had not left much. A few crusts, two apple cores and some potato peelings were all he found and, as he uncovered each treasure, he sat in the rain and ate it.

Vincent was just resifting the refuse to be sure that he had missed nothing when something – he did not know what, there had been no sound – made him turn around.

Five yards away, pointing a rifle with a fixed bayonet at him, stood a man and beside him a woman. The man took a quick step forward and said something in German that Vincent took to mean 'hands up'. There was no escape. The man motioned him towards the house and Vincent walked quietly through the door.

The woman lit a lamp and then, at a curt command from her husband who stood apart with rifle at the ready, she felt Vincent's pockets for weapons.

She found the knife from his escape boots and handed it to the man. Now he knew Vincent was unarmed, he relaxed. He was older than Vincent, probably in his late thirties, and the uniform he wore made him look shorter and stockier than he was. His hair was cut short and his eyes were small and close together, but when the lamplight caught them they were a vivid blue.

He asked if Vincent spoke German and Vincent shook his head. The woman, who had been looking at Vincent as though he were some fascinating creature at the zoo, spoke softly to her husband. They had a quick, brusque conversation and she left the room. Her husband motioned Vincent to sit down and almost immediately the woman returned and placed before him a bowl of hot soup.

Food! *Hot* food! Vincent thanked her with his eyes, and he started to gulp the thick, salty soup. He had taken a dozen mouthfuls in greedy, noisy haste when he realised they were both watching him; the man dispassionately, the woman with pity.

Vincent blushed, then ate his soup more slowly; nervously, like a dog eating in strange surroundings being watched by people it fears. When he had finished the soup she brought him a slice of sausage on a plate and beside it a stuffed parsnip and some boiled potatoes. Beside his plate she placed an apple.

The man then spoke to her and she backed away from Vincent as if she could not take her eyes from him, felt behind her for a coat hanging on the wall, put it on and left the house.

That act, and the fact that hunger was starting to retreat and free his mind for thoughts of escape, set Vincent's mind alert. He was now alone with this man – this armed soldier. The woman had obviously gone to bring aid. After she returned, escape might be impossible. *This* was the time when escape was easiest, the lecturers always said. *Before* you were locked up. To keep out is easier than to get out. But first Vincent wanted to finish his meal; he thought he would have time for that and it may be days before he ate again ...

Rifle on one knee, the German sat on the opposite side of the table from Vincent, and about five feet beyond. While he ate, Vincent judged the width of the table and decided that if he flung it forward it would not be wide enough to hit his captor.

Then he tried to guess what the table weighed. If was about six feet by four and made of pine. If he tipped it up he should be able to half-throw it at the same time, and that way it might strike the German's knee or his rifle and then if Vincent could reach the light ...

Vincent picked up the apple and went to bite it, but polished it on his sleeve instead. As he did so, he looked up at the German and smiled. The German half-smiled in reply. Again Vincent went to bite the apple, but again he changed his mind and indicated that he would put the apple in his pocket.

The moment his hands were below the level of the table he grasped its edge and lifted and pushed the heavy wood with every ounce of his twelve stone behind it. In the same instant he jumped to his feet and leapt to his right. If there was to be any shooting he wanted to be a moving target.

The soldier grasped his rifle as he saw the table move. But indoors, and from a sitting position, a rifle is a clumsy weapon. The table hit the rifle butt then crashed against the German's thigh. Vincent watched, surprised, as the heavy table seemed to fly through the air. He rushed forward to follow up his advantage and struck the German on the jaw.

A jab of pain shot up his arm, reminding him of his burns, but without pausing he grabbed the rifle and wrenched it from his captor. With a whoop of joy he swung and struck the soldier on the side of the head with the butt. The German dropped unconscious, his head cut and bleeding. He trod on the German's collar, flattening the cloth against the floor, then drove the bayonet through the collar deep into the floorboards.

On the mantel stood the bowl of apples. Vincent filled his pockets and hurried out of the door.

He made for the creek, groping and stumbling along the slippery banks, cursing the rain for spoiling the footholds but blessing its covering noise. He blessed, too, his stroke of luck that one soldier, alone with a compassionate wife who fed prisoners, should be his captor and host for such a precious meal. The capture had certainly done more good than harm.

Then, hurrying through the dark of the creek bed, Vincent started to worry about his pursuers. The creek was rather an obvious thing to follow, so he left the dark of the valley and climbed a hill which lead up to a ridge running south. They would probably guess he had come from the wrecked N-Nuts, so a change of course seemed a wise precaution.

At the hilltop he paused to watch the flashes and count the seconds. Forty-four!

Less than ten miles!

They were closer now. The Allies must be advancing again. Even if those flashes were the German's rear artillery – the Allies would not be much more than fifteen miles distant.

Vincent could have cheered with joy. Tomorrow he might be free. He just had to lie low and let the front pass over him.

He hurried on, excitement and fear mounting inside him. He must get far away from that farm and find a safe place to hide before dawn. From his emergency kit he still had the Benzedrine pills – the drug that gave strength to carry on just a little longer in an emergency. He'd take those now, then spurt ahead and be safe. Then he could sleep them off; they always said you must sleep afterwards, you couldn't press on once the Benzedrine wore off.[3]

Vincent fumbled for the tablets and swallowed them while he jog-trotted towards the rumbles and flashes of the battle.

Soon he was laughing to himself as he headed for the big cliff that loomed above him. He had been smart. He had tricked the

Germans into giving him food and then escaped. What if he had fractured the man's skull? 'Stupid German farmer! He got off light! Earlier I thought I might eat his baby; I let him off light. He'd rather I cracked his skull than ate his baby. I've killed babies before. Yes, I've killed babies – but I've never seen their broken little bodies; I've never killed them with my own hands. Bombing is different; bombing is civilized. How many prize bomber crews, with hundreds of women and children to their credit, could take a child and kill it with their hands?'

'The Japanese do,' Vincent reflected. 'And I saw a German bayonet an adolescent Greek girl when she showed too much fight. Which is worse: to bayonet a girl because she would not submit to sex or to kill a baby animal for food? The babies I have killed – the babies we have all killed, not only the bombers but the men who built the planes and the people who paid for them, everybody – these babies in Berlin and Nürnberg and Stuttgart ... I was less right, morally, to have killed them than I would be in killing a baby for food.'[4]

That made Vincent laugh again to himself. Why was it funny? Why could he think things now which at other times his mind refused to face? Vincent was not sure what he was doing and he no longer controlled his thoughts. He had his eye fixed on the cliffs and he was hurrying toward them as quickly and as quietly as he could. But his mind would not take things seriously; he felt that he had not a care in the world once he reached that cliff.

Why was it funny that he had hit that German, and maybe killed him, and that if he were captured he could be shot? He did not know why; he only knew he had to reach the cliff. He had to reach the big cliff and go to sleep and then, when he woke up, everything would be all right ...

He did reach the cliff, though it took another four hours. He could hardly stand when he came to three great rocks which had fallen to form a triangular cave, a massive wigwam of stone against the cliff-face. The noise and crash of battle was all around him, but he stumbled into the damp, cold cave smiling happily. He knew he had made it. He knew now he could sleep.

Vivid flashes filled the cave with paroxysms of ghostly light, revealing Vincent's sleeping form, his features muddy, his gloved hands twisted. He shivered and sometimes groaned as he lay in his filthy, rain-drenched uniform, drugged into the sleep of the exhausted – but on his face was a smile.

'Say, bum, who you tink you are, eh? Rip van Winkle?'

Vincent stirred and blinked through the stupidness of half-awakening at the giant, steel-helmeted American who stood, legs apart, glaring down at him. 'Hmmm?'

'Who you tink you are, sleepin' t'rough a battle? You ain't Snow White, dat's for sure.'

Vincent looked at his watch. It was eight o'clock. Morning. His mind was foggy and his head ached but quickly he realised he was saved. Saved! He was free!

The morning was noisy with bass artillery played fortissimo, staccato machine-guns and a choir of syncopated shouting – Vincent's overture to escape. He jumped up and ran towards his rescuer.

'Steady, Mac,' said the American; then Vincent noticed a .38 revolver pointing right at him. 'Not so fast, Fritz! You don't give Uncle Lem the skip dat easy.'

Vincent laughed and said, 'But I'm British. RAF, you know.'

Nonetheless he stopped and looked unhappily at the dispassionate barrel.

'British, huh?', said the American. 'Den what you doin' wearin' dat scarf?'

'This scarf?' Vincent was puzzled. 'I always wear a scarf when I fly.'

'But you ain't flyin' now, Superman.'

'No. I was shot down. Raiding Groninberg four days ago.'

'Yeah? I reckon you're a paratrooper.'

'Honestly, I'm British. Look, here's my identity card.'

'Paratroopers always got identity cards. Why you wearin' dat scarf?'

'I told you I always wear a scarf.'

'Day before yesterday orders says 'no scarves'. You know why?

Because we got German paratroopers around here and dey all wear scarves as a sign. Why don't you follow de order?'[5]

'I was behind German lines. I didn't know about it.'

'I'll say you was behind German lines; you're a German, dat's why and just t'prove it I'm gonna shoot you right in da belly.'

From the joy of a moment before, the situation had suddenly become as desperate as it could be.

'Say your prayers, Fritz, 'cos here's where you get yours.'

'Stop! Listen! *Check* before you shoot me. I'm willing to write a request that you, personally, be allowed to shoot me if I'm a German. But check first.'

'You'll write dat?'

'Yes. Gladly.'

'Dat'll make a swell souvenir. Okay! Write it here in my notebook.'

Nervously, speaking each word as he put it down, Vincent wrote; 'I, P/O Vincent Farlow, hereby request that – er, what's your name? – that Sergeant Lem Rizonico be permitted, personally, to shoot me ...'

'In de belly.'

'... by all means! To shoot me in the belly if I am shown to be a German paratrooper. How's that?'

'Sign it.'

'Okay.' Vincent signed it with a flourish since it was destined to remain a treasured souvenir.

'But you're just stallin' for time. If you wasn't German ...'

Eventually Vincent persuaded his new and infinitely more dangerous captor to take him to Field HQ. There, to his surprise, he was treated with less suspicion than he had been by the burly sergeant. Suspicion he did not mind, however; at HQ there was less shoot-'im-in-de-belly feeling.

All that day Vincent waited for confirmation of his identity. He waited while Field HQ contacted Area HQ, who contacted Division HQ, and so on through Army Group, US Army HQ, Allied combined services liaison, British HQ, RAF HQ Europe, RAF HQ UK, Bomber Command, Group, Base and finally 101 Squadron who finally said, 'Yes, he's British', and then the message returned by the same tortuous route.

The US Army then arranged for transport to Juvincourt. A bleak aerodrome, its many bomb craters shovelled full of earth, its bullet-riddled huts unlined and chill, its flying control patched and makeshift: Juvincourt represented the RAF in the US Sector.[6]

A few dozen men had been dropped on the wrecked 'drome soon after its capture, ordered to make it into an emergency landing field. They had few supplies, fewer arms. They had achieved wonders. They had even devised a kind of FIDO: if a stricken plane wanted to land at night or in poor visibility, the RAF erks would run along beside the runway exploding incendiaries salvaged from the German bomb dump. They received mail once a fortnight. They were forgotten men, they said, and they were not happy.

The German advance had come within a few miles of them and, two nights before, their entire guard had been found naked and stabbed to death at their posts, killed for their clothing by German paratroopers.

The next day Vincent begged a lift in an American Dakota flying back to England. They took him right to Ludford, landing without even calling control, and dumping Vincent in the middle of the 16 runway. Then, with a gay wave, they took off again while Vincent went in to see the puzzled control officer and tell him what was happening.

Vincent asked if any others of his crew were back.

They were not.

Was he again, as when he had first come to Ludford, an only flying survivor?

He turned into the met office. The sight of him stunned the girls for an instant. Then Wendy said, 'Oh, hello, Vincent,' almost casually.

But at the same instant, Paps shrieked, 'Vincent!' and rushed up to him and flung her arms around his neck. Vincent was surprised at how much he liked it and at the same time he realised how much he had suddenly come to want such attention.

'I can do with a lot more of this,' he said.

— 2 —

As soon as Vincent heard that Krink, Chiltern and Yarpi were safe he started organising a party. Any important event demanded a party and the escape of even half a crew from behind the German lines was certainly important. Bill was already reported a prisoner safe in a German camp and even Magnetic could still turn up – after all he had hurt his ankle and that would naturally make him slower. Perhaps the wretched Smiff would be their only casualty; such a successful escape from so dicey a do demanded a jolly party indeed.

Jackal was invited and came with Half-pint; he was still in plaster and so, he explained, Half-pint had circles under her thighs. For Krink he brought a black-eyed, long-haired, pale-skinned girl six inches taller than Krink himself. Her name was Petunia but Jackal had called her Sonja from the moment they met and now she was known as nothing else.

Vincent invited Paps. He had never taken her out before simply because he feared her reputation. He enjoyed her company in the Met office where she showed herself to be intelligent and even refined, but when by chance they met in a pub or at a dance her manner became suddenly sensuous and he knew he could not be more friendly with her and keep it platonic. She had accused him, once, of avoiding her and he had admitted it. 'That,' she said in just the seductive tone that Vincent feared, 'only makes me all the keener.'

H-H and Barbara were invited, and they brought two magic twin dogs, visible only to themselves. The twins were introduced to everybody and everybody had to discover what they were up to from what H-H and Barbara said.

'He doesn't seem to like you, old man,' H-H would say. 'I'm not surprised; even ordinary moustaches frighten him and your P/O Prune effort could stampede wild horses.'

Barbara would order her twin to beg or shake hands with some-body and, quickly, she would say, 'Uh-uh, darling, other paw! There's Mummy's angel; now you can go and sit by the fire.'

Suddenly H-H screamed at Jackal; 'Careful, you clumsy clot! You trod on Tinker!'

'What sort of a dog is it?', asked Jackal.

'A brown dog,' H-H answered blandly. 'Very rare.'

Whenever the dogs kissed, H-H and Barbara had to kiss too. As the evening wore on and the alcohol wore in, Tinker and Tinkerbell kissed more and more frequently.

Johnnie, resplendent in his new pilot officer's uniform, invited Wendy. To Vincent's embarrassment and Paps' annoyance, she came. Johnnie looked a little more dignified but acted even shyer than usual, so that with the reticent Wendy he made small impression in the generally rollicking company. But Barbara let Wendy nurse Tinkerbell and later invited Wendy and Johnnie to tea. Vincent overheard Johnnie accept and it made him furious.

Yarpi brought a sixteen-year-old called Laura. They were not a happy couple.

She stood in awe whenever the lovely Barbara or important-looking Wendy came near. Nor did Yarpi's company ease her mind. His face was disfigured with a mass of small cuts brown with cordite stains and he jumped a foot when H-H announced that Tinker was about to bite him.

Chiltern declined to attend; whether because Wendy was with Johnnie or because there was Drink (which he always spoke of with a capital 'D') nobody knew.[1]

Joe was out of hospital at last so for him the party celebrated his release as well as the return of his friends. He had found an Australian girl – a WRAN attached to some Navy post in Grimsby – and they amused each other immensely by exchanging graphic Australianisms, displaying so full a vocabulary of risque phrases that H-H suggested blending basic English with base Australian and dispensing with drawing-room French altogether.[2]

For some reason known only to themselves Joe and his red-headed companion (whom he called 'Blue') would collapse in spasms of laughter when either of them said; 'How's your dirty rotten form?'[3]

Krink observed that nothing like this had hit the States since

'Why did the chicken cross the road?'. 'And even that,' he pointed out, 'needed an answer.'

Paps was on duty in met at midnight and since the party was in the village, a mile and a half from control, she had to leave at about twenty past eleven. They feared that they would be a little unsteady on their bicycles, so Vincent said he would walk with her. He found it pleasant as they walked arm in arm through the cold night and he wondered to himself why, for more than a year, he had scrupulously avoided this girl's company.

Paps was flushed when they went into the light of the met office. Her normal high colouring shone even more glowingly against her clear, fair skin.

'I'm afraid night air and alcohol don't mix,' she said.

'Would you like me to stay a little longer?,' asked the girl Paps was relieving.

'Oh, no, dear! Thanks all the same,' said Paps quickly. She turned her face from Vincent to the Waaf and winked.

'Oh! Then I'll leave you two to, er, hold the fort.'

When they were alone Paps took off her jacket and loosened her collar, then stoked up the fire to a blaze. Vincent did not speak but watched her as she moved around the room. She walked over to the teleprinter and watched the weather messages ticking away to themselves. Then she drew her hand across her eyes and said, 'Oh, dear, I *am* tipsy. I can't even read these symbols.'

She walked unsteadily over to the rest-bed. 'I think I'll lie down for a moment.'

Vincent moved uneasily. He said, 'Would you like me to make you a cup of tea?'

'Oh, you are most dreadfully English!', said Paps crossly. Then, before Vincent could be offended, she added in her most provoca-tive tone, smooth as a whisper; 'No, dear, thanks. Come and sit here and talk to me.'

He paused, and Paps said, 'Switch off the lights; we can see by the fire.'

'I knew it would be like this,' Vincent said to himself as he looked at her nestling into the pillow, her fair hair waving around her face, her deep grey eyes half-closing a little slatternly, her lips almost trembling as they dimpled into a smile. 'I knew she would arrange this situation; why did I allow it?'

And, from his depths, he heard a voice say, 'Because you wanted her too, you fool! She excites you, she obviously wants you, take her and revel in it.'

He turned and took Paps' shoulders in his hands, bent over her and kissed her. She responded hungrily. She took his hands in hers and held them to her ample breasts, then ran them down her body and around her hips. Then with sudden tenderness she placed her hands behind his head and kissed him lingeringly, holding her body close to his, her eyes closed now, her breath fast and tremulous. Then she took his head in her hands and looked at him.

'You've nearly driven me crazy,' she said. 'You've tried so hard to be good I just couldn't resist you. Do you know what we've nick-named you in the Waaf's mess? 'Tall, blond and righteous', and we're all agreed it's a scandalous waste. Well, from now on you're my tall, blond and passionate.'

She ran a hand through his hair. 'Now go and make me that tea,' she said. 'I'm even less capable of working than I feared; I'm drunk as a skunk and I love it. When you bring me that tea I'll be inside this bed like a grown-up girl and I like plenty of sugar.'

'But you don't take sugar.'

'Tonight I want everything you have to give me; plenty of sugar ...'

'There I was,' said Jackal, 'forty thousand feet over the target, nothing on the clock but the maker's name, on my back, the navi-gator taking astro-sights out of the bomb-baby, and still going up.'

'What on earth are you talking about?', asked H-H.

'I'm telling Krink how to shoot his shot-down-in-flames-behind-the-German-front-and-escaped line.'

'Surely Krink can shoot that line himself.'

'The only line he shoots to me,' said Sonja languidly, 'is about what he's going to do now that he's back. And I wouldn't have him change that story for the world.'

'That story never changes,' said Jackal. 'It's just recast occasionally.'

'Is he really an Honourable?', whispered the Wran to Joe.

'Yep. A fair-dinkum Honourable.'

'Stone the crows!'

'Aw, that's nothing,' said Joe, loath to be outdone. 'I would've been a Lord if one of my crusading ancestors hadn't castrated himself negotiating a double chastity belt.'

'Gee, but you're fabulous, darl! Trust your dirty rotten form.'

Their laughter was rudely cut short. An air-raid siren sounded – so loud that it seemed to be in the next room. Immediately the lights went out amid surprised whispers.

'The Huns have got a bloody cheek,' Jackal's voice was heard to say. 'Raiding us at this time of the war, and with a party on.'

'And with the weather as foul as it is.'

'I don't believe it is a raid.'

As if to give this view the lie, there came a thud like a muffled explosion, and almost instantly the room was lit with a ghastly glare and filled with putrid smoke.

'Incendiary!', exclaimed a voice. 'Put it out, quick!'

There was instant confusion; people running everywhere, a spate of bumping into and tumbling over ...

Then the light switched on and standing in the doorway ...

'Magnetic!' yelled Krink.

'You old bastard!' approved Joe, in his most affectionate tones.

'That entrance,' said Jackal, 'leaves Mephistopheles gasping in the wings. Please accept this honorary rank of ASM,' and whipping out his pen-knife, Jackal snipped six inches off Magnetic's tie and dangled the trophy from his breast pocket.

'You mean there isn't an air raid?' asked the Wran.

'I am the air raid!' said Magnetic, grandly.

'And a very welcome one,' said Jackal. 'Despite the fact that you overplay the part.'

'Oh, you are a lousy lot of cows,' said the Wran, quite unaware that what passes for tea-table chatter at the Methodist Lady's College in Wagga Wagga might be impolite for an English sergeant-major's wife. 'I've never been in an air raid and I thought I was going to see one at last.'

'While it lasted, that was as good as any air raid,' said Joe. 'Magnetic, what did you toss in here? A Molotov cocktail?'

'No. Just a Very pistol cartridge, green. Down the chimney.'

'Wacko!', said Joe. 'The green light! Just what we've been waiting for.'

'How's your dirty, rotten form?'

Magnetic glanced around the room. 'Is Vincent back?'

'The green light,' repeated Joe. 'He's doing fine.'[4]

— 3 —

Krink, Magnetic and Yarpi were in Squadron Leader Chiltern's office, standing at attention in front of his desk. Chiltern sat straight-backed behind it, looking at some notes in his hand.

'I had to write a report on our trip to Groninberg,' he said. 'One cannot lose a Lancaster without explaining it in some way. Naturally, I cannot know everything that happened. So I have you here to supply what little information I can't be quite sure of myself.

I'll read you what I've already written: I took off at thirteen-fifty-seven hours from Ludford Magna ... that's all routine stuff, until we come to – ah, yes, here. Approximately fifteen miles before reaching the target we received, without warning, three direct hits from anti-aircraft shells ... yes, Farlow, what is it?'

'First, sir, may we stand at ease?'

'What? By the look of you all sprawling about I thought you were at ease. Yes; fall over if you haven't got spines to hold yourselves up. And, Farlow, don't interrupt if you have nothing important to say.'

'I have, sir. Three corrections. We were twenty-five miles from the target, there were two direct hits and one near miss, and Graham distinctly gave you, not only warning, but an order for evasive action.'

'Really, Farlow. I said approximately fifteen, which is near enough, and often a near miss is worse than a direct hit and this is to be a *concise* account – I cannot record every syllable that our hysterical Graham uttered or I'd fill ten volumes. And please do not interrupt, Mr Farlow. You are not here to correct what I have written but to fill in a few blanks with answers that I could not know. I shall continue: The port-outer instantly became unserviceable allowing the captain no opportunity to feather ... yes, Farlow, what is it now?'

'To be more *concise*, sir, you have only to say, 'the port-outer seized'.'

'Farlow! It so happens that I am conscious of whom I am writing to and how to put my report as best as they will understand it.' Chiltern was so annoyed that he was losing control of himself.

It was useless to try to correct or even assist Chiltern. He had them here, it seemed, to read them his story so that they would substantiate it. They had been hit without warning, they actually bombed an observed German concentration although the bomb aimer, abandoning his post in the face of the enemy, deserted the aircraft. They did not fly in circles above where they were hit, nor was there at any time a shred of doubt in the captain's mind that N-Nuts was doomed; it could never have reached the Allied lines. Times were altered to fit his story (that was why they were fifteen, and not twenty-five miles from the target – to allow for the time spent circling) and at no point was Squadron Leader Chiltern made to appear less glorious or more fallible than in fact he had been. Indeed, Squadron Leader Chiltern emerged and unerring and heroic master of a terrible and, it seemed, almost single-handed ordeal.

They were all surprised when Chiltern said; 'Flying Officer Krynkiwski. As you were the senior officer in the area of the fire I am recommending you for the DFC.'

'But, sir ...' stammered Krink, bewildered.

'You must therefore have been in charge of what efforts were made there to save the stricken aircraft. I shall therefore suggest that you be decorated.'

'You were the senior ranking officer up aft,' said Chiltern. 'You must therefore have been in charge of what efforts were made there to save the stricken aircraft. I shall therefore suggest you be decorated.'

Chiltern took a letter from his 'Out' tray and said; 'This has been dealt with but since it is addressed to you all I am going to read it to you. It is a maudlin letter addressed to 'The Crewmates of Sgt Smith', from his mother and sisters. 'We heard as how some of you got back and we want to write to ask you to tell us just how our dear Jack got killed. He meant the world to us. Jack was our only man about the house. Please write and tell us the true story because we want to know.' I've written and told them what happened.'

'Is that kind, sir?' said Krink. 'A letter can be kept and cause sorrow for years. A personal visit and a soothing talk would be better. I'll gladly go if you're too busy, sir.'

'A novel way to wangle a trip to Blackpool, Krynkiwski. But how can you deliver a soothing talk when you tell a mother that her son was burnt to death?'

'Oh, I wouldn't tell her that, sir. Just say he died instantly; hero's way out … all that guff. It would be terribly unkind to tell his family he died in agony; they have enough sorrow already.'

'Do you never give any consideration to honesty and truth when you speak, Krynkiwski? The woman asked for the truth and you would fling her a pack of lies.'

'Decency is often more important than truth, sir.'

'Observing your company of late, Mr Krynkiwski, I am surprised to hear you speak of decency.'

'I mean decency in the big things, sir.'

'Surely morals are big things,' sneered Chiltern. 'These women have written a letter to this crew. As captain of this crew I have answered it. I told them the truth, as they requested; that Smiff was burnt to death having been badly wounded.'

Vincent was suddenly more angry than he could ever remember having been before. The true story of Smiff's death trembled on his lips, but instead, he said; 'You cannot know how Smiff died, sir. Perhaps he died of shock the instant he was hit. It would be monstrous to send your letter.'

'He did not die instantly, Farlow. You have told me yourselves that he was alive.'

'Possibly muscular reaction, sir …'

'You know and I know perfectly well that Smiff burnt to death, and that is what I have written.'

Outside Chiltern's office the four men exploded with protests to each other.

'He's deliberately altered the whole thing.'

'But only, he insists, to keep the account concise and uncomplicated.'

'I just can't see why he's put me up for a DFC,' said Krink.

'Can't you? I thought it was obvious.'

'I feel like starting a riot.'

'I feel like a drink.'

'I'll settle for a drink of tea,' said Vincent, and he strode off towards the met office.

Vincent was still so annoyed that he forgot to feel sheepish as he entered the scene of his recent revels. He was already inside when he noticed that Squadron Leader Gaffer was there, having strayed down from flying control. Joe was there too, and Wendy. Paps was off duty.

'Hello there,' said Wendy. She spoke brightly enough but her glance was cool. 'Enter the meteorological wizard!'

'What do you mean?', asked Vincent.

'This,' said Wendy, as she pointed to a map stuck on the wall. It was the map of a synoptic situation, and Vincent recognised it as the hurried work that he and Paps had done just a few hours before through the fug of romance and alcohol. Now Vincent blushed.

'It is without doubt the most remarkable weather ever to have been recorded over the British Isles,' said Wendy. She laughed and carried on; 'I notice with amazement that Moreton-in-the-Marsh not only had gale-force winds but also fog, in addition they experienced snow out of ten-tenths of cirro-stratus, despite the fact that the temperature was well above dew point. One cold front runs, not only *into*, but right *through* a centre of low pressure, and there it proceeds to *cross* a warm front like a glacier through the Gulf Stream.'

'How did you know it was my work?', asked Vincent.

'Because it not only shows your particular frontal technique, it also bears your signature. Like a true, proud artist you've signed it boldly.'

Vincent laughed. Then he became more serious. 'It won't matter, will it? I mean, nobody will get into trouble?'

'Luckily for you, and for Corporal Bartlet, no. There'll be no flying while this weather keeps up. So your neck is saved. Though it could have been serious.'

'That's what just occurred to me,' and Vincent's furious frown returned. 'Chiltern is just in the mood to court martial me on the slightest pretext.'

'Really?', said the Gaffer. 'Why?'

The whole tale came bubbling out; the bumptious report, the distortion of facts, the alteration of intent, the glorification of the writer.

'And what annoys me the most,' concluded Vincent, 'is that he caused the whole damned thing.'

'How do you mean, he caused it?', asked Gaffer.

'By being pig-headed about captain's prerogative. Bill gave him evasive action which he ignored.'

'Do you mean that Squadron Leader Chiltern's stupidity caused you to be hit?'

'Not quite. We'd have been hit anyway. But not badly enough to be shot down. And the stupid thing is that, apart from being slow off the mark, he did jolly well. He succeeded in flying the thing when I'm sure most pilots would have baled out, as Bill did. We'd all be prisoners now were it not for Chiltern. He could have told the real story and still come out well. But that's not good enough for Chiltern; his report must be text-book to the last.'

'In other words, his report is just a pack of lies?'

'Well, hardly that bad. He did lie about 'no warning', but mostly it's just avoiding relevant facts or using misleading words.'

'He has always struck me as a particularly honest man.'

'Oh, he gives that impression. And at times he is so damned honest it's a crime ...'

Vincent told the story of Smiff and the letter from his unhappy family.

'You mean he told them that Smiff burnt to death?' Wendy asked incredulously. 'Oh, the heartless beast! I feel I could ...'

She struggled for words that were polite and chose: '... could bang his head!'

'From what he has told me,' said Squadron Leader Gaffer, 'I had gathered that those were not your feelings at all.'

Wendy looked quickly at Gaffer and coloured to the roots of her hair. She dared not catch Vincent's eye. Gaffer sensed that he had hit a touchy spot and changed the subject.

'Anyway, Farlow, why aren't you wearing your Flight Lieutenant rank?'

'It isn't through yet, sir.'

'On the contrary, I know that it is. Something or somebody must be holding it up.'

With that Gaffer turned to Wendy. 'Well, if you're quite sure there can't be any operational flying, I'm off.'

Squadron Leader Gaffer encountered one aspect of Chiltern that very afternoon which reminded him of what Vincent had said. Chiltern had borrowed the GC's Oxford to fly down to RAF Hemswell[1] to see some friends. Weather bad enough to ground Bomber Command did not awe Chiltern. Gaffer was not in flying control when Chiltern took off, so Gaffer did not recognize the Oxford when it returned.

It so happened that at conference that very morning the squadron call-sign had been changed. Chiltern remembered, on returning to Ludford, that it had been changed but could not remember what the new code was. He decided to bluff his way out of it.

'Oxford Fox to Ludford,' he said on radio. 'Request permission to land.'

'Ludford to Oxford Fox,' said Gaffer. 'You can't land here.'

'I must land at Ludford. I must land at Ludford. Over.'

'Ludford to Oxford Fox. Are you in trouble? Over.'

'Not in trouble, Ludford. Not in trouble. Over.'

'Then bugger off back to Training Command. You can't land here; this is an operational squadron. *Out!*' said Gaffer firmly, making it obvious that he would stand no nonsense.

Squadron Leader Chiltern had to be careful what he said on radio in case the Germans picked up his message. He was also particularly eager not to mention his own name on radio in case somebody important heard it and realised that he had boobed. He decided on a very drastic course.

'Oxford Fox to Ludford,' he said. 'I am coming in to land. I am coming in to land. *Out.*'

Squadron Leader Gaffer could hardly believe his ears. He yelled and bellowed into the radio but the Oxford continued its approach. He fired red Very lights and flashed the red Aldis until flying control looked like pre-war Picadilly Circus.

Still the Oxford droned down. Gaffer picked up the phone and called the guardroom. 'Hello, sergeant? Arm yourself then hurry out to an Oxford that is just landing. Take the pilot into custody and bring him in, at pistol-point if necessary, to me, here, now.'

The sergeant did not march Squadron Leader Chiltern in at pistol-point. When he saw who the pilot was the sergeant, with admirable quick-wittedness, said; 'Er, I rather think flying control would like to see you, sir.'

Without answering and white with rage at his own stupidity, Chiltern strode past him. What the Gaffer said to Chiltern the ear-straining erks could not overhear, but when they emerged again into control office the two senior officers seemed quite friendly.

'Life,' said Krink, 'grows too complicated.'

'Cheer up,' said Jackal, 'it'll solve itself.'

'Solve itself?', moaned Krink. 'I dare not leave this bar. I am doomed to stare into this flat, watery beer for ever. Outside in the lounge, two women are waiting for me. One of them believes that wounds received on the Groninberg trip have rendered me impotent. The other believes, or wants me to believe, that the child she finds she is going to have is mine. How can I walk out there and face them *both together*? What one thing can I say to make them both happy and leave me clear? Was there ever a situation less likely to solve itself?'

'Oh, do introduce them! The dialogue between those two girls has such possibilities. But why are you worried about the girl who thinks you've been castrated?'

'She wants to marry me.'

'Despite your sad loss?'

'Yeah! It's incredible. She was playing hard to get and preaching marriage and things so I said, 'Well, let's get married some time', and it worked like a charm. Then, when I wanted to back out, I told her about my distressing wounds and she said – you'd hardly believe this – that sex isn't all that important and she'd marry me anyway.'

Jackal laughed and burst out singing; 'No balls at all, no balls at all. She married a man who had no balls at all.'

Krink grinned unhappily and said, 'Aw, hell, this ain't funny.'

Jackal stopped singing and spoke seriously. 'You can get rid of the fiancee by playing it noble,' he said. 'Give her the routine about, 'You would make this sacrifice for me? Oh, sweetest, how my selfish heart longs to accept. But I cannot let you do this thing. It is too much. The price is too high ...'

'Sure, sure,' interrupted Krink. 'I get the trend; 'I cannot let you do this thing.''

'Well, yes. Reduced to essentials I suppose that's it. But play it up a bit. Develop the theme.'

'Look,' said Krink. 'Why don't you tell her? Say I'm too upset.'

'But I've never met the girl.'

'Say I described her to you and you recognised her beauty the instant you walked in.'

'You don't get rid of a girl by telling her that! Hasn't she got a wart on her nose I could recognise her by? That might do the trick without further effort.'

They peeped through the door.

'That's the fiancee with the two-way-stretch nose. And that's the little mother, sitting near Vincent and Paps, the one with the pink gin and the expectant expression.'

Jackal was back in four minutes, during which time Krink had lit and thrown away three Lucky Strikes.

'Has she gone?', Krink asked nervously.

'Straight to join a nunnery and weeping as she goes.'

'She was cut up, huh?'

'All joy is fled from her life.'

'I feel a cad.'

'You are a cad. Now, what about our little mother ...'

'What about her?'

'I've got a theory ...'

Vincent was sitting in a corner looking ill-at-ease. He kept twisting his drink between his fingers nervously as he looked at Paps who, on the other hand, looked radiant and eager.

She leaned close to Vincent as she spoke. 'Honestly, darling,' she was saying, 'I feel alive for the first time in months. You've no idea how long and how much I've wanted you.'

'Truly? I didn't know girls felt that way.'

'Don't you believe it! There were times when I was with you and I didn't know what you were saying. I only knew that you were close and my body ached for you. You must have felt like that, haven't you?'

'I – I don't know. I don't think I have; not without some expression of affection beforehand.'

'Oh, you wonderful boy! You really are innocent, aren't you? Don't ever change. Keep that manner though you become a *roué*. It will win you mistresses galore.'

'Would you approve if I became a *roué*?'

'Approve? Why should I care? I probably won't even know you then.'

'Do you mean that now, even now, you assume that ...'

'That this affair won't last? Oh, my sweetest Vincent, you really are a poppet! Never spoil good sex by wondering if it's going to last.' She closed her eyes an instant and then said quickly; 'For God's sake book a room in this frowzy bug-house and take me upstairs to bed before I tear you to pieces.'

Vincent looked very steadily at his glass, but his voice was unsteady when he replied, 'I don't know that I want to.'

Paps' eyes, which he had seen so warm and tender, suddenly grew hard and cold and furious. 'You're a fool,' she said. 'There isn't a man in this pub who wouldn't envy you my company tonight. With my figure and my talents I'm the most bedogenic woman in this town.'

He started. 'The most – what?', he asked.

'You heard!'

'Excuse me,' Vincent said, rising. 'I have to see a man about a bitch.'

He stormed from the lounge into the crowded bar and ordered a drink. Vincent had been shocked. He admitted to himself that he had been a prig when he was eighteen but he thought he had grown out of that in the last three years. Suddenly he wished that he had never changed; if *that* was where the trend from puritanism led then he would revert to puritan.

'The celibate life,' he reflected, 'precluded these risks. Perhaps one sacrificed the greatest pleasures but one also avoided the greatest indignities, the greatest heartaches, the greatest shames. And,' he concluded his particular train of thought, 'the greatest mistakes.'

Suddenly he realised what impulse, what powerful weakness, had made him victim to Paps' lure. Reaction to fear; that's all it was. He had experienced it before, he now remembered, but that experience had been rather beautiful, with a sweet girl he had loved and with whom, under different circumstances, he felt sure he could be happily married.

The importance of the Paps mistake rushed upon his mind and swamped it. He had chosen her because he had wanted somebody and she had flung herself into his arms with such hot welcome, such ready response, that he had grasped the easy goal without considering whether or not it was the goal he wanted. The person he had wanted then and still wanted, wanted now more than ever, was Wendy. And now Wendy knew all about Paps; she had seen the swift *affaire* from the beginning and would now guess its ugly end ...

His introspection was cut short when he felt a heavy slap on the back.

'Vincent! Don't look so glum. Have a drink; help me celebrate.'

It was Krink and, looking as pleased as a dog in a forest, the wide-smiling Jackal.

'Celebrate?'

'Sure! An hour ago I felt a doomed man. I had two women after me. Waiting for me, they were. Lurking like anything. Sinister.

Inescapable. Now I am a free man. They are both gone – phoof! – forever. Thanks to Jackal.'

'Thanks, as you say, entirely to me,' agreed Jackal.

'You should've seen him,' Krink said to Vincent. 'This night-fighter had told me she was pregnant and wanted forty quid to get it fixed. But Jackal figured he could scare her off.'

'I first diagnosed the case,' explained Jackal, eager to present Vincent with the facts. 'She said she was pregnant, but she was drinking and smoking. But most girls go off smoking and drinking at such a time. Makes 'em sick. So I assumed she was lying.'

'Yeah,' said Krink, unwilling to have his story told for him. 'So Jackal says to her, 'You needn't give this horrible abortionist forty pounds – I shall attend to you with greater skill and without charge.' So we sling her in the car and shoot up to Lighthouse Hill.'

'And there we spread my greasy blanket on the ground and Jackal says, 'Now, my dear, if you will just lie down there I think we can manage this by moonlight and without anaesthetic', and he pulls out a shiny cut-throat razor.'

'You don't mention my acting, dear boy. The quiet intensity of tone, the flashing of the blade in the steely starlight ...'

'And when she sees him this dame just yells, 'No! Don't touch me! I'm not pregnant! Honestly, I'm not pregnant at all. Truly!' And she flees down the hill like a runaway ghost.'

'Leaving us with nothing to do but climb back into the car and return here to buy you a drink, dear Vincent. What will you have?'

'Terrific, it was,' Krink continued. 'Imagine. Got rid of two dames as easy as that. Would you believe it could be that easy to get rid of two dames?'

'Sometimes,' said Vincent. 'Sometimes it's dead easy.'

'Squadron Leader Chiltern sends his compliments, sir, and asks will you please come over to his flight office straight away.'

The messenger was a young sprog pilot newly posted to B Flight and the urgency of his message surprised Vincent. He hurried over to see Chiltern.

'Come in, Farlow,' Chiltern said as soon as he arrived. 'And close the door carefully behind you.'

Chiltern sat at his desk for quite a few seconds, looking Vincent in the eye.

Then he leant forward and said, 'So you believe that I murdered Smiff, do you, Farlow?'

The question was meant to surprise Vincent, and it did. But it did not surprise him as much as Chiltern hoped it would. Instantly Vincent realised what must have happened. Squadron Leader Gaffer always seemed a friendly, easy-going chap, but senior rank is quite a bond. Gaffer had obviously told Chiltern what Vincent had said; 'He caused the whole thing.'

Vincent glared back at Chiltern and thought, 'How like you to put it like that! To accuse crudely and hope to shock the other fellow onto the defensive. Well, I refuse to be put off by you; you ask me a brutal question and I'll give you a brutal answer.'

'Yes, sir. I think you did.'

Chiltern leapt to his feet. 'What?'

'It is not how I would have put it myself, sir,' said Vincent. 'It was not quite murder. But I have every respect for your regard for the truth. You asked me what I believed. I answered you truthfully. Yes, I do believe that you murdered Smiff.'

'Do you realise what you are saying, Farlow?'

'Only too well, sir. You didn't watch Smiff die. I did.'

For just one moment Chiltern was shaken. 'But I couldn't have caused it,' he said, and there was almost pleading in his voice.

Very quickly, however, he controlled himself. One could almost watch his mind at work; 'It was a mistake to have said that. I must assert myself before any possible thought of guilt gains sway.'

Chiltern looked sternly at Vincent. 'I couldn't have caused it,' he repeated, firmly. 'There was no opportunity to evade.'

'Graham ordered evasive action, sir.'

'It was an unorthodox order.'

'There wasn't time for polite preamble. As we now see, a man's life was at stake.'

Chiltern did not like this conversation at all. He had never supposed that he would be obliged to defend himself against this accusation. He had absolutely no doubt in his mind, now that he thought about it clearly. His action had been correct. A sudden shout in his ear to 'Dive port' is not correct evasive procedure. A captain must know what is happening, who is speaking, why advice is given; he is not just a servant to leap without thought or question to any order from any person. Chiltern did his best to square his receding jaw. His flabby cheeks still shook with indignation and his round, weak face shone with nervous perspiration, but his small eyes glinted pale and hard.

'Graham's decision was incorrect. If we were hit as a result of anyone's mistake that person was Graham. He should have given the correct order and he did not. The man was hysterical. That is evidenced by his very next action: deserting the aircraft – an act of cowardice for which I have recommended he be demoted to Ac/1 while he is held prisoner and dishonourably discharged when he is released.'

Chiltern looked at Vincent as if defying him to comment on this latest news. Seeing that Vincent was about to speak, however, Chiltern held up a hand for silence him and continued speaking himself.

'I once said to you, Farlow, and the whole crew, that I would make my crew the finest on this squadron. I also said that any man who tried to stop me I would remove. I was not speaking idly. I am glad Graham has gone, he did not please me. Another crew member who does not please me, Farlow, is you. I am therefore insisting that you be removed from my crew.'

He paused for just a moment but this time Vincent looked grimly at the wall behind Chiltern's head; he did not attempt to speak.

A trace of a smile touched Chiltern's lips. He thought he saw, in Vincent's silence, mute acceptance of his own authority and compliance of his own strength of will. 'In order to save you the embarrassment of this demotion from the flight commander's crew, however,' continued Chiltern, 'I shall request the Squadron Commander post you from this squadron. It is fortunate that I have been able to postpone you the acting rank that accompanies the post of navigation leader. In view of your conduct, of course, you will be posted as an ordinary member of aircrew and that will save you the added embarrassment of relinquishing rank that you would have only held for a week or so. Considering the seriousness of your offence, Farlow, I hope you will agree that I am being extremely lenient. A less just man may have let his personal feelings influence him. I was tempted to do so, believe me, but I can more readily forgive a hurt against myself, such as yours, than I can a hurt against my king, such as Graham's. This demotion is not yet official, of course; I am simply being as fair as I can and warning you what to expect. This way you can vacate your post more gracefully.'

'Thank you, sir.'

'Not at all, Farlow. I am sorry this has happened.'

'We are all sorry this happened, sir.'

Chiltern raised an eyebrow. Was this man still trying to fight him?

'Let me remind you, Farlow, it could have been far more serious.'

Yessir,' said Vincent. 'You might have killed us all.'

— 4 —

'... in a letter I wrote when I first came here I said it would be strange having a new crew. But I never expected anything as strange as this. The last burst of six ops we did in nine days. In that time we stopped a fixed gun over Saarbrücken wounding the bomb aimer. Then our Special baled out on Dortmund – virtually driven to it by this maniac skipper. That hectic Duisburg-Duisburg-Wilhelmshaven bash came in only forty hours (we did Wilhelmshaven without Gee, and my ex-skipper was killed by FIDO). And then he capped the lot by getting us shot down on Groninberg – bomb aimer captured and rear gunner killed. Imagine, all that lot in nine days! Plus a four day walk home. And now this caper. I'll leave Ludford almost happily just to be rid of the man ...'

'How formal are they on formal mess night?' asked Johnnie. 'I don't want to put up a black, especially when I'm with Wendy.'

'Judging by how it used to sound from inside the sergeants' mess, the officers are quite informal by about ten o'clock,' said Magnetic.

'Well, I've only been to one formal night myself,' said Vincent. 'It's not formal at all by comparison with peacetime. No ceremonial swords or passing the port.[1] Just best blues and rather a better dinner than usual, and dancing afterwards. The Air Vice-Marshal always comes. Oh, and you must be careful of his daughter – don't pick her if you feel like getting fresh with a popsie. If you really want to crawl to the brass hats, dance with their wives. They're so bloody happy to get them off their hands and drink with the boys. You must be dainty at supper, too, or Gaffer has a dig at you. He eats enough to choke a horse himself, but lowly pilot officers must nibble like mice. Personally, I think I'll leave after dinner.'

'Nonsense,' said Magnetic. 'Stay for a drink, anyway. I'll buy you one. Meet me in the bar straight after dinner.'

'Well … if you insist. But I'll be dull company.'

The bar after dinner was everyone's rendezvous. Small as it was, Vincent had been there some time before Magnetic found him. They bought two beers and took them outside into the lounge.

Magnetic had never seen Vincent so depressed. Yet it was not a hang-dog depression: it was militant, aggressive. Vincent had not told anybody of his clash with Chiltern and its impending sequel. The only explanation Magnetic could think of was that, since this was the officers' mess and Paps was only a corporal, Vincent could not bring her along and felt annoyed about it.

When, after a few drinks, Vincent had still not attempted to unburden his unhappy heart, Magnetic decided to follow this tack and see how far it got him.

'Not dancing tonight?', he asked.

'Dancing?', mocked Vincent. 'You dance with women and women are the devil.'

'Is that true bitterness I perceive in your voice, or are you just being true to Paps?'

Vincent banged his glass down. 'If women are the devil, then Paps is hell itself.'

'But I thought you two had fused together at last.'

'Fused? Yes, that's the word. We fused! But it caused a spark that blew us straight apart again. Too much voltage for me.'

'Then, if women are the devil and Paps is hell itself, what is Wendy?'

'Huh! I wonder.'

Vincent stopped staring at his empty glass, caught a steward's eye and ordered another drink. 'I wonder if it's Wendy. Or Chiltern.'

'Ah!' said Magnetic. 'That's it, eh? Chiltern!'

The steward brought the drinks. As he put them down Vincent said to him, 'Bring the same again.'

'We can't sir, I'm sorry. We're short of glasses.'

Vincent took his glass and drained it at a gulp. 'Then fill that one up again,' he said.

There was an intensity in the way Vincent drank and ordered another that Magnetic had never seen in him before. He was not drinking for the pleasure it could give. He was not even drinking to forget; he was drinking, it seemed, to help him remember, to intensify the misery he felt. Magnetic decided to try to change Vincent's mood.

'You mentioned your stupid illusion of success just now. Why illusions?'

'Because I'm a triple flop. A flop at being an aviator. A flop at being virtuous. A flop at being wicked.'

'I wouldn't call winning the BEM being a flop.'

'Oh, that! It signifieth nothing.'[2]

'Let me decide that, will you? Tell me how you won it.'

'Shoot my line?'

'Yes. 'There I was …' Tell me how a flop wins a gong or else I can't agree that you're a flop.'

'It was a fiddle.'

'Nonsense! As a flop you're a failure and unless you tell me the story I insist you're a success.'

'All right!'

Vincent looked Magnetic in the eye with something of an alcoholic twinkle. 'But first, where's that bloody steward? I want a drink.'

'It was in Crete,' Vincent started. 'I had just baled out for the third time in a month. I landed in the town we had been bombing and found it empty. I had been shot down raiding a deserted town. To top it all, inside ten minutes the Germans started raiding it too.

Isn't war intelligent? Twenty-four Dorniers gave it hell – and me the only Allied target for miles. It's damned funny. And they didn't even scratch me.'[3]

'When the raid was over I started looking around, for food et cetera to sustain me while I tried to catch up with the Allies. The most interesting establishment which had been hit was a bank; I hid in its vault during the German raid. Almost next door was a shop with suitcases. So, on a hunch, I took the largest suitcase, put in it a few scraps of food I found, then crammed the rest of the space with money, the largest denomination notes I could see. Then I hurried after the retreating Australians.[4]

I caught them at the coast and managed to join the evacuation, then made my way to Alexandria. The first thing I did there (where's that bloody steward? I want a drink!), was go to a bank. I dumped my money on the counter not very hopefully and said, 'I suppose this stuff is valueless?'

The teller looked at it, counted it, and said, 'On the contrary, it's worth almost three thousand pounds.'

And then I spoke a very good line. I said, 'Well, I'd like to open an account.'

'This, remember, was straight after being shot down for the third time in one month – an astonishing run of luck, both good and bad – and I was very fed up. I had money. Nobody knew who or where I was. I didn't feel like flying any more.[5] So I decided to stay in Alex. I rented an apartment, bought a car, found myself an exotic Greek mistress and went out that first night and painted the town red. Next night we went out and gave it another coat. There wasn't much money couldn't buy in Alex despite the war, and I started living like a king.'

Magnetic raised an eyebrow. This seemed strangely unlike Vincent. But he said nothing, and Vincent continued.

'But it was costing money. Real money. After five months I only had a few hundred left. The end was coming. It only accelerated things, then, when my Greek lovely pinched what cash was left, stole my car and vanished.

'I couldn't afford to be investigated; I just had to let her go. But

I had been thinking about this day for some time. I had planned what I should do. So I started growing a beard and set off to walk to Cairo.[6] I took my time, I didn't eat much, I let myself get generally run-down so that by the time I reported to the RAF in Cairo I looked pretty dreadful.

'But I dragged myself into RAF HQ, saluted as smartly as I could, and said, 'Sergeant Farlow reporting for duty, sir' – another rather good line.'

'Naturally, they asked me where I had been and what I had been doing. I told them that I had been picked up by the Germans after baling out, but managed to escape. *Then*, I told them, I joined up with a gang of resistance bods and started the Voice of Crete anti-German broadcast.[7]

'Now, it so happened that there had been such a radio on Crete, and it had operated until just about the time I left Alex. The leader had some code name and the Germans put a price on his head. They must have got him because he vanished and the radio stopped.

'So I told RAF HQ that I was this chap! That I had worked with the resistance for five months but was advised to leave when the reward was offered because Crete was incredibly poor and for that much money I would probably be betrayed. Resistance found a small boat, I explained, and with one other chap, I set out to sail for Africa. The other bloke died of exposure, I committed his body to the deep, but I made it, so; 'Sergeant Farlow reporting for duty, sir.'

'They couldn't really check my story. The beginning was true: I had been shot down. The end was true: this fellow had vanished from Crete. I had even brought a boat to show them ... They believed my story and gave me the BEM. *That* makes me a flop, surely.'[8]

Magnetic's puzzled frown softened. 'It was a just reward for effort,' he said. 'Look at all the hard work you did to get it.'

Then he added, 'Watch my beer, will you?', and walked away into the crowd, exchanging a word with Johnnie and Wendy on the edge of the dance-floor.

Wendy, thought Johnnie, was undoubtedly the prettiest girl in the mess, and she had danced with him more often than with anyone else. In her company, with his new officer's uniform and the dignity he felt it gave him, he seemed almost suave.

Watching them, Vincent held his glass so tightly that his knuckles strained white. He hoped the glass would break, and cut his hand. He felt vicious.

'Would you mind if I take that glass, sir?' The steward was back again.

'That's Pilot Officer North's beer. You can't have it.'

'But we're very short of glasses, sir.'

'Well, you can't have that one.'

The steward went away and left Vincent with his thoughts; heavy, black, unpleasant thoughts. 'Hey, come back!', he called the steward. 'Bring me another drink.'

'Do you really think you want another drink, sir?' The steward was old enough to be Vincent's father.

'Of course I want another drink,' slurred Vincent vindictively. 'Why d'ya think I ordered it?'

'Very well, sir.'

Vincent was trying to think about Chiltern and the war and how much he hated them both. But time and again he found himself thinking about women: Wendy and Paps. He had been a fool on both counts, he told himself. He could have won Wendy if only he had done something about it instead of acting shy. And Paps! What a coy, inexperienced fool he had been with Paps. She was a magnificent creature and she had shown herself tender and sweet at times, too. He could have had his pick: a beautiful woman as his girlfriend or a beautiful woman as his mistress. And he had lost them both; one because he would not be too audacious and the other because he would not be audacious enough.

'Really, sir,' said the steward beside him, 'we must have that glass. Mr North isn't in the mess. And the beer's flat anyway.'

'Look!', said Vincent. 'Go t'hell. That's m'friend's beer.'

His voice started to rise in pitch and volume. 'He told me t'watch it. Can't pinch m'friend's beer. Go t'hell! M'frien's ...'

'Hey, Vincent, quiet,' said H-H, who had suddenly appeared beside him.

'He wants t'pinch m'friend's beer.'

'No, he doesn't. He just wants the glass. We're short of glases.'

'He *does* want t'pinch m'friend's beer!' roared Vincent.

'Quiet.'

'I won't be quiet. I'll punch anyone's nose who lays a hand on Magnetic's beer.'

'But Magnetic doesn't want it. He's gone. He's taken a popsie home.'

'He has not!' snapped Vincent. 'He hates popsies. The last thing he said was 'women are the devil and grog's the shot, now watch m'beer'. That's what he said. Now you're all trying to pinch m'frien's beer ...'

H-H looked around him. He caught Jackal's eye and beckoned him over. Vincent was still waving his arms and making a lot of noise.

'Quiet,' hissed H-H. 'The Air Vice-Marshal's daughter is over there.'

'To hell with the AVM's daughter!' bawled Vincent. 'She can't have m'frien's beer ...'

Between H-H and Jackal, Vincent was dragged from the mess, heels trailing in the carpet, bawling 'M'friend's beer!' and 'To hell with the AVM's daughter!' in a loud but befuddled voice. Not many people saw it. Those who did and who recognised him said that he could not be himself tonight; there was nobody less likely than Farlow to be drunk and disorderly, they said.

At the Squadron Commander's conference next morning Vincent said he was not feeling up to *faux pas*.[9] He was not sure what official attitude was adopted to young men who were dragged out of formal mess calling down curses on AVM's daughters. He feared that he may not have heard the last of it.

The conference was short. Weather was still terrible and Bomber Command could not fly although the army were in strife again and crying out for support. But as they were leaving, Vincent's heart leapt to his throat when the Squadron Commander said; 'Don't you go yet, Mr Farlow; I want to have a word with you.'

Vincent sat down again as the others left.

'I've been hearing a lot of things about you lately,' said the Squadron Commander. 'Mostly from Mr Chiltern. He tells me that you have spread malicious slander against him. Is this true?'

'That is not true, sir. Though it is not without basis. I disagreed with Mr Chiltern over our Groninberg report.'

'Tell me exactly what you disagreed with in that report. Be frank. This will go no further. I have to judge the truth from the facts I have and after hearing both sides of the story.'

'Well, first, that we were hit without warning. Graham did say, 'Dive, port, go', and Chiltern ignored it. Next, that we bombed a target. I let the cookie go because we were on fire and losing height. We were still over German territory but that's all I can vouch for. The rest of the bombs we simply hadn't time to drop; they were still on when we crash-landed.'

'I know. We found them in the wreck.'

This was an indication that the Squadron Commander was not against him and Vincent drew heart from it.

'As for spreading the story around, sir, that is an exaggeration. I was steamed up about it after hearing the report and I mentioned it in met office. Unfortunately it was overheard by Gaffer and I think that's who took the story back to Chiltern.'

The Squadron Commander leaned back.

'Yes. That is what I imagined had happened. Well, I must tell you that you have upset Mr Chiltern very much and that he has asked me to post you from the squadron, and to see that your promotion is stopped. Normally I might have done so. But you are lucky that, at the time Mr Chiltern was telling me what a fine chap he is and what a rotter you are, there were two reports on my desk. One was about him making a damned fool mistake forgetting his own call-sign, the other was a note that Group have accepted your wind idea and are putting it into practice officially. Then Mr Chiltern recommended his w/op for the DFC and I could see no justification for it. His real aim was to get himself recommended as well, because a crew member is seldom decorated and not his skipper.[10] So I was not prepared to take his word and I checked. Now I've heard your story it fits in with the facts I have. And I'm going to reverse Squadron

Leader Chiltern's requests completely. Your Flight Lieutenant rank is through, and you can put it up straight away and consider the appointment as Navigation Leader as official. But Mr Chiltern is right when he says the two of you would clash if you remained here. So I am posting *him* from 101. He hasn't a crew here now. I feel he's a valuable man if we can put him in the right place. So I'm kicking him upstairs. I've found an all-officer, all permanent-RAF crew in PFF. I'll send him there. He's a good pilot and a brave man. He'll consider a PFF posting a promotion and there he'll have a good chance of winning his precious gong.'

All Vincent's thoughts of the arrogance of office and the blindness of authority, which had festered in his mind during the last twenty-four hours, faded humbly away. A Squadron Leader has half a ring more than a Flight Lieutenant and can make life difficult for him, but a Wing Commander has half a ring more than the Squadron Leader and will often put things to rights.

'Thank you, sir,' said Vincent.

'You've earned it. By the way, I'll let you pick your own skipper this time, within reason. Got any ideas?'

'Haven't thought about it. Somebody bright, sir. Not a sprog. And not too brave to dodge a shell.'

'Then what about Cahill? He'll be flying again soon.'

'Jackal! Oh, fine! Yes, sir, I approve of Jackal.'

'Right. That's all then, Farlow.'

Vincent was about to salute and leave, but the Squadron Commander stopped him.

'And by the way,' he said, 'the AVM's daughter says junior officers never relax with her. She complains that they are awed by her father's position. So she asked me to tell you that, though frank, your comments were refreshing.'

— 5 —

Dear Vincent,

Since the liberation of Crete I've been trying everywhere to find out if you were dead or if you survived the boat ride to Alex.

As this letter testifies, I managed to last it out. We revived your broadcasts from time to time. The last winter was tough, but generally I think we managed to remain a thorn in Jerry's flesh.

I'm back in Australia now and finding it hard to live civilized; you will insist we aren't civilized, so you'll just have to come out here and let me show you. My family were pretty pleased when I turned up.

This letter is partly on behalf of the Cretan authorities. They asked me to find you; they want us both to go back to testify against war criminals and unveil a memorial to the underground and all that rot ...

Vincent could not keep his Crete exploits a secret now; when the time came he would want special leave and transport to Crete and all manner of official assistance. But he felt he had no need to fear transfer off flying at this stage. Surely a squadron navigation leader was more important than a radio announcer ...[1]

'There I shall be,' said Jackal, 'forty thousand feet over the target, on my back ...'

'Well, you'll be on your own. I'm not hanging around while you fly aerobatics over Germany.'

The new crew laughed. They laughed wholeheartedly, not like a new crew at all. Snow Fry, who had flown with Jackal before, was bomb aimer. Joe was back in the rear turret. All the others were the same except the new Special, Felix Newman, a tall Canadian Flying Officer inevitably known as 'Pussy'.

Dark with huge grey eyes and eyelashes which women swore were wasted on a man, Pussy's face was long and solemn, but when he smiled it came to broad life like lighting a Hallowe'en pumpkin with large, fine teeth. His spine, like everything else about him, seemed elastic. When he jived, which he did whenever he heard music (and whether or not he had a partner), he looked like a rubber cartoon character; one could picture him wearing a thin sailor-suit and doing a Disney hornpipe.[2]

For their first fortnight as a crew they were never sure whether they were at war or off duty. Every day they were briefed to fly and every day the weather stopped them. Sometimes they were briefed twice. It was their share of the Battle of the Bulge.

Protected from the Allied air forces by December fogs, the Germans counter-attacked and broke through the American sector. The American line cracked; a great slice of her army was cut off, then battered. Most of them were killed; Rundstedt took few prisoners. The army was learning again what it means to fight a war without aerial superiority.

Meanwhile the Germans had poured through the gap at Ardennes and advanced through Luxembourg and deep into Belgium, planning to reach the coast at Antwerp and cut the Allied armies in half. German propaganda promised to push the invasion back into the sea and, without an Allied air force to dispute it, the Wehrmacht advanced more than a hundred miles towards that goal and nothing seemed able to stop them.[3]

At dawn on Christmas Day, 1944, 101 Squadron were briefed, the take-off time was put back and back until noon. Then the trip was scrubbed – for the nineteenth time in fourteen days.

'Half a tour of abortions,' said Pussy.

'Abortives,' corrected Jackal.

'My mistake.'

'Not at all. Easy really. Same root.'

'At least we didn't get halfway there this time and have to turn back. I hate landing with a bombload.'

'Really? *You* worry about your landings too, do you?'

It was no joke; nineteen briefings, seven take-offs and no ops. But they made it fun.

On the night of the twenty-fifth, however, the Allies got their Christmas present: good weather at home and over Europe.

On Boxing Day they bombed Rundstedt's supply centres at St Vith. While the weather lasted, so did the attacks. The Allied armies countered: British and Canadians hit from the north, Americans from the south, to snip off Hitler's bulge. This time, too, when they called for air support they got it. Soon the pincers met; the bulge was cut off and the front was back in Germany. The Allied armies had more respect for the air force after that.

On this first trip since Nürnberg, Jackal was troubled with altitude toothache.[4] A faulty filling had caused acute pain in the reduced air-pressure at altitude. Jackal had had the same trouble during training, but it had responded to treatment.

'But now they're using real bullets,' he told the dentist. 'So take it out.'

'That is the only sure cure,' said the dentist, and took it out.

Jackal showed the tooth to Krink afterwards.

'Tonight,' he said, 'if I put it under my pillow it might turn into a ballet dancer. And if it does, after a respectable interval I shall give her to you.'

'And after that?'

'After that just call me 'Gummy'.'

Flying became fun again. After one daylight raid (the ratio of day to night flying was by now about fifty-fifty) five B Flight pilots moved into formation with Jackal leading. They were skimming level cloud-top at about 8,000 feet. Jackal was highest, with each following plane stepped down about fifty feet. Gradually he let down until the lowest plane touched the cloud. He forced them still lower and the bottom Lancaster was seen to cut a channel through the cloud. Still lower and the second bottom Lancaster was cutting the top layer off the cloud, with the bottom Lancaster still visible between two cloud-walls towering on either side. So they fell into line-astern and dropped down and down, their combined twenty-five thousand horse-power eventually cutting the hundred-foot-thick cloud layer right in half. Thereafter, whenever conditions permitted, cloud-cutting became a regular game.

Flying became beautiful, too. One early morning they took off through fog and burst into brilliant sunshine. Below them, fog lay thick and smooth over Lincolnshire. Just one hill rose to fog-top and on it, like a fairy castle supported by the clouds, stood Lincoln Minster, magnificent in stately solitude. It was a magic sight, mystic and unreal.[5]

'Vincent,' said Jackal, 'you're the photographer. Take the f2.8 and get a hand-held oblique of that.'

They unhitched the aerial camera and Jackal flew low circuits while Vincent captured the momentary magic.[6]

Another day over the channel they were flying behind a cold front when they flew out of a shower and saw, far below, the shadow of their own aircraft *surrounded* by a complete circle of rainbow. Jackal tipped up on one wing so they could all see their dazzling halo.[7]

Such experiences sent them on their way with a little wonder in their hearts. With Chiltern the sky had been a vast parade-ground, now they rediscovered it as an endless wonderland.

Jackal often made flying into a game. Returning from one night target Joe reported an unidentified aircraft.

'It looks like a jet, skip,' he said.

Magnetic, the Londoner, had a look. 'It's a buzz bomb,' he announced.

'Where is it?' asked Jackal.

'A few miles behind, fifteen starboard, low.'

'Steer me in front of it.'

'Okay, skipper. Five starboard.'

They watched the 300 mph buzz bomb close in behind them until it was slightly starboard and a hundred feet lower. At that moment Jackal dropped a wing, jabbed on right rudder and dived right across the buzz bomb's nose.

The buzz bomb bounced in the slipstream, rolled over and crashed. Jackal had toppled the automatic pilot and they all cheered lustily at this bloodless victory.

Back at Ludford they were full of their story. They reported it to Intelligence and Jackal claimed an enemy aircraft destroyed. Next day he was sent for by the CO. The greeting surprised him.

'Your function is to bomb Germany,' he was told, 'not to risk valuable bombers and lives fooling around with a ton of high explosive doing three hundred miles an hour. You're a damned fool. Let Fighter Command or Ack Ack deal with those things.'

Jackal told the crew of his dressing-down.

'But it was great fun, wasn't it? Let me know if you see any more, gunners, and we'll do it again. But this time we won't tell old Blood-and-Thunder.'[8]

Something that amused the crew but not Jackal was the return of Jackal's altitude toothache.

'I knew it must've been the wrong tooth when it didn't turn into a ballerina,' said Krink.

'It's all right for you but I've only got twenty-nine left.'

'Well, at one per trip they'll finish this tour!'[9]

Once again flying was fun, flying was beautiful, war could be a game. But flying could still be tough.

The target was Leipzig; a twelve hundred mile round trip against Rundstedt's revitalised Germans: fighting Germans; attacking, advancing Germans. This target demanded respect.

Against average opposition they bombed in a concentrated attack. They had almost left Leipzig's defences behind and were breathing easier again when flak burst nearby.

At first it did not seem serious, but next moment the starboard outer was on fire. Jackal cut the engine and feathered, then set off the built-in fire extinguisher in the engine nacelle but the foam failed to smother the flames.

And then, while Jackal and Magnetic were discussing what to do next an urgent voice screamed; *'Dive port! Go!'*

M-Mother spun down port but Jackal was an instant too late. Tracer streaked around the bomber and the shudder of her own guns was syncopated with dull, off-beat thuds as German cannon shells hit home.

Suddenly there came a scream that no man in that aircraft ever forgot: a shriek of fear and terror.

It was followed by a voice almost as terrible; 'Christ! Me bum!' I'll bleed to death!'

That was all Snow said.

His voice died in gurgles and gaspings for breath. They could not turn off the sickening sounds: horrifying rattles and dwindling, struggling breaths followed them as they twisted madly through the sky.

The wounded M-Mother flew Joe's hectic spirals sluggishly. She was not reluctant; her heart was in the fight. But she was weak.

Miraculously the tumult ended.

'I think we've lost 'em,' reported Joe.

Jackal brought M-Mother back to straight and level. He sent Magnetic into the nose to help Snow, then started checking the damage. Everybody else reported okay.

'Sorry, skip,' Joe added, after saying he was all right. 'I saw the bloke on our port first, but another one came in from starb'd.'

'So that's why my evasive action seemed too slow,' Jackal thought. But over the intercom, he said, 'Okay, gunners. We did very well to lose them.'

The fire which had beckoned their attackers had been blown out in the dive, but the port inner had seized and the port outer was over-heating. Jackal feared they might have to finish the trip on one engine.

'Navigator, we've lost some height but we're still at seventeen thousand. Work me out a gradual dive to bring us straight over Manston at one thousand feet.'

When Jackal finished speaking Magnetic reported; 'I think Snow's dead. He's hit in the buttocks. The muscles are all turned inside-out like lumps of cauliflower.'

Jackal did not comment, replying; 'Watch the port outer.'

They were in trouble this time. Five hundred miles was too far to fly happily on two; it would probably be impossible on one.

Vincent had bad news, too. 'A straight line for Manston takes us over the Ruhr. I suggest we go south. That way we reach our front earlier and we have a shorter sea-leg, and we can put down at Juvincourt if things get worse.'

'Right-ho, Nav. But work out what height we should maintain. In one long shallow dive we might make it, even on one.'

Vincent computed a course to take them home on the fastest safe route. He prepared a graph dropping to one thousand feet over England's east coast.

Manston was specially equipped: squads of ambulances, fire engines, crash crews and bulldozers there could handle a crash a minute.[10] Vincent's graph showed that in one hour they should be over a point north of Wiesbaden at 11,200 feet.

In fact, they reached it a few minutes late and by then they had fallen to 6,500 feet.

'Do you want a course for Juvincourt, skip?', asked Vincent. 'Champagne sells for eight bob a bottle and we could be in Rheims tomorrow.'

'I'd rather make Manston, nav. Better hospital there in case Snow's alive. We'll be right if the port outer holds.'

After two hours they should have been almost to Brussels and at 7,100 feet. But the port outer cracked. Temperature and oil pressure went simultaneously and Magnetic and Jackal feathered just in time. They flew past Brussels 4,600 feet below schedule height and sixteen minutes behind time.

'Shall I switch the IFF on to 'Distress'?,' asked Vincent.

'Might as well, nav,' said Jackal. 'If we're going to ditch we might as well have them ready for us.'

IFF (Identification, Friend or Foe) was an automatic SOS radio. Once on 'distress' it would be picked up and followed by the RAF rescue teams.

M-Mother was now flying only on her starboard inner. On one-quarter power she was limping home; slow, tired and dangerously low. Fortunately she was as light as possible: the bombs were gone and most of her petrol was used. Jackal did not agree with throwing guns and gear overboard; those few pounds made no real difference to the weight of a huge aircraft. Everything depended on that one Rolls-Royce Merlin.[11]

Their rate of descent had been terrifyingly steep at first, but as they fell into heavier air their fall decreased. At Wiesbaden they had been 4,800 feet below schedule. At Brussels they were 4,600 feet below schedule. At the coast of Belgium they were 1,800 feet below schedule.

But Vincent's schedule was only 2,700 feet.

They slid out over the sea at 900 feet.

This was the tricky stretch. Sixty miles of freezing sea. There was nothing they could do but wait. They simply looked at that starboard inner and prayed it would hold. It showed no sign of going wrong. Every note was correct; every gauge read perfection. Still it could not keep them at height.

Gradually, foot by painful foot, M-Mother was sinking toward the waves. That engine had to last another twenty-five minutes, that was all. It had flown hundreds of hours and tens of thousands of miles. Now it *had* to last a little longer: just half of one hour, another fifty-odd miles.

They were at 350 feet when they saw the coast. Manston was lit, waiting for them. While they had watched that starboard inner, hoping helplessly, a hundred faces on shore had tracked them across the channel.

'It's happening as you see it in the films', thought Krink. 'A scene of the aircraft skimming the water. A scene of the crew watching, praying. Then a flash to rescue control, with worried friends watching the plot. All it needed was a girlfriend in air-sea rescue and this was the peak of a dozen scenarios; a chance for some wizard silent acting. All the actors a-tip-toe with the audience, were dreading the splutter that would spell disaster by just a shrinking gap of water.'

They came over Manston at 200 feet. 'Liedown-Mother on one,' said Jackal. 'Wounded on board. Request emergency landing.'

Control answered, 'Roger Liedown-Mother. Standing by. You may pancake.'

The Manston runway is huge; Tiger Moths can take off across its width without leaving the tarmac.

But Jackal could not manoeuvre, he had to land the way he was heading.

M-Mother was off the runway and bumping on turf when she finally stopped.

As he cut that one wonderful engine, Jackal spoke a line that was often quoted thereafter; 'I have two firm friends: Mr Rolls and Mr Royce.'[12]

The doctor said that Snow was dead. 'He died almost instantly. Shock. His wounds are frightening but they shouldn't have killed him.'

All the crew suffered shock.

For the first time, Joe had been sick in the air. Yarpi was pale and shaken. Jackal was cursing the dentist. In the midst of their combat he had been attacked with toothache.

Least upset was Pussy Newman. But he had only recently started flying. This was his first dicey do and the effect of such experiences is cumulative.[13]

The crew waited at Manston so as to bring both the patched M-Mother and their dead comrade back to Ludford. Pussy was horrified at the sight of Snow's beard. He had never seen a corpse before and did not know that human hair grows many days after death.[14]

Joe could no longer keep his illness a secret. The MO at Manston had questioned him at length, and impressed on him that he must report sick as soon as he returned to base. Joe was embarrassed by this spotlight on his weakness and reverted to Australian vernacular to cover his blushes. 'Dicken a bloke didn't feel much of a grouse old galah,' he said.[15]

Jackal reported his return of altitude toothache.

'I'll tell you what's really been happening,' the dentist said. 'You have had an altitude toothache once and once only. That was the first time you got it during training. But your subconscious mind associated toothache with altitude and there began your trouble. Right. When you started flying ops again after a long rest your subconscious was upset about it. Our subconscious mind wants to make cowards of us all. So it tried to give you toothache so severe that you wouldn't be able to concentrate on flying. I thought this was so the first time you came to see me. But I still took the tooth out because that was the best form of psychological treatment. If you remember, I also gave you a long speech of why this would cure it. All psychiatric suggestion. When it happened a second time I *knew* it was psychological but I still thought the subconscious might respond to physical treatment so I extracted that one, too. It is possible that, in time, this method might cure you.'

He smiled. 'But you may not have enough teeth to finish the treatment. Now you have shown me which tooth you want extracted this time I must refuse. You have terrible teeth. As a dentist I assure you they are dreadful. But amidst this rubbish is one fine, flawless, perfect tooth and this is the one you want me to extract.[16]

'Instead, I want you to do this. Recall the trips when you have had toothache. They've been the tough trips; the times you were worried, yes? Well, that proves that it's psychological. Were it physical, you'd *always* get it at exactly the same altitude. But this time you got it when you were actually going *down*. Impossible. So when it happens again, if it does, just say to yourself; 'I have not got toothache, it is imagination', and you'll find it will go away.'

'Might it be a similar thing that makes my rear gunner sick?'

'Almost certainly.'

'But the MO has dismissed natural medical grounds as a cause and wants to reclassify him LMF.'

'Oh, dear, I shall be in trouble with the MO. Don't tell the MO I suggested it, then, but advise your gunner to appeal to the Senior Base MO straight away. If it has a psychological origin, they'll find it.'

They were given a rest before they flew again. When they returned to duty a new bomb aimer and a new rear gunner awaited them. They were both Londoners who had flown together before. Bomb aimer Bob Kellogg was a huge boy, over six feet tall, fifteen stone and shapeless, with black hair, a round face and a delightful voice.

Bob had more nicknames than any other man on the squadron; Corn Flakes; Crispie; Snap, Crackle or Pop; Dog's Breakfast; All Bran: Bob answered to them all, but the most popular one was Roughage. His girlfriend was known as Regular, and everywhere they went they were greeted by cries of; 'Keep Regular with Kellogg Roughage!'

Their new rear gunner was a cockney named Ray Payne. He was slight and nimble with bright black eyes and a flashing smile. Payne wore a DFM, won during his first tour. Both newcomers were Pilot Officers so that Yarpi became the only non-commissioned member of the crew.

They were named 'the dice crew' almost immediately. Between them they had certainly survived more than their share of dicey-do's. Bob, Vincent and Ray had baled out and wore golden caterpillars. Everybody but Pussy Newman had been shot down at least once, Bob and Ray had been shot down twice and Vincent four times. They once worked out that, between them all, they had written off over twenty aircraft worth almost a million pounds.

Their first target was Tomaszow in Poland. The story was that, under political pressure, the RAF had been committed to give close support to the Russian army.

''Ere!', said Ray. 'Wot do they mean 'close' support? Russia ain't close, it's two farsand bleedin' miles away!'

The target was a bridge seventeen miles from the Russian front. To fly to Poland and back would leave very little weight for bombs, so the authorities suggested going on to land in Russia after bombing Tomaszow, then reloading and bombing another target for the Russians *en route* home. The Russians replied; 'We can't spare the petrol.'

It was a disappointing answer but not altogether unreasonable. To fuel five hundred bombers for the return trip would take over a million gallons of petrol. Perhaps it genuinely was more than the Russians could spare.

So the RAF had to plan it differently. Navigation was the main problem. Poland was far beyond Gee range. H2S would be effective but not all aircraft had it and up-to-date maps of Poland were not available even for those who had H2S. They could not afford to waste petrol searching for the target, so they asked the Russians to send out one aircraft a few minutes before TOT to drop a flare over the bridge.

And the Russians replied; 'We can't spare the petrol.'

Britain could spare 500 bombers and 3,500 valuable men and £2,500,000 worth of bombs, but Russia could not send one small plane seventeen miles!

Nobody was very surprised. Any man who was obliged to deal directly with Russians knew how infuriatingly unco-operative they always were. Even, as in this case, when you were trying to help them.

'They were not only unco-operative,' said the intelligence officer, 'they were downright hostile. They seemed to be thinking: 'You've promised to fly this raid and we're going to make you keep that promise. We don't intend to help you. One of these days we're going to fight you, and the more British airmen who are killed now the less we'll have to kill then.'

Krink summed up squadron feelings when he said; 'We might as well fly the few extra miles and bomb Moscow straight away. We've got the power to do it, now. It'll save a lot of trouble later on.'[17]

They all resented the prospect of this dreadful, useless, wasted trip. With heavy hearts they walked out to their aircraft.

Jackal had gone out early to see if he had left his helmet in his cockpit after their morning air test. As he climbed into M-Mother, he heard a noise up forward. Looking up quickly, he saw Yarpi in the cabin. The covers were off the magneto switches.

Yarpi spun around. His eyes were frightened. He stood, trembling, a screwdriver in one hand and a spanner in the other.

'Were you tinkering with those switches?'

Yarpi did not speak. He looked wild-eyed at Jackal and his moist mouth quivered.

'You've disconnected those wires,' Jackal said. 'I can see them from here.'

And he added, incredulously, 'That's sabotage!'

'Yes,' screamed Yarpi suddenly. 'It's sabotage!' He turned back and started pounding the instrument panel wildly, plunging the screwdriver through dials. He smashed the rows of switches with the spanner, screaming, 'Sabotage! It's sabotage! It's always been sabotage and it's always been me! Not Schydt but me!'

Yarpi hit the heavy windscreen so hard it cracked. He struck it again, furiously, and then again, enraged because it would not break.

'I'm glad you caught me,' he screamed. 'Now you can gaol me or shoot me. But I won't have to fly. I won't get burned again or hear my friends get killed.'

Jackal restrained him. Yarpi offered no opposition and started to blubber. 'What do they expect? I can't stand it. Long ago I had a fit. I could have been grounded then. But I flew on. Really, I've been brave.'

He whined miserably, tears lining his pathetic, exhausted little face.

'Yes, Yarpi,' said Jackal, leading him away. 'Really, you've been brave.'

— **6** —

The Specials' section was delighted. It had been decided that Specials could fly on all raids, including daylights. It had been argued, previously, that Specials were only needed to jam night-fighter messages. Now it was agreed that most daylight raids were close support against the German army who used radio, and that army messages could be jammed while the force flew over the front in the same way 101 had jammed them on D-Day.

Almost immediately they were given a daylight raid on Essen. Met had forecast cloud and light winds over the Ruhr so PFF used a new technique. Aircraft equipped with H2S sets which enabled targets to be bombed accurately through cloud released, not candle bombs, but coloured parachute flares at the point at cloud-top where bombs to hit the target should reach the clouds.

Bombs aimed accurately at the floating flares should land just as accurately as if they had been aimed at markers on the ground. True, the flare would slowly drift off the target, but each flare only lasted a short while. Target flares would be constantly renewed and the master bomber would order by radio which flare was currently accurate and was to be used for aiming. Any sceptic who thought the ruse inaccurate was soon silenced by the results.[1]

Cloud-top was a little higher than forecast, at 8,500 feet. If this attack missed the target it would be an expensive failure; more than a thousand heavies were engaged. Opposition was not inconsiderable even for the Ruhr, but German fighters seldom managed to burst through the RAF fighter cover.

The bombers found it frankly dull. All that was to be seen of the target was a green or red flare floating beneath a tiny parachute, above a passive, dead calm ocean of cloud.

Then suddenly the cloud shook, and rapid ripples destroyed its calm, like the smashing of clear reflections when a trout jumps from a placid pool.

Instantly every bomber in the force was shaken by a blast-wave from some mighty, as yet unseen, explosion. And then, as they looked down a little fearfully, they saw the cloud-top open in a mighty billow. That endless cloud, almost two miles high, was broken open and flung aside by the flame and force of the greatest explosion that any of them had ever seen. A mushroom of smoke poured up through the cloud and, curling and rumbling, rose to the height of the bombers themselves, telling its terrible story of destruction.

In awe, that mighty bomber force turned for home, a little fearful of what they had done.

At debriefing, Vincent was talking with Krink and Magnetic when Johnnie Muller drew them aside.

'You saw that great explosion?', he asked.

'Of course.'

'My bomb!', said Johnnie.

In undiminished hate of Nazis, Johnnie still dropped his eleven and a half pound bomb every trip.

That night's newspapers told the story:

'After the biggest of all daylight raids, by a force of well over a thousand RAF heavy bombers, Essen is tonight a city of fires and smoking ruins. This mighty blow by a mixed force of our heaviest bombers, which dropped between four and five thousand tons in half an hour, brings the total on Essen during the war to over 35,000 tons. The 450 square miles of the Ruhr contain not a single town of any industrial importance and not a single major factory of any value. It has been devastated beyond recognition.'[2]

The flyers were happy. The RAF had flown the 'biggest of all daylight raids'. They had led the way in the air, and now that changed conditions made the tactics wiser, they had outdone the Americans at their own game.

But a little of the Specials' elation had gone. Two 101 aircraft were missing. Two Specials who would have been in the mess tonight had they not started flying daylights.

Altogether, war in the air was not becoming as easy as most of them had hoped. Losses generally hovered between two and four percent. It was better than the old days, much better; and now that they were flying so successfully it seemed more justified. But a tour had been increased from thirty to thirty-six trips.

In thirty-six trips at three percent losses, a crew had a 108 percent chance of being killed in one tour.

Some men on the squadron had flown over sixty trips, but the experienced flyers flew better and were safer. More flyers were lost on their first six trips than at any other stage of their flying. Until then, they lacked the experience that training cannot teach. War itself is the final schooling. After five trips a keen crew are alert to most of the enemy's tricks. They have learnt not to gawk in wonder at what goes on around them but to recognise each event for what it is and, if necessary, get out of the way of trouble.[3]

But even the best crews could be unlucky. In fact, good crews could even be murdered.

The target was Wanne Eickel, Eastern Ruhr. It was a daylight attack.[4]

The Squadron Commander was flying S-Sugar, one of those fantastic aircraft that never die. She had passed the hundred trips mark, more than twice as many operations as any other aircraft on the squadron, and still she flew and always came back. She had just been in for a 'major' – a complete overhaul. She had four new engines, all American Merlins, for Rolls-Royce could no longer meet the demand for these engines and had supplied the blueprints to the United States.

Taking off for Wanne Eickel, S-Sugar lost her starboard inner. To 'go round on three' was not particularly healthy, but it had often been done before. They set course a few minutes early hoping, at reduced speed, to start ahead of the main force and still be with them at the target.

Somewhere over France another engine had to be feathered. Valiant S-Sugar flew on with two engines, dropping back further and further.

They watched her, a mile or so behind, plugging on to the target.

Foolish? If it were foolish then World War II was won by fools. Bomber Command did not turn back. S-Sugar had bombed a hundred times and she would bomb again. That was the spirit which drove her.

But it takes more than spirit to drive an aeroplane; it takes engines. And S-Sugar had only half her engines. They watched her, and they watched a new Messerschmitt rocket fighter flash up behind her, 100 mph faster than any Allied fighter.[5]

S-Sugar had hardly started to evade when she blew up.

Back at Ludford, Barbara was sitting in the Riley as usual, waiting for H-H.

As one of the last crews was walking in, she asked, 'Has the Squadron Commander landed yet?'

'No, Ma'am. And he's not going to. A squirt put a burst into his bomb bay and he blew up.'

Barbara said, 'Thank you', and let out the clutch.

Not until they saw her driving off alone did they remember that H-H flew with the Squadron Commander.

They watched the snappy little Riley, a streak of green speeding along the perimeter track. They noticed that it did not turn off towards the village. It was going straight, faster and faster, skimming over the mile-straight stretch of tarmac. It seemed to bounce a little at the end.

That was when it ran off the tarmac and over the turf. Then they saw a sudden, vivid orange flash and, a few seconds later, heard the muffled, grinding roar as the Riley hit a tree at full speed and exploded.

Not long afterwards the American Merlin was withdrawn from bomber operations and existing stocks relegated to Training Command.[6]

— 7 —

'I enclose a copy of *The Med Student* which includes your article on altitude toothache. Your extraction treatment for a psychological ache was considered extreme. The Learned Company supported you, though, pointing out that RAF practice would be more conversant with altitude toothache than we students. (Why are professors always so dashed pompous?) Anyway, Robert, thanks for writing a jolly provoking article. Which brings me to my reason for writing.

An article on morals in the services (with a medical slant somewhere to make it qualify) would give *The Med Student* quite a fillip. Do you think you could write it for us? I mentioned it to old Potter and he said that the topic was not only unsuitable but that he had known you from a boy and was certain you would not know sufficient of the subject to write on it, and he most definitely thought we should be overstepping the mark to ask you to enter the fray, as it were, in order to find out. But if you could see your way clear …'

Jackal flicked the letter with the back of his hand. 'So from here on, dear boy,' he said, 'sex for me is a Medical Challenge. 'Pardon me, madam,' I shall say, 'I am conducting a poll.' And then I shall do any damned thing I like and lay my conscience at the feet of science.

'Come off it,' said Vincent. 'Don't blame science because you're a rake. You're like one of my navigators who swore his calculations were right and tried to blame a ten mile error on astronomy. 'The fault, dear Brutus, lies not in our stars but in ourselves.'[1] You should at least have the courage of your seductions.'

'Do they always talk like this?' asked a smooth, swarthy sergeant sitting next to Magnetic.

'Not always,' said Magnetic. 'Sometimes they talk about food.'

The sergeant was their new gunner. Yarpi was awaiting court martial. The sergeant looked the kind of man sometimes seen around ill-lit bars in smoky night-clubs sipping pernod and wearing sunglasses.[2] Actually his manner belied his appearance. He was respectful and unassuming. His name was Alan Nuffield. Before he joined the RAF he had never been out of Wales.

The first trip Alan flew with his new crew was full of excitement. Once more it was in daylight, once more it was the Ruhr.

When Bomber Comand flew in close support of the army they needed perfect weather. A few clouds over the target had prevented many a raid because, in doubtful visibility there would be scope for the tragic mistake of bombing the wrong army.[3]

It was expensive, however, to plan a raid, fly to the target, then turn back without bombing. Even a small force of three hundred bombers would waste more than half a million gallons of petrol. Some bombs they could bring back, but it was too dangerous to land with cookies so they always had to be jettisoned in the channel. In addition, it upset the aircrews. Even if they flew over a target, unless they bombed it was not counted as an operation and that hurt morale.

So Command hit on the 'free lance' idea. If a close support target was obscured, the master bomber could give the force permission to bomb free lance. They must then fly at least a further five minutes into Germany, where they could select any target they saw and bomb it. It showed what superiority the Allies now had in the air, though crews soon discovered that this new game could be dangerous.

The target was obscured when they arrived, and the master bomber gave them free lance. The whole force droned on over almost continuous cloud. After five minutes, one by one the Lancasters bombed and turned back. But M-Mother seemed unlucky. Underneath she saw only solid cloud. The sky around them was growing very empty and still they saw no cloud break with a target under it. Big Bob in the bombing compartment was growing quite anxious, but still he refused to bomb until he saw a target worth the trouble they had gone to.

After sixteen minutes, when they were sixty miles into Germany, all but one of the main force had bombed and turned back. Their only companion was another Lancaster with 460 Squadron markings which was flying beside them and had shared their patch of cloud-filled sky.[4]

It was bright daylight, and they were now without fighter escort. They were one of just two bombers wandering into almost central Germany looking, it seemed, for somewhere to be shot down.

'Germany is like some parts of the female anatomy,' said Jackal. 'The nearer you get to it the worse it looks.'

At last Jackal said, 'There's a gap! Fifteen port! It's small but you might see something.'

He swung M-Mother towards the patch of clear sky. As they

turned, the other Lancaster decided to come with them. Suddenly Bob spoke.

'I can see railway lines! Right five, skip. Bit more! Steadee. There's a rail-head down there; it looks like a coalmine. Right, right, steady. Steadee, bombs away.'

It had been a very quick run up, and so small was the gap that the other Lancaster had been unable to bomb. Jackal kept on course just long enough to get his target photographs, then they turned gladly for home. The other Lancaster turned with them, obviously deciding against flying on alone.

For ten minutes they droned westward and still he did not bomb. There were a few cloud breaks but underneath was always open meadow. It is surprising how little of any country constitutes a target.

Still the other Lancaster did not bomb. And still, thank God, the Germans ignored them. Within two minutes they would be within ten miles of the front. Unless he bombed now it would be too late.

Then they saw the village. They did not give it more than a glance; a village is not a target.

'Hell! He's opening his bomb bays,' announced Magnetic.

'Oh! the rotten bastard!'

They looked down at the darling little village. It had, perhaps, fifty houses. A creek ran through it from north to south, and a road crossed over a bridge then ran into a forest. It looked sleepy and delightful, a sweet little village which might have been in Devon or Oxfordshire or Westmorland. And now this oaf was going to bomb it!

The bombs went curling down toward the quiet villagers, all unmindful of their doom. M-Mother's crew watched the furthest bombs grow smaller as they fell, like a tapered row of church organ pipes, sharp-tipped and grey.

It was a perfect piece of bombing. The eleven bombs fell in one straight line, starting at the eastern tip of the village. There were ten thousand pounders and one cookie. The thousands straddled the whole village, one hit the bridge, then the cookie landed just on the edge of the forest.

As it did so, even before its own explosion had subsided, it was followed by another and even greater blast. Two more eruptions followed, deeper into the forest; sympathetic explosions set off by the first. They had unknowingly bombed a precious ammunition dump.[5]

Back on the squadron, Yarpi and Joe had been making a fuss.

Joe had reported to Base and, within a few minutes, his illness had been diagnosed as neuro-diabetes. When excited and over-anxious about flying he suddenly had an involuntary attack of diabetes – the effect was intense though short-lived. Joe insisted that the MO who wanted to reclassify him LMF was either a fool or a spiteful villain, and should be punished. Nobody paid any real attention to Joe's pleas. Few bothered to wonder how a man would feel to be innocently branded LMF. Joe lay in hospital and sulked.

Yarpi was doing everything in his power to avoid what looked like an extremely serious charge. Sabotage of one's own aircraft was so rare and serious a crime that he knew his punishment would not be light. He, too, was appealing for medical justice. It really was a pity that he had not reported his epilepsy when it occurred. Few people would blame him for being sick. But sabotage was a different and far more serious matter. The medical people were not being very helpful. Even if they proved the illness, they explained, that did not excuse sabotage.

Yarpi's real hopes were just blossoming. He was trying to exert political influence in South Africa and through the Union officials in Britain. Perhaps, if he could show that his case really came under Union and not RAF jurisdiction, perhaps then he had a chance …

The next time the squadron flew over the Ruhr they flew only a few hundred feet high, in daylight, and they flew without loss. The Ruhr, Hitler's arsenal and Europe's most difficult and most bombed target, had fallen at last to the Allies.

The Ruhr, the army said, fell without any great battle.

Without any great battle! The battle of the Ruhr was never seen by soldiers. It had been a hybrid battle between a defence system and an air force. It was a battle which takes its place amongst the military giants. It had been waged throughout terrible years, back and forth, at fearful cost and sickening loss. It had ended, like all mammoth battles, in a crashing climax of attackers utterly triumphant and defenders utterly routed.

After the battle came the army.

A very different battle, smaller but as desperately contested, was decided after waging and waning between two continents, between two governments, between two corps of diplomats and two air forces. It was called in the Kroonstad Press 'The Battle of Hero-Harry van Rijn', and it hinged on a sabotage charge which they said was trumped up by jealous senior officers.[6]

The Jaapie supporters had won. To Britain and the RAF, Yarpi's future hardly warranted international tension.

When he took his jubilant departure, Yarpi destroyed any good feeling his old crew might otherwise have felt by saying, 'Next time you're crashing in flames, man, think of me sipping iced rum and cokes on the sundeck of the SS *Port Elizabeth*.'

— 8 —

When fear is new and the sight of death has novelty, men will buffet danger to test their strength.

When the novelty has gone, replaced by confidence and determination, then operations become a challenge. Halfway through a tour, the end is still distant.

Trip by trip the end is being overtaken but is still too uncertain to dwell upon. It is not until the remaining trips number only five, then four, then three, that their minds dare to compute the cold statistics of deliverance.

With three more trips to fly, at three per cent losses, the chance is 108 to 9 of living.

Then it is 108 to 6.

And then it is the final deal: 108 to 3, good odds but the heart is beating faster and the hand that deals the cards is trembling. It is all or nothing for the final jackpot.

Men pray for an easy target as their last. They beg the chance to get it over quickly. A final trip to Stettin would seem a cruel omen.

Even as men's minds pondered the end of a tour, so, now, were spirits bent upon the end of the war. To end a tour meant a six month reprieve; to end the war meant more than most of them had dared to think on more than lightly.

When Magnetic expressed the fear that Chiltern would kill them all they had agreed. Unconsciously, it seemed each mind had seen the gamble for life with dice loaded against them. Against loaded dice they had won through. The unexpected could happen. Now the war must soon end, and it seemed that at last the dice were loaded in their favour, yet could not the unexpected happen again?

Men still flew and men still died. Luck could desert them.

As Germany shrunk between the closing jaws of east and west the last few trips all seemed to be to Stettin. The army forced its eastward way and soon the only targets left were Halle, Magdeburg, hated Leipzig or far Berlin. The ten or twelve remaining German cities had gathered about them all the defences of the dwindling Reich and each determined to sell its capture dearly. Only distant targets remained and almost all of these had such a vicious reputation that their names still demanded respect even when the attackers knew that victory must soon be theirs.

Thus the war in the air raged to the end with its old intensity. Here was no falling-off. This was not a mighty army opposing a collapsing, routed force. This was the old battle of planes against cities. The flyers fought with some misgivings. Were they not entitled to want to live after winning so near the goal?

On 101 Squadron, particularly, the war's ending would bring disturbing thoughts. The Specials, heart of this unique squadron, still included many Germans. What did unconditional German surrender offer to them? What did the end of the war mean to Johnnie Muller? Berlin was his home but Berlin was in ruins. He would go first to Switzerland and his mother. But England was more his home than Switzerland and England, with his help, was now delivering the death-blow to his homeland. He strove to find the ideal solution, the one right course which would satisfy every justice.

But after the battle, what would the war have gained? Nazism would have been defeated but the spirit of Nazism might not have been purged from the German heart. The evil of Nazism, defeated by the evil of war, might still be potent: the war might have been fought to prove that two evils don't make a good. And who was to say that an aggression worse than German aggression and a doctrine more evil than Nazism might not take its place?

For Johnnie the war held fewer problems than the peace. And so he clung to war and resolved to deal with the peace when it arrived.

Ulm in daylight was a sobering thought. Deep into southern Germany, almost to Switzerland, and by day. It would have been impossible while the Germans held the line along the Rhine. Perhaps it was still impossible but it was their target so they would soon know ...

As they flew south into the strengthening April sunshine it did not seem thinkable that this could be a rendezvous with war. High above a budding earth sugar-coated with dainty clouds, it was a delight to be alive. The morning sun, rising higher and higher above the dazzling Alps, comforted their cabins with warmth and cheerful light.

Astonishingly the picture changed as, charcoal grey with pointed ochre centres, crackling flak-bursts drew a smoky road down which they flew.

Many crews who had flown a first tour in the helter-skelter days after D-Day and screened – often inside two months and with less than a hundred hours of operational flying – were now flying their next tour and found the end of the war more dangerous than before.

A year before, with 1943's losses ringing in their ears, Command had ventured little. To fly by day at all was tempting Fate enough. Since then, Command had learned to say; 'We rule the skies. We fly when and where we please. If men get killed? Well, we have plenty of men and planes. We can spare them. All we must do now is end the war quickly.'

Nowadays, Command actually routed night attacks over flak areas *intentionally*. To waken a million workers, spoil their sleep and their morrow's work, was considered worth losing a bomber or two.

So had run their ever-quickening course. New weapons and new aids meant only fiercer fighting. The bombers were asked to do more and more.

For the last two hundred miles the bombers had had no fighter escort, and they watched forebodingly the skies around them. But German fighters did not come. Perhaps the fighters felt, like the bomber crews, that this would be a damned silly time to get killed.[1]

An anti-aircraft gunner, on the other hand, fighting desperately on the ground, although he knows in his heart that all is lost, is not exposed to greater personal risk. He will fight with all the ferocity of hopelessness. He will try to win revenge with his last shell, try to cost the hated enemy one more dead.

Most of the way to Ulm, Jackal held M-Mother straight and fast. Occasionally Bob, in the nose, or Ray in the rear, called for swift evasion of predicted flak, but shells needed to be close indeed to turn them aside.

Bob saw the shell which was to mean so much to them. He called a quick evasion, Jackal dropped the nose and M-Mother shuddered as the next shells burst above her.

Instantly Alan shouted to look up, but Jackal had already seen it. The Lancaster above them had been hit, her starboard engines were afire and her wingtip shot right off.

Suddenly she was barely inches above M-Mother, weaving and waffling, impossible to avoid because her course was unpredictable.

Jackal shoved the controls forward and M-Mother fell away, but still the burning aircraft fell above them, followed them down, glued to them as if she had impaled herself on M-Mother's tall XYZ aerials and now planned twin suicide.

There came a sudden crash and Magnetic shouted surprise as perspex shattered all over him. The trailing radio aerial from the stricken plane above fouled M-Mother's starboard inner, its lead weight hurling itself against their cabin. In that moment of confusion, Jackal did not know what was happening. Alan cried; 'She's falling port!', and then they could not see through the smoke as the burning plane poured over them.

Six hectic seconds and it was all over. Jackal eased carefully starboard and, as they burst out of the trail of smoke they saw the stricken bomber half-flying, half-falling away to port. Her plight seemed desperate but, remembering N-Nuts and Groninberg, Magnetic thought they might make safety. As they watched the burning plane falling below the bomber stream they saw her turn off towards friendly Switzerland.

Then they saw her aerials. It was an XYZ aircraft, one of themselves.

They looked at the letter.

'Who's flying Charlie?', asked Jackal.

'Hell! That's Johnnie Muller's crew,' said Magnetic.

'They bloody nearly collected us. But I sure wish them luck.'[2]

The next day was Sunday and they did not fly. The 101 Squadron hangars echoed to a new military sound: of shouted orders and of marching feet. Now that the war was far away and air raids could not reach them it was safe to hold a formal church parade.

There were roll calls and inspections. Waafs whose uninspected hair had grown luxuriantly all winter were ordered, 'Have it cut. This isn't a beauty parlour, it's an air force.' Sergeants whose boots had not been polished since the last squadron dance were loudly and publicly upbraided. Officers who had been sergeants the last time they were on parade found themselves in charge of flights and wished the ground could open up and swallow them. Here, indeed, was evidence that peace was coming soon.

'All present and correct, sir!', came the shouts.

So many were not present, but few minds thought of that. For most of the thousand and more men and women this was the true beginning of the end, time to get out, time to leave the air force to playing at toy soldiers.

'Roman Catholics and Jews fall out on the left!' roared the SWO. Everybody else would attend a non-denominational service.

But men at war take ill to parades and pomp. Bright-eyed Jackal found grounds for protest. He stepped out of position and the Adjutant asked what was the matter.

'Sir,' said Jackal seriously, 'what about Druids?'

'Don't talk rot, Cahill. There aren't any Druids.'

'I beg your pardon, sir,' said Jackal, with great mock sincerity.

'I am a Druid, sir. When I enlisted I was asked my religion. I said, 'Christian'. But they insisted that I be Methodist or Presbyterian, and I pointed out that these were not religions but denominations. I had no denomination, so they wanted to put me down as Church of England, which they said was fundamental to this country. But I pointed out that this country can be more fundamental than that and specified myself as Druid – officially. So, sir, is there a Church Parade for Druids, sir?'

Jackal was really being too polite. The Adjutant called over the SWO for a whispered conference. Then the SWO made a flamboyant about turn and yelled; 'Roman Catholics, Jews *and Druids* fall out on the left.'

Alone, Jackal clicked his heels, stepped forward, and joined the renegade band.

Even parades could not keep war away, near though the disciplinarians' dreams were coming. When next they flew to what remained of Germany, it was by night to Kiel.

This delighted them. If fly they must, then Kiel – one of those German targets which did not seem to put its heart into the fight – was more harmless than most. Most German cities fought lustily with all the skill and all the venom they could muster. Leipzig, Stuttgart, Berlin, Düsseldorf were four cities which made of war in the air a spiteful, personal feud.

Perhaps the people of Kiel felt that, not their city but their dockyards and their naval base were the targets. The navy was the target; let the navy defend themselves.

No matter what the reason, Kiel was far from being a dreaded target in April 1945. Moreover, this attack offered something new: the pocket battleship *Admiral Scheer*, which had shelled Spanish civilians in 1937, was in dock.

Kiel was an uncomplicated target: sea-leg all the way there, bomb, then out and sea-leg all the way home again. There was only the target to lend any interest at all. That target, however, was a pyrotechnic marvel to behold. Navy ack-ack defences are built mainly to counter low-flying aircraft. Tonight's attack was from high-flying aircraft but, nothing daunted, the German gunners still sequinned the velvet sky with every gun they had.

Then the background lit with dangling flares, the marker bombs opened like eyes and blinked up at the unexpected brilliance. The master bomber said; 'The reds are spot-on. Bomb the reds. Bomb the reds.'

Jackal, Magnetic and Vincent each spoke one line after bombing.

'Wizard prang!'

'Jolly fine show.'

'Very pretty target.'

Then they flew home.

Pussy Newman was writing the raid into his flying logbook. He looked up and asked, 'How do you spell *Admiral Scheer*?'

'Why bother?' asked Krink. 'There's a swell picture of it in the paper. 'This picture', it says, 'shows the battleship *Admiral Scheer* upside down at Kiel. She has been written off by Lancasters which bombed her on Monday night at the cost of ten planes missing. The capsized ship now looks very much like the *Tirpitz* did after the RAF had finished with her in Tromsoe Fiord.'

'But how do you spell 'Scheer'? repeated Pussy.

'You mean you're not going to paste in the clipping?'

'This,' said Pussy with dignity, 'is a logbook, not a scrapbook.'[3]

Cured of his diabetes and fit again for flying, Joe returned to Ludford. His first visit was to the hospital where he, a flight sergeant, told the MO, a Flight Lieutenant, what he thought of him. The MO did not actually apologise to Joe, but he did say that he now saw that Europe was too fierce a theatre of war for his poor, colonial nerves, and assured Joe that he would arrange, on medical grounds, a quick removal from local operations and a posting to a quieter squadron in Burma.[4]

— 9 —

H-H, now Johnnie – both lost in daylight. One by one the old gang were going. Hyde had gone long ago. It seemed cruel that some of them should have lasted almost to the end …[1]

The wreck of Johnnie's plane was found without survivors. They had crashed high in the Alps, and their would-be rescuers had been forced to leave the frozen bodies there beneath a simple cairn, ringed-in with rugged peaks.

Vincent was in the mess having an after-dinner drink with Wendy, when the new Specials leader came over and told them that he had just had the confirmation.

Wendy received the news quietly. She remembered Johnnie saying; 'We have all the time in the world and suddenly I have faith that romance will come.'

'All the time in the world,' she mused. 'How little we know. Johnnie's tender patience was his charm. I think I loved him for that.' She had never truly faced the question because he had always said there was plenty of time. And yet, within a little month …

She wanted to feel sad, and lounging in the mess with a drink at her elbow seemed wrong.

Vincent's voice interrupted her thoughts. 'May I see you home?'

In his voice was the same soft, sympathetic note that she had found so reassuring when she had heard it before, when she had walked out on Hyde at their DFC party. But that time Vincent was a flight sergeant and he added, 'Ma'am'. Now he out-ranked her. Now he seemed older and stronger in every way.

Vincent had brought her home that night, and been the perfect Galahad. For one moment, at her doorstep, she thought he would become the Don Juan, but again he called her 'Ma'am', and rank had stifled whatever he might have said. And so was set the pattern of their friendship.

She had asked him over to met for tea. He had come, shyly at first, but always she had looked forward to his coming. And then he brought Magnetic and they had suddenly become a part of the office. The four of them: Vincent, Magnetic, Johnnie and Joe. They made the office so alive!

Wendy remembered, when she had wondered about Chiltern, the chill she felt when she had tried to imagine how she would react if anything happened to those four. Well, now Joe was gone and Johnnie was dead. Somehow she could not feel any more seriously about the one than about the other. She was furious about the dirty trick that Joe had suffered. She felt infinitely sorry for Johnnie, and in her mind she used the phrase: poor little Johnnie.

She checked herself now and seemed to understand herself. Could she have loved a man she thought of as 'poor little Johnnie'? Vincent spoke and she stopped in mid-thought to listen.

'Why are men so brutal?', he asked. 'Once you beat a foe, must you pound him to pulp? After Dunkirk, Hitler vowed that he would pursue all enemies to their 'total annihilation'. We, a little later, demanded nothing less than 'unconditional surrender'. I'm sure the fighting and flying that is going on now is unnecessary. Did we need to bomb Ulm? Did Johnnie have to get killed?'

'Ours not to reason why ...'

'Ours *is* to reason why!', corrected Vincent. Johnnie's death had annoyed him. 'In wartime we dare not reason why aloud but the war is ending now. When it is over, men *must* reason why.'[2]

They walked from the mess, silent for a moment, and then Wendy noticed that their arms were linked. Vincent noticed it almost with surprise too, because they were suddenly both conscious of it.

They had reached Wendy's hut. Although they had walked slower and slower as they drew near, they were bound to arrive eventually. They paused, but before they actually stopped, Vincent tugged her arm and said, 'Overshoot. Let's go round again.'

He stopped and turned and looked at her. The new spring air had enhanced the lovely colouring of her skin; crisp moonlight burnished her hair, casting soft shadows to highlight her aristocratic cheekbones and her baby nose. Her eyes, in shadow, were dark and soft, and her tender lips were trembling into a smile.

This was the moment to kiss her. But then Vincent thought of Johnnie. Wendy was upset. It was because she was upset that he was seeing her home.

Their silence grew intense as they resumed their walk. Both of them were tinglingly aware of what had not been said. Wendy realised anew how much she liked this shy, casually graceful young man. He had masculine confidence, and he knew his mind and had thoughts and convictions, right or wrong, that he was not afraid to express. Yet he was shy and she was glad. She knew, now, that she could match his pace.

'This is a precious moment,' he said. 'It is just right, except that it has come on an unpropitious night. And it is a week or so too early. Do you think we can recapture this moment?'

'Why must we?'

'There is a little time must pass by first. Don't fret. The war can't last more than a few weeks. And then we can speak boldly and we won't be mourning friends.'

She shivered slightly in his arms and he kissed her, lightly and tenderly, and suddenly he knew that he was right not to be carried away tonight. It could all happen so easily and uncontrollably and tonight it would be irreverent: a thought, perhaps, to haunt them.

He smiled at her, admiring the way her mouth remained oval and small as he had kissed it. He said; 'We have all the time in the world.'

'Oh, Vincent, please don't.' She pressed her hand to his lips and, in answer to his look of surprise she explained, 'Johnnie said that. Those very words.'

'Oh,' he said, softly.

'He is haunting us tonight.'

'Yes. But don't be sad, please, 'for here lies Juliet, and her beauty makes this vault a feasting presence full of light'.'

'Is Juliet in a vault?'

'Yes. But only sleeping. she is about to waken to her lover.'

Standing on the step of her hut, she could almost look straight into his eyes and she could see that they were laughing again. He kissed her softly.

Then pressing her hands in his, he kissed them, too, and whispered; 'Tomorrow.'

He smiled again, then left her. Sadly she watched him go. 'About to waken to her lover,' she repeated. 'But in that story, when Juliet awakened, her lover was dead.'[3]

'We always have put you in the picture,' said the Squadron Commander, 'and we shall this time, too. Though it's rather a different picture. Your target is Dresden.

'Dresden is an art city and has never been bombed. For that reason, refugees have flocked there. Its population, usually half a million, is now over three millions.

'Right! The Big Three have agreed that it should be Russia's honour to capture Berlin. The British weren't happy about that when it was decided, and we're a damned sight less happy about it now, because Stalin has halted his armies outside Berlin and is making a dash for the Mediterranean to cut off all Eastern Europe. If he does that then we, the British, have lost the war. We entered it to prevent Hitler from upsetting the European balance of power. If Stalin wins all eastern Germany and cuts off Czechoslovakia and Austria and Hungary and Jugoslavia (as he is attempting and as he will if we don't stop him), then the balance of power in Europe is haywire anyway and we have fought for nothing.

'So we must stop him – and those millions of refugees in Dresden are going to help us do it. The trick is a German one. Before Dunkirk, you remember, Germany bombed Rotterdam to force refugees on to the roads to block our retreat. Right, that's what we plan: to use German refugees to block the Russians. Dresden is not a target in the normal way, but I think you can see that it may suddenly prove your most important mission of the war.'[4]

Dresden was not, as the Wing Commander had warned, a normal target. The bombers flew through almost no opposition. The precious guns which had guarded Dresden had long been moved to more vital targets. In a city which had never needed air raid shelters, refugees in their thousands had turned the shelters into homes. Hotels, shops and houses were crammed with refugees; some people were living in the streets. And into this defenceless mass the bombs struck terror.

That was exactly what they were supposed to do. Had those people but known it, the British aim in stopping Russia was Germany's aim, too, but blind fear knows no logic. It was not a big raid; less than three hundred bombers, and it lasted only a few minutes. But the German papers said that in those few minutes 600,000 people died.[5]

The RAF have great respect for the German nation. They stood and fought and took a frightful beating and did not cry. Dresden is the only raid that they resent. To wipe out Berlin, Cologne, Hamburg, Nürnberg, Düsseldorf; all that they understood and forgave. This was total war, they had started it.[6]

But Dresden, they said, was not a target. They speak of Dresden as the British speak of Coventry. True, the Coventry Cathedral was destroyed, but nobody can deny that Coventry proper was a legitimate target.

What, we might wonder, do the Luftwaffe think of British towns? They are bound to speak with respect. By London and by Fighter Command the Luftwaffe was defeated. They could hardly say; 'This man is not a fighter yet he beat me.'

So the refugees were frightened out from Dresden; out onto the roads to block the Russians. But we had over-estimated Russian compassion. Their guns and tanks and transports thundered as well over refugees as through blank streets.[7] They had orders to strike south, to the Adriatic at least, and only guns, not people, could stop them. The Russians reached Trieste. Dresden had suffered in vain and Yalta had lost us the war.

Jackal flung the paper aside.

'Well, that looks like it,' he said. 'Germany announces Hitler's death and the next day Berlin falls. They won't carry on now. We can all go home.'

'Who can call a halt if Hitler's dead?' asked Vincent.

'Anybody. The generals. The admirals. I say the war's over and the first thing I want to do is trounce you for your table tennis title.'

'The G-C forbade it.'

'Nonsense. You're talking like an ex-champion already. Now come along and bring two beers.'

Vincent won the first game. Jackal won the second. The third would be the decider. They had started it when Flight Lieutenant Lane, the met officer, stuck his head into the games room and asked if they had seen Wendy.

Then he said, 'Hello! Not playing him for his title are you, Jackal?'

'Not really playing him for it. Playing *with* him for it is nearer the truth. Stick around and be the first to congratulate the new champ.'

Jackal was as good as his word. He was in fine spirits, whereas Vincent's heart was not in his game. Jackal crashed home the winning drive, then flung his bat in the air.

'Shake my hand, Mr Met-man', he said. 'Congratulate me.'

'I'll shake your hand, but in condolence, not praise. You realise that now you've beaten this man you're doomed.'

'Rubbish!' They were both laughing. 'The war's over. And anyway, I can't get killed because he flies with me.'

'At that rate you're both doomed. Better play him again and let him win this time.'

'Not on your life! If I did play him again he probably would win.'

'Well, let me buy you a farewell drink. The bar's as likely a place as any to find Wendy.'

They never did have that drink. As they walked from the games room the Tannoy called all navigators to prepare for another raid.

The announcement of Hitler's death had struck Command as unconvincing. He was to be war criminal number one: naturally he would try to escape. A fake death would deliver him from his own people too; his memory of Mussolini's fate would still be fresh in his mind. It was quite possible that he had fled, and if so they knew where he would be – Berchtesgaden. Command decided, therefore, to beard him in his lair.[8]

Berchtesgaden by day! It was more amusing than ever. Way down to the Alps to find a hole in a mountain-top and fill it in. Ulm had surprised them, now they must fly past Ulm, past dread Munich itself, to the farthest point of the war, over mountains where crash landings were unthinkable and to bale out meant death from cold upon some glacier – and in daylight.

The crews drew some excitement, however, from what must have seemed the most personal attack of the war. This was not an air raid, it was a manhunt and the quarry was Hitler himself.

The setting for this raid was even lovelier than it had been for Ulm. This time they were flying right along the line of the Alps. The sun, hurrying up from the south now spring gained momentum, rose even higher.

Jackal and Magnetic in their flying glasshouse, were soon flying in shirt-sleeves. Beyond Strasbourg they found themselves atop a newborn world of ice and glacier.

On they droned, south-east. The world was rugged, steep and still: a petrified ocean with gigantic waves of stone struck motionless, their white tops frozen into foam-flecked ice.

Navigation over such country would have been impossible had there not been well-mapped lakes here and there between the peaks.

Bombing presented one unique problem. Although altimeters showed four miles above sea-level, the Lancasters were struggling to gain sufficient bombing height above land-level. It was a new sensation when the world itself reached up to threaten them in the sky. They hoped they would not run into flak. Although they had climbed over 20,000 feet from base, the guns up here would be less than a mile below them.

The target-markers went down, pinpointing impregnable Berchtesgaden skulking deep in the mountainside; and immediately the flak came at them, heavy guns from the valleys and light guns from the peaks, all staining the clear Alpine air.

Vincent had passed the target wind to the bomb aimer and was about to go forward to watch the attack when he saw a row of neat round holes advancing in a jagged line along M-Mother's fuselage.

'Dive starb'd, go!' he yelled.

It must have been light flak, Vincent thought as M-Mother tumbled from the line of fire. He had not heard them, not had they shaken the aircraft.

M-Mother levelled out. 'Was that you, nav?' asked Jackal, surprised to hear evasive directions from inside the aircraft.

'Yes, skip.'

'Then what the hell was that for?'

'Light flak. There were bullet holes appearing along the fuselage.'

'I felt nothing.'

'You would've if we hadn't dived. They were moving straight towards you!'

Instantly the two men remembered the jinx of the table tennis title, but there was no time to think of it.

'Overshoot the greens one second,' said the master bomber. The bomb aimer gave a correction. Jackal turned M-Mother onto their last target.

'Bombs gone!'

Immediately three shells hit the nose, the third only a foot in front of Jackal's head.

Before the fourth could strike they had dived beneath the line of fire.

Then they both seemed to know what they could not believe. This fantastic thing was happening. The jinx was hunting Jackal.

He set M-Mother climbing again. Two evasive dives over this high ground did not leave them much sky to manoeuvre in when the next shells came. Jackal seemed to know that they would come, but when they did, there was no warning. Suddenly a draught gushed through the cockpit and the perspex roof above him shattered.

Vincent screamed; 'Dive starb'd!', but even as he called he saw Jackal jerk in his seat. A gash had appeared in his shirt behind the right shoulder-blade, and another at the side of his throat where the twenty millimetre shell came out.

Magnetic leapt across and grabbed the control column. But only Jackal could reach the rudder bars and, in pain, he was pressing with his right foot so that M-Mother skidded in wide, untidy turns.

At least they were not losing much height, but Magnetic was no pilot and these pointless turns were getting them nowhere.

It was about twenty seconds before Jackal recovered from the shock and was able to take an interest in the flying again. Straightening his feet on the rudder bars he went to take the controls.

As he moved his arms, however, a grimace of pain contorted his face and he waited another few seconds before taking the stick with his left hand only.

He took it off again almost immediately to switch on his microphone. Then he looked at Vincent with a twisted grin.

'What course, Champ?', he said.

Vincent tried to grin back. He leant forward and set the course on Jackal's compass.

Magnetic had to act as Jackal's other hand; to work the throttles, turn the trim, to push or pull whatever knob was needed.

Meanwhile Vincent had ripped Jackal's shirt from his shattered shoulder and was trying to patch the wounds with first-aid dressings. The shell had gouged an inch-wide gash above Jackal's shoulder-blade, then entered the shoulder itself and tore its way up through bone and flesh.

Vincent recognised arterial blood but could not staunch the flow which welled up from Jackal's throat. He pressed two pads into the wound and bound them tightly, but he had scarcely finished before ugly red patches appeared and grew again.

The colour left Jackal's face and, with an undramatic little grunt, he slumped back.

Magnetic grabbed the controls again and M-Mother renewed her wavering, sliding course.

Vincent studied the wound again, painlessly now, and by binding the torn artery tightly against a bone he reduced the bleeding considerably. He put another dressing on the wound, then forced some hot coffee through Jackal's lips.

Jackal opened his eyes.

'Steady, skipper,' said Vincent. 'You're losing blood. You'll have to land as soon as we see somewhere to get her down.'

'Can't land on this mountaintop,' said Jackal thickly.

'Try to hold out till we find somewhere.'

Jackal relapsed into unconsciousness, but his feet remained more or less steady on the rudder bars whilst Magnetic held the controls as steady as he could. To try to change places with only a few thousand feet between them and the Alps was unthinkable.

Another sip of coffee brought Jackal round again. He blinked through half-closed eyes. Then painfully he reached forward and took the controls.

Vincent put the new course out of the Alps on Jackal's compass and sluggishly they turned north. Vincent noticed that they were in a shallow dive. He pointed to the artificial horizon on Jackal's panel.

Jackal nodded painfully but still he did not lift M-Mother level.

Vincent watched more with compassion than with fear while Jackal struggled against his weakness to hold M-Mother in the air.

It was obvious that Jackal's failing strength would soon be gone completely. They had already been forced off course to miss a mountaintop, and now they flew along a valley with great cliffs towering around.

Twice Jackal actually dropped the control column, so Magnetic took his hand and held it on the stick. Jackal looked up at him and nodded slowly; he tried to speak but no sound came.

Then he beckoned Vincent close. 'Find – place to land,' he whispered. 'Must – land – now.'

Vincent looked round them. This country was impossible.

'There's nothing yet, skip. Try to hold on.'

'Must – land now,' slurred Jackal.

'Hold on, skip, hold on.'

'Must – land ...'

'Hold on.'

'... now.'

Magnetic touched Vincent's shoulder and pointed forward. The valley they were following turned sharp right. At first Vincent thought Magnetic pointed it out as a warning, in fear that Jackal would not see it or could not negotiate it. But then Vincent saw the smoke.

Smoke! A wispy ribbon of blue smoke, almost too slight to see as they rushed towards it, was curling up from around the corner. Smoke meant a fire, perhaps a house. That might mean a field or a road. Somewhere to make a forced landing.

'Skipper, look! Some smoke! Turn starboard, slowly now. Then ready to turn pretty hard and put her down if there's space.'

Vincent turned to Magnetic. 'Throttle-back and flaps,' he said.

But Jackal was bringing them around too slowly. The far cliff was rushing at them.

'Starboard!' said Vincent, softly but intensely. 'Follow that smoke.'

'Smoke?', gurgled Jackal, faintly. 'Can't – see ...'

Then he slumped over the controls. M-Mother nosed sharply

down. Magnetic and Vincent both snatched at the stick to pull M-Mother back up and towards a tiny clearing with a shack and blue smoke now suddenly visible, but before they had steadied her, or before Jackal could recover for just a few more seconds, M-Mother jolted and shuddered, and there came a dreadful rending and tearing of metal.

'Here's a hopeful beginning to the peace,' said Flight Lieutenant Lane, looking up from the newspaper and glancing at the faces around his met office.

'Monty and Ike *and* the German Chief of Staff all agree that the war was won in the air. The German says so without reserve, Eisenhower says it was bombs that beat Germany and even admits that more than half of those victory-bringing bombs were dropped by the RAF.'

Montgomery is not so sweeping. He says; 'The mighty weapon of Air Power enabled us to win a great victory quickly, and to win that victory with fewer casualties. The figures show 60,000 aircrew lost since D-Day, but he estimates that they saved a million troops.'[9]

'Sixty thousand since D-Day? Or altogether?' asked Paps.

Wendy answered her. 'Yes, sixty thousand since D-Day. The bomber losses for the whole war were forty-two thousand planes and fifty-nine thousand aircrew.'

Her voice came flat and lifeless. 'The first ones died over Wilhelmshaven the day the war started, and they were still dying over Berchtesgaden up to the day it ended.'[10]

Wendy went on staring at the paper. Then, suddenly and convulsively, she gripped it between her hands and buried her face in the crumpled sheets. Paps put a reassuring arm around Wendy's shoulder.

'They might show up yet,' she said.

'From country like that?' Wendy spoke into the paper and her question ended with a tiny sob she could not stifle.

'Stranger things have happened. You never know.'

'Barbara knew. She drove into a tree and ended it quickly. The fifth wife to kill herself on this squadron. They all knew. None of their men came back.'

She was crying now. For the first time in the days since Vincent had gone missing she had really broken down. Paps did not try to say any more, just tried to comfort her silently.

There was a quick knock on the door and Squadron Leader Gaffer hurried in. He was talking before he looked around. 'How is visibility at Cottesmore?' he asked.

Then he noticed Wendy with Paps kneeling beside her. Gaffer was embarrassed, and wanted not to intrude, but his question was important.

'I've just slipped down from control,' he explained. 'An American Dakota has just landed to drop survivors and they want to return to Cottesmore. But there's fog around. Will they be able to get in?'

Wendy had heard only one word, but it was Paps who spoke it.

'Survivors?'

'Yes, seven bods they picked up on the Continent.'

'Seven? One missing! Do you know whose crew it is?'

'Why only seven?' asked Wendy, hardly daring to come out of her daze. 'Who is missing?'

'I don't know who they are or who is missing. But I do know there's a Dakota waiting on my runway for a visibility report,' he almost shouted. 'Is there fog at Cottesmore?'

Paps rushed to the map. 'No!', she said. 'It's fine. It's ten-tenths sunshine. It will be just wonderful.'

She turned to Wendy as Gaffer went grumbling away. 'I wonder ... can it be them?'

'I wonder ...'

'It must be. Is there anybody else it could be? It *must* be them.'

'And I look a wreck!'

There was a knock and a voice outside the door said; 'May we come in?', and at the sound of it their hearts stopped beating.

The door opened and Vincent stood there.

'Vincent!' cried Paps, and went to rush towards him.

'One moment, dear,' said Wendy, holding Paps back. 'My turn.'

And she turned towards the door and said, 'Oh, Vincent,' very softly.

It was many minutes before they could tell their story. Even the high emotions at their return and the fact that it had happened days before could not hide the amazement they still felt at their escape.

'It was quite impossible country,' they explained. 'And then we saw this smoke. Jackal was almost done but we made the corner and there was this unbelievable clearing with a tiny hut in it. We actually clipped a crag and ripped our bomb bays out, but Jackal revived at the noise and set her down, rough but safe. Our position had seemed impossible, and yet we landed, almost – miraculously.

Then, walking towards us from the hut came a man, a young man with a beard, and when we looked we all swore it was Johnnie Muller.'

'Johnnie! Alive?'

'But it wasn't Johnnie. Rather, I don't think it was Johnnie. We rushed up to him but he didn't know us. He spoke very little English. When we said we knew him and that he had flown with us, he said he had been in the Alps for as long as he cared to remember.'

'But *was* it Johnnie?'

'I would swear it was. But it couldn't be. However, we hadn't time to discuss it because Jackal was hurt so badly. We made a stretcher, and this hermit chap gave him some sort of medicine and that seemed to help. Then he led us to a village and sent us on alone. He would not come with us. He said that nobody knew he was there and that he was happier alone. I couldn't help feeling – *hoping* – it was Johnnie.'

'Poor little Johnnie,' Wendy said. Then, seeing questioning eyes upon her, she added, 'And how about the Jackal?'

'We don't know. The village was German. We were taken prisoner and he was sent to hospital. Johnnie, er, that is, the hermit, had said his only hope was to get to hospital quickly. So we just don't know.'

Vincent shook his head. 'He *was* a strange chap; mysterious and yet – simple.'

'But was it *Johnnie*?'

'I could have sworn ... And yet, had Johnnie time to grow a beard?'

Nobody answered.

Then Krink clapped his hands loudly and said, 'He hadn't time, really. So that's solved. Now, snap out of it; we've got a party to fix.'

'And don't forget that we're all expectant,' added Magnetic.

'Expectant?' asked Paps, puzzled.

'Sure!', said Krink. 'All ex-prisoners are on expectant mothers' rations and that means bags of orange juice. So let's get cracking. Who's going to organise the gin?'[11]

Ray Ollis: A chequered career

Robert Brokenmouth

'I think the ones who survived weren't as lucky as the ones who were lost. The ones who survived had so much more to cope with.' – Margaret Ollis

'... it should never be forgotten that in war everything is confused. At all levels it is hard to see clearly ...' – John Grigg

Briefing

101 Nights is a play on Richard Burton's *Arabian Nights* and 'crusader knights'; and it tells the story of 101 Squadron, the first Radio Countermeasures (RCM) squadron, during WW2.

Ollis's approach is very typical. Most Bomber Command servicemen felt they were embarked on a moral crusade; that they were 'knights of the air' was an obvious, if unspoken, subtext. Many who served in the Navy and Army felt much the same way.

> we felt that the Germans were going to wreck this world of ours and that we would have to stop them ... The war we were involved in was very clear cut. It really was a crusade. – Ross Munro (Canadian correspondent in World War II, Knightley)

The war waged by the Luftwaffe and Bomber Command was one of brutal, bludgeoning attrition, of constantly changing methodology, equipment and tactics. Initially determined not to target civilians, Britain's bombing policy became primarily directed not by a carefully considered plan to win the war, but by a complex series of powerful, furious actions and reactions by the enemy. The uncertainty of target types further confused the circumstances and led to necessary, and unnecessary, evils. For it is evil we must discuss here. Not evil people, but ordinary people employed in an evil business.

'Bob' Braham, a night-fighter pilot in May 1940, explains:

> the Luftwaffe ... had got away with relatively light losses considering the terrible damage they had inflicted on the civilian population [of Britain]. It made me furiously angry to see our cities burning beneath me as I flew ... through the night sky, trying to stop what, at that time, seemed pointless murder of helpless people ... I could never see why the Germans thought these murderous bomber raids would help them. The destruction merely hardened the hearts of the British people against them.

Britain may not have been a decent man's paradise, but the British firmly believed themselves to be decent. Their colonies were considered profitable, semi-civilised places which, with tutelage, would in time govern themselves in a civilised way.

By contrast, the Germans led by Adolf Hitler, believed that they were better than the people in the countries around them; it was natural to conquer their neighbours and expand their country into other people's territory.

The key difference between the British and the Germans in WW2 is intent. Initially the British attacked military targets, holding back from attacking German cities until their own cities were bombed with considerable damage and loss of civilian life. The Germans, however, were deliberately bombing civilians in 1937, before WW2 started.

But first, to *101 Nights* (1957), a striking, vivid war novel published within ten years of the war. The publisher is prestigious; the House of Cassell included writers such as Winston Churchill, Quentin Reynolds, Sir William Slim and Sir John Slessor. Only a few night-bomber and German-pilot memoirs had so far appeared, with modest success; Cassell took a punt on *101 Nights*.

Yet there is little to show for Ray Ollis's life-long energy, drive and ambition, and we wonder why. Ray's dustjacket photograph shows us a handsome, talented, confident man, whose 'own experiences in the air with 101 Squadron are guarantee enough of its authenticity.' We wonder how much of *101 Nights* is true and how much fiction.

This is a delicate balancing act. Unnoticed, Ian Fleming slid his own experiences and opinions into his novels. Popular books described as non-fiction often tweak facts to ensure a better read. Paul Brickhill's non-fiction thrillers could not be clogged with too much fiddly detail.

All writers try to present an essential truth to their readers, sometimes deciding that in setting down their experiences the factual gorge is too hazardous to negotiate without fiction's bridge. In a 'story', truths may be told which would not have the same impact if told in an autobiographical account.

Anglophile Raymond Chandler's bitter-on-the-outside character Phillip Marlowe stifled his inner romanticism. Drawing his character's name firstly from Sir Phillip Sidney, one of Elizabeth I's courtier-warrior knights, and from Christopher Marlowe, an Elizabethan playwright whose surface bitterness and butchery emphasises a profound morality, Chandler was a man out of place (if not time).

By contrast, Nevil Shute Norway was an engineer who wrote popular and significant novels, often drawing on his personal experience. Thomas Malory (*Le Morte D'Arthur*) was one of Shute's – and 'Dambuster' Guy Gibson's – favourite authors.

Born in Waratah, New South Wales on 4 February 1924, Raymond Bernard Ollis was the youngest of three sons.

If Ray had developed an interest in flying, it would have come from the huge publicity generated by the numerous long-distance flights and air-races from Britain to Australia, and such pioneers as Captain Ross Smith and Keith Smith, and later C.A.W. Scott and A.E. Clouston, and Great War heroes like Ball, McCudden and the fictional Biggles.

The characters of *101 Nights* emerge from a British literary and social tradition stretching back centuries. In their childhood, these young men of Empire were encouraged to regard themselves as, if not born gentlemen, then part of a creed and philosophy which allowed them to become gentlemen. Thomas Arnold and his muscular decency had firmly influenced the public schools – and the working class boys who aspired to greater things – for sixty years. Thomas Hughes' best-selling autobiographical novel *Tom Brown's Schooldays* (Macmillan, 1869) was enthusiastically read and reread by 'old boys' of every age, as were magazines like *The Magnet* or *The Boys Own Paper*.[1] The young men of Empire looked back towards an Old World on the far side of the ocean.

Excited about ideas and experiences, Ray was larger than life to those lucky enough to come into his orbit. He played the piano beautifully, had an excellent singing voice, and was well-read in what his widow Margaret calls 'high-brow' literature.

A connoisseur of art and music, and the old and rare, Ray delighted in scouring junkshops and bookshops. Ray's love and pursuit of music, art and literature is principally responsible for our reading *101 Nights* today, far more so than his experiences in Bomber Command.

Bombing cities from the skies had its infancy in the German Zeppelin raids on London in WW1. Hanson describes 'the Fire Plan', Germany's ' secret strategy that was to be employed to bring England to its knees ... England shall be destroyed by fire'. Air-dropped incendiary bombs would create firestorms engulfing entire districts of London, creating mass panic and popular unrest that would 'render it doubtful that the war can continue', and force the British Government to sue for peace'.

Delve quotes the 1920s Trenchard Doctrine; 'the nation that would stand being bombed longest would win in the end ... to win it will be necessary to pursue a relentless offensive by bombing the enemy's country, destroying his sources of supply of aircraft and engines, and breaking the morale of his people', but Trenchard was following the lead of Italian aviator General Giulio Douhet's 1922 *Command of the Air*. The modern, machine-age warrior thought ahead.

When, in support of General Franco, the Luftwaffe deliberately bombed the town and people of Guernica in 1937 it caused worldwide revulsion – the bombing was cruel, unnecessary and brutal. Although the stated purpose was to assist the soldiers, 'morale bombing' was first practised by the Germans. Morale, to the military mind, is the will to resist, the will to fight. Another war seemed inevitable, that the bomber would be a key component, and that Europe's cities would suffer grievously equally inevitable.

As former diplomat Harold Butler remarked, Hitler 'calculated correctly on the spinelessness of the French Government and the complacency of the British Government, without whose active aid [Hitler's] future victims in eastern Europe were at his mercy'.

Germany revelled not just in militarism, but in the destruction it could cause. The feeling in Europe was that Europe was modern, civilised, that The Great War had been a hideous mistake, and no-one in their right mind would again plunge Europe into war.

When considering the Germans' invasion of other people's countries we must also consider: on what grounds is this acceptable? At what point does the bombing and shelling of other peoples' cities in the pursuit of expansionism become justifiable? What possible justification does an invading country have for enslaving the invaded country's inhabitants?

In December 1938, Ray Ollis passed his practical examination in pianoforte and won a scholarship to Sydney's prestigious St Andrews College; his older brothers had gone to college in Newcastle. In 1939 Franco won the Spanish Civil War – with Germany's help.

The British Empire had slowly concluded that the Germans were neither savoury nor honest. Their bombing of English civilians in the Great War still provoked anger. Their hateful treatment of Jews was well-known. To put it bluntly, the Germans had been behaving like cads. They were indecent, beastly. Chamberlain's declaration of war, preceded by his guarantee of support for Poland, was made because he and his ministers believe that Hitler should be stopped.

In the mindset of the times the concept of English decency was that, regardless of the odds and opposition, the tyrant must be resisted, and that the chivalric knights must ride forth to slay the dragon. In *101 Nights*, Vincent Farlow declares, 'Decency is often more important than truth', the core crusader belief.

The core German belief is for a titanic struggle in which the best one can hope for is a glorious death on the field of battle. Mistaking the English sense of decency and determination for their own beliefs, the Germans saw the English as brothers united in the pursuit of war. In 1920, Junger commented;

> Of all the troops who were opposed to the Germans on the great battlefields the English were not only the most formidable but the manliest and the most chivalrous.

Hitler may have been portrayed as a Teutonic knight on propaganda posters, but the Nazis saw themselves as a new version of conquering Rome. 'Nazi' became synonymous with evil.

Britain became the only country in Europe that could fight for what was right, so her Empire's young men hurried to fight for the Old Country and to repel the Nazis. The lure of the air was compelling for a generation of young men growing up with stories of the filth and mud of the trenches. Yet Delve quotes Ludlow Hewitt on the RAF: 'Entirely unprepared for war, unable to operate except in fair weather and extremely vulnerable in the air and on the ground.'

The German bombing of Guernica, Rotterdam, Poland, Holland, France and England provoked significant rage. In November 1940 Ray Ollis's second-oldest brother Ron turned 21 and enlisted in the Australian Army. New Prime Minister Churchill decided to bomb targets (oil facilities, train yards) in Germany, still cautioning the RAF not to hit civilians. The Battle of Britain had been won, but Britain's cities were being bombed almost every night.

Serving with the 2/30 Battalion in Malaya in 1941, Ron and John Ollis were taken prisoner by the Japanese at the fall of Singapore.[2]

*****

Service Number 423478

Ray Ollis's first job was at the *Herald Sun* as a newspaper copy boy, journalist being the first step in a writer's career (Quentin Reynolds and Ernest Hemingway being greatly admired). One imagines Ray, the compulsive diarist, following the Nazis' progress across Europe, into the Mediterranean, Africa and Russia.

When the Luftwaffe bombed Coventry on 13 November 1940, it was 'the first time ever [that] air power was massively applied against a city of small proportions with the object of ensuring its obliteration ... in terms of its reputation as a centre of industrial excellence, the Germans viewed Coventry as a legitimate target in their attempts to break Britain's economy'. John Ray also points out that any military intention could not help but be also intended to induce terror.

Hitler had made speeches threatening to destroy British cities for many years, remarking to his intimates that it would be enjoyable to burn London, and now he was doing just that. Speer recalled that, had the Germans possessed heavier bombers with heavier, more destructive bomb-loads, they would not have hesitated to use them, any more than they would have hesitated to use an atomic bomb.

John Ray again; 'For the Germans, the Coventry raid was hailed as a huge success ... a German High Command communique referred to 'the utmost devastation'. A new word entered both languages – *koventrieren*, or 'to Coventrate', meaning to devastate a place by aerial bombing. By what reasoning can such gloating in destroying the helpless be called justifiable?[3]

When WW2 began, German bombs were more effective; it was not until early 1941 that the British, copying the German's example, introduced bombs with more explosive, thinner casings and better fuzes. The initial impact of Bomber Command was quite small; until early 1943, the tonnage and accuracy of RAF bombing was limited. When critics of Bomber Command point out that their bombing campaign caused far greater destruction and death than Germany, they miss the point. Most Germans acknowledge that 'they started it'; and they were led by men not given to sense or surrender. Germany's forces had killed thousands of civilians, terrorised millions more, and were convinced that this was only to be expected, the normal way of conquest.

1941 was a year of dreadful set-back for Britain, with bombed cities, retreats in Africa, Greece and Crete and savage attrition in the Atlantic. In 1941 Bomber Command was the only weapon the RAF had which enabled the British to fight back.

USA was forced into the war by the Japanese, frustrated at the USA's refusal to sell them more oil so they could expand their brutal conquest of China and Indo-China.

Churchill accurately represented the British Empire; 'What kind of a people do they think we are? Is it possible they do not realise that we shall never cease to persevere against them, until they have been taught a lesson which they and the world will never forget?'

Ray waited for his eighteenth birthday in February 1942 when he asked his parents for their consent to enlist. With John and Ron's fates still unknown, the three week delay between Ray's birthday and his enlistment was probably because Ray's parents were not pleased about their last son also dashing off to war.

'Going into the RAAF was a huge adventure. Ray couldn't wait to get there; all the rest of his family were there. His mother must have had fits worrying about them' (Margaret Ollis). Yet it would have been difficult to refuse Ray; the war was going badly and the Empire needed every man it could get to fight the aggressors.

With their deliberate intention of precisely bombing carefully-considered targets, the Americans (like the British at the beginning) had the right idea, the right targets in mind (oil, synthetic oil, and ball-bearing plants) but (again, like the British at the beginning) would find that they were unable to bomb effectively.

Appointed Commander-in-Chief of Bomber Command the day before Ray Ollis joined the RAAF, Air Marshal Arthur 'Bert' Harris' force had less than 70 heavy bombers, and '378 serviceable aircraft with crews', 50 of which were light bombers. 'In effect, this meant that we had an average force of 250 medium and 50 heavy bombers until such time as the Command really began to expand' (Harris, *Bomber*).

Harris did not make the policy nor the decisions regarding area bombing, nor did he believe in 'morale bombing'. As Probert comments, 'the policy of area bombing was not conceived by Harris, as all too many critics have suggested. It was determined by the Air Ministry under Portal's direction, with the support of the other Chiefs of Staff and the War Cabinet.'

By early 1942 too much had been invested for Bomber Command to be diverted from its purpose, and it gathered momentum. America and Britain needed to cement their new relationship with the newly formidable Russia; for if Russia took Europe, then Britain and America would be obliged to take Europe back – resulting in a much longer and unimaginably more costly war.

Harris's first three major successes after he was appointed Commander in Chief of Bomber Command were Lübeck (a medieval port used to supply the German occupying forces in Norway), Rostock (a medieval town with a Heinkel factory) and Cologne – the latter the famous '1000 Bomber Raid'. All three targets burned and were extensively damaged; all three were on the list of targets Harris had been directed to bomb.

Perhaps if Hitler had not been Germany's leader, the Germans might have sued for peace then; Germany did not need a potentially devastating war on two fronts. Instead, Hitler retaliated; between April and June 1942, the Germans bombed British cities noted for their history and cultural importance.

Harris used 1942 to reduce Bomber Command's weaknesses, consolidate its strengths, improve its bombs and navigational equipment, and expand. Lighter, more vulnerable bombers were either shorn off or removed entirely while newer types were phased in.

To combat the German night-fighters and flak, Radio Counter-measures (RCM) and better radar navigational systems (such as Gee, H2S and Oboe) were introduced, as were the Pathfinder Force (PFF) and the bomber stream. Tactics shifted to combat the German defences. Allied night fighters were equipped with airborne radar.

The British public regarded themselves as having been pushed too far by a playground bully. The fight was on, regardless of its practicality, and they believed they would win, simply because they stood on the side of right and the Germans stood on the side of wrong.

In 1942 the mood in Britain remained determined, but an air of resignation had crept in. Noticing this, Shute wrote *Most Secret* 'to perpetuate the mood of bitterness and hate which evolved in England in the latter stages of the War' (Anderson).

> 'Who could have guessed these Germans were not people like ourselves?'
>
> 'We were told often enough,' said Simon grimly. 'All the world told us that the Germans were a murderous and an uncivilized people, without decent codes of conduct. But when they conquered us, we thought they would be people like ourselves.'
>
> …
>
> 'The Germans do that sort of thing. They do it for a policy, because they think it makes people afraid. And if we mean to win this war we must do horrible, beastly things to them. Torturing things, like they have done to us.'

Most Secret was intended to remind Shute's readers of their anger and bitterness towards the Germans, who had hurt the British so much that they now didn't care how badly they behaved as long as the Germans were hurt, mangled, crippled in return;

'I would put on my best clothes and go to watch the young men tie the Germans up in bundles and pour petrol over them and light the petrol. That is the way to deal with lice,' I said. 'With a blow-lamp.'

When we read *Most Secret* from our own distant perspective we are tempted to align the writer's intentions and feelings with our own. Yet Shute's description of deliberately burning helpless Germans was not intended as a condemnatory metaphor to the burning of German cities, but as justified rage (or 'the decency of hate', to use Humfrey Jordan's phrase[4]); 'I don't mind looking at that Jerry. I wouldn't mind a hundred or so like him, all stretched out in rows and stinking.'

Most Secret's bitter rage at the unjustifiable bombing of Britain and brutalisation of civilised Europe does not merely reflect the mood of the time; most of Britain wanted to strike back at the men Shute describes as 'Satan and his messenger at Berchtesgaden'.

What we now call the Holocaust is all too familiar to us now, but in 1942 it was horrific, unimaginable, too awful to contemplate.

On 13 December 1942 Ed Murrow's regular broadcast, *This is London*, reached across Britain to the USA; 'What is happening is this: millions of human beings, most of them Jews, are being gathered up with ruthless efficiency and murdered ... moral depravity unequalled in the history of the world. It is a horror beyond what imagination can grasp.'

To the aircrews, Hitler and the Nazis needed to be destroyed; knowledge of the Holocaust merely added fire to Britain's 'holy rage', and the Americans' determination to fight the evil of Germany.

Ray was training with an artillery unit when his call-up came several months later.

Musgrove, Braham and Grigg contend that in February 1943, when Roosevelt announced to newspapermen at the Casablanca Conference that the Allies were seeking nothing less than the 'unconditional surrender' of Germany, this made the Germans that much more determined not to surrender. From that moment, the war became an extended exercise in madness, butchery and mayhem.

In March 1943 several hundred servicemen sailed for Canada. If you were on a converted cruise liner you could be in a luxury cabin unaffordable in peace-time. This is where Ray got the taste of the travelling life. Even so, for most the troopship was to be endured; too cold or too hot, cramped, smelly and vomitous.[5]

Ray attended Number 2 Air Observer School at Edmonton; it was an intensive three months. Air navigation was the principal subject, map reading was crucial; once Ray could complete a simulated flight in the classroom using Dead Reckoning (DR) he was allowed up in an aircraft to apply what he'd learned. Once the aircraft's position was located on the map, Ray was able to work out the aircraft's groundspeed, wind direction, wind speed and compare this with the intended route. If the aircraft was off-course, the navigator had to give a correctly-timed correction to the pilot.

After obtaining an average of 75%, Ray qualified as an Air Navigator; the class then travelled by train across Canada to the port of Halifax before sailing to Britain, where he arrived at Gourock, Scotland in December.

Ray arrived in a country with a grim and determined past. Having withstood repeated German attacks and an attempted invasion Britain was beginning to repay the Germans for their unacceptable behaviour. Ray waited out the winter until a place came up in February 1944 at Halfpenny Green, No. 3 (Observer's) Advanced Flying Unit, where his skills were tested in foggy, smoggy England with its four seasons in a day. Two weeks later his Chief Instructor passed this 'keen and conscientious worker. Satisfactory ...'

Loosely inserted in Ray's logbook is a typewritten account describing Ray's training and operational experiences. Titled, *'Copy. Extract, Flying log-book, R.B. Ollis'*, it runs concurrently with his logbook from April 1944.

The 'Extract' allowed Ray to make comments he couldn't in the logbook. In April, he was transferred to No. 21 Operational Training Unit, navigating Wellington 10s from Enstone around the countryside.

It is here that Ray found his first crew; Warrant Officer Walter Hrynkiw (J86647, RCAF), Wireless Operator P/O B.J. Keynes, Bomb Aimer Sgt Gordon Smart, Mid-Upper Gunner Sgt Jack Squire, and Rear Gunner Sgt Joe Lightfoot. It is probable that Ray bases at least one of his most significant characters on Hrynkiw.

Pilot Walter Hrynkiw had already survived ten ops on Halifaxes with the famous 78 Squadron. 78 flew the most operations of 4 Group, with the highest losses 'and highest percentage losses in any Halifax squadron' and the greatest losses in 4 Group (Middlebrook and Everitt).[6]

Hrynkiw's ops with 78 Squadron were eventful; as Ray arrived in Scotland, an old battered Halifax (JD118, EY-E) took off just before sunset. Over the target Hrynkiw's aircraft was badly hit by flak, killing Sgt Valley, his navigator, and seriously wounding Sgt G. Creer. Hrynkiw was able to return, but lost control, crashing in Yorkshire.

Hrynkiw's last op with 78 Squadron was on 21 February 1944. Hrynkiw's boys found and bombed Stuttgart just after 4 am. Again badly hit by flak, Hrynkiw's navigator was killed and two others seriously wounded. Hrynkiw struggled home; running low on petrol they were diverted to RAF Dunsfold in Surrey. As they landed, the undercarriage collapsed, causing the Halifax to swing a full 90 degrees; Hyrnkiw attempted to take off again, but crashed into trees.

Hrynkiw was then transferred to No. 21 OTU where, two months later, he found a new crew. It says much of Hrynkiw's personality that the 'sprogs' thought him a confident and determined man, particularly after he explained that he could only do twenty ops to the crew's thirty; the crew would then have to make up their remaining ten ops with other pilots.

By May, the crew were working hard to get into the fight before the invasion started, flying night cross-countries, bombing practice and 'fighter affiliation' (where a fighter practices attacking the bomber, and the bomber practices evasion and gunnery).

It was an exciting time to be in England; for several years the city streets were filled with uniforms, then, suddenly, in early June, most of them vanished as the invasion armadas assembled. Ray was on leave as the Allies' invasion of Europe began, and when flying bombs first fell on England, particularly London. Hitler's spiteful mini-blitz was as needless as it was cruel; however, by the apparently careless targeting standard set by the Allies' bombing, to the Germans the mini-blitz would have seemed appropriate (if insufficient) revenge.

Morale bombing is a double-edged sword. During the Battle of Britain, the Luftwaffe were frequently told the RAF had no more aircraft, yet the Hurricanes and Spitfires kept appearing; Luftwaffe morale drooped. Three years later during the Battle of Berlin, the Germans knew that if they maintained a high enough rate of attrition among the British and American bombers, the aircrew would begin to rebel. It took time for the German Vengeance weapons to be contained; while their impact certainly affected public morale, the V weapons never threatened the invasion.

By early July Hrynkiw and his crew were at 1662 Heavy Conversion Unit at Blyton, one of hundreds of temporary airfields built for the duration of the war. Blyton operated the Halifax; Flight Engineer Sgt Roger Grantham-Hill joined them for the next three weeks' training.

One of Ray's logbook entries stands out: 'July 17, Duty: Passenger. Remarks: Dental-Check.'

Unless it were common practice for all crew to undergo an 'altitude toothache check' before entering operations, it seems that Ray went up (as a passenger) with P/O Lyons, presumably with a medical officer, to ascertain whether his condition was real or psychosomatic.

Deighton remarks that

granted courage by ignorance and the inhibitory effect that curiosity has upon fear, [a crew's] morale was high for the first five operations, after which ... a crack-up point was reached by the eleventh or twelfth trip ... [which] was marked by more subtle defensive changes in the crew: a fatalism, a brutalising, a callousness about the deaths of friends and a marked change in demeanour ... this was the time in which the case-histories of ulcers, deafness, and other stress-induced nervous diseases that were to follow the survivors through their later years, actually began ...

Such 'defensive changes' need not, of course, confine themselves precisely to 'the eleventh or twelfth trip'; they could easily occur earlier.

The day after Ray's dental-check, Hrynkiw's crew provide 'Diversion for Ruhr. Zuider-Zee, 60 E'.

The heartland of German military manufacturing, the Ruhr (nicknamed 'Happy Valley') was much-visited and much-feared by Bomber Command airmen. The 'diversion' sent some 115 aircraft out over the North Sea in order to either fool or divide the attention of the enemy fighters from the two major raids on oil installations; Middlebrook and Everitt leave an impression of skies crowded with radio traffic and noisy radio jamming, feints, double-bluffs, spoofs, bombs, mines, anti-aircraft rockets, V1s and flak.

On 19 July the crew performed a seven-hour 'Bulls-Eye' in this case 'stooging around the enemy coast generally making a nuisance of themselves' (Feast) – baiting the enemy searchlights along the Dutch and French coast to confuse the German night-fighter defences.

Again, almost an op. But only if they'd dropped bombs.

As the pilot's controls and crew positions in a Lancaster were in different places to the Halifax, Hrynkiw and his crew then did day and night exercises at Number 1 Lancaster Finishing School, a busy training station, then taking two weeks' leave before reporting for duty at Number 101 Squadron, Ludford Magna.

***

Mens Agitat Molem

101 Squadron's history included bombing the German Army in France and Belgium in 1917; the squadron motto, *mens agitat molem* ('mind over matter') was coined during WW1.

Ground Cigar used fifteen land-based VHF transmitters to jam the German night-fighter controller's channels. Because the jamming could not be pushed far enough east, a similar jamming system that could be carried in aircraft was developed; in October 1943, 101 Squadron was selected to carry the new Airborne Cigar (ABC).

ABC equipment weighed over 600 pounds, including receivers, power units, transmitters, generators, aerials and so on. The receiver swept for signals 25 times per second. Headphones enabled the operator to hear the German transmissions, but a cathode ray tube was also used, depicting the German bandwidth as a horizontal line, and German transmissions as a vertical line. The Special Operator could aim his own transmitter at the vertical line, and tune in. If he heard a German transmission, he would tune his control to the German's frequency, transmitting a loud warbling sound, obliterating the vertical line. ABC's three transmitters could jam three German signals at once; the Special could return to check if the German was still there, or had shifted frequency. Alexander reports that the first

German transmission ABC heard was 'Achtung English bastards coming!'

The savage battle of attrition from November 1943 to March 1944 (known as the Battle of Berlin), the bitter losses of the Nuremburg raid, the savage Mailly-le-Camp raid in May might have been only half a year past, but on a bomber squadron three weeks ago was an eternity.

The lead-up to D-Day, the softening of the German defences and the dislocation of the transport and communication networks were also gone. Now all that remained was for the Germans to fold their cards, get up and go home. But Germany did not surrender.

While not blind to the mistakes of Britain and Australia, Ray regarded the Germans in the same way all Allied bomber crew did. The Germans deserved the bombing because they started it and, if they were not stopped, they would continue to devastate and enslave Europe, the Mediterranean, Russia, the Middle East, Africa, America ...

Searby's comment is accurate:

> Whatever one's reaction to the bombing of cities ... it was [the enemy's] own choice – that the shooting war should be conducted against the civilian population – when, after failing to defeat our fighter squadrons in 1940, he drenched London in a sea of fire and slaughter; thereby planting the seeds of [his] final defeat.

In late August 1944, Hyrinkiw's crew arrived at Number 14 Base, Ludford Magna, where 101 Squadron had between 44 and 50 Lancs on station at any one time (the equivalent of two squadrons). Ludford Magna was very small, but nearby village pubs the White Hart and the Black Horse catered to local farmers and their labourers.

A Bomber Command squadron was (and is) an enclosed world. Aircrew maintained a rough, dark, sardonic sense of humour regarding their work and the increasing likelihood of their painful deaths.

Hrynkiw's crew were given a week to familiarise themselves with squadron life and their aircraft; a period which also allowed their superiors to assess whether they were properly trained and suitable for ops.

A few more exercises later and Hrynkiw's crew were ready. All raids were eventful. But some raids were more eventful than others ... what we would consider the battle of a lifetime today, many logbooks do not bother to record an impression.

Four early ops were on Le Havre; their Gee set 'packed up' and their 'starboard outer oil-line [was] holed by flak' on their first op, but their second was 'Quiet' as were their next two raids.

Hours after the last raid, on 11 September, the Germans surrendered after a British ground attack which cost 50 British soldiers their lives in exchange for 11,000 German prisoners. Only two Bomber Command aircraft had been lost.

Hrynkiw's crew had done five ops in a week. The sprogs may have thought that in six weeks they'd be home for Christmas.

The crew's next op, Stuttgart, was a harsh baptism. Ray did not fly with the crew, his place taken by a man called Castle. One of just over 200 Lancasters, on 12 September Rays' crew took off into the dusk at ten to five and left Stuttgart in a firestorm a little after half past eight.

On returning the crew found themselves over Karlsruhe; flak killed Irish bomb aimer Gordon Smart (the aircraft was holed 17 times). Despite this, Hrynkiw pressed on and bombed the target. This would have been hard on Hrynkiw; his last op to Stuttgart had been a 'dicey do' resulting in two crew hospitalised and one dead.

Ray does not explain his absence on this op. When asked if Ray had suffered from a minor feature of *101 Nights*, 'altitude toothache', Margaret Ollis replied that 'a lot of the fellows had this problem', and that 'Ray had had a couple of teeth removed'.

If Ray did suffer from altitude toothache, it is not hard to imagine that Ray would have felt uneasy (if not guilty) at Smart's death; perhaps if Ray were navigating instead of Castle this would not have happened. But we cannot know; the simplest of errors of navigation could have the worst consequences.

Other ops were laid on, but many were cancelled. Also, there were more ops for 101 than for most squadrons because 101's ABC services were essential. On the few days that ops were not on, nearby farm-houses offered food different to the mess, and a homey, human atmosphere. There were pubs, but not every man headed there. Some crews stuck together, some split up. There were books to read, letters to write, games to play to pass the time – and griefs. But above all it was waiting, waiting for the next op.

Ray's sixth op, followed by an abort, was to Calais. For his eighth op Ray navigated for F/L Haycraft, taking off into the darkening dusk for the Siegfried Line where the roads and railways around Saarbrücken were bombed in support of the Third Army. Ray found the target marking by the Pathfinder Force 'poor', commenting, 'PFF Pull Your Finger Out', most of the bombs were on target. He also added, rather laconically, 'combat'.

Now we notice something significant. Many Bomber Command memoirs include a moment where the navigator 'appear[ed] from behind his curtain and was momentarily terrified by what he saw which was surely the work of Lucifer. "Bloody hell!" he said, and disappeared back to the relative safety of his navigator's position. He was happier not to know what was going on outside' (Feast).

It seems that, unlike most Bomber Command navigators, Ray was emerging from behind his screen and work-table to look at the target. His irritated comment is on an operational aspect which other navigators would not have added because they did not see it.

Ray's next raid elicits, 'Reich by day!', adding a newspaper clipping to his logbook: 'Bombers were flying through absolutely ten tenths flak. I saw several hit and going down in flames, but I saw no fighters attack them'. One wonders if this is what Ray saw. The public, radio and newspapers were thirsty for heroes; if you survived, the war might provide a quick route to fame and fortune.

From here, Ray's logbook resembles a film-fan's scrapbook. When, in *101 Nights*, Ray makes a derogatory remark about a logbook resembling a scrapbook, at the time it was mostly young women who kept film-star scrap-books; autograph books were a more acceptable pursuit for boys, but not men.

Their new bomb-aimer, F/S R.S. Symonds (RAAF) joins for bombing practice. On 14 October Hrynkiw's crew embark on the first of three operations in thirty-six hours, intended to demonstrate the speed and power with which Bomber Command could now operate; Operation Hurricane.

Duisburg twice, Wilhelmshaven once. Finding clear skies over

Duisburg over 950 heavy bombers left a large part of the Ruhr in flames, and were back inside five hours. Bomber Command lost fourteen aircraft.

In *101 Nights*, Ray writes, 'The men could see their vicious handiwork and such is the hate that war creates, the men delighted in it.' We wonder if this refers to his crew or himself.

A few minutes before midnight, nearly a thousand aircraft flew to the same target, returning to Ludford a little over five hours later for the loss of seven aircraft.

Ray's clippings tell part of the story; 'Early yesterday morning Duisburg was on fire from end to end ... some of the thousands who manned the bombers on the first raid by daylight ... also made the double trip. They rose before 4 am and after their return, before lunch-time, only had time for a wash, a meal, a quick nap, before preparing for the night raid from which they returned early yesterday morning – almost 24 hours after the first take-off.'

The crews were woken to prepare for a 5.30 pm take-off for Wilhelmshaven.

Not getting much sleep before going off on another raid is not like going to see a show, coming home for a nap and heading off to work. The toll of ops was cumulative; the enormous nervous tension, the constant attention to small detail, always aware that the next moment could be your last, is a pressure that wearies the spirit in such a way that the damage is done before the individual is aware there might be a problem. As Deighton points out, around the eleventh op is about when changes in behaviour typically began to occur; 'Noisy men became quiet and reflective while the shy ones often became clamourous.'

Ray tells us; 'sea leg both ways and lost Gee! Our third op in 40 hours with only 8 hours sleep. Astro leading-line to target bang on', but despite the apparently good marking and the bomber stream coming down below the clouds Wilhelmshaven was not destroyed, (though its historic Rathaus was).

A few nights later Hrynkiw heads for Stuttgart. Ray's Extract is blunt, 'First time skipper on Stuttgart returned without a dead crewman'. Deighton observes:

perhaps it was the relief of surviving the thirteenth operation that made [morale] climb after it. Men had seen death at close quarters and were shocked to discover their own fear of it. But recognising the same shameful fears in the eyes of their friends helped their morale, and after a slight recovery it remained constant until about the twenty-second trip ...

Their next trip, on the 23rd to Essen saw their Air Speed Indicator, Air Position Indicator, Bomb-Sight and 'Z' (code for the Special Duties Operator's ABC equipment) all fail 25 minutes before reaching the target; without them they could not find the target; even if they did, they would be bombing by guesstimate. Realising the futility and the unnecessary danger of continuing, Hrynkiw turned around, jettisoning his bombs in the Channel. Because they did not bomb the target, there was 'no op' to count towards their tour.

Two days later they returned to Essen, returning 'holed by flak'.

On the 28th, they flew on a daylight raid to Cologne: 'Direct hit on Krupps ... Layer cloud at 8,000 feet shattered by blast of explosion below'. It is fair to assume that Ray witnessed this.

Two nights later they again visited Cologne. Again, their ASI and API both failed. But most unusually, their robust Distant Reading Compass also failed. Icing was clearly a factor here, but Feast relates an incident involving 'magnetic links in the chain to the control column' rendering the DRC unserviceable. Perhaps Hrynkiw's crew wondered aloud about sabotage.

However, the crew 'pressed on to atone C.O. bawl-out re Essen abort (23/10/44) ... 2 combats'. The loss of these instruments, particularly the DRC, could have resulted in the crew being killed; however the Bomber Command attitude was that if it was at all possible to 'press on' and bomb the enemy, the crew should continue.

On this raid 'enormous damage was caused in Braunsfeld, Lindenthal, Klettenberg and Sulz, which were "*regelrecht umgepflugt*" – "thoroughly ploughed up" ...' (Middlebrook and Everitt).

Halloween sees Hrynkiw's boys return to Cologne. As an ammunition train blew up, Ray's logbook remarks 'Wizard Prang' and 'Fuck Their Horrible Luck!'; it seems likely Ray saw the huge explosion.

Ray Ollis completed his eighteenth op over Düsseldorf on

2 November, and on the 4th found Bochum. No doubt mindful of the C.O.'s bawling-out, the Extract reveals, 'Lost starboard inner on take-off. Started immediate climb and set course 7 mins early. Bombed on 3 [engines], 6 minutes late and 2000ft low. Very hot trip.'

Extra strain on the remaining three engines immediately after take-off meant that SR-C would struggle to lift off, and would continue to struggle to maintain height and speed. That they bombed 2000 feet below the bomber stream meant they avoided the icing at higher altitude; they were lucky not to have been hit by bombs falling from above, or been damaged by the upward blasts of exploding cookies.[7] Ray was luckier than he knew; of 749 aircraft despatched 28 were lost.

Ray's twentieth op was to the Nordstern synthetic oil factory in Gelsenkirchen, his twenty-first the oil refinery at Wanne Eickel. Heavy cloud obscured the target; Middlebrook and Everitt report the Master-Bomber directing 'the force to bomb any built-up area'. Ray's remarks are succinct: 'Shamozzle!'.

On Remembrance Day they flew to Dortmund's Hoesch Benzin synthetic oil factory, a momentous occasion. Hyrinkiw had finished his tour, and their wireless operator his second; 'thus busts a swell crew'.

Two weeks later 'New Crew. S/Ldr Warner ... (Pilot, joined RAF 1937, on first op.)'. Squadron Leader Warner joined 101 in early September; it was two months before he made his first op: Freiburg. This Lancaster, PB 237, was five months old and, having endured numerous ops, would have been considered by operational standards either a lucky kite or a weary old cantankerous creature.

Not only was this trip Warner's first, it was Ray Ollis's 22nd after which, Deighton explains, morale 'sloped downwards without recovery'.

Ray's logbook; 'first [op] with new crew. [A] quiet trip [to] Freiburg (population 135,000) wrecked, 30,000 killed.'

Two nights later Warner's crew found Neuss, at a quite unusual 4.30 am local time, to catch the fire-fighters unprepared. 'Bright moon. Pilot aghast, but quiet for Ruhr.'

Barely two weeks later, on 16 December the Germans launched a counter-offensive through the Ardennes forest, intending to split the Allied armies and reach Antwerp and Brussels. The Battle of the Bulge was deliberately launched in bad weather to hamper Allied air cover.

The next day Warner's boys helped destroy or damage truck factories and military barracks in Ulm. Ray comments, 'Under "duty" for this op, I have entered "?" because pilot, given small alteration, refused to fly it. As my flight commander Warner was required to sign my monthly summary, he questioned my "?". I explained it. He proceeded no further ... just signed the summary.'

The Germans' advance through the freezing, cloud-covered Ardennes toward Allied fuel dumps could not be located until finally, on a frosty, foggy Boxing Day 290 aircraft bombed German troops near St Vith with considerable success.

This, Ray Ollis's 25th op, was the most significant in his career, and forms the most extraordinary story in *101 Nights*.

Chorley records 'Homebound, forced-landed 1627 near Reims. F/S Jackson is buried at Clichy Northern Cemetery.'

S/L Warner's crew took off in their usual Lanc (SR-M, PB 237) from Ludford Magna at a quarter to one in the afternoon. Ray's logbook says, 'Ops St Vith. Hit and set on fire over St Hubert. R/Gunner killed – B/A baled out. Made successful forced landing at Rheims.' There is a later emendation: 'Pilot and W/Op awarded DFC'. They were in the air for three hours and forty minutes.

Ray's Extract is emphatic:

Approaching St Hubert B.A. ordered 'Dive port GO!'. Aircraft continued straight and level. Hit by three heavy flak shells, one engine stopped, both fins damaged, rear guns blown onto Rear Gunner's legs and aircraft set on fire from main spar aft.

Fell (from memory) 1,000 to 6,000 [feet]. Bomb-Aimer, looking UP, saw self and W/op with parachutes coming forward to bale out. He could not see pilot. I gave thumbs down and he jettisoned hatch and baled out. Pilot sent us back to fight fire. W/op returned to his set and did not budge. Flight Engineer and I fought the fire. Rear Gunner had lost one leg, the other trapped under the guns. He was on fire ... hydraulic oil spraying over him and burning. I tried to remove him, couldn't free leg. I killed him. With Flight Engineer I fought a bit of fire, returned to my log.

We were flying in broken circles above the guns that had hit us! DR/C was out and the pilot was turning slow circles under influence of fire on metal skin circuit. These circles the pilot was slavishly following. I estimated a relative course to the sun for Juvincourt.

I returned to fight fire. I returned to get orders re bombs. Skipper said 'Jettison'. I descended into the bombing compartment (which had no floor), Flight Engineer with right arm through my para-chute harness and left arm around cabin upright. I selected all bomb stations, pressed the tit, and though the arm rotated no bombs fell. The circuits were burnt away. I went aft and dropped the cookie (I had to trip the manual lever with my ruler; it was red hot). The 10 x 1000 pounders we had to ignore in the press of other business. We flew over Rheims airport. Warner asked 'Is this Juvincourt?'. I knew it was Rheims but answered 'Yes'. I knew we might fall out of control any instant. It took Warner 15 minutes to land; on impact the aircraft broke up from the mid-upper turret back. Warner said to me 'Weston (the W/op) was the senior officer; he MUST have been charge aft'. Warner and Weston were awarded DFCs. The reports read: (*Sunday Graphic*) 'Ablaze but they bombed target. With the rear gunner dead, two turrets blazing, and ammunition exploding, a Lancaster went on to its target at St Vith, bombed it, and returned home, the crew fighting the fire all the way. Flak smashed the intercom and bomb-release mechanism. Bombs had to be dropped by hand. For their great courage two of the crew, Squadron Leader Warner and Flight Officer David Weston have been awarded the DFC.' (Big laugh: Warner had caused the loss and Dave had done nothing. We did NOT bomb the target and we did NOT 'return home'). Another Sunday paper printed the same misrepresentation under the heading 'Bombed by hand they get DFC'. Warner was shot down and captured shortly afterwards; Weston was killed.

Ray must have made some official representation about the accuracy of Warner's report of the St Vith raid (and, by implication, the circum-stances under which Warner and Weston won their DFCs), because he was later Gazetted to receive the DFC on 7 December 1945.

A later newspaper story:

I had been shot down in Luxemburg, and … while passing through Rheims, [an] American soldier sold me the painting for 600 francs, [then] about £3/16/-. I bought the painting because it was obviously very good and was signed in the Van Dyck manner, AVD 1633. The painting had evidently been cut from its original frame and remounted. I gathered it had at one time been looted and could well be valuable.

His head and hands in bandages and clutching his painting, Ray arrived back at Ludford, '4 days, one hour after original take-off!'.

RAF records provided by David Champion reveal that F/S Colin 'Col' Dearnley Donohue, after evading capture in the forest for a little over two days, was taken prisoner by a resting German motorcyclist asking for his papers. Warner, Sgt W. Harthill, F/O D.W. Weston and Sgt E.C. Roberts survived and made their way to friendly lines.

Ollis's recuperative leave is short; on 15 January Ollis joins Warner's crew for Merseburg; 'two orbits. Heavy flak'; meaning the crew orbited the target, amid heavy flak, twice.

With 26 ops completed, Ollis appears to be once more without a crew. On 10 February, Joe Lightfoot (Rear Gunner) is 'posted N/F, sick, with 26 ops completed'.

Two weeks later, Squadron Leader Warner took off for Duisberg. Over 360 Lancasters successfully bombed the town. Seven Lancasters were lost; three crashed in Allied territory.

Warner, Sgt W. Harthill, P/O A. Jeffcoat, W/O J.A.M. Bird and Sgt E.C. Roberts survived to be taken prisoner; F/O G.L. Halsell (RCAF), F/O D.W. Weston DFC and Sgt S.J. Stephens were killed. Ray's incorrect comment, 'Since 20.2.45 – Dortmund – I am the only one of Hrynkiw's crew alive' clearly reflects his isolation among the thousands at Ludford.

On 5 March F/Lt Harrison's crew and their new navigator Ray Ollis take off for Chemnitz. 'Chamozzle! First with new "dice" crew. Quiet trip'.

Part of Operation Thunderclap, these raids on far-east German cities were designed partly to hasten the Reich's internal breakdown while appearing to help the Russians advance. The intent was actually to hamper the Russian advance by clogging the roads with refugees. This double bluff did not work; the Russians were careless of the refugees, and their presence seems not to have hindered them at all.

At 27 ops, Bushby explains, 'we had all reached that delightful state of being "flak-happy". This manifested itself in a feeling that since we had come so far along the road by which so many had failed what was to stop us going on to the end? ... The self-deluding logic was unassailable.'

Two days later Harrison's crew headed for Dessau, 60 miles southwest of Berlin. Jules Roy had an engine failure and, rather than lose time and effort without notching up another op, decided 'We'll push on deep into Germany to be sure that we can drop our bombs there and then we'll make for home.'

On 11 March, Harrison's boys climbed through the stratus into the bright blinding sky above where hundreds of fighters carved condensation trails and over a thousand bombers headed for Essen. 'Ruhr, once "hot plus", now almost undefended'. A cutting continues, '… Essen is tonight a city of fires and smoking ruins … The 450 square miles of the Ruhr contain not a single town of any industrial importance and not a single major factory of any value. It has been devastated beyond recognition.' Ray comments, 'compare with London Blitz'.

This might be where in *101 Nights* Ollis describes a 460 Squadron Lancaster unloading its bombs on an apparently non-military village.

One of just over 250 aircraft, Harrison's boys took off for an oil refinery at Lutzendorf. After returning from a diversion to Great Dunmow, Ray's triumph was palpable: 'That's number 30! From here on in, it's sheer zeal!'.

On 9 April they were off to Kiel: 'good prang, very pretty target, sunk *Admiral Scheer* … bags of light flak'. The U-boat yards, the *Admiral Hipper* and the *Emden* were also badly hit.

On the 11th Ray added a comment: 'Warner reported POW – hence Germany's internal collapse?'.

Five days later, Harrison took off at 6 pm on Ray's 32nd and last raid, and Bomber Command's last big raid: Berlin's military barracks and rail yards, but many bombs fell into the city. Grimly, Ollis has written; 'combat'. Only one aircraft was lost on this raid, to a nightfighter; the Luftwaffe could muster few fighters by now.

When Ray adds 'fitting climax to a chequered tour' he was luckier than he knew.

Feast observes that during WW2 there were 1,074 men killed while serving with 101 Squadron; 178 became POWs.

Ray Ollis would never be the same again.

***

Adelaidian Interlude

> We have become connoisseurs of ruin in this war. We have learned
> to distinguish between the bombed, the shelled, the burned, the
> blasted ... a town that has the the sour stench of a rubbish heap from
> one end to another, and where the only sound is the drip of water
> from the broken roofs ... One does not pity the people of the town,
> nor does one hate them. One says, 'they did it to us', but one is left
> just staring. ... The terrible thing is that one has no feeling at all ...
> One is stripped of every feeling, the humane and the inhumane ...
>
> (V.S. Pritchett (*New Statesman and Nation*, 7 April 1945) via
> Knightley)

In his despair at Britain's victory, Pritchett seems to have forgotten
the British motivating force: hatred at the German's callous, brutal
behaviour for more than a decade.

Ray Ollis shared neither Britain's bitter rage nor Pritchett's despair.
Ray went to war because he believed it to be the right thing to do,
and it was an extraordinarily exciting adventure where he might reap
rewards. Just as the tempest of war ends somewhat anticlimactically,
101 Nights ends with the survivors looking forward to the next party.

The victory parties celebrated the living, but were also part of the
unable-to-be-forgotten grief for the vast numbers of dead, maimed
and missing. Just briefly the world was a tainted, wonderful place.

Britain was stricken with rationing, shortages of food, jobs and
housing, and a rampant black market. For all the later hand-wringing
over the Allied bombing of Germany, we must remember that the
Allies aided Germany to rebuild, to some extent against the wishes of
the British public, when Britain also needed rebuilding.

The late 1940s and early 1950s form an idealistic decade, riven
with doubt and fear. The Second World War had left an enormous
impression; for many years every minor war the former Allies became
involved in was another potential world conflict. The Russians
exploded an atomic bomb in 1949. The Korean War began in
1950. Many ex-servicemen felt that war with Russia was inevitable;
'bombing Moscow' was a succinct expression of how many people felt,
the unspoken subtext was 'bomb Moscow *first*'.

Handsome, charismatic, talented, musical, ambitious Ray Ollis, 21, had the world at his feet. Having risen from schoolboy to adult, he had a rich experience of life, the sure confidence of extraordinary achievement and an independence of movement undreamt-of by his parents less than a decade ago. He had experienced extraordinary euphoria, and the pinnacle of his life so far was to witness the vast crusade to liberate the world, watching great, momentous events happen beneath him. In spite of all the shells, tracer and explosives aimed at him, Ray Ollis had survived. Many such men felt they were bulletproof.

Posted first to Brighton, Ray sailed back to Australia and a training school at Mallala, some 35 miles north of Adelaide.

In this small and sleepy town in the South Australian wheatbelt Ray met 'country girl' Marjorie Adams, whom he married shortly afterwards.

Although Ray was gazetted to receive the Distinguished Flying Cross it would have been a grim leave; by now the Ollises had been told of their oldest son's death as a POW.

Discharged shortly after his 22nd birthday in February 1946, Ray now had 'an appalling stutter' (Margaret Ollis). There is a well-founded theory that illnesses such as aphasia are linked to left-handedness and lesions on the brain. Ray's stutter may have been linked to an injury incurred in childhood, or in one of his several crash-landings, or an emotional aftershock.

A doctor advised Ray to force himself to talk publicly, so he got a job with Australian Broadcasting Commission (ABC) radio, and also sold Gestetner printers to offices. Talking cured the stutter. But Ray had another illness.

The American Psychiatric Association describes Bi-Polar (called manic depression for many decades) as experiencing 'dramatic mood swings – from high and feeling on top of the world, or uncomfortably irritable and "revved up", to sad and hopeless, often with periods of normal moods in between. The periods of highs and lows are called episodes of mania and depression.'[8]

People going through a manic phase experience euphoric states lasting days, weeks or even months where they are careless of objects, money and other people and their feelings. When their mood has died down, the enormity of their behaviour can hit home with devastating impact, not assisted by the illness's other side, depression. Percy Bysshe Shelley's lines from *Prince Athanase*:

> My brain is wild, my breath comes quick –
> The blood is listening in my frame,
> And thronging shadows, fast and thick,
> Fall on my overflowing eyes.

Rowe argues 'that depression is not an illness or a mental disorder but a defence against pain and fear … an unwanted consequence of how we see ourselves and the world'; manic depression is a different matter. Mental illness itself used to be seen as demonic, and the sufferer's illness 'their demons'.

Yet every manic depressive's condition is different. Many creative people – even geniuses – have been manic-depressive; Ray's son Timothy confided that 'many parts of Ray were borderline genius'. Ray's illness fuelled his frantic, restless creativity, and Ray seems to have considered his euphoric and creative states to be normal, and his 'down' states to be the illness.

Hershman and Lieb suggest that

> manic-depressives have been a part of all of the accomplishments on which we as human beings pride ourselves – the arts, sciences, industry, scholarship, philosophy, religion – and also those which have brought more dubious benefits to humankind – war and politics.

Partly as a result of Ray's obvious good looks, talent and ability, his appearances in the newspapers and national competitions, it seems clear that Ray Ollis saw himself not as a survivor returning to civilian life, but a triumphant crusader knight; a man for whom things will inevitably succeed.

It might be argued that when the niggling realities intruded, overdue bills among them, that depression descended because, like Vincent Farlow, he was not who he believed or wanted himself to be. Also, it is significant that two of Farlow's doomed skippers are a slight pun – Jackal, and Hyde are clearly intended to remind us of Robert Louis Stevenson's famous story *Strange Case of Dr Jekyll and Mr Hyde*.

Ray was either in denial of his symptoms or more likely not properly diagnosed. In the 1940s, there simply weren't any generally available books on manic depression. Most doctors would not have recognised its symptoms; it was only when Ray's behaviour became noticeably florid and erratic in later years that his condition became evident.

By 1947, Ray and Marjorie lived in an Adelaide much smaller than today, little more than a large, charming country town with blocks of industrial metal sheds, surrounded by a moat-like parkland bordered by period mansions.

While Adelaide maintained a strong, nationalistic clamour of intellectual dissent, waging war against the artistic hegemony of Melbourne and Sydney, Ray had a very different intellectual – and political – intent.

Determined to make his living by writing, Ray also enrolled to study creative writing under Dr Biaggini at Adelaide University. When Ray's logbook asks us to 'see diary, volume 2, page 345', we realise the seriousness of his ambition; that's a lot of diary for someone under twenty-one.

While the Jindyworobaks movement and the Mary Martin Bookshop had particular links to the Adelaide University, Ray was an Anglophile who yearned for the old Europe which he had fought for and helped destroy. Indeed, his main character in *101 Nights* is based on himself, but he made Farlow an Englishman.

Ray was more focused on Europe, his education was European; while in Britain and France he had collected, in a modest way, rare art and books.[9] While Adelaide and Ray shared an intellectual dilletantism which harboured a strong Romantic tendency, Ray had seen too much political reality to be swayed by gatherings of leftish theosophers.

Ray applied for copyright for several plays and musicals, each tinged with shades of his own life, but it seems they were never performed; Ray approached theatrical agents but Adelaide audiences would have found his work too morally challenging.

Gestetner promoted him to advertising copywriter, and the couple joined Adelaide's large dance and art scenes. A local newspaper featured a series of articles on the looted, possibly Van Dyck, painting he purchased in Europe. The couple reached the final of a national dancing competition, but Ray's 1951 letter to the *Mail* spoke of a disgruntled restlessness with tidy, provincial Adelaide.

In March 1952 Ray applied for copyright for another musical, *Sunbeams from Above*, with the same dispiriting result. Three months later, having sold the 'Van Dyck', Marjorie and Ray sold up and took a passenger liner to England. It is hard to avoid the feeling that Ray was escaping back to the Europe he knew, to the grander, bigger stage he expected.

The world was about to change. Stalin, the 'Man of Steel', died on 5 March 1953, Kenya was beginning to rebel, Elizabeth II was crowned in June, the Korean War grudgingly ground to a cease-fire in July and the following year saw the French defeated in Vietnam.

Although Nevil Shute and James Riddell's flight from England to Australia (in a Percival Proctor) in late 1948 was given coverage inter-state, it was not covered in Adelaide newspapers.[10] As Shute said to one Australian newspaper, 'If you stay too long in one place, you get run down. The battery needs recharging.'

***

Escape to Write

Sometime in late 1953, after somehow wangling a trip as '2nd navigator' on a round trip from Topcliffe to Tokyo, Gestetner gave Ray a three-year contract to the British colony of Kenya.

On 26 November 1953, about the time the politicians in London were realising they needed to deal with the problem in Kenya, Ray Ollis arrived in Nairobi where, it seems, his friends were friends with Sir Evelyn Baring, Governor-General of Kenya (1952–1959); Ray apparently enjoyed parties and receptions in their circle.[11]

'Ray drove an old diesel-run Mercedes around East Africa with a shotgun under the seat', visiting countries such as Rhodesia and Uganda (Margaret Ollis), where 'most Europeans carried a gun at all times', but 'things weren't so bad so long as you were prepared for anything, and took no chances.'

He also embarked on a novel; there were things he wanted to say which, were they to appear in an autobiography, might be questioned – if not denied. Ray may also have read Long's *Greece, Crete and Syria*; which includes several remarkable survival stories not unlike Farlow's (such as Private Carroll).

Kenya between 1954 and 1956 was a time and place of muddy colonial morality and no small danger.[12] Appropriately, *101 Nights* portrays a muddy, dangerous moral quagmire from an operative's perspective, especially since Ludford's nickname, 'Mudford Magma' had been awarded with good reason.

With only a few years to gain perspective on his years in Bomber Command, it is fair to say that much of *101 Nights* was culled from Ray's still-fresh memory, his logbook and his lengthy diaries. For colour, he also drew on some of his greatest influences.

Ray chose a forceful and lyrical image to weave into *101 Nights*; initially a literal reference to the West Wind, which several times forced Bomber Command into a chaotic night. However, the West Wind was also Bomber Command, battling the night-fighters and the flak with their 'violent tempest of hail and rain … attended by that magnificent thunder and lightning' (Shelley's note to *Ode to the West Wind*).[13]

Ray depicts the operational and moral complexity of Bomber Command, the vast scale of wartime operations in a way that, until then, had not appeared before the public. He makes it clear that bombing dealt in death and destruction, that he knew he had killed not just the enemy, but civilians as well.[14]

It is our own perception of ourselves which tends to dominate our more rational capabilities. This is one major reason for depression, that the mind finds too easily the gap between expectation and miserable reality. It may be observed that, no matter what it is they are writing, a writer always writes about an aspect of themselves, often confessing their darkest truths in the guise of fiction.

Writing in a new world, in a colonial corner where old ways were dying and new dynasties were bubbling up, Ray Ollis's depiction of the crusading knights of the air is provocative and thoughtful, as much a part of the story of modern alienation as it is of Bomber Command.

World War Two was a time for heroes. Mostly they were created for public consumption in aid of the war effort; journalists and writers went out to find them. Leonard Cheshire's *Bomber Pilot* was regarded by his peers as letting the side down, 'shooting a line' (or grandstanding). Realising this, Cheshire was embarrassed by its publication.

Ray's Farlow is a war-damaged hero who describes his bravery as 'failure'; in best T.E. Lawrence style, Farlow must be heaved into the limelight; his modesty making him more heroic. In Farlow Ray writes about himself; he does not want to say that he wants fame and the approval of the masses, public success, yet he clearly feels that what he is and what he is capable of merits all these things.

Ray creates another doomed hero, Jackal, one of thousands of ordinary heroes, and his flipside, Hyde, a man who is two men; the capable, roistering warrior who becomes the crippled, fearful man who is no longer as capable as he once was. Hyde dies like warrior knight Richard Hillary, wrestling at the controls of his aircraft with clumsy, burn-cramped hands. In Hyde, Ray reveals his manic and depressive selves, his capable and incapable selves. Hillary's *The Last Enemy* was a story loosely based on fact; Hillary disguised his ambitious nature with a heroic, moving tale of a reluctant hero facing up to his fears and weaknesses, mirroring the plight of the public at the time.

Ray compares Jackal and Hyde with the methodical ambition of Chiltern, his lack of regard for the stuff of life, while Jackal and Hyde plunge into the warp and weft of wartime night-life. However much Chiltern is based on Warner, in Chiltern Ray also tells us of his own determined ambition, and his luxury-loving, lascivious side. *101 Nights* reads like an encoded memoir; it would be as unjust to assume that Farlow is pure Ollis as it would to assume that Chiltern is pure Warner. Ollis has altered his memoir to serve his story.

In quoting Shakespeare, Ray chose fiercely appropriate lines. Take 'With busy hammers closing rivets up/ Give dreadful note of preparation' from Part One. Taken from Shakespeare's patriotic play *Henry V*, the quote refers to the construction of knight's armour and other preparations prior to battle, but a fuller quotation may as well be a slice of everyday life in Bomber Command;

> Now entertain conjecture of a time
> When creeping murmur and the poring dark
> Fills the wide vessel of the universe.
> From camp to camp, through the foul womb of night
> The hum of either army stilly sounds
> That the fix'd sentinels almost receive

> The secret whispers of each other's watch
> Fire answers fire, and through their paly flames
> Each battle sees the other's umber'd face;
> Steed threatens steed, in high and boastful neighs
> Piercing the night's dull ear, and from the tents
> The armourers, accomplishing the knights
> With busy hammers closing rivets up
> Give dreadful note of preparation.

Ollis directly aligns the bomber crews with the medieval British knights.

There is a sense of despair and bitterness which runs through *101 Nights*. Kubler-Ross remarks that death 'is an integral part of our lives that gives meaning to human existence. It sets a limit on our time in this life, urging us on to do something productive with that time as long as it is ours to use.'

Few of us comprehend this in our day to day lives, even if we work among the doomed or dying ourselves, as everyone did at an operational airfield in WW2. Ollis refers to suicide so often one wonders just how bad his depressions really were; his quotations from *Romeo and Juliet* and *Macbeth* snarl at the waste and loss.

Ollis pays much attention to the women on the ground, many of whom lived a nightmare of anxiety each time their man flew on a raid. Barbara Cunard comforts the distraught Mrs Hardy by saying, 'It might kill me to stay silent, but I would let nothing hurt that memory.' When she hears about her husband's death, Cunard immediately kills herself, in her mind perhaps preserving her memory of him forever.

Ollis describes Jeschonnek's suicide as an expression of failure to maintain a chosen life.

Schydt and Yarpi's acts are so self-destructive they may as well be suicides; if taken to courts-martial, both would have been found guilty and probably shot.

These impulsive suicidal acts reject the cards fate has laid, reject the truth of things. As if a risk is only acceptable if it brings dividends; if the result is unbearably negative, 'there's always one way out, and they can't stop me'. Suicide is a mortal sin against God, and God's will is not considered; here Ray Ollis is a modern writer, balancing the debt to the past and the everyday wonder of the present.

At some point during the late 1960s, Ray Ollis's mental health began to break down, and at this point he appears to have been diagnosed as manic-depressive, which goes a long way to explain why he was unable to focus on a relationship and why, increasingly as he arrived in one country, he felt so restless he would board another ship to escape. Timothy Ollis noted: 'He liked being shot at! He loved the adrenalin, of putting himself in danger. Look at his three years in Kenya ...', during the Mau-Mau Uprising, his dangerous journey in a Proctor called 'Old Gert', courting danger ...

Once committed to a psychiatric institution, Ray exercised all his skill and powers of persuasion to be released, legally sane in 1972. Deciding to kill himself, he then annotated a will, wrote a letter to his brother Ron, loaded his shotgun, and headed to see Margaret and the children for a final showdown.

Ray Ollis took his own life in a moment of dreadful impulse. For decades he had combatted an unspeakable urge; insanity was the end.

It is true that we cannot know a man by his words alone, but also by his actions. In analysing his words, we may read too much into Ray Ollis, or reveal too much which he would have preferred to have kept hidden. Songwriter Rowland S. Howard observed: 'people don't understand that if something has been written in an oblique way, it's oblique for a reason'.[15]

Don Bennett's *Pathfinder* was published the year after *101 Nights*;

> ... the second German war was officially fought as a 'war without aim' ... [Churchill] made frequent statements to the effect that Germany would never rise again to be a scourge against mankind. Thus we asked our young men to fight and die without any clear ideals such as liberty, fair play or justice ...

For an individual, whether they be within the organisation as Dyson and Bennett were, or operating at its edge, as Ray Ollis was, perspective is difficult to maintain at the best of times.

Some historians compare numbers. British deaths through German bombing were much lower than German deaths through RAF bombing. But again we must return to the intent behind the bombing.

Grayling puts his finger on the main problem when he writes:

if Allied bombing in the Second World War was in whole or part morally wrong, it is nowhere near equivalent in scale of moral atrocity to the Holocaust of European Jewry, or the death and destruction all over the world for which Nazi and Japanese aggression was collectively responsible: a total of some twenty-five million dead, according to responsible estimates. Allied bombing ... claimed the lives of about 800,000 civilian women, children and men ... [to say] nothing about the injured, traumatised and homeless, who in many respects suffered worse ... The bombing of the aggressor Axis states was aimed at weakening their ability and will to make war; the murder of six million Jews was an act of racist genocide. There are very big differences here.

It is the intent which still separates the acts of evil men from evil acts by men. There was a moral crusade, certainly, but the crusade bore a momentum which prevented effective analysis of intent versus results.

Lowe remarked:

many people do not care if the Germans suffered or not. During my research I have spoken to scores of people – Jews, Gypsies, Poles, Danes, Dutchmen, Frenchmen ... who have listened to my descriptions of the Hamburg firestorm and merely shrugged their shoulders. 'It was their own fault,' is the standard reply. 'They started it.'

'They started it'. And 'it' was not just bad, but indecently bad, evil almost beyond imagining. The trouble with evil is that once evil has been seen, we become accustomed to it. This is essentially both the truth of and the emotional justification why the Allies, in particular Britain, expanded the bombing war in Europe, and why the USA firebombed Japanese cities with no pretence of precision targeting.

'They started it' was partly the reason why Roosevelt demanded 'unconditional surrender', regardless of the tactical necessities or realistic consequences.

Interestingly, Lowe also finds that the Germans' response 'exactly mirrors the sentiments of their enemies': "We started it." Or, even more tellingly, "We deserved it."'

101 Nights was written less than a decade-and-a-half a world away from a 1945 when Ollis and thousands of men peered down upon Duisburg. Jean Calmel wrote:

The spectacle was grandiose, but it was no longer human. Against the blood red of the city the latticework of streets was marked by black lines which at times were effaced by an avalanche of flames. ... Immense spirals of smoke rose to the sky, almost tangible in their density.

In the same way as the fighter who has just shot down his opponent in flames savours his triumph, we had accomplished an identical exploit and felt the same moral satisfaction.

The grim, determined misery of 'survivor's guilt', when you are the only survivor out of hundreds of men ... this guilt drove men to apply for Pathfinders, returning to ops again and again to atone for the dreadful indecent sin of living while their comrades died, often in flames ...

These men, who had become one with the wild West Wind of Bomber Command, were they Eliot's 'hollow men' who forgot that they fought for decency, because they had become indecent, corrupt?

Despite Blake's view that experience may not always corrupt, in the real world this is but wishful thinking, there can be no return to innocence from a state of corruption.'

Ray's wartime experiences, as well as his time in Kenya, would seem to embody such an ongoing moral battle, a world where 'even the good ... were deluded into considering evil a necessary portion of humanity'.

Bomber Command operated with optimism, with the best of intentions, but a primary policy insufficiently flexible to force the war to a more rapid conclusion.

'They deserved it' may have been the driving force behind Bomber Command's West Wind, and Ray ends *101 Nights* with the future:

Men should mourn their friends, but they must not go on mourning, piling grief upon grief, lamenting more and ever more dead comrades. That way madness lies: a madness that in war is suicide.

By August 1956 Ray had mailed his novel to Cassell in London, received a positive reply and written his 'Briefing' from Fort Smith. It is likely he had also written – in Swahili – the bulk of his notes for a second book, on the Mau-Mau Uprising. However, Cassell were about to release Nicholas Monsarrat's novel *The Tribe that Lost Its Head*, and translating Ray's book from Swahili might have seemed an expensive risk; Ray never translated it himself.

Ray Ollis left Africa when his contract with Gestetner expired; Kenya was granted independence in 1963 and declared itself a republic a year later.[16]

***

Publication ... and After

For the next few years Ray's passage is vivid, bright; however, afterwards, real information is sketchy. Ray bounces between Africa, Britain and Australia, even navigating on a long-distance flight from London to Darwin in emulation of the pioneer aviators.

Ray, 'nightclub singer' Geoff Layton (owner-pilot) and dentist Matt Deen (second pilot) arrived in Layton's Mew Gull in Darwin on 22 November 1956, their epic 13,000 mile journey having taken the three musketeers a little over 106 hours.

> Decorators were repainting the hotel in Darwin where we called to celebrate. On the walls were signatures of Ross and Keith Smith, Amy Johnson, Kingsford-Smith, Bert Hinkler, Jean Batten ... and, while we drank, a workman painted them over. He was a young workman and our protests puzzled him – perhaps he had never even heard of Amy Johnson.[16]

These names were instantly recognisable to the three fliers, in particular Ray, who makes it clear he was following in the footsteps of his boyhood heroes.

Ray's restlessness continued as he worked his passage as a steward between the continents on the cruise ships. In one letter, dated 3 May 1957, he writes,

> I'd love to fall in love right now. It's exactly what I need ... for my morale and my work. Sydney is so DULL. ... There was a time when I had hopes of fixing a flight back to London about this time. But it's fallen through. So I'm thrown back onto the ships ...

His letters and logbook make him appear extremely restless. The next day Ray went on a 42 minute 'flip in Australia's first (1929) plane', Genairco VH-UOD, his duty (still) being navigator to Dr Morris's pilot. This was the first single-engined aircraft built in Australia; production was limited and ceased in the early 1930s.

A few weeks later, Ray had again worked his way back to England on a cruise ship where he attended Cassell's publication event for *101 Nights*, which did well enough to earn a reprint, a paperback and a translated paperback; even a radio serial was considered.

All the while Ray is writing. Three days before his ship, the *Orontes*[17] sailed for Australia on 29 October he reveals:

> The news about my play is not encouraging, I'm afraid. The agents say it's clever and good theatre … but add that it's definitely TOO HOT TO PRODUCE. I admit the theme is grim. So I put a lot of comedy into it to soften it a bit. They say the injection of incest into a 'domestic comedy – almost a farce' is not in good taste and would probably upset most theatre-goers … I hope to be able to write during this trip. I've never managed to get any writing down at sea before … either as passenger or crew … but this trip I hope I will … If I do, my next novel will be finished by the end of the voyage.

Neither the play nor his 'next novel' seem to have gained much interest; and his by-now established routine of travel, writing and 'flips' continue; in September 1961 Layton and he were '200 feet over Wilhelmshaven', a place he last saw on 15 October 1944 after two raids on Duisburg inside 24 hours.

In Sydney in late 1961, Ray met Margaret 'at a dinner party thrown for him by a friend of mine'. Margaret Hall (née Pearce) grew up in the village of Addington, near Biggin Hill RAF airfield. She and other girls would wave to the fighter boys as they scrambled off to meet the Germans. 'I've been bombed more times than I can count,' she states implacably.

There was a hill which led down to their house; one day a German bomber flew down the hill so close Margaret could see his leather flying helmet and chinstrap. Her mother stuffed her children under a hedge while the German went on to shoot up their greenhouse.

It wasn't the first time that happened; like all the local women her mother was furious with the Germans. When they parachuted down the Home Guard had a tough time protecting the Germans from irate women armed with rolling pins – and worse.

I always knew what I wanted. I wanted to join Norman Hartnell[18] and make dresses for the Queen. I'd been to college, but they didn't want that, they wanted a clean sheet, straight from school, so they could mould you, so I just turned up every day, very polite, well-dressed, and asked for a job, every day for a year. They gave me a job because they were so sick of the sight of me.

Margaret had married Hall, a New Zealand mariner, but he died at 32 of a heart attack. Margaret was 26.

When Margaret met Ray 'he was charismatic, talented, full of beans and knew what he wanted', she remembers. 'When I fell in love with him he was sensitive, caring man who'd been through a hell of a lot, never had it easy (although it wasn't an easy time before the war)'.

'He had to write, he was always writing, articles for newspapers and magazines, the *Herald*, *Pix*, *People*, and was always dashing off for some story. He didn't earn that much, he wasn't able to contribute much to the household.'

They married in 1964, honeymooning in New Guinea.

It was only in passing that Ray talked about the war. He would mention that they bombed a lot of carburettor factories – without a carburettor, of course, an engine won't go. He had a lot of mates from all the squadrons. One night he came home from the pub, he'd met Thomas Kenneally, who'd asked him all sorts of questions about his service in Bomber Command.[19]

I think he was happy with his lot at Ludford, you were sent where you were needed and just got on with it. He told me about Ludford, and its mist, and that Ludford was so high that it was the last to go under into the fog, so they had everybody arrive.

He was particularly moved by the plight of the rear gunner, who, he said, had the worst and most dangerous job in the crew. He was very upset over the role of the rear gunner. They all would've wanted that [the mercy killing of rear gunner John Jackson] done to them if they were in the same circumstance.

Although Ray had been in several crashes at Ludford, he hated Boxing Day – that was the day he was burned, when he was obliged to dispatch the rear gunner, and of the crash which was caused by the pilot.

Ray was very badly burned, all his skin, especially on his back … his back was very scarred with graftings, it was all bright red. His hands were a bit peculiar, serviceable, and yes, possibly that was due to burn injuries. He was not good around a bonfire, he had a physical and emotional reaction to fire.'

Apparently their marriage encountered problems around 1966; one reason for this was Ray's working hours (6 pm to 2 am), another his restlessness; one day in May 1968 he raced out to follow the Endeavour replica from Sydney to Mackay.

Six weeks later, Ray flew to London via Hong Kong, Teheran and Vienna, the trip taking four days. Whatever it was he was doing in London, he worked his passage for the return journey to Australia.

Margaret describes Ray as 'an adventurer. What he'd seen could not compare to dull peace-time reality, he always wanted more, big experiences.' The day to day life of peacetime just wasn't exciting enough for him.

Margaret Ollis recalls, 'He did have dark moods. There were times where I just picked up the boys and we stayed at a girlfriend's place, just to remove them from his influence.'

It seems likely that Ray described his moods in *101 Nights*:

Magnetic had never seen Vincent so depressed. Yet it was not a hang-dog depression: it was militant, aggressive ... [Vincent] was not drinking for the pleasure it could give. He was not even drinking to forget; he was drinking, it seemed, to help him remember, to intensify the misery he felt.

Rowe describes 'an idea which is central ... that depression can be our response to the discovery that there is a serious discrepancy between what we thought our life was and what it actually is.'

Rowe goes on to suggest 'that depression and anxiety, and other mental disorders, are defences, not illness[es]' and, quoting Gwyneth Lewis,

depression is a lie detector of last resort ... it says the way you've been living is unbearable, it's not for you ... if you can ... come through it without committing suicide – the disease's most serious side-effect ... it teaches you slowly how to live in a way that suits you infinitely better.

However, it is one thing to carry a shotgun under the car seat as one drives about Kenya during a militant uprising, and another to buy a sawn-off shotgun in peace-time 1960s Sydney.

Ray had tried to kill himself before. What part of Ray Ollis's death was caused by illness and what part added to by his time in Bomber Command, we will never know.

Margaret now thinks that 'the ones who survived weren't as lucky as the ones who were lost. The ones who survived had so much more to cope with.'

Many soldiers would concur with Smiff's reasoning: 'I would *thank* a man for killing me if I were dying in agony. To shoot him now would be kindness.' One wonders if Ray Ollis saw death as a solution to an unsolvable problem.

Certainly many felt guilty. Sir Arthur 'Bert' Harris (as quoted by Probert); 'There was nothing to be ashamed of, except in the sense that everybody might be ashamed of the sort of thing that has to be done in every way, as of war itself.'

After Ray's death, Margaret 'didn't have time to be upset, I had two children and a home to support – there was no help from the government in those days'.

Final debriefing
Jonathon and Timothy Ollis both have families. Ray Ollis would have been proud of Margaret's achievements, proud of his two boys and their families.

'Bomber Command lost more than twice as many aircrew on operations as did all the other RAF Commands put together', its operational losses were 47,120, with a further non-operational 8,090, and 530 ground staff killed during World War II' (Richards). This does not include those who died as POWs or were wounded while on duty – over 9,000 – nor the losses of aircraft in Training Command, HCUs, EATS, Coastal Command, losses of aircrew at sea ... nor civilians killed as a result of RAF crashes, the wives and girlfriends who committed suicide, nor Harris's 'old lags' who committed suicide ...

The price of war is heavy:

Ray Ollis: A chequered career

This fiend whose ghastly presence ever
Beside thee like thy shadow hangs.
(Shelley)

It's not about the numbers or statistics, but the loss of individuals who did their best against forces they could not always successfully combat.

Ray Ollis remains someone to remember. That he survived his illness long enough for his account of Bomber Command to be published is to our benefit.

Today, Margaret Ollis remembers Ray best as a fair man of slim build, talented, charismatic, handsome, walking around the room humming, beating time with a sheet of music, or playing the piano beautifully, his talent sparkling throughout the house. Margaret remembers a determined writer of articles, songs, musicals and plays, a book on the Mau-Mau uprising and a memorable Bomber Command novel.

We should remember a man who could have been anything and gone anywhere, but who died at a suburban railway station, fighting the temporary perception of himself, his unacceptable circumstances, in a moment of misguided impulse knowing he was unable to alter them.

I could lie down like a tired child
And weep away the life of care
Which I have borne and yet must bear,
Till death like sleep might steal on me,
And I might feel in the warm air
My cheek grow cold, and hear the sea ...'

Shelley, from *Lines Written in Dejection near Naples*

I am indebted to Margaret Ollis, Ray's widow;
Jonathon and Timothy Ollis, Ray's two sons;
and Marjorie Ollis, the family genealogist,
and Steve Oakley.

Notes

One

1   101 Squadron (pronounced 'one oh one'), then of Number 1
Group, Bomber Command, was one of several secretive, special
Allied squadrons. Based south of the then-small villages of Ludford
Magna and Ludford Parva, Ludford aerodrome was high up in
the Lincolnshire Wolds (a series of low treeless hills on a chalk
base). *101 Nights* is set in a fictitious amalgam of 1942 and 1943,
becoming more chronologically precise as the book progresses.

From early 1942, the Lancaster became the premier English
bomber during the Second World War, usually operating with a
crew of seven. Of the many books, start with McKinstry.

2   'Buckley' is a black joke: to say someone 'had Buckley's' was to
say they had no chance: Ollis makes us think the new crew have
'Buckley's' of surviving their first operation.

3   There were three aerials, the thickest being less than 6 inches at
the base and about two inches at the tips; one behind the pilot's
cabin, another just behind the rear turret; the third projected
out below the pilot's cabin, giving the overall impression that the
aircraft would have difficulty landing.

Not all 101 Squadron aircraft were equipped with ABC aerials
('XYZ' in Ollis); and the Luftwaffe also developed their own
'special duties' squadrons – see P.W. Stahl, *KG 200. The True Story*
(Jane's Publishing Company, 1981).

4   Not true, they did. The evolving series of battles over occupied
Europe, particularly from the end of 1942, is extraordinarily
exciting; see Knoke, Gunston, or David P. Williams, *Hunters of
the Reich. Night Fighters* (Tempus Publishing, 2001); Theo Boiten's
excellent *The Night Fighter versus Bomber War over the Third
Reich 1939–45* (Crowood Press, 1997), and Boiten and Michael
Bowman's *Battles with the Nachtjagd ...* (Schiffer, 2006) tell the
story from the German perspective.

5   'Men of many nationalities with a mixture of qualifications, were
required to speak German ... some of them, known as Special
Operators, are thought to have been Germans whom the Nazis
expelled from Germany. Their task was to seek out, jam and
confuse the enemy Wireless Transmitter and Radio Transmitter

instructions, not to mention the broadcasting of false information to German fighters while imitating their controllers. Known as "Airborne Cigar" (ABC), this operation was an additional duty, as the Lancasters still carried a normal bomb load to the target' (Alexander).

The secrecy surrounding the ABC Lancasters was as much to protect the safety of the German-speaking Specials as the ABC equipment itself; being able to speak German was regarded by most British as not only suspicious, but probably traitorous. Without the secrecy, resentful rumours involving 'local Germans' would certainly have formed; the Specials were isolated from the Squadron at large, sleeping apart from their crews. 'Ray always said that the Specials never deserted or baled out – they were part and parcel of their missions. It did upset them that they weren't treated like members of the crew – but the crews knew this and tried to make them feel better about it' (Margaret Ollis).

'Airborne Cigar' consisted of a receiver and three transmitters (the three aerials) ... The jamming signal was an undulating, warbling, almost musical note; or, as Parke explains, the clatter of one of the Lanc's engines. The receiver included a cathode ray tube which gave a visual indication of every signal within the waveband covered. As soon as a signal appeared, the special operator tuned his receiver to it, and, having identified it, one of the transmitters would be tuned to the same frequency and switched on. He would then continue to search the band for other signals. In the early days the SDOs transmitted in German but the Germans soon overcame this by broadcasting on several wavelengths ... but after [this] was discontinued ... the SDOs simply searched for – and jammed – the messages etc.' From Mike Garbett and Brian Goulding's *The Lancaster at War* (Ian Allen, 1971, the first in a series). See Appendix 1.

Feast, over Nuremberg on 30/31 March 1944; 'Every available [German] fighter was being thrown into the assault by means of the running commentary. The Germans were switching between nine different speech channels and two Morse channels; at the height of the battle the running commentary was being broadcast on five separate channels ... the transmissions were so powerful, and so many frequencies being utilised, that his jamming had little effect ... they had also lost three ABC aircraft, and were about to lose their fourth.'

6   Night fighters could and did locate 101's Lancasters by their radio transmissions; Chorlton: 'after the war it was discovered that the

Germans had developed an electronic countermeasure which enabled their fighters to home in on the ABC aircraft's jamming transmissions'; more usually the Luftwaffe Nachjagd used then-sophisticated airborne radar able to isolate aircraft inside Window's jamming; today, aircraft using the Marconi's Zeus ECM have a radar warning receiver which can locate – and jam – over 1000 searching radar signals.

Ward and Smith: 'From October 1943 onwards a sprinkling of 101 Squadron Lancasters accompanied most major operations, whether or not 1 Group was on the order of battle, and as a result, 101 Squadron sustained the highest casualties of any heavy squadron.' The 'sprinkling' was usually about six, sometimes one or two more. 'By 1945 101 Squadron had flown 2,477 ABC sorties and lost 145 Lancasters (including 33 in crashes).'

Chorlton also states that 1,176 men from 101 Squadron were killed on operations during WW2 – more than were killed at Pearl Harbor. Only 460, 103, 207 and 61 Squadrons lost more Lancasters on operations than 101 Squadron with 140, 135, 131 and 116 respectively. See also Price.

7   'Trinket' is a made-up surname; perhaps Ollis intended the name to imply that, to the British, Australians were all 'trinkets'; cheap expendable jewellery. If the expression 'Grog's the shot!' followed by the gulping of half a pint didn't announce itself clearly enough, Trinket's manner is distinctly Australian, and Australians of the day would have smiled in recognition of the 'Australian in a strange land'. Lancaster LM 739, of 100 Squadron, wore a foaming tankard inscribed 'Grog's the Shot'. This Lancaster survived the end of the war and was immortalised in kit-form by Revell in 2012.

8   '"O" wing'. Sometimes referred to as 'the Flying Arsehole', the Observer's badge featured an 'O' surmounted with a wing. In March 1942 Bomber Command decreed that the title 'observer' be changed to 'navigator' (a flying 'N') and that a 'bomb aimer' (a flying bomb) be introduced so the navigator didn't have to leave his post at a critical moment.

Joe knows Farlow has been in (and survived) the RAF for some years, as opposed to the newer or sprog crews such as Buckley's (who were told to 'touch nothing'). Usually won on the ground, the BEM, or British Empire Medal, was an unusual medal for an airman (usually being won on the ground), and would have drawn instant attention to Farlow in any RAF mess.

9   After several weeks of bombing and air-skirmishes, the Germans invaded Crete on 20 May 1941; the subsequent brutalising battle was over in twelve days. Casualties were high.

10 Krynkiwski is a fictitious surname, Ollis's first 101 squadron pilot was Walter Hrynkiw DFC; 'Krink' may have been his nickname.

11 The cumulative effect of the strain of operations caused several types of aberrant nervous behaviour. 'The operational word for nerves was "the twitch". You could see it at the bar any time. Facial muscles would twitch involuntarily without the owner's awareness. ... Some would flutter an eye, some would stutter slightly as their mouths jumped around.' (Harvey).

12 'Hyde' Parke is a double pun – Hyde Park is a famous public park in London; the darker pun implies 'Jekyll and Hyde', that Hyde has two personalities.

Two

1   Though the author represents 101 Squadron during 1943, Wing Commander R.I. Alexander DFC commanded 101 from January 1944 until after the war; Ollis did not know his predecessor.

2   Leipzig is deep in the German heartland toward Berlin, where the Saale and Elster rivers and numerous railway lines meet. Although partly a cultural centre, factories made and assembled aircraft, engines and aircraft components. It was farther to fly to Leipzig than Hamburg; Dresden is some 75 miles south-east.

3   'The weather briefing ... was eagerly awaited by all crews for the inane nonsense and tension relief it provided ... in all our weather briefings I never heard one that was coherent ...' (Harvey). In RAF slang 'cloudy' came to mean 'shady or unreliable'.

    Specials Leader 'The Hon. Holbrook-Hardwicke' is a fictitious, stylised hybrid name representing the son of a Lord, an old aristocratic family. Ollis is emphasising what is less obvious to us now: during the war the RAF mixed together people from all walks of life, including classes that would rarely if ever meet.

4   Timing in the bombing war was critical in terms of navigation, enabling a large number of aircraft to bomb in swift, successive waves; accurate timing also assisted accurate reporting.

5   4 Group. Part of 3 Group since July 1941, 101 Squadron were transferred to 1 Group in September 1942. At about the time *101 Nights* begins, there were seven Bomber Command Groups in England: 1, 2, 3, 4, 5, 6 and 8 (Pathfinder Force); 100 Group,

dedicated to RCM (Radio Countermeasures), became operational in November 1943.

6   The RAF was formed by amalgamating the Royal Flying Corps (RFC) and the Royal Naval Air Service (RNAS) during the First World War, so the RAF described their aircraft in nautical terms and maintained Naval traditions.

Crews varied their in-aircraft patter depending on how, when and where they were taught, and how they adapted to battle conditions in the air. In order to prevent confusion, crews rarely called each other by name in the air, but by their job; 'skipper', 'rear gunner' and 'bomb aimer'.

7   Ground speed would always be greater than air-speed, because the higher above the ground you are, the further there is to fly, so even if you're flying at 150 mph three miles up, you're travelling slower than that 'on the ground'. Hence 'indicated' (meaning 'indicated air speed') versus 'ground speed'. Other variables were the wind speed and direction.

8   In west Germany, the Ruhr was a 30-mile long tightly packed industrial area near the Rhine which produced large quantities of guns, transport, bombs, ammunition and other militarily helpful products. Usually wreathed in drifting smoke and fog haze, it withstood numerous (relatively ineffective) attacks by the RAF until late October 1944. See also Cooper, *The Air Battle of the Ruhr* ... and Botting *From the Ruins of the Reich: Germany 1945–1949*.

9   Flak battery. A concentration of anti-aircraft guns.

10 The Handley Page Halifax was England's other major four-engined bomber. Renaut: 'I had now great faith in the Halifax and its handling qualities and I had seen how it stood up to a battering. Mind you, it took strength in the forearms and wrists to hurl it about the sky, and unlike the Lancaster it responded slowly and heavily ... the Lancaster was much gentler to fly but give me the Halifax for a battering every time.' Although Dyson points out that the successful bale-out rate was higher in 'Hallybags' than Lancasters (whose main escape hatch was quite small), more comforting to the Lancaster crews was their considerably higher operational ceiling, which may partly explain why Halifaxes had a higher successful bale-out rate: they were hit more often by the German flak. An August 1942 memorandum from Harris to Portal; '[the performance of the Halifax is] little better than the [two-engined] Wellington. The Lancaster ... at the same

all-up weight as the Halifax (59,000 lbs) can carry 3000 lbs more bombs or fly 550 miles further. In addition, it is faster and is more manoeuvrable ...' (McKinstry).

11 Q-Queenie. Since RFC days the RAF used letters and familiar words to help identify each aircraft over the radio, and prevent misheard letters. For the majority of WW2, no RAF squadron had more than 26 operational aircraft (although 101 was an exception), so each aircraft was unique. The letters which identified each aircraft (and its radio call-sign) were painted in large letters on both sides of the aircraft fuselage, after the two-letter squadron designation code. 101 Squadron's designation was SR; each aircraft also wore a serial number, painted in much smaller letters on the aircraft's tail.

Radio call-signs in WW2 varied slightly; RAF call-signs were later superseded by the NATO phonetic alphabet (i.e., Alpha, Bravo, Charlie, Delta, Echo, etc).

12 With GPS beyond imagining, night bombers used radio beams to find their way. Without them, they were reduced to triangulating their position by the stars, gauging windspeed and groundspeed and hoping their compass was working. The result was often inaccurate bombing.

13 The corkscrew is sometimes misleading in description; from a novel written by a Lancaster veteran: 'the standard night-flying evasive action tactic in Bomber Command ... the manoeuvre consisted of flying the bomber on a flight path paralleling that of a corkscrew. If the gunners, for instance, reported a nightfighter closing in from the rear port quarter – or eight o'clock – the pilot dived to port in a turn, pulled out and made a climbing turn to port, rolled over into a climbing turn to starboard and, then, completing the cycle, dived to port again. Carried out at night under combat conditions, [the corkscrew] proved itself against German nightfighters whose pilots had found it difficult, in the darkness, to keep a well-corkscrewed Lancaster or Halifax in clear view long enough to line it up in their gunsights for an accurate burst of fire.' (Geoff Taylor, *Beware the Wounded Tiger*, Peter Davies, 1971).

14 '... we struck our first fighter, a decoy with all lights ablaze flying 1000 yards astern. This was strictly for the birds and, instead of catching us unaware, alerted the entire crew so that when the fighter who was tracking us on instruments started his attack from 5 o'clock we turned smartly into it and he ran through a long

burst which so disillusioned him he disappeared into the night. His decoy also doused lights and possibly went in search of more gullible victims'. (Cusack)

15 Flying a dog-leg 'meant deliberately to cut across the path of one's fellow aircraft on leaving or re-entering the stream. It meant running the risk of collision and throwing the advancing war machine out of gear. And yet no one dreamed of arguing. The orders were formal. You had to be on time'. (Calmel)

A curve of pursuit 'consisted of the positioning period, when the attacker flew a parallel course some 1,500 yards behind to the right or left of the aircraft, estimating the course and speed of the other plane. Having assessed this, if he was on the bomber's starboard or right wing he would bank, drop his port or left wing, and start his attack towards the tail of his target. At approximately 800 yards he would straighten up, pull his sights on to the target, drop his right wing and come in for the attack proper. To nullify this, as soon as he banked the second time, the gunner who had been watching and giving a running commentary to his pilot, knew the enemy was committed to attack and ready to open fire. At 600 yards he gave the command "Turn starboard, go" at which the bomber pilot threw the bomber into a violent turn right. If everything had been estimated correctly, the fighter pilot, already launched on his final thrust, would be unable to turn, and travelling at 150 miles per hour faster than the bomber, would go skidding past its tail. The gunner, estimating distance on his illuminated sight at 600 yards, was supposed to open fire ahead of the plane so that it passed through his fire.' (Cusack)

16 'Hitting' a slipstream; while the initial tube of disturbed air behind each propellor did dissipate into a long cone, crossing the disturbed air could vary from a slight judder to the physical jolt when a car hits a speed hump on the road, which could cause the aircraft to buck.

17 By this stage of the war, 'bombing blind on ETA' was recognised as unreliable. 'Every deviation from course, every variation in airspeed or alteration in height, adds another mile to the final error. A difference of one degree gives an error of one mile in sixty, and on the compass one degree is almost indistinguishable. On a flight of 600 miles, then, it will be a good crew that has less than a ten-mile error' (Cheshire).

With no official records and only his log-book and diary, and perhaps only Harris's *Bomber Offensive* available to him, Ollis's depiction of 101's earlier career is remarkably accurate.

18   Cheshire; 'Half our job was to drop the bombs in the right place, the other half to get back intact and fit to fly again. Then navigation: to make use of all available aids; to check the "met" winds by visual pin-point if possible: if not, by taking drifts or Astro sights, or in the last resort by W/T. ... we sorted out the navigational equipment and stowed it in the satchel. I never knew there could be so much stuff for what I imagined was a simple operation. Maps, rulers, compass, dividers, CSC, pencils, rubber, penknife, code books, computer, plotter, Astro tables, watch, sextant, planisphere, protractor, log book and Very cartridges.'

19   Taxying: the aircraft travelling on the ground. The 'pens', 'pans' or 'frying pans' were just off the perimeter track; aircraft travelled from the perimeter track along a shorter track which ended in a large flat circular area (the pen) where the aircraft were parked between ops, and where the ground crew usually worked on them. The pen was also called a pan because it looked like a frying pan from above.

20   A firkin is an old English unit of measure applied to volume – thereby liquid, implicitly beer. Today the term is modestly ribald. *101 Nights* was published in 1957, when 'fucking' could not have been published in any mainstream English book.

21   For three navigators to be killed with the same pilot – and on the same tour – is long (but not impossible) odds.

Three

1   'Pearly Oyster' is a powerfully lewd sexual innuendo.
    Aircrew were often housed in Nissen huts. Harvey: 'The Nissen hut was nothing more than a concrete pad over which corrugated iron sheets were bolted in a continuous arch from one side to the other. The end walls were made of wood. A door and two tiny windows were located at one of the ends. It was large enough to house a row of six iron cots on either side of a central aisle, which was the only spot where you could stand fully erect. Heat was supposedly supplied by a tiny iron stove, erected in and blocking the centre aisle ... it was perfectly heat proof.'

2   The watches used by the RAF during World War 2 were made by several companies but are usually referred to as Longines.
    Once Bomber Command began operating by night, navigation became a struggle to blend arithmetic and geometry into a practical method of keeping a large aircraft on track in the dark. Dead reckoning computed the speed of the aircraft, the height

of the aircraft, and the local wind speed and applied it to a map. Astro navigation assisted to pin-point the aircraft's position with reference to the stars. Both methods require precision timekeeping – the Mark XI navigator's watch had a second-hand. The Mark XI also had to be waterproof, vibration-proof and – as aircraft flew higher – temperature and pressure-proof.

3 By the 1930s, dockworkers were regarded as the most militant and communist of labour groups. Dockworkers were renowned for dropping tools at inopportune moments; in October 1943 London dockworkers went on strike, demanding 'extra danger money' to unload American ammunition ships. In May 1943 Sydney dockworkers struck and American soldiers had to give up part of their leave in order to unload ships; in Wellington, New Zealand, the dockworkers struck just before the Marines were due to ship out to Guadalcanal, with the result that the Marines loaded their own gear, adding to the shemozzle on the landing beaches. Such strikes must have worked; many RAF airmen were surprised to find that labourers digging latrine trenches at their aerodrome earned more than they did, partly because of the 'danger' involved in working at a wartime 'target'. See Hal Colebatch's *Australia's Secret War. How Unions Sabotaged Our Troops in World War II* (2014).

4 A suitably obscene song.

5 It was not unusual for crew members to experience loose bowels or vomit before (or even during) an operation. Sometimes the captain reported it, sometimes he didn't. It was only when such an illness interfered with the crew member's ability to perform his duties that it became a problem.

6 A logbook entry describing 'intense light flak' or 'moderate heavy flak' refers to the calibre and type of shell used, not the intensity.

   German defenders used mostly 88 mm guns and 105 mm guns. The 88s were 'heavy flak' and had a ceiling of up to 49,000 feet. The explosive shell had a mechanical time fuze, so it would explode where the bombers were. Heavier flak was later fitted with a proximity fuze to detect a large body (such as an aircraft), exploding regardless of height. 105 mms fired even heavier 32 lb shells but at a much lower height. Medium flak fired more slowly and aircraft had to be flying quite low for light flak to be effective. See Hogg.

7 The Short Stirling was the first four-engined British heavy bomber of the Second World War. Designed and built by Short Brothers to a 1936 Air Ministry specification the Stirling entered service

in 1941, being relegated to second line duties from 1943 when the
Halifax and Lancaster took over its role.

8   There is no reason not to accept both Harris (in *Despatch*) and
Garbett and Goulding that instructions were indeed issued 'in
the early days'. Martin Bowman reports that, on their first night
of operation, 7/8 October 1944, that ABC Specials from 101
Squadron, broadcast 'the order "All butterflies go home" ... on the
German night fighter frequency, resulting in many enemy night-
fighter pilots returning to their airfields!' (*Confounding the Reich* ...).
This technique was code-named CORONA: Countermeasures
against Running Commentary.

      Harris (in *Bomber*); 'We had evidence of the effectiveness of this
method when we began to hear the enemy controllers lose their
tempers.'

      CORONA first operated on Kassel on the night of 22/23
October 1943 where the bombs and incendiaries created a
firestorm. The three factories constructing V1 bombs were badly
affected, delaying the start and degree of the V1 attacks. On the 17
November raid on Ludwigshafen, the CORONA operator told the
German nightfighters to land because of fog; most landed early for
the loss of only one Lancaster.

9   Hans Jeschonnek. A career Nazi who transferred to the Luftwaffe
in 1933, he became Chief of the General Staff of the Luftwaffe
only six years later.

10   Remscheid, just south east of the Ruhr. 'The Heinkel He
100D single-seat fighter was, for a considerable period of the
war, an enigma. Allocated the designation 'He 113' by the
Reichsluftfahrtministerium and much publicised under this type
number by the German Propaganda Ministry, the fighter never, in
fact, bore this appellation ... it was generally believed that the He
100 (alias He 113) had entered service with the Luftwaffe, but the
fighter was never accepted for service use. Only twelve production
He 100D-1 fighters were built and, in a successful attempt to
mislead Allied Intelligence, these were repainted with different
insignia several times and many propaganda photographs of the
fighter distributed, leading to the erroneous belief that the He 100
was in widespread use' (Green).

      The 30/31 July 1943 raid on Remscheid 'marks the true end
of the Battle of the Ruhr'. Middlebrook and Everitt do not
mention the Heinkel factory, but 'the post-war British Bombing
Survey estimated that 83% of the town was devastated [with] 107
industrial buildings ... destroyed; the town's industry, generally,

lost 3 months' production and never fully regained previous levels'. This raid pre-dates 101's first use of ABC on 7–8 October.

11 Commanded by the famous VC winner Hughie Edwards, 460 (RAAF) Squadron also flew Lancasters. Based at Binbrook, a few miles north of Ludford. 100 Squadron, based at Waltham, a few miles north of Binbrook, was the first choice for ABC but, already fitted with the new H2S radar, could not carry both.

12 It was not unusual for a crew member to drop 'a little something extra' with the bomb-load – a brick, a bottle or two or a small practice bomb.

13 Blackpool Illuminations. Prior to World War I, Blackpool was known for a spectacular display of nearly ten thousand arranged electric light bulbs. Removed during the war, the display returned in 1925 on a much grander scale. The lights went out again in September 1939, returning ten years later.

14 Perhaps. Deighton (in *Bomber*); 'In cash, at 1943 prices with profits pared to a minimum, each Lancaster cost £42,000.'

Harris, *Bomber Offensive*; 'The education of a member of a bomber crew was the most expensive in the world; it cost some £10,000 for each man, enough to send ten men to Oxford or Cambridge for three years.' Deighton continues, 'Add another £13,000 for bombs, fuel, servicing and ground-crew training at bargain prices and each bomber was a public investment of £120,000.'

15 However, putting extra strain on an engine can cause it to break down, later leading to serious problems – if not loss of life.

16 While this incident was rare, it did happen that an airman might faint or swoon under pressure. Calmel even confesses that on the way home, all the crew but the pilot were asleep!

17 Odds of survival were heatedly discussed in Bomber Command, which had the harshest casualty rate of the British Services in WW2. Of all aircraft on ops, the 1943 average loss was 3.6%, so 33% of all crews might survive a first tour, but only 16% or so would survive a second. But the radar battle in the night skies over Europe shifted rapidly from late 1943, and the odds shrank ...

18 101 Squadron lost two aircraft on the 'Thousand Bomber' raid on Cologne on 30 May 1942; 101 Squadron performed its first ABC operation (7/8 October 1943 against Stuttgart). 1942 was Bomber Command's year of demonstration and consolidation; the great Bomber Offensive did not start in earnest until 1943.

19 After much argument, The Pathfinder Force (PFF) was formed in
    January 1943.
20 On numerous raids the German fighters were drawn north or
    simply away from the RAF's intended target areas by diversionary
    raids, course changes in the bomber stream, and misleading
    transmissions in German from an RCM station in England.
21 In the popular newspaper comic strip *Blondie* (from 1930) by Chic
    Young, Blondie Bumstead was the top-heavy blonde and Daisy the
    family dog. Blondie and Daisy would have been instantly familiar.
22 Krink's almost says, 'mistress', which would imply that Blondie
    was a prostitute or loose woman, which Blondie would have found
    insulting. Sensibly, Krink dries up.

Four

1 Krink isn't the only one who cheats on his partner; his American
   wife's room-mate appears to either have two boyfriends or Krink's
   wife has slipped up and she has a new boyfriend – presumably
   Ruffles (referring to Ruffles and Flourishes, the fanfare which
   ushers in dignitaries). This is a loaded paragraph; there are several
   controversial points. The B-17 Flying Fortress did fly faster and
   higher than the Lancaster, but the Lanc carried more bombs
   further than the Fortress day-only bomber. The debate continues.
2 'Miss Barbara Cunard' is intended to represent a member of the
   fabulously wealthy family of Cunard Line shipping company fame;
   Ollis loved the cruise liners.
3 Cusack differs: 'At briefing, in addition to the Groupy and Wingco
   was a middle-aged florid officer with bags of rings who was finally
   pin-pointed as the Group Air Vice-Marshal. An English pilot with
   twenty ops to his credit remarked, 'I don't like the look of this.
   These bloody AVMs mean a lousy target.'
      Air Vice Marshal E.A.B. Rice served 1 Group from 24 February
   1943 until 11 May 1945.
4 Only six weeks after ABC was introduced, and only a month after
   CORONA was introduced, German women gave instructions to
   the night-fighters; German-speaking WAAFs were used for the
   first time on 23/24 November on the third attack in the long-
   running Battle of Berlin, and directed the German pilots to land.
   Many did.
5 The first PFF raid is infamous. On the night of 17/18 August 1942
   the Flensburg U-boat construction yards were raided, led by the
   PFF. Don Bennett, their commanding officer, furiously objected,

citing the bad weather and the four different aircraft the PFF had been issued with, each of which had a different ceiling and speed. The met wind prediction was wrong and the bombers drifted north; towns in Denmark were bombed instead.

6   There were still Avro Manchester squadrons as the Lancaster came onto operations. Harris despised the bureaucrats who insisted on using the inadequate Napier Vulture engines on the Manchester.

7   The planners tried to stagger the different types of aircraft and their operational heights to minimise 'friendly' bombing. But many RAF aircraft were destroyed like this, others returning with holes or unexploded ordnance. On the first Thousand Bomber Raid, statisticians calculated that the number of bombers likely to collide was two; Bomber Command considered this an acceptable risk given that without the bomber stream, many more bombers would be shot down.

Five

1   Introduced in March 1942, Gee was a variant on the German Knickebein target location system. The Gee set was a cathode ray tube – rather like a primitive television. By August 1942 the Germans had developed Heinrich, which jammed Gee ground transmissions; by November Gee was unusable; the British countered with Oboe in December.

2   Window was used on the first of four massive RAF raids on Hamburg, on 24/25 July 1943, predating the use of ABC and Corona. The 27/28 July raid caused a firestorm.

    Window consisted of bundles of 2,200 strips of coarse black paper with aluminium foil stuck to one side. These metallised strips could swamp German radar sets – particularly the Wurzburgs and Lichtensteins – with false echoes making them useless.

3   Window was introduced reluctantly, lest it affect allied defences. Nevertheless it was estimated that its use in the six major raids which comprised the Battle of Hamburg 'saved' over 100 bombers aircraft. The Luftwaffe's version was called Duppel (i.e., double).

4   A googly is a ball bowled in cricket which turns in the direction opposite to what the batsman might expect, deceiving him. 'Every ball a wicket' means that for every ball bowled, a batsman is dismissed – an almost impossible success. At the time, the British surface attitude to war as a game of cricket was mirrored in the RAF.

5   On 14 May 1940, the Germans threatened to bomb Rotterdam
    unless it surrendered, which it did. Some bombers already
    despatched didn't receive the cancellation order and about
    800 civilians died, causing worldwide outrage. The Germans
    considered bombing Rotterdam to be strategic, and later bombed
    Coventry and London to destroy targets like oil, food, supplies
    and military-manufacturing. The British, outraged by what
    they considered deliberate, cowardly and unnecessary attacks on
    civilians, learned a great deal from the German bombing. With
    the assistance of America and its Lend-Lease loans, in the final
    eighteen months of the war the Allies devastated German cities in
    kind, diverting millions to the air defence of the Reich rather than
    resisting Allied invasion forces.

6   A fire-storm from the air. 'On a wide horizon, from north to south,
    a single fiery glow; above this, while we had a clear starry sky
    above us, an enormous cloud whirled and billowed upon itself over
    the city, reaching to the sky with sharp, threatening edges. I was
    reminded of a volcano eruption ...' (Dr Franz Termer as quoted in
    Lowe).
        Nuremberg had avoided major destruction in previous raids; the
    most destructive raid on the city was on 2/3 January 1945 where,
    although great damage was caused by fire, there was no actual
    firestorm; Ollis did not fly on this raid. Martin Middlebrook's *The
    Nuremberg Raid* deals with the 'Night of the Big Winds' (the worst
    of several), which resulted in the loss of almost 100 bombers.

7   Aircrew were guarded around 'correspondents'.

8   This statement, even in 1943 (as opposed to 1940), would have
    been hotly denied by many pilots. However Ottaway quotes Guy
    Gibson, at a talk at a gunnery school in Quebec, 'navigators were
    rapidly taking the place of the pilot as the "main man" in a bomber
    crew. He didn't like to say this as he was a pilot himself, but it was
    true.' Fighter and fighter-bomber pilots were their own navigators.

9   Of Group Captain Leonard Cheshire, Morris quotes Flight
    Lieutenant Ron A. Read; '[*Bomber Pilot*] breached the 'line-
    shooting' code of the RAF, and [Cheshire] was regarded with
    some suspicion by many who read it, including most of my
    contemporaries. We couldn't accept that anyone who could
    break the code in such a way, obtaining considerable publicity
    while doing so, could still be a genuine, down-to-earth, ordinary
    operational pilot.' Cheshire was later awarded the Victoria Cross
    for numerous acts of gallantry.

10 Reminiscent of the 27/28 July 'firestorm' raid on Hamburg. Joe's comment seems brutal – if pragmatic – about the unspeakable horror of burning thousands of civilians to death. Given Ollis's earlier remark about 'useless, helpless civilians' (above), every crew knew they were flying an extremely flammable aircraft into a 'very hot' place, that on each raid they were running a small but significant risk of being burned alive ... as they flew through the hot air and cloud of a burning city, many would smell burning human flesh.

11 '... in addition to their bombing role, some elements of V/KG 2 began to intercept bombers over England and from late August ...1943, intruders once more presented a threat to Bomber Command.' Parry, *Intruders over Britain: The Luftwaffe Night Fighter Offensive 1940–1945* (1987).

Regular German intruder operations lasted until April 1944. Parry relates; 'the only 101 Squadron Lancaster brought down by a German intruder was Lancaster III ED410, early in the morning of the 28 September 1943. Refused permission to land at Ludford, Pilot Officer Skipper had been diverted to Lindholm where, over the Wickenby airfield, Oberleutnant Abrahamczik shot the Lanc down ... none of the eight crew had time to escape before the aircraft crashed and exploded in flames.'

12 The role of the 'Master Bomber' (or 'Raid Controller') was introduced by Guy Gibson on the Dams Raid of 16 May 1943. Gibson performed this job once more, on the raid of 19 September 1944 on Rheydt and Monchengladbach on which he was shot down by Bernard McCormack, the mid-upper gunner in a returning Lancaster of 61 Squadron.

13 Peenemunde was the German secret research and development site on the Baltic, catering principally to the V2 rockets. The raid was essential; the master bomber was Group Captain John H. Searby (*The Everlasting Arms*, 1988). It is thought that this raid delayed the appearance of the V2 over Britain by two months. Forty-four allied aircraft were lost, partly due to the attack being deliberately made in moonlight, and partly because the Germans had just introduced Schrage Musik (two upward-firing cannons) in their Me 110 night-fighters.

14 At 8 am on 18 August, Jeschonnek received a call; 'Peenemunde, which, as the birthplace of the V-weapons, was the apple of [Jeschonnek's] eye, had been the target of an extremely heavy precision air attack.' Half an hour later Jeschonnek was found dead

on the floor, his pistol beside him. He left a note: 'I can no longer work together with the Reichsmarschall. Long live the Fuhrer' (E.R. Hooton, *Eagle in Flames. The Fall of the Luftwaffe*, 1999). The damage to Peenemunde was less than first thought; neither the testing blocks nor the irreplaceable construction drawings had been destroyed (Cajus Bekker: *The Luftwaffe War Diaries*, 1967); even so, the Peenemunde raid was the last straw for Jeschonnek. The Luftwaffe was losing control over events. Jeschonnek was caught between 'the truculence of Hitler, whom he greatly admired, and Goring'; he was a scapegoat for other men's failings.

Six

1   Cricketers. William Joseph 'Bill' O'Reilly (1905–1992) was a great Australian bowler; Harold Larwood (1904–1995) was a precise English fast bowler.

2   Many bomber airfields were close to railway lines; B-17s flying low near trains would have been an everyday sight. There were numerous occasions where an aircraft would, against standing orders, fly too low and 'buzz' a train; there were many deaths.

3   The original is delightfully rude. Also, singing anything like this near US flyers was asking for a fight.

   'To get good results with the Norden the bombardier needed to make an undisturbed straight and level bomb run lasting three minutes (about nine miles) and be able to observe the target through his sighting telescope during that time … Under operational conditions bomb aiming errors could be anything up to five times as great as those on practice ranges, for visual bombing.' Ethell and Price, *Target Berlin. Mission 250: 6 March 1944* (1981).

   There is a complex, involved history behind Carl Norden's bomb-sight; only the two lead B-17s used the sight and the rest of the bombers dropped their bombs when they saw the lead bomber's load drop, so there was considerable margin for error.

   Calais is the nearest European port to England and was regarded by the RAF as a cushy target, despite being heavily fortified because the Germans expected the Allies to land there. The Germans fired large calibre guns at England from Calais, later building V1 flying bomb launch ramps.

4   Coger's is still pronounced 'Koh-jers'.

5   Purple Heart. American medal awarded for receiving an injury, regardless of how slight or catastrophic.

6 *Queens Die Proudly* by William Lindsay White (1943); *How to Lose a War* was metaphorical. Farlow's remark, 'I seem to recall the evacuation of Manila was none too glorious' refers to White's *They Were Expendable* (1942).

7 The actual paragraph is: 'Side by side, the Dutch and the Australians plunged through that outer ring of Jap submarines. The American forces took up the last defensive position, skirting the back edge, firing on the run. It was our duty not to dissipate ourselves in lost causes, but to do what damage we could, and conserve our strength to strike again.' See Roberts, *Age Shall Not Weary Them* ... (1941?); McKie, *Proud Echo* (1953) and Payne, *HMAS Perth ... 1936–1942* (1978).

8 The question is, 'which country bore the brunt of the majority of the fighting, Britain and its Empire, or the Americans (who sometimes appear to believe they won it all by themselves)?' Most combatants in WW2 knew the previous war's peace had been botched and felt that WW2 was a continuation of The Great War.

9 On 30 January 1943, the tenth anniversary of the Nazi's coming to power, three De Havilland Mosquitoes from 105 Squadron bombed Berlin as Goering was about to address the nation, forcing the speech to be postponed. 139 Squadron did the same to Goebbels a few hours later.

10 See Gallagher, *Retreat in the East* (1942) and Clive and Knight's *Milne Bay 1942* (2000); also Graeme-Evans' two-volume *Of Storms and Rainbows. The ... 2/12th Battalion AIF ...* (1991).

11 Peter Fitzsimons' popular overview, *Tobruk* (2006) should be read alongside Maughan, *Tobruk and El Alamein* (1966).

12 Meaning Russia. In April 1945 Knoke wrote; 'Communism has now reached the heart of Europe ... The destruction of the German Reich means that the last bulwark against Red world-revolution has been overthrown. Over Berlin the Red Flag now flies. There we have the real victor in this war. The way is now open to Stalin. When will his tanks roll across Europe?'

13 They were lucky to avoid the more likely scenario of an enthusiastic brawl ending only with the arrival of the Military Police. Disputes and brawls were common.

14 Riley specialised in making in sports and racing cars.

Seven

1 The equipment and extra person in a 101 Lanc certainly pushed up
the cost. The young pilot officer, by his public schoolboyish slang
and this deliberate misquotation, represents England's privileged
upper class. The phrase is attributed to the Duke of Wellington
as he passed a cricket match at Eton many years after his victory
at Waterloo; according to Sir Edward Creasy, Wellington actually
said; 'There grows the stuff that won Waterloo' – a reference to the
quality of the young men of England, not of Eton specifically.

2 Ollis did not fly on this raid, and his description seems to be a
composite of the last major RAF raid on Berlin, on 24/25 March
1944 ('the night of the big winds'), and the Nuremberg raid on
30/31 March 1944, which incurred heavy losses.

3 Percy Bysshe Shelley's, *Ode to the West Wind* first appeared in
Prometheus Unbound (1820). Ollis is referring to the unexpectedly
powerful west wind which wrought such havoc on this raid.

4 At altitude, ice could build up on an aircraft's upper surfaces so
quickly and thickly that the aircraft could suddenly drop from the
sky; the pilot needed skill, courage and luck to be able to recover
from such a dive. Ice was also one reason the Air Speed Indicator
stopped working.
    When RAF aircraft weren't 'kites', 'crates' or 'machines', they
were 'she' (despite this particular aircraft being V-Victor). Another
hold-over from the Royal Navy.

5 When Hyde (as Shelley) wants to become part of the 'wild west
wind', one wonders at the paradox; to the Germans, the 'wild west
wind' was Bomber Command.

6 The aerodrome would set up a radio signal, the pilot would hear
an 'error' sound when the aircraft was not 'on the beam', and a
different note when the aircraft was on track. SBA (Standard Beam
Approach) was not infallible and required practice to get right.
    '... fog to an Air Force that had yet to be introduced to the
wonders of radar and the blind approaches it made possible, all
too often sealed pilots off from the ground until they ran out of
fuel and the only safe way home was on the end of a parachute ...'
(Mackersey). The aircraft would have been abandoned in the air, to
fall where it may.

7 Shelley's *Ode to the West Wind*.

8 Middlebrook (*The Nuremberg Raid*) cites 101 Squadron as
dispatching 26 ABC Lancasters. Of these, 20 bombed, 6 were
missing, one was wrecked in a crash. 47 men were killed, 8 were

POWs and one evader. Feast describes the dining room after the raid; '... he was surprised to find the room devoid of any of the WAAF girls who were usually there with a friendly smile and a greeting to serve them their meal. The serving cabinet was filled ... but there were no waitresses. Instead, there was a notice pinned to the wall that simply instructed them to help themselves ... The WAAFs ... were in the rest room, in tears.' Otter quotes Marjorie Dymond on her first day at Ludford Magna, the day after the Nuremberg raid; 'there was a gloom over the place I hadn't met before in my service ... 101 Squadron had lost nine aircraft and their crews the night before.' (*Maximum Effort III* ... 1993).

Eight

1   More aircrew were killed on this Nuremberg raid than in the Battle of Britain.

2   Lack of Moral Fibre. RAF code for cowardice, as opposed to being unable to fly for medical reasons (the German term was *Kanalkrank*).

3   In the week following Nuremberg, Bomber Command mounted only a few small raids. 101 missed the next major raid, by 5 Group on 5/6 April, but sent seven Lancs to Villeneuve-St-Georges on 9/10 April.

4   In April 1942 Bomber Command forbade wives to live inside 40 miles of an operational station. The effect a devastated wife could have on active station life was disconcerting, but many COs turned a blind eye to the practice.

5   Established in 1938 as an aircraft maintenance, storage and training unit, RAF Cosford also housed a hospital.

6   The Croix de Guerre is a prestigious French medal.

7   Archibald McIndoe pioneered plastic surgery for severe burns before, during and after World War II.

8   Winston Churchill was Prime Minister of Britain for most of World War 2.
     'The night of 16/17 October 1940 was particularly unfortunate. During raids by seventy-three bombers on various German targets, only three aircraft were shot down, but ten Hampdens and four Wellingtons crashed in England when attempting to land at their fog-covered bases on return. When this was brought to the attention of Winston Churchill, he immediately memoed his chief of air staff, who had only been in the job for two weeks: "What

arrangements have we got for blind landings for aircraft? How many aircraft are so fitted? It ought to be possible to guide them down quite safely as commercial craft were before the war in spite of fog. Let me have full particulars. The accidents last night are very serious." (Williams). This memo lead to the development and widespread use of the beam approach or glide path landing.

9   Ollis seems to assess the cost of each Lancaster at around £42,000; by 1943 standards it was over £45,000, several thousands of times the yearly salary of a flight-sergeant or pilot officer.

10   FIDO (Fog Intensive Dispersal Operation) at Ludford was clearly necessary because Ludford was usually the last airfield in the area to disappear beneath the fog, and 101's RCM were critical. Construction of FIDO at Ludford started in summer 1943, the squadron running ops around the workers until it finally became operational in March 1944.

     Landing at Ludford was more difficult than at other south-west to north-west airfields because of the potential cross-wind, and landing at Ludford with a cross-wind and FIDO lit up was even more hazardous (partly because the heat could be blown away). Then factor in Otter; 'the air space around Ludford was particularly busy as the circuits for Binbrook, Kelstern and Ludford virtually overlapped' (*Maximum Effort, The Untold Stories*, 1993).

     '... to get back to base and find the place fog-bound isn't comforting. FIDO ... was, to say the least, slightly Heath Robinsonish ... pipes along both sides of the landing strip; steel hosepipes, with holes drilled along the top. Come the fog, and the return of the wandering boys, all you have to do is belt high-octane fuel into the pipes, until the juice squirts out of the holes; then (in effect) drop a match. The fog goes like magic. But it's a little like landing in the mouth of hell, and you'd better not fishtail off *that* bloody runway. I, for one, never fell in love with FIDO' (Wainwright, *Tail-end Charlie. One Man's Journey Through a War*, 1978).

     FIDO saved thousands of lives, but FIDO's flames did reach up to some injured aircraft and blow them apart. *Tee Emm* (May 1944) attempts to dispel doubt; 'Prune followed the instructions and found himself safe on the ground. He said the experience was rather like descending into hell; he had half-expected to find Mephistopheles in person standing by the blood wagon.'

11   Shakespeare's *Henry V*, referring to the construction of knight's armour and other preparations prior to battle. Ollis directly aligns

the bomber crews with the knights who fought the French for Calais. The build-up to D-Day was phenomenally complex.

12 Speer; 'I shall never forget the date May 12 [1944]... On that day the technological war was decided. Until then we had managed to produce approximately as many weapons as the armed forces needed, in spite of their considerable losses. But with the attack of 935 daylight bombers of the American Eighth Air Force upon several fuel plants in central and eastern Germany, a new era in the air war began. It meant the end of German armaments production.'

13 Ryan only says that the window-dropping force (617 and 218 Squadrons) 'confused' the German radar stations because the window 'snowed the screens'; although partly correct, this is ultimately misleading. *101 Nights* was published three years before *The Longest Day*, and here Ollis explains that the Window-dropping force (operations Glimmer and Taxable) pretended to be an invasion fleet. Operation ABC had five B-17s from 214 Squadron (of 100 Group) and 24 101 ABC Squadron Lancasters flying in a great rectangle (roughly from Eastborne to le Traport), their radio emissions pretending to be part of a huge bomber stream; the ABC aircraft were intended to draw the German fighters. Due to engine failures, P/O M.J. Steele's ABC Lancaster L-Love was ditched 25 miles off Beachy Head at 0050 hrs; the crew were quickly retrieved.

14 Aircrew often preferred older aircraft because they had always returned. See Franks, *Ton-up Lancs* (2005).

15 There were four airborne deception operations in the evening and early morning. Operations Glimmer (performed by 218 Squadron between Eastbourne and Boulogne) and Taxable (performed by 617 and 50 Squadrons between the middle of the Channel opposite Littlehampton and the Cap d'Antifer) consisted of pushing out bundles of Window at precise intervals as the aircraft flew at a precise low level and slow speed, producing radar signals which simulated an invasion fleet. Similarly, Operations Titanic I, II, III and IV (performed by 149, 138, 90, 199 and 803 Squadrons) simulated an airborne invasion near Caen and the Cap d'Antifer, dropping hundreds of dummy paratroops (armed with sound and light-producing devices) through a huge cloud of Window. Mandrel was twelve ships producing emissions from the Channel to jam the German early warning radars from picking up the actual invasion fleet.

'All the German night fighters that operated were put up against
the patrol of ABC aircraft ... on their arrival in the area, the
fighters found that they were being subjected to serious jamming
on the R/T communications channel; then the fighter control
plotting became confused due to the presence of German fighters
in among the jammers. The fighters returned towards their control
points, but appear to have received instructions to go on hunting
in the [non-existent] bomber stream as there was sporadic fighter
activity in that area between 0105 hr and 0355 hr. The result of
all this confusion was that the Airborne Forces met no opposition
in the air and landed with negligible casualties – a remarkable
achievement when it is remembered that a casualty rate of at least
25% was expected' (Brookes); also see Price.

16   101 had no respite after D-Day; there were just too many
important ops, some supporting the invasion, some to V1
launching sites. From here onwards Ray seems to be describing his
own operational experiences.

17   This may be how Glenn Miller died; heading for Paris on a foggy
15 December 1944 his C-64 transport aircraft flew into an area
allocated for jettisoning bombs, and was hit by bombs dropped by
recalled Lancasters. If a pilot needed to jettison his load, ultimately
he was going to drop it where-ever he could.

18   Middlebrook and Everitt state that the RAF lost 53 Bomber
Command aircraft from the night of 5 June to the morning of
the 9th, not including Fighter Command (Air Defence of Great
Britain), Coastal Command, nor the Second Tactical Air Force
losses; the USAAF 8th and 9th Air Forces were also involved in
D-Day. There are many books detailing the land and airborne
forces on D-Day; but at the time Ollis was writing, the air and
naval aspects of D-Day were all but forgotten; to some extent it
remains so today. See Delve, *D-Day. The Air Battle* (1994).

PART TWO

One

1   A deliberately chosen name. Matthew the Evangelist died a martyr.
Thomas A'Beckett (1118–1170) was Henry II's 'turbulent priest'.
The Chilterns are the chalk flatlands spread over much of southern
and eastern England, including Lincolnshire; it seems that Ollis
is describing Chiltern as a chalky, flaky man whose natural goal

is martyrdom because he angers people enough they want to kill him.

2   During WW2 the RAF dropped unnecessary formality. On operational stations saluting was unnecessary given the stress and strain of operations. But saluting and proper RAF conduct was rigorously enforced at training stations, and some newly arrived aircrew found this lack of discipline initially confusing, with awkward or embarrassing results. See also Cusack.

3   The only person dressed up in full pomp and regalia at the Lord Mayor's Show in a local village or town, would be the Mayor and a few dignitaries; everyone else would be dressed more casually.

4   Actual battle conditions could not be simulated, and the rapid pace of the night war meant that what was current six months ago would not be current by the time the new crew arrived at an operational squadron, Training Command was not highly regarded by operational crews.

5   In the lead-up to the invasion of Europe, the RAF began flying short, daylight missions.

6   'Screened from operations'. Johnnie had reached the end of his tour. A second tour of operations was 20 ops, after which aircrew could no longer be ordered to fly on operations. The exception was the Pathfinder Force, whose first tour was 45 operations, and 15 optional. Many crews opted to continue after completing the 'magic 60', some flying over 100 ops.

7   Invoking the battle cry 'England, Bomber Harris and Christmas turkey at home!', light-heartedly reprises Shakespeare's famous war cry, 'Cry 'God for England, Harry and Saint George!' (*Henry V*).

8   A deviation of aim of only a few degrees would result in the bombs being wasted; bombs often fell outside the target area, even miles from the aiming-point. When a crew bombed a few seconds early, their bombs would not reach the target. Bombing planners learned to place the aiming-point slightly ahead of the bomber stream, so most of this 'creep-back' would land on target.

9   The fighting was bitter but by 10 July the British held Caen.

10 At almost 270 kilometres long, the Dortmund-Ems Canal was used to transport war material from the Ruhr. Although its banks were easily repairable it was at its most vulnerable along a raised aqueduct near the Munster lock. Ollis is probably referring to the raid of 23/24 September 1944, although he did not fly that day.

11 Introduced in January 1943 for Pathfinder aircraft, H2S produced a self-contained radar topographical image. Although the Germans

could neither jam or alter the image, it was helpful to the navigator but unreliable as a target locator. 101 aircraft could not carry ABC as well as H2S.

12   The Englishman who 'provoked the War of American Independence' was General Thomas Gage.

13   An excellent point. Similarly, many in the RAF's upper reaches opposed the appointment of Don Bennett as head of the Pathfinder Force. Bennett had a significant civilian aviation background and made mighty contributions to the RAF; see Alan Branson's *Master Airman* (1985).

Two

1   Most aircrew did not want to be seen to over-exaggerate their achievements; 'shooting a line' attracted much derision. Farlow's answer of 'a bit of a fiddle between Crete and Cairo', was meant to be a self-effacing 'bit of a mix-up', but the Squadron Commander thinks Farlow means that he 'fiddled' or 'wangled' the medal. Cusack uses the term 'fiddly' to mean a one-pound note, the sum for which a favour would be done.

2   Ollis flew to Emmerich on 7 October 1944, noting 'Reich by day!'. Middlebrook and Everitt report a successful raid on elements of the German army in the town; more than six times the number of civilians as soldiers were killed.

3   Aircraft today have electronic fly-by-wire – the equivalent of power-steering – but a Lanc had to be physically hauled about the sky. Flying in the slipstreams of other aircraft would be tiring as Chiltern would have to fight to keep the sometimes bucking aircraft on an even keel within the bomber stream. Note that Chiltern accepts that he is placing the aircraft – and the lives of his crew – in the way of a potentially lethal fighter attack.

4   A dialect pronunciation; he and his family pronounce his name 'Smiff', not 'Smith'.

5   Given that Ollis had suffered burns in combat, he may well be describing his own hands.

6   In the Halifax, the wireless operator and the navigator both sat below and in front of the pilot and flight engineer's seats, with the bomb aimer's position further forward. In the Lancaster the bomb aimer either lay or stood below them, above the escape hatch 'just twenty-two inches wide'. Behind a curtain, the navigator's desk was immediately behind the pilot (facing port), the astrodome above him. The radio operator sat behind the navigator. 'From the older

types of British night bomber, Halifax and Stirling, about twenty-five per cent [escaped]. From Lancasters, fifteen per cent. ... The Lancaster hatch was in various ways more awkward and harder to squeeze through [and] probably cost the lives of several thousand boys' (Dyson).

7   On the night of 5/6 October, Ollis navigated for a crew lead by F/L Haycraft. On the Siegfried Line, the roads and railways around Saarbrücken were bombed to assist the Third Army. Despite the thousands of houses ruined, only 344 people died.

Three

1   Cusack was also over-age when he enlisted in the RAAF; many Free French pilots who flew with the RAF were also above the maximum allowable age.

2   Snow's Australian variation of 'get your finger out' or 'pull your finger out' emphasises the unpleasant implication that the person being addressed has their finger up their bottom instead of doing their job. This was such a common term that *Tee Emm* published '*This Month's Prunery: The Most Highly Derogatory Order of the Irremovable Finger*' (OIF), delivering a pithy piece on an aviator's foolishness. 'Get your finger out' also gave rise to superb terms like 'finger trouble' or 'digititis', meaning that someone wasn't very competent.

3   'The great Australian adjective' used to be 'bloody'. These days, 'bloody' is barely a swear word. When many people were far more strict in their beliefs, 'bloody' was not merely naughty, but crude, crass and ugly. 'Fuck' and 'piss' were shocking to many; the 'c' word was utterly beyond the pale. Even so, in the 1940s a greater percentage of Australians swore more fluently than the British.

4   Ray told Margaret Ollis that 'Specials never deserted or baled out; they were part and parcel of the thing. It did upset them that they weren't treated as important; it was the crew who made them feel better, and more included.' His disclaimer, 'I know of no true instance ... where a German "Special" baled out over his homeland' seems designed to make one wonder if such an incident did occur. In fact, 101's Operations Record Book reveals that Special Operator F. Urch did bale out over Hannover during evasive action, on 18 October 1943, leaving Sergeant D. Langford and the rest of his crew of A for Apple behind.

Some aircrew did bale out during operations, preferring to face the enemy or the sea rather than another operation or the stigma of 'going LMF'. Also, when an aircraft had been fatally hit, aircrew would occasionally be caught by the aircraft as it plunged. In *Laughter-Silvered Wings* (1984), J. Douglas Harvey recounts the tale of a mid-upper gunner baling out during a German raid on London; 'as soon as the gunner got back to base he went LMF and refused to fly again. When he had landed in London ... he had been set upon by irate Londoners who assumed he was German ...' See also Renaut and Calmel.

Four

1   The Battle of Arnhem (17 to 26 September 1944) was a critical part of Operation Market Garden, mostly involving British troops.

2   During the Battle of Britain, the Messerchmitt Bf 109 was faster and more manoeuvrable than the Hawker Hurricane, and difficult for the Supermarine Spitfire to beat – but it could only stay a short time over England. In later years the Bf 109 lagged behind improved marks of Spitfire. The FW 190 arrived in mid-1941. Designed by the superbly-named Kurt Tank, the Focke-Wulf FW 190A flew at over 410 mph and was armed with four 20 mm cannon. Pilots of the Spitfire V received a rude awakening.

The North American P-51 Mustang came into its own in early 1944, when fitted with the new Rolls-Royce Merlin 61. The Mustang also carried new disposable drop-tanks. The P-51 then escorted bombers as far as Berlin.

At the time Ollis flew, the umbrella of fighters protecting the RAF daylight bombers were hundreds strong. *101 Nights* describes what is the Battle of Germany.

3   The huge shock-waves from the bursting bombs were from the 4,000 pound (or 8,000 pound, or 12,000 pound) 'cookies' which, when seen in daylight, appeared to expand like gigantic bubbles.

4   Operation Hurricane. The two back-to-back raids on Duisberg took place on 14 and 15 October 1944. After arriving back at Ludford just after 5 am after their second Duisberg op, the crews were woken to prepare for a 5.30 take-off for Wilhelmshaven, their 'third op in 40 hours' as Ollis notes.

Calmel on the first Duisburg raid: 'In the sea of clouds ... they found a single gap and below this was the target ... the bombing was impeccable. The gap was quickly filled with thick black smoke from the explosions of 4,500 tons of bombs.' On the second raid, Duisburg was visible as 'a red gleam ... 130 miles away ... Gigantic fires reddened the sky ... Nearly the whole city was ablaze.

Visibility was excellent, and the flak, obliterated by the hail of bombs that morning, was practically non-existent ... The spectacle was grandiose, but it was no longer human.'

Ollis's log-book; 'Four journalists were to have flown these dual trips to Duisburg. Only one survived'. William Troughton's report on these raids made the front page of the *Daily Express*.

Journalists habitually clamoured to fly on raids, and many were lost. Ed Murrow was the only journalist to survive out of the four who accompanied 101's neighbouring Squadrons 50 and 460 on the 2/3 December 1943 raid on Berlin.

5 By this time the weight of bombs dropped by the USAAF and RAF well exceeded the weight dropped by the Germans on England; 'the greater the tonnage of bombs dropped, the better the effect' seemed to be the mantra. The inability of the Allies to hit precisely the right target lead to a blunting of civilised sensibilities; Harris enthusiastically pointed to large areas of cities laid waste, assuming that an area in ruins could no longer produce aircraft, tanks, trucks etc. This was disproved when Albert Speer was interviewed for the Nuremberg trials.

6 Tarmac – even if the runway was concrete, as it was here, the runway was always referred to as 'tarmac'.

Five

1 RAF heroes. In the October 2011 issue of *Britain at War,* James Cutler revealed that on the night of 19 September 1944, Guy Gibson had been shot down by 61 Squadron Lancaster mid-upper gunner Bernard McCormack, who thought Gibson's Mosquito was a Ju 88 night fighter. Gibson's book, *Enemy Coast Ahead*, tells of his experiences up until the end of the Dams Raid on 16/17 May 1943.

Edgar James 'Cobber' Kain DFC (1918–1940) was a New Zealand Hurricane fighter ace with 17 credited victories in the Battle of France, won the war's first DFC, and died while 'beating up' the airfield prior to flying home.

Douglas Bader was a British Hurricane fighter ace with 20 credited victories. Shot down and captured over France; between escape attempts the rest of Bader's war was spent tormenting his German guards at Colditz.

Paddy Finucane was a Spitfire fighter ace with 26 credited victories; the youngest wing commander, he was killed in action on 15 July 1942 – his death is as Ollis describes.

2 The raid on St Vith, Boxing Day, 1944.

PART THREE

One

1 Escape kits were developed by Clayton Hutton. '[Butch Harris] fingered the supple leather approvingly and asked me what was the idea of the strip of webbing running round the boot at ankle level. By way of answer I extracted a tiny knife blade from the cloth loop at the top of one of the boots and with it I cut through the webbing. "There you are, sir," I said, as I separated the two sections. "The perfect escape boot. Two compasses and a powerful saw in the lace, the bottom part easily detachable to make an ordinary walking shoe; the top half, lined with fur, can be used with the top half of the other boot to provide a warm winter waistcoat"' (Hutton).

2 Hawker Typhoons were equipped with rockets in late 1943. Ollis's comment is not strictly accurate, but the Tiffy's eight 60 lb rocket projectiles were deadly for German armour and shipping.

3 *Tee Emm*, June 1943: 'Drugs of the benzedrine, ephedrine and pervitin type, if taken in small doses of 5 to 10 milligrammes, stave off sleepiness and increase the sense of well-being, but after a time they decrease the desire to work, and by postponing the desire to sleep they will in the end kill the ability to do so. They should therefore only be used under the medical officer's supervision in an occasional temporary emergency in which the possible dangers from sleepiness are greater than those from work fatigue'.

First appearing in inhalers for asthmatics, benzedrine was also used to treat narcolepsy but, because of the easy availability of the drug for aircrew and soldiers, was used 'recreationally' during WW2.

'Wakey-wakey' pills were given to aircrew to take before an operation; in the event of an op being scrubbed, those who had taken the pills before take-off were kept awake for the rest of the night. Side-effects – critical for aircrew – included an increasing inability to make sound decisions, which also included a 'willingness to take risks' and therefore an increase in aircraft losses. It is now illegal for commercial pilots to take benzedrine or any other amphetamine.

4 Johnny Evans: '... the escaper's greatest enemy is hunger ... When a man is starving, he very soon becomes reckless and insensitive. He takes unnecessary risks. He approaches farm buildings and the dogs give him away. He hunts for food in the fields ... Once

a man's belly is empty he makes a hundred and one mistakes ...'
(Hutton).

5   German paratroopers, like the Allied paratroopers, were highly
    trained and well-disciplined. '[O]ne particular item that became
    something of a Fallschirmjager trademark in North Africa and
    later, was a brightly coloured neckerchief or silk scarf. Some
    regiments even adopted uniform colours: FJR 5's, for example,
    were dark blue with white polka dots.' From *Fallschirmjäger.
    German Paratroopers 1935–45*, by Bruce Quarrie (Osprey, 2001).

6   The grass airfield near Juvincourt-et-Damary in northern France
    was built during 1938 and 1939; the Germans added three concrete
    runways, a railway and extensive support facilities. The Luftwaffe's
    largest French airfield, Juvincourt was a frequent target in the
    lead-up to D-Day. Taken from the Germans on 5 September, 1944;
    the Americans repaired Juvincourt and used it for many USAAF
    units (mostly fighters) and an emergency airfield for the USAAF
    and (secondarily) the RAF.

Two

1   There have been many movements attempting to ban 'Drink, with
    a capital D'. Books like Frank Russell's *Prohibition Does Work. An
    Australian Investigator's Opinion* (1930) were not uncommon.

2   The surreal world of now-obsolete Australian slang repays
    investigation.

3   'Blue' has long been an Australian nickname for anyone with red
    hair. 'Form', good or bad, is how well you behave with accepted
    modes of behaviour. 'To "know someone's form" is to have
    summed him up unfavourably; 'How's your rotten form?' is a
    jeering reproach, given currency in WW2 slang.

4   Setting off sirens, dropping lit Very cartridges down chimneys and
    snipping off ties were all common party games enjoyed by men of
    the time.

    Vyacheslav Molotov was the Soviet foreign minister responsible
    for breaking up Finland (November 1939 – March 1940); of
    necessity the Finns weapon created the contemptuously-named
    Molotov cocktail (petrol or some other flammable substance in a
    bottle, with a rag in the neck as a wick. When thrown the bottle
    shatters and the rag lights the petrol). Molotov was not amused.

Three

1   The Group Captain's aircraft is an Airspeed Oxford; Airspeed was an aviation company set up by, among others, Nevil Shute Norway in 1934. About 13 miles north of Lincoln, from November 1944 Hemswell was home to Nos 150 and 170 Squadrons.

Four

1   RAF 'formal nights' followed a tradition passed down from the Navy. Ollis's passing negative reference to passing the port is more satirically expressed in Cusack.

2   From William Shakespeare's *Macbeth*.

3   Two bombing raids on a town deserted except for our hero seems worthy of Joseph Heller. Although the situation was certainly confused, and the story half-fits the Blenheim IV bombing raids by 14, 45 and 55 Squadrons on Maleme airfield and around Herakleon, this particular situation did not occur.

4   Servicemen liberating funds from a bank is not unique.

5   'I was very fed up' is a classic British understatement. The stress of operational flying – and its effects – is a subject for many books.

6   From Alexandria to Cairo is under 200 miles.

7   There was a Voice of Greece (not Crete) anti-German radio station. Fiction or not, Farlow would not have been the first or last flyer to land among the partisans and fight with them.

8   A tale worthy of Flashman. Had Farlow's absence after the Greek lovely pinched his cash and car been explained in this manner to the RAF, instead of the explanation he does provide, he would have been court-martialled for desertion.

9   A wry joke; the correct expression is borrowed from golf – 'not up to par' means 'below normal'; a faux pas means literally 'a false step', and therefore a breach of conduct or manners. Being 'not up to faux pas' would mean 'not being up to his bad behaviour'.

10 Chiltern was betting on the snobbery within the RAF whereby the officers got the gong but the other ranks didn't; this is why the Victoria Cross was initiated, so that 'nobodies' of the services could receive an appropriate medal. While this snobbery persisted during WW2, with the introduction of so many officers from the lower and middle classes, as Ollis demonstrates here, it was by no means the rule.

Five

1 Farlow's BEM was, then, not 'a bit of a fiddle between Crete and Cairo', and the story he told Magnetic to excuse his desertion by impressing the RAF was in fact true. Crete was liberated from the Nazis in October 1944.

2 A Disney hornpipe. A hornpipe is a naval dance; cartoons acquired a musical soundtrack in the late 1920s and the characters cavorted in exaggerated and improbable time with 'silly symphonies'.

3 See Charles Whiting, *The Last Assault* (1994) or Alex Kershaw, *The Longest Winter* (2004). To see the rest of Ray Ollis's tour in context with the battle in Europe and the immediate aftermath, see the DVD *Britain's Victory in Europe* (1995).

4 This type of neurosis is mentioned in Mae Mills Link and Hubert A. Coleman's *Medical Support. Army Air Forces in World War II* (1992).

5 Lincoln Cathedral (née Lincoln Minster), on the highest hill in Lincoln, was an iconic landmark for thousands of aircrew.

6 F-numbers describe the size of the camera's aperture compared to the focal length of the lens. Farlow's removal of a sophisticated and expensive camera from its mounting and aiming it like a Kodak Box Brownie is extraordinary; if he'd broken it he'd probably face court-martial.

7 A circular rainbow can only be seen from a position in the air: as rainbows appear relative to the observer, your aircraft's shadow will be at the centre of the rainbow.

8 The hydraulically operated automatic pilot was attached to the Directional Indicator ('a gyroscopic heading indicator') and an attitude indicator. The aircraft would then fly straight on a compass course. The Royal Aircraft Establishment produced a variation in 1930, the invisible pilot ('George' or 'Elmer') which improved during the war.

    The 1944 V1 attacks on England lasted from June to October; the V1 flying bomb, buzz bomb or doodlebug flew on automatic pilot; if an aircraft could get close enough to waggle its wings beneath the bomb's wing, the mixed slipstreams would cause the gimbals to re-adjust – and the bomb would fly straight down. Most V1s were brought down by flak, and rockets from Typhoons or Tempests, but this incident is feasible; although the V1 travelled at 350 mph between 3000 and 4000 feet, even a close pass could cause the V1's gyro to topple.

Ogley states: 'The 2,419 V1s which dropped in the London boroughs killed 5,126 people. Outside London, 2,789 flying bombs caused another 350 deaths. In terms of casualties the "doodlebugs" were worse than the Blitz.' Harris (in *Bomber*) points out that the Germans never achieved their intention of launching 6000 V1s per day; only being 'able to launch an average of 95 a day between the middle of June and the end of August. Of these only two-thirds made landfall and less than a third reached Greater London.'

9   In August 1942 Harris ruled that a tour was 30 ops; the airmen then did six months as an instructor. Anyone surviving as an instructor was only required to do a 20-op second tour. This altered several times during the last months of the war.

The ballerina reference is another lewd joke; flexible and bendy, ballerinas were reputed to be superb fun in bed.

10 Williams: 'The idea of emergency aerodromes, capable of accepting aircraft in distress regardless of weather conditions, emanated from a Flight Lieutenant Broadhead of 5 Group ... in October 1941 ... On the Isle of Thanet in east Kent, [Manston] ... was the last of three emergency aerodromes to be constructed in England during the Second World War', and was operational by the end of May 1944.'

'... the total landings at Manston during September 1944 were estimated to be nearly 6,000, and 600 of these were reckoned to be emergencies, with, so far as records confirm, about a score with the use of FIDO'. That's 200 landings per day, 20 of which were emergencies ... 'it was estimated that a total of 5,796 emergency landings had been made at Manston in its time as an emergency runway ...'

11 Many pilots would disagree; six machine guns, ammunition and oxygen bottles would certainly have made a difference to the aircraft's overall weight; when an aircraft is barely flying, removing weight alleviates the stress on the airframe and engines. When the first Manchester prototypes attempted to get off the ground with a full complement of men, weapons and bombs, the aircraft refused to unstick. The surface of the wings was therefore reduced in thickness, unfortunately allowing the early Manchester to fly – with some strain – into battle.

12 Rolls-Royce was formed by Mr Charles Stewart Rolls and Sir Henry Royce in 1904, initially designing and manufacturing motor-car engines.

13   Hastings, Wright and Glueck describe cases of Functional Symptoms owing to Combat Flying; 'which are precipitated or caused by the stress of combat flying ... occurring individuals who have little or no previous history of personality maladjustment and have been regarded as average or normal until they began combat flying. These conditions tend to be cumulative ...'.

14   Hair and nails do appear to lengthen after death, an illusion caused by the skin shrinking.

15   Wilkes: dicken (or dickon) was 'an expression of disbelief or rejection'; a bloke is a man; grouse is 'excellent or outstanding' and a galah is 'an ass, a nincompoop' (based on the galah's often daft behaviour); so 'I can't believe I was such an extraordinary idiot', might be a fair translation.

16   English teeth are appalling due to the lack of fluoride in the water (and, in the 1930s, toothpaste; the editor's father used coal dust).

17   The Polish Resistance (Armia Krajowa) timed their rebellion to free Warsaw from the Nazis as the Russians approached, but the Russians stopped, refusing to enter the city or provide assistance. The Nazis crushed the Polish rebellion (extremely hazardous supply drops from the RAF had little effect).The Russians let the Nazis destroy the city and its people before they entered.

   'Bombing Moscow' is a common mid-40s to mid-50s sentiment. General George Patton expressed this view in public, embarrassing the US government; his death now appears suspicious (one theory being that the Russians assassinated him in 'self-protection').

Six

1   Wanganui; Musical Wanganui was blind sky marking by Oboe-equipped aircraft. Wind could blow the flares away, forcing more markers to be dropped while the Master Bomber issued instructions.

2   Ollis flew on this raid on 11 March 1945; the last raid to hit Essen, it paralysed the area. Allied troops entered shortly after, to minimal resistance. Of the 12/13 March 1943 raid on Essen, Goebbels recorded 'things simply cannot go on like this'.

3   Dyson: 'My analysis was based on complete records [and] my conclusion was unambiguous: the decrease of loss rate with experience which existed in 1942 had ceased to exist in 1944 ... The disappearance of the correlation between experience and loss rate ought to have been recognized by Bomber Command as a warning signal, telling us that we were up against something new.'

In *Men of Air. The Doomed Youth of Bomber Command* (2007), Kevin Wilson demonstrates the wide difference between the average loss rate and that when a raid goes horribly awry, as on the Magdeburg raid 21/22 January 1944. Middlebrook and Everitt's figures concur, the total loss rate of 6.9 percent (58 aircraft) for the entire Magdeburg raid, while the Halifax loss rate was 15.6 percent (35 aircraft).

4   Wanne Eickel was bombed many times; Ollis flew on the 9 November 1944 raid. Pathfinder flares vanished into a huge cloud which reared 20,000 feet over the target. The Master Bomber instructed the bombers to bomb any buildings; as Wanne Eickel sustained little damage in this raid the bombs fell more or less indiscriminately around the Ruhr.

5   The 'new Messerschmitt rocket fighter' implies this is the Me 163 Komet, but the fighter was more likely to have been the more common German jet fighter, the Me 262 – the two were often confused.

6   It was not unusual for a wife of a member of aircrew to commit suicide, and it was several decades before cars were installed with self-sealing petrol tanks.

   Built under licence by Packard, American Merlin engines were identical to British Merlins. Lancaster B-Is used Rolls-Royce Merlin 20, 22 or 24s; Lancaster B-IIIs used Packard Merlins (of either type 28 or 38); from the outside, a B-I looked like a B-III. Of the minor modifications to the B-III, the only difference which could lead to an unexpected crash was that the Packard Merlins used Bendix Stromberg 'pressure-injection' carburettors, necessitating the inclusion of 'slow-running cut-off switches' in the cockpit.

Seven

1   William Shakespeare, *Julius Caesar:* 'Men at some time are masters of their fates:/ The fault, dear Brutus, is not in our stars/ But in ourselves, that we are underlings.'

2   Ollis is describing a spiv. To a seedy, unsophisticated man Pernod (a French aperitif) seems exotic and sophisticated so, wanting to look sophisticated, he drinks it at night.

3   For example, the raid against seven German Troop positions facing the 3rd Canadian Division during the battle to close the Falaise Gap on 14 August 1944. The Master Bomber systematically guided the force through the seven targets. The 12th Canadian

Field Regiment used yellow marker flares which the bombers mistook for their own markers; seventy aircraft bombed the flares. Men were killed and injured, weapons and transport was also hit.

4 Otter states that 460 Squadron 'was to lose more than 800 aircrew' while at Binbrook. 460 flew an astounding 5,700 Lancaster sorties – the most operations by any squadron on one type of aircraft – for the loss of 140 aircraft. The 'night of 18 August [1943,] saw one of the most riotous parties of the year on Cleethorpes Pier, so riotous in fact that the ... Mayor ... wrote to Wing Commander Edwards to tell him his men were no longer welcome in the town!'

5 Cost and work factors were beginning to over-rule humanitarian factors. Chuck Yeager remembers; 'Atrocities were committed by both sides. That fall our fighter group received orders from the Eighth Air Force to stage a maximum effort. Our seventy-five Mustangs were assigned an area fifty miles by fifty miles inside Germany and ordered to strafe anything that moved ... It was a miserable, dirty mission, but we all took off on time and did it ...' (Yeager and Janos, *Yeager. An Autobiography*, 1985).

Ollis did not intend us to think that 460's Lanc had spotted the ammunition dump before unloading on the quiet village, but that it was lucky to hit a legitimate target. Although Bomber Command policy at this time involved 'targets of convenience' when the main target was inappropriate, Ollis's point is that you can't trust how an enemy appears.

6 *Kroonstad Press* was a popular Dutch newspaper; van Rijn is Rembrandt's surname.

Eight

1 Not the case; German aircraft factories were producing hundreds of fighters but, with factories, the transportation network and the oil manufacturing plants being destroyed, there were many pilots but not enough aviation fuel. Bomber Command's bureaucracy (not just Harris) miscalculated far too early in the war; a determined, combined offensive against oil, transportation and aircraft factories might have brought Germany to a halt much earlier. However, as Harris famously observed, trying to win a war by bombing the enemy 'has never been tried before, and we shall see.'

2 Ollis did not go on this raid, but bombers colliding was not uncommon – surviving such a near-miss showed remarkable skill and a coolness under pressure from the pilot(s).

3   The *Admiral Scheer* was sunk at Kiel on 9/10 April 1945. After
fighting the Russians since November 1944, the ship's guns
were dangerously worn and her last captain, Ernst-Ludwig
Thienemann, had put in to Kiel for replacement and repair. This
raid also damaged the *Emden* and *Admiral Hipper.*
    The captain who, obeying orders, shelled the Spanish town of
Almeria on 31 May 1937 was Wilhelm Marschall (1886–1976). His
autobiography has so far not been published in English.

4   Joe may be partly based on 'Joe Lightfoot posted N/F, sick, with
twenty-six completed'.

Nine

1   Ollis nails the special nastiness about the ending of the war. For
sheer unnecessary tragedy, Renaut: 'Just before I left Scampton
[in early 1946] there was a horrible accident. The aircrew who
were mostly unemployed, were put on to cleaning out the flight
offices on the first floor of the hangars. A gang of aircrew were
busy cleaning the linoleum floor with buckets of petrol and some
fool said: 'I know how to dry it out', and before anyone could
stop him he struck a match and the whole floor caught fire in a
minor explosion. The aircrew were burned to death, overcome by
flames and suffocation in seconds. It seemed to me such a senseless
tragedy to die like that after having survived an operational
tour ...'

2   'Ours not to reason why ...' is from the well-known poem *The
Charge of the Light Brigade* by Sir Alfred Lord Tennyson, which
eulogises the heroic sacrifice of a brigade of British cavalry.

3   'For here lies Juliet, and her beauty makes/This vault a feasting
presence full of light'. William Shakespeare, *Romeo and Juliet.*
Shakespeare portrays their love as mad and dangerous, not
romantic. In his own copy, Ollis underlined two lines further
down; 'Shall I believe/ That unsubstantial Death is amorous'...
ominous given the manner of Ollis's own death.

4   Apart from Harris' *Bomber Offensive, 101 Nights* is one of the first
books to discuss the pivotal significance of the 13/14 February
1945 Dresden raid, now the subject of numerous books and
documentaries. By then almost every major city in Germany
lay in ruins and Auschwitz had been captured by the Red Army.
Predating Russia's request for huge raids at Yalta, 'Operation
Thunderclap' had been planned as a series of raids to break down
the organisation and administration of the German war economy,

to be delivered at a critical point in the Allied advance. As the Allies moved into Germany, more distant targets like Stuttgart and Dresden could be approached and the Luftwaffe more easily avoided.

The Combined Strategic Targets Committee issued Harris with a directive 'listing ten towns from the East and for military transportation on the Eastern Front' (Probert). Berlin was first; Dresden second. Harris: 'by this time [Dresden was] the main centre of communications for the defence of Germany on the southern half of the Eastern Front'; the raids were also intended to block German reinforcements heading toward the Russians, and were linked to Churchill's fear that Russia's armies would surge southwards to take most of western Europe.

The Allies expected the Russians to halt their drive into Europe in deference to the refugees, but the Russians ploughed on regardless, indifferent to the mass of refugees, '... Soviet tank columns simply crushed any refugee farm carts in the way and raked them with machine gun fire. When a detachment of tank troops overtook a refugee column on 19 January, 'the passengers on the carts and vehicles were butchered'.' (Beevor, *Berlin. The Downfall 1945* (2002).

'In the three months of the air battle of eastern Europe we lost 780 men and facilitated the Red Army's savage advance to Berlin. This is my regret about Dresden: that it helped the Russians establish themselves deep inside Europe with appalling ferocity, and prevented the very balance of power that we had fought to restore' (Musgrove).

McKee, a soldier who saw the devastating effects of area bombing and wrote the second major work on Dresden; 'The difference between these few fire-blitzed streets [in English cities] and a great city which has been almost totally destroyed is titanic, and not to be apprehended by the intellect; it is a matter of emotion. And yet the survivors in the fire-stormed cities of Germany, which had been between 75 and 95% erased from the earth, spoke after the war of what happened in Dresden as if it had been infinitely worse.'

The first major work on Dresden was the detailed but seriously flawed David Irving's *The Destruction of Dresden*. The repositioning of the Dresden raid in the public's imaginative zeitgeist on both sides of the Atlantic reached a peak with Kurt Vonnegut's bestseller, *Slaughterhouse 5*, which seems to be where the spark of anti-Bomber Command revisionism in the 1980s and 1990s was lit.

Ollis did not take part, but he seems to be the first to nail 'the problem of Dresden'.

5   If the German papers really did publish such a shockingly high (and inaccurate) figure, it was exaggerated to frighten the German people into misguided heroics in the face of defeat. Over two raids, slightly over 800 Bomber Command aircraft dropped nearly 1,500 tons of high explosive and nearly 1,200 tons of incendiaries; the USAAF raid did not cause as much damage. The firestorm, significantly aided by the dry weather, burned out a very large part of the city. The number of dead remains in dispute but estimates of 45,000 to 50,000 seem balanced.

6   '… they had started it'. Essentially both the truth and the emotional justification why the Allies, particularly Britain, expanded the bombing war and is, I believe, why the Allies demanded 'unconditional surrender', regardless of the tactical necessities.

Sebald (*On the Natural History of Destruction*, 1999) quotes Speer to demonstrate that both Goering and Hitler would have cheerfully reduced London to rubble and ash in 1940 had they been able.

7   Russian callousness is well-documented. Toppe, in *Night Combat* (1982); 'Russian Commanders had no scruples about casualties when a mine field had to be cleared in a hurry. On 28 December 1942 on the Kerch Peninsula, for instance, a Russian penal battalion was driven across a particularly dense German mine field during the hours of darkness which preceded the attack. The casualties were very high, but several lanes were cleared for the follow-up units.'

8   Benito Mussolini (and his mistress) were executed by Italian partisans and strung upside-down in a public square in Milan.

Hibbert's *Benito Mussolini* (1962) more closely matches the Anglo view of Mussolini held by Ollis.

Ollis did not fly on the 25 April 1945 raid to Berchtesgaden.

9   Eisenhower sent Harris and Spaatz 'excellently worded letters suitable for both internal and external publication'. 'As the Allied Armies advance into the former industrialised area of the Rhineland they are everywhere confronted with striking evidence of the effectiveness of the bombing campaigns carried on for years by Bomber Command and, since 1942, but the 8th Air Force … the effect on the war economy of Germany has obviously been tremendous …' (Probert).

In the letter Montgomery wrote to the Royal Air Force on 5 May 1945, he also praises 'the brave and brilliant work of your gallant pilots and crews and the devotion to duty of the ground staffs have aroused our profound admiration.' In *The Memoirs of Field-Marshall the Viscount Montgomery of Alamein, KG* (1958), Monty writes, 'No-one knew better than I how much we soldiers owed to the Royal Navy and The Royal Air Force ... My relations with the RAF had been very close ...'

10   RAF Station Logbooks did not record airmen as 'dead', but 'missing' or 'failed to return'; a term which included POWs, the dead and the missing. 'The fatal casualties to Bomber Command aircrew, including those who died while prisoners of war and a few killed by German bombing, totalled 55,000' (Richards). Dyson had access to the raw data: 'When the total casualty figures for Bomber Command were added up at the end of the war, the results were as follows: Killed on operations, 47,130. Bailed out and survived, 12,790, including 138 who died as prisoners of war. Escape rate, 21.3 percent.' Even so, these figures do not include losses incurred during training.

The first Bomber Command sortie of WW2 was an unsuccessful search for German warships north of Wilhelmshaven. The next day 30 aircraft were despatched to bomb the warships; five Blenheims and two Wellingtons were lost (Holmes: *The Battle of Heligoland Bight, 1939* ..., 2009). After several more daylight raids with devastating losses to the 'invincible' bombers (without self-sealing fuel tanks), Bomber Command changed to night bombing.

The last raid of the war was on the night of 2/3 May 1945 when 231 aircraft were despatched to Kiel. 15 aircrew died.

11   Ex-POWs received pregnant women's rations, which were double the normal allowance.

APPENDIX – Ray Ollis: A chequered career

1   *The Magnet* (1908–1940) and *The Boys Own Paper* (1879 to 1963) were London-based weekly magazines with a serial story in each issue as well as other stories or articles; deprived of paper during the war, their sales fell. *The Magnet* featured Billy Bunter.

2   See Barber's *Sinister Twilight: the Fall and Rise Again of Singapore* (1968) and Farrell's *The Defence and Fall of Singapore, 1940–1942* (2006).

3   Hastings' *Bomber Command* (1980) gives some indication of the beginnings of a war at least partly constructed on outrage and

reprisal, as does Ray; for an emphatic read on the morality of bombing, Grayling is provocative, as are Grigg and Ellis.

4   *Decency of Hate* (1943).

5   See Charlewood: *Troopship Memories: A Dip in the Ocean* (1996).

6   Holland: *Nobody Unprepared: Nemo Non Paratus: The History of No. 78 Squadron* (2002).

7   There were three main types of 'cookie' blast bomb. The first was 4,000 pounds; the second was simply two 4,000 pounders bolted together ... and the third was three 4,000 pounders bolted together.

8   www.psychiatry.org

9   On his leaves Ray travelled to London, Oxford, and Brighton where he bought first editions such as *Little Dorrit*, *Barnaby Rudge*, *The Old Curiosity Shop*, *Childe Harold* by Byron, *Fables* by Dryden, the *Life of Walter Raleigh* and a religious treatise by Robert Bolton.

10 See Riddell *Flight of Fancy*, (1951).

11 See Douglas-Home, *Evelyn Baring. The Last Proconsul* (1978).

12 See Cobain's *Cruel Britannia: A Secret History of Torture* (2012) and W.B. 'Sandy' Thomas's *The Touch of Pitch* (1958).

13 This would be no disservice to Shelley, whose work is peppered with what Strong called 'The Sinister'.

14 As did such heroes as Guy Gibson. Ottaway; 'when the bombers went on a big raid to a target such as Bremen, they did not worry too much about placing their bombs on military targets. In Guy's own words: 'We just plunk them down in the middle of the town.'

15 Interview with the editor, 1994.

16 See Grenfell Price, *The Skies Remember: The Story of Ross and Keith Smith* (Angus & 1969); MacKenzie, *Solo. The Bert Hinkler Story* (1979); Kieza, *Bert Hinkler: The Most Daring Man in the World* (2012); Babington Smith, *Amy Johnson* (1967); Mackersey, *Smithy: The Life of Sir Charles Kingsford Smith* (1999); *Jean Batten: The Garbo of the Skies* (1991); Gillie, *Amy Johnson, Queen of the Air* (Weidenfeld & Nicolson, 2003); see also Scott, *Scott's Book ...* (1934) and Clouston *The Dangerous Skies* (1954).

17 The English 'Bodyline' cricket team sailed to Australia on the *Orontes* in 1932.

18 Hartnell, *Silver and Gold* (1955).

19 Kenneally's *Act of Grace* was published under the pseudonym William Coyle.

Glossary

Turnover of personnel was necessarily intense, so RAF and other Services slang varied from and period to period and area to area (much like a dialect).

Ac/1: Aircraftsman Class 1. Then the second-lowest RAF rank, only Ac/2 was lower.

Ac/w: Aircraftswoman.

Adjutant: (and either Adj as a name or 'the Adj' as a title) The officer charged with keeping the aerodrome running smoothly, organising everything from equipment, personnel, concert parties and punishments.

Airfield: an aerodrome. Usually laid in an 'A', the longest leg from south-west to north-west – except Ollis' airfield, Ludford Magna.

Ailerons: A long, hinged flap at the rear (trailing) edge of an aeroplane's wing. The aileron on one wing moves in the opposite direction to other, causing the aircraft to bank or roll. From French; 'aile', meaning 'wing'.

Aldis, or Aldis lamp: A large lamp with shutters which, by rapidly opening and closing the shutters, allows ships and aircraft to communicate visually using Morse code. Invented by Arthur Cyril Webb Aldis (1878–1953).

ASI: Air Speed Indicator. Dial showing the actual speed the aircraft is flying at, taking into consideration the wind. The airspeed came in through the pitot head.

ATS girl: The Auxiliary Territorial Service (ATS) was one of the women's services.

AVM: Air Vice-Marshal. In the 1940s, the officer in charge of a Group; roughly equivalent to a Major General in the Army.

Base, or Base HQ: Introduced in late 1943, a Base was a headquarters which handled two or three airfields; Ludford was 14 Base. Most RAF airfields were just airfields; an RAF station is a more permanent.

Blackout and Blackouts: Curtains made of thick heavy material to prevent the slightest light from emitting and assisting enemy aircraft, a nightly procedure known as 'the blackout'; 'blackouts' were also 'a Waaf's winter-weight knickers'. (Partridge)

Bloodsheet: Also known as the Chopsheet, Chop List or Chop Docket. The Battle Order, the list of aircrews available to fly on operations, usually at the entrance to the mess or at Flight. The Bloodwagon is the ambulance. See Chop.

Bods: 'Bodies', as in 'chaps', so often used to denote either Englishmen or 'our chaps', as in 'our bods'.

Boffin: Scientific chap.

Bullsh: Bullshit.

Byronic: After the manner of Byron or his poetry, but also to be irresistibly attractive to women despite being essentially a cad.

Cad: an ill-bred man, often vulgar.

Candle bombs: a bomb that detonated with an intense flame, used as a target indicator or marker.

Chiefy: Or chiefie. On the ground, a flight sergeant or 'chiefy' was in charge of each flight of bombers.

Chop, the: Killed, dying on active service Other euphemisms include the American 'bought the farm' and the English 'bought it' or 'had it', 'cashed his chips' or 'gone for a Burton' (from a famous 1930's poster campaign advertising Burton's Ale).

Clot: an idiot, but a gentle, joshing derogative.

Collected: killed.

Continent, the: What the British call Europe, but not what Europe calls Europe.

Cut-throat razor: a steel blade which folded into a handle.

Dandy: A vain and overly-fashionable man.

Dakota: The Douglas DC-3, or Dakota. Developed with more power and accommodation than the DC-2, it first flew on 17 December 1935. The Dakota's reliability, easy serviceability and robust structure indicated it could be converted for other military uses.

Dice: as in 'dicey do', 'dicing' etc. Risky, threatening, dangerous.

Dispersals: Flight dispersals. Outdoor pan of concrete where the aircraft were parked, fuelled, loaded and rearmed – and usually serviced – in almost all weathers.

Don Juan: A man who is outrageously successful with women. Based on Lord Byron's epic satire.

Dornier: The Dornier Do 17, or 'Flying Pencil', German bomber.

Elsan: Chemical toilet made by Elsan, located toward the rear of the bomber. Much derided, little used, as after the aircraft had been thrown around the sky the Elsan could tip and spill its contents.

Erk: RAF slang for aircraftsman, a mechanic who works on aircraft.

ETA: Estimated Time of Arrival. The most careless way to bomb.

Glossary

Extinguishers: Fire extinguishers for Lancasters were located in the engine nacelles. Often referred to as 'graviners' after Graviner, the company that developed and manufactured them.

Fair Dinkum: Then-common Australian slang for 'true' or 'really?'.

Fillip: From flip, to give a sharp rap with the fingernails. A brief urging gesture. Interestingly, a flip was the term used in the 1930s to a joy-flight in an aircraft.

Flak: German anti-aircraft fire. The name is either 'Fliegerabwehrkanonen' i.e., flyer-army-guns or the German abbreviation Flugzeug-Abwehr-Kanone (anti-aircraft gun).

Flak-happy: Reckless, careless behaviour through cumulative exposure to flak.

Flak ship: a small ship loaded with anti-aircraft guns. These ships would try to position themselves beneath the bomber stream; they accounted for many lives.

Flap: as in 'ginormous flap'. Panic, excitement or consternation.

Flap: large flaps on the inner, rear surface of the wing, which can be extended to increase lift during take-off and landing.

Flight: of a person, short for Flight Sergeant. Of aircraft, a Flight of aircraft was usually between eight and twelve, and designated 'A Flight' and 'B Flight'; two flights made a squadron. Of a place: short for Flight Dispersal; hence 'being at Flight'; the hangars where the aircraft – in peacetime – were stored prior to being wheeled out for take-off.

Flying control: what we now call Air Traffic Control. The place from where aircraft are guided down to land via radio and radar.

Fritz: German or Germans. The enemy, the Hun; from WW1.

Gaffer: British slang for 'the boss'.

Galahad: A heroic saviour, an honourable man.

Game: (adj.) plucky, up for it.

GC: Group Captain (or Groupy). Senior to a Wing Commander; roughly equivalent to a Colonel in the Army.

Gin-and-it: A contraction of 'Gin and Italian', the 'gin-and-it' comprised two shots of gin, one shot of sweet vermouth, perhaps a dash of bitters to taste, a handful of ice.

Gink: American slang; pejorative slang for a fellow.

Ginormous: 'Very large'; blended from 'gigantic' and 'enormous'.

Gong: a medal.

Grog: alcohol or beer.

Ground loop: A ground-loop occurs where, on the ground, there is too much power coming from either a strong cross-wind or the engine(s) on one side of the aircraft without corrective use of brakes or flaps to maintain the aircraft's stability. Essentially, the more powered side of the aircraft then attempts to fly, tipping the other side into the ground, often spinning the aircraft around in circles.

Guff: Empty talk, foolish bluff, nonsense.

H2S: Airborne Radar Navigational and Target Location Device.

Had it: in this sense, been destroyed or been finished..

Half-pint: Humorously derogative way of describing a short person. A more polite version of 'short-arse'.

HE: High Explosive.

Hide (as in, 'you've got a hide!'): 'you've got a hide!' means 'you've got a cheek' or 'you've got a nerve'. Impudent.

Hillman: English car.

Huns: At the time, a derogatory term for German, or Germans (also Fritz, Jerry, Boche). Brickhill describes Kommandant Rumpel interrogating Douglas Bader, who is consistently rude. Rumpel says 'we know you call us Jerries, but ...' 'No, we don't,' Bader snapped. 'We call you Huns!'. The charm fled from Rumpel and he shot up, face cold and rigid, and stalked out.'

Hyde Park: large public park in London, famous for its Speakers Corner.

i/c: In Charge of.

Intercom: Inter-communication device similar to the telephone allowing the crew to communicate with each other.

Ju 88: Junkers Ju 88, German twin-engined fighter/ bomber which handled a variety of roles. The radar-equipped night-fighter Ju 88 proved very successful from mid-1942.

Kiwi: a New Zealander.

L'affaire de coeur: French, literally 'an affair of the heart', but usually intended to mean 'a love affair'.

Lark: a frolicsome adventure or spree, and to make fun of, tease, or play the fool.

Limies, or Limeys: American term, from lime-juicer for English sailors; Royal Navy orders to their seamen to eat limes to prevent scurvy.

Looked daggers at: glared hard at, as if the glare could stab or kill. A venomous look.

Glossary

Luckies, or Lucky Strikes: Manufactured tobacco cigarettes, usually (but not always) referring to the brand Lucky Strike.

Mae West: An inflatable life-jacket intended to keep an airman afloat; after the famously buxom sex-siren cinema star. Also rhyming slang: Mae West = breast.

Main spar: The huge main wing strut crossing at right angles within an aircraft's fuselage. In the Lancaster, it was above hip height, and had to be scrambled over to move between the cockpit and the rear of the plan.

Me 110e: Me 110e Messerschmitt Bf 110, also referred to as the Me 110 or Zerstörer ('destroyer'). A twin-engine heavy fighter which, although outclassed in daylight, adapted well to becoming the most common German night-fighter.

Mephistopheles: The Devil.

Mess: Sergeant's Mess, or Officer's Mess. Where the sergeants, or officers, ate, drank and tried to relax.

Met: Meteorological Office.

Mid-upper: the mid-upper gun turret, about half-way down the spine of the Lancaster. Armed with two Browning .303 machine guns, with a tracer round usually every twelve or so bullets, this gunner had a commanding view above the Lancaster.

Morse: Morse code. Letters coded as dots and dashes.

Natter: talking aimlessly, endlessly, irritatingly; to talk when speech is forbidden.

NCO: Non-Commissioned Officer.

Nightfighter (when not an aircraft): a sexually active (if not predatory) woman, who may or may not be a prostitute.

Nuisance raid: a few fast twin-engined bombers (e.g. Mosquitos) dropping bombs on a target as a diversion while the main force head elsewhere; also used to provoke to disturb the sleep of the inhabitants. See spoof.

Oboe: Ground-controlled Blind-bombing Radar System. Intended to increase the accuracy of bomb-aiming or target marking under all weather conditions. An aircraft followed radio beam and its position was calculated by measuring its distance from a second point.

Observer (also 'O wing'): Until 1942, the man responsible for navigation and bomb-aiming, and sundry other tasks.

Olio-leg: Oleo leg; the two main oil-damped shock-absorbing undercarriage legs of a heavy bomber, to which the main wheels are attached.

Odd bods: Spare people; unattached airmen who flew with an unfamiliar crew missing a member.

OTU: Operational Training Unit. It was rare for a crew to be returned to an OTU, and regarded as a great disgrace for the crew and the OTU itself.

Over: and Out. In radio transmission, a simple method to indicate that someone has finished talking and is waiting for a reply by saying 'Over' at the end of a sentence. 'Out' means that the speaker is finished speaking and does not expect a reply.

Paps: large breasts.

Perimeter track: Taxying lane leading off and around the three runways, enabling the bombers to get onto their pan quickly.

Perspex: Transparent, plastic and shatter-proof substance which acted as a window in bomber gun turrets, astro domes, bomb aiming positions and cockpits.

Piccadilly Circus: metaphorically, somewhere very busy indeed.

Pinpoint: a precise time matched to a visually identified place enabling the navigator to confirm speed and direction, and plot accordingly.

Pongo: Derogatory RAF slang for a member of the Army, supposedly because they don't wash as often.

Popsie: RAF slang for wench, a woman of easy virtue or frivolous nature.

Press-on gong: a medal for continuing the attack in spite of damage to the aircraft, aircrew or other difficulties normally necessitating an early return to base.

Prune, P/O: Pilot Officer Prune. A pilot who takes unnecessary risks, and generally loses his neck through 'prunery'; a pilot who has several 'prangs' on his record.

Put up a black: do something bad which is brought to a superior officer's attention.

Radar: the acronym RADAR (Radio Detection and Ranging) was first used in 1940–1941 by both the British and the US Navy, although the term RDF (Radio Direction Finding) was used by the British for several years. By the end of the war, 'radar' was in conversational use.

Radio silence: not transmitting radio signals, which could be picked up by the enemy and used to detect the transmitter's location.

Rag: noisy, disorderly conduct, great high spirits.

Rake: an immoral or dissipated man.

Rip van Winkle: someone not connected with current events (Rip van Winkle slept for 20 years and awoke to find that things had changed).

Roué: a man who leads, a life of pleasure and sensuality.

Rolling-stock works: A factory that makes and repairs the vehicles which use a railway, from carriages and engines to cattle-trucks.

Romance wreckers: Also known as Passion Killers, Blackouts or Official Issue. Voluminously virtuous women's bloomers as worn by the various branches of the women's Armed Services, WAAFs, WRENs etc.

Scoop: news obtained and printed in advance of a rival newspaper.

Second Dickie: (also Second Dickey, or the Dickey Pilot): a pilot flying with an experienced pilot for instructional purposes.

Section: a section of aircraft was between two to six; but usually four. Thus a Flight Commander outranks a Section Leader.

Sextant: an instrument that measures the angle between two objects, such as a planet or star, and the horizon: the angle combined with the time measured allow the navigator to compute a position line on a chart.

Shooting a line: to talk too much, especially to boast.

Shower: a large number (pejorative), e.g. 'a shower of shit'.

Show her his etchings: (or, show you my etchings) to entice a girl home, code for a request for sex.

Sideslip: when attempting to land in a cross-wind, aiming the aircraft into the wind so that the aircraft's flightpath follows the aircraft's intended direction (rather than simply flying straight, which will allow the wind to push the aircraft off the runway).

SOS: the international request for urgent assistance; the letters were chosen because their Morse pattern was easy to remember (three short dashes, three long, and three short).

Spitfire: the Supermarine Spitfire, the most flexible and effective fighter aircraft of the Second World War.

Spiv: a borderline criminal, an unreliable opportunist.

Spoof: to fool or to trick. A spoof attack was where the bomber stream would apparently head for one target, only to change direction to another. Later raids would sometimes use more than four changes of direction in order to spoof the defenders.

Sprog: a new recruit, especially a raw one.

Squadron: An RAF squadron consisted of up to 24 aircraft. Wartime supply difficulties, damage and attrition meant that a squadron might be whatever the aerodrome could put up.

Stinko: exceedingly drunk.

Stringers: strips of light metal which hold the frames of the fuselage rigid.

SWO: Station Warrant Officer.

Swuffled: from *swung* and *waffle*.

Tannoy: Public address system made by Tannoy.

Teleprinter: a device for sending a typed message via telephone line to one or many destinations, where the message was printed by the teleprinter at its destination.

Tit: The bomb-release button in British bombers. A pressable nipple on the end of a cord.

TOT: Time On Target.

Tracer: Tracer bullets. A bullet which has a small charge at the bottom; the charge burns brightly (red, in World War II) when ignited which reveals its trajectory, allowing the gunner to adjust his aim.

Trailing Radio Aerial: A lengthy wire aerial unwound behind the aircraft to enable the wireless operator to receive transmissions from the home aerodrome.

Trim: keeping the aircraft balanced in flight; hence 'trim tabs', which are the small flaps attached to the wing's trailing edge, intended to assist in maintaining trim.

Tucker: food, rations.

USAF: The USAAF, United States Army Air Force, became the USAF in 1947.

Very lights, Very pistol: a single shot flare gun which fired a lighted flare into the sky.

VC: The highest British medal possible: the Victoria Cross.

Waaf: a member of the Women's Auxiliary Air Force; the acronym WAAF was simply pronounced 'waff', or, as the author writes it, 'waaf'. Australian WAAFs were WAAAFs.

Wing: Several squadrons of aircraft, usually three or four.

Glossary

Wings: (or pilot's wings). Named for the cloth patch that all pilots wore on their shoulder. 'Getting your wings' meaning 'qualifying'.

Wizard prang: RAF slang via Public School slang: 'wizard' meaning 'exceptionally good' or 'exceptionally spectacular', and 'prang' for crash, destruction; after a successful bombing run, an exclamation of relief and joy at the destruction, reducing the enormity of the event to a schoolboy game.

WRAN: Women's Royal Australian Naval Service. The British equivalent was Women's Royal Naval Service (WREN).

Wurtzburg: giant radar dishes which the Germans used to direct night fighters, searchlights and anti-aircraft fire. Also spelled Wurzburg or Wuerzburg.

Bibliography

These skeletal publishing details quoted are of the original publication unless otherwise stated, and should enable the intrepid reader to locate the reference; there were many other references consulted.

Raymond Alexander, *Special Operations No 101 Squadron*, (The Author, Anglesey, 1979).

John Anderson, *Parallel Motion. A Biography of Nevil Shute Norway* (The Paper Tiger, 2011).

D.C.T. Bennett, *Pathfinder* (Frederick Muller, 1958).

Patrick Bishop, *Bomber Boys. Fighting Back, 1940–1945* (Harper, 2007).

Paul Brickhill, *Reach for the Sky* (William Collins, 1954).

J.R.D. 'Bob' Braham, *Scramble!* (Frederick Muller, 1961).

Andrew Brookes, *Bomber Squadron at War* (Ian Allan, 1983).

Richard Burton, *The Book of The Thousand Nights and A Night*, (10 volumes, Kama Shastra Society, 1885; popularly known as *The Arabian Nights* or *The Thousand and One Nights*).

John Bushby, *Gunner's Moon* (Ian Allan, 1972).

Harold Butler, *The Lost Peace. A Personal Impression* (Faber, 1941).

Christy Campbell, *Target London. Under Attack from the V-Weapons* (Little, Brown, 2012).

Colonel Jean Calmel, *Night Pilot* (William Kimber, 1955).

Raymond Chandler, *The Big Sleep* (Hamish Hamilton, 1939).

Leonard Cheshire, *Bomber Pilot* (Hutchinson, 1943).

W.R. Chorley, *Royal Air Force Bomber Command Losses of the Second World War* series; several volumes, Midland Press. Now published by Ian Allan, they are also available online, with updates.

Martyn Chorlton, *To Serve Was Their Highest Aim* (Aeroplane, Kelsey Publishing Group, June 2012).

H.I. Cozens and Brian Johnson, *Night Bombers* (DVD; 'Archive at War', Oracle, 2009).

John Bede Cusack, *They Hosed Them Out* (revised and expanded edition, 2012, Wakefield Press).

Len Deighton, *Bomber* (Jonathan Cape, 1970).

Ken Delve, *Bomber Command 1936–1968. An Operational and Historical Record* (Pen and Sword, 2005).

Freeman Dyson, *Disturbing the Universe* (Harper and Row, 1979).

John Ellis, *Brute Force: Allied Strategy and Tactics in the Second World War* (Andre Deutsch, 1990).

Sean Feast, *Carried on the Wind. Wartime Experiences of a Special Duties Operator with 101 Squadron RAF Bomber Command* (Woodfield, 2003).

Guy Gibson, *Enemy Coast Ahead – Uncensored* (Crecy, 2003). In comparing passages quoted by Richard Morris (who worked from the manuscript) with this edition, one realises that the Crecy edition is not complete.

A.C. Grayling, *Among the Dead Cities. Is the Targeting of Civilians Ever Justified?* (Bloomsbury, 2006.

William Green, *War Planes of the Second World War. Volume One: Fighters* (Macdonald, 1960).

John Grigg, *1943. The Victory That Never Was* (Eyre Methuen, 1980).

Bill Gunston, *Night Fighters. A Development and Combat History* (Patrick Stephens Limited, 1976).

Nick Hanson: *First Blitz. The Secret Plan to Raze London to the Ground in 1918* (Doubleday, 2008).

Arthur Harris, *Bomber Offensive* (Collins, 1947).

Sir Arthur T. Harris, *Despatch on War Operations* (Frank Cass, 1995).

J. Douglas Harvey, *Boys, Bombs and Brussels Sprouts* (McClelland and Stewart, 1981).

Donald W. Hastings, David G. Wright and Bernard C. Glueck, *Psychiatric Experiences of the Eighth Air Force. First Year of Combat* (Josiah Macy Foundation, August, 1944).

D. Jablow Hershman and Julian Lieb, *Manic Depression and Creativity* (Prometheus Books, 1998).

Richard Hillary, *The Last Enemy* (Macmillan, 1942).

Ian V. Hogg, *Anti-Aircraft. A History of Air Defence* (Macdonald and Jane's, 1978).

Clayton Hutton, *Official Secret* (Max Parrish, 1960).

Ernst Junger, *The Storm of Steel* (Originally published in 1920), but translated by Basil Creighton for Chatto and Windus, May 1929. Junger revised the book many times, and the current edition (Penguin, 2003) is a new translation of the last revision; I have quoted from the 1929 edition.

Phillip Knightley, *The First Casualty: The War Correspondent as Hero, Propagandist and Myth Maker* (Andre Deutsch, 1975).

Heinz Knoke, *I Flew for the Fuhrer* (Evans Brothers, 1953).

Elisabeth Kubler-Ross, *Death. The Final Stage of Growth* (Spectrum, 1975)

Gavin Long, *Official History of Australia in the Second World War, Volume II: Greece, Crete and Syria* (Australian War Memorial, 1953 – .

Norman Longmate, *Air Raid. The Bombing of Coventry, 1940* (D. McKay, 1978).

Keith Lowe, *Inferno. The Devastation of Hamburg 1943* (Viking, 2007).

Ian Mackersey, *Into the Silk* (Robert Hale, 1956).

Alexander McKee, *Dresden 1945. The Devil's Tinderbox* (Souvenir Press, 1982).

Leo McKinstry, *Lancaster. The Second World War's Greatest Bomber* (John Murray, 2009).

Sir Thomas Malory, *Morte D'Arthur* (Caxton, 1485; but significantly reprinted in 1819).

J.C. Masterman, *The Double-Cross System in the War of 1939–1945* (Yale University Press, 1972).

Martin Middlebrook and Chris Everett, *The Bomber Command War Diaries* (Viking, 1985).

Richard Morris, *Cheshire. The Biography of Leonard Cheshire, VC, OM* (Viking, 2000).

Edward Murrow *In Search of Light: The broadcasts of Edward R. Murrow, 1938–1961* (Alfred A. Knopf, 1967).

Frank Musgrove, *Dresden and the Heavy Bombers. An RAF Navigator's Perspective* (Pen and Sword, 2005).

(OED) *The Oxford English Dictionary* (The Clarendon Press, 1933).

Bob Ogley, *Doodlebugs and Rockets. The Battle of the Flying Bombs* (Froglets, 1992).

Susan Ottaway, *Dambuster. The Life of Guy Gibson VC* (Pen and Sword, 1994).

Patrick Otter, *Lincolnshire Airfields in the Second World War* (Countryside Books, 2012 revised).

Eric Partridge, *A Dictionary of Slang and Unconventional English* (Routledge and Kegan Paul, 1970 (revised and enlarged), 1961. Posthumous editions revised after the eighth edition in 1984 have been 'politically sanitised', and therefore historically unbalanced.

Alfred Price, *Instruments of Darkness. The History of Electronic Warfare* (Macdonald and Jane's, 1977, revised).

Bibliography

Henry Probert, *Bomber Harris: His Life and Times* (Greenhill Books, 2001).

John Ray, *The Night Blitz, 1940–1941* (Arms and Armour Press, 1996).

Michael Renaut, *Terror by Night* (William Kimber, 1982).

Denis Richard, *The Hardest Victory* (Hodder, 1994).

Dorothy Rowe, *Depression* 3rd edn (Routledge, 2003).

Jules Roy, *Return From Hell* (Kimber, 1954).

Cornelius Ryan, *The Longest Day* (Gollancz, 1960).

John Searby, *The Everlasting Arms. The War Memoirs of Air Commodore John Searby DSO, DFC* (William Kimber, 1988).

Percy Bysshe Shelley, *The Complete Poetical Works* (ed. Thomas Hutchinson), Oxford, 1927.

Albert Speer, *Inside The Third Reich. Memoirs* (Macmillan, 1970).

Archibald T. Strong: *Three Studies in Shelley*, Oxford University Press, 1921

Tee Emm. (facsimile set published by Commonwealth of Australia, 1986).

M.J. Trow, *War Crimes. Underworld Britain in the Second World War* (Pen and Sword, 2008).

Chris Ward and Steve Smith, *3 Group Bomber Command. An Operational Record* (Pen and Sword, 2008).

Sir Charles Webster and Noble Frankland: *The Strategic Air Offensive Against Germany* (HMSO, 1961).

Mark K. Wells, *Courage and Air Warfare. The Allied Aircrew Experience in the Second World War* (Frank Cass, 1995).

G.A. Wilkes, *A Dictionary of Australian Colloquialisms* (Sydney University Press, 1978).

Kevin Wilson, *Men of Air. The Doomed Youth of Bomber Command*, (Weidenfeld and Nicholson, 2007).

Geoffrey Williams, *Flying Through Fire* (Grange Books, 1995).

Wakefield Press is an independent publishing and
distribution company based in Adelaide, South Australia.
We love good stories and publish beautiful books.
To see our full range of books, please visit our website at
www.wakefieldpress.com.au
where all titles are available for purchase.

Find us!

Twitter: www.twitter.com/wakefieldpress
Facebook: www.facebook.com/wakefield.press
Instagram: instagram.com/wakefieldpress